OKSA POLLOCK
the Last Hope

ANNE PLICHOTA
CENDRINE WOLF

Translated by Sue Rose

PUSHKIN
CHILDREN'S

Pushkin Children's Books
71-75 Shelton Street
London WC2H 9JQ

Translation © XO Editions / Sue Rose 2013

Oksa Pollock: The Last Hope first published in French
as *Oksa Pollock: l'inespérée* by XO Editions in 2010

Original text © XO Editions, 2010. All Rights Reserved.

This edition published by Pushkin Children's Books in 2013

ISBN 978-1-78269-000-9

Set in 12 on 16 Arno Pro by Tetragon, London
Printed in Great Britain by CPI Group (UK) Ltd
www.pushkinpress.com

OKSA POLLOCK
the Last Hope

PROLOGUE

A BOY WOULD HAVE RULED OUT ANY POSSIBILITY, destroying their last and final hope.

Pavel Pollock jumped up and, in an attempt to mask his agitation, leant over the cradle where a tiny baby girl lay sleeping. His daughter. Everything now hinged on his little girl—he knew it—and the thought was already eating him up inside. Gloomy joy filled his heart and yet his eyes were shining with happiness at becoming a father. He turned to look at his wife, blinking away a few tears. Marie Pollock smiled back at him. Would he ever learn to be less of a worrier, she wondered. Less anxious? Deep down, though, she knew she loved him just the way he was.

Suddenly a cry from the cradle made them both jump: their baby girl had just expressed herself with surprising force. Eyes wide open, she was trying to prop herself up on her little arms, but despite her fierce determination, her head with its dark, silky curls kept falling back onto the pillow. Her father went over and picked her up, his heart thudding.

"Is this okay? Am I being too rough? I'm not hurting her, am I?" he asked his wife, frowning with concern.

"Don't worry, you're doing fine," she replied easily. "Well, look who's here! Hello, Dragomira!"

Everything Pavel's mother's did had a touch of exuberance and today was no exception: hidden behind the largest bunch of flowers they'd ever seen, Dragomira was also carrying a variety of bulky bags in every colour, overflowing with gifts—bags she dropped as soon as she laid eyes on the baby in her son's arms.

"Oksa!" she cried. "You're awake, my little treasure! I'm so happy!" she exclaimed to Marie and Pavel, kissing each of them in turn.

"Hmmm, I think her nappy needs changing," remarked Pavel, horrified at the thought.

"I'll deal with it!" volunteered Dragomira. "If you don't mind, Marie, of course," she added, with an imploring look.

A few seconds later, little Oksa was wriggling on the changing table while her gran wrestled with her sleepsuit. Pavel stood beside her to watch, careful not to miss a thing.

"Oksa... our last hope," murmured Dragomira almost inaudibly.

Pavel shuddered and his face darkened with annoyance. He allowed his mother to finish dressing the baby, then asked her firmly to follow him into the corridor of the maternity hospital.

"Mum!" he hissed angrily through his teeth. "You couldn't help it, could you? You just couldn't stop yourself! If you think I didn't hear you—"

"Hear what, my dear Pavel?" asked Dragomira, her blue eyes gazing deep into her son's.

"I know exactly what you're all thinking! But you're basing your hopes on a very slim chance. You might just as well rely on the wind!"

"But ships rely on the wind to sail across the sea," continued Dragomira in a low voice. "We'll never give up hope, Pavel, never."

"You're not taking my daughter there," insisted Pavel, placing heavy emphasis on every word as he leant against the wall. "I won't let you, so get that into your head! I'm her father and I want my daughter to have a *normal* upbringing. As normal as possible anyway," he added, correcting himself, looking strained.

They glared at each other silently in the corridor, ignoring the passing nurses and patients in dressing gowns who stole glances at the pair as they locked eyes, each of them trying to convince the other. It was Dragomira who broke the tense silence:

"My dear son, I love you deeply but you mustn't forget that you're bound to our land, just as we are. And whether you like it or not, Oksa is too—and there's nothing you can do about that. If there's even the slightest chance we might be able to return home, you know very well we'll grab it with both hands. We owe it to those who stayed behind, those who've been living in the grip of Evil since the Great Chaos!"

"Mum," replied Pavel, finding it hard to hide his resentment, "I have huge respect for you, but I won't allow it. You have no idea what I'm capable of doing to keep my daughter out of all that. We have to forget. It's too late now. It's over."

"I'm afraid fate is stronger than all of us, Pavel," concluded Dragomira with a firmness that surprised even her. "There's no point tearing each other apart, because fate will decide for us, make no mistake."

1

MULTILEVEL MOBILIZATION

SOME TWELVE YEARS LATER. BIGTOE SQUARE. LONDON. Oksa squeezed between the removal boxes to reach the window of her room. She raised the blind and pressed her nose against the cold glass. The square was filled with activity that morning, and she watched the comings and goings for a moment with a doubtful expression, then gave a deep sigh.

"Bigtoe Square… I'll just have to get used to it," she murmured, a faraway look in her slate-grey eyes.

The Pollock family—first, second and third generations—had left Paris for London a few days earlier on what appeared to be a sudden whim by Pavel Pollock. After hours of secret meetings which had been off-limits to Oksa, her father had made a formal announcement with his customary solemnity: for the past ten years, he'd held the coveted job of head chef in a renowned restaurant, but now at long last he had the opportunity to open his own restaurant. In London. This small detail had been added so casually that Oksa had suddenly wondered whether she'd heard correctly.

"You mean… London… England?" she'd asked after pausing for a few seconds.

Her father had nodded with obvious satisfaction and, at the sight of her stunned expression, had added immediately that, of course, if his wife and daughter didn't want to move, he'd respect their decision, even though it was a dream opportunity.

"This is a once-in-a-lifetime chance for me!" he'd stressed.

Marie Pollock hadn't taken long to think about it: her husband had been very jumpy of late and she'd told herself that a complete change of scene would do the whole family good. As for Oksa, did she really have a say in any of this? Although she was almost thirteen, the important decisions were out of her hands. She didn't want to leave Paris, even less France. But she'd get used to it. The main thing was that her gran and her best friend were coming with them. After all, there was no way she could live without Dragomira—her Baba!—and Gus.

※

After absent-mindedly watching the traffic driving around the square, Oksa turned away from the window. Hands on hips, she looked around and gave a long whistle.

"What a mess! It'll take months to unpack everything! Such a hassle."

In every room, umpteen boxes took up what little space wasn't already occupied by furniture. Although there was less room here than in their Paris apartment, the Pollocks had been incredibly lucky to find a typically English red-brick Victorian house, with steps leading up from street level to the front door, a bow window and a tiny garden enclosed by wrought-iron railings through which you could glimpse the basement windows. The ground floor and first floor were occupied by Oksa and her parents and the second by her gran, Dragomira, who'd lived with them for as long as Oksa could remember. She looked up at the ceiling.

"What on earth is Baba doing?" she wondered, running her fingers through her chestnut hair. "*It sounds like she's skipping or something! Anyway, I should probably start getting ready if I don't want to be late,*" she thought with a start, heading for the wardrobe. Being late on her first day at school would be all she needed!

※

The scene upstairs where Dragomira had her apartment was much more unusual. The baroque living room, hung with lustrous bronze drapes, was in total chaos. This was the work of the mischievous magical creatures which seemed to be vying with each other to see who could make the most mess. Two tiny golden birds were lending a helping hand; after a few joyful test flights around the crystal chandelier, they were tormenting what looked like a large, frizzy-haired potato as it ambled over the crimson wool carpet, dive-bombing the creature as if they were fighter planes.

"Down with the dictatorship of the gastropods!" chanted the tiny birds. "It's time to stop living under the yoke! We must play our part in the struggle against mollusc imperialism, my friends!"

"Hey, I might be a little short in the legs, but I'm no mollusc, I'm a Getorix! And I have fabulous hair," it replied, puffing out its little chest and tossing its hair back to one side.

"Bombs awaaaay! Long live the liberation of oppressed nations!" shouted the birds in reply.

With these fighting words, they dropped their missiles: ten or so sunflower seeds, which bounced off the back of the Getorix.

"Talk about the oppressed," it grumbled, picking up the seeds and munching them.

The plants, easily upset by this commotion, were wailing and writhing frantically in their pots. One of them, which was perched on an antique gold pedestal table and seemed more nervous than the others, appeared to be trembling and all its leaves were drooping.

"THAT WILL DO!" yelled Dragomira. "Look how stressed the Goranov is now." The old lady gathered up the folds of her purple velvet dress and knelt on the floor. The terrified plant was sighing pathetically and she massaged its leaves, humming a soft tune. "If you go on like this," she continued, eyeing the troublemakers severely, "I'll have to send you all to stay with my brother. And you know what that would mean: a very long journey!"

12

These words had the immediate effect of silencing the creatures and plants. They had very bad memories of their last journey, when Dragomira had suddenly embarked on what they'd regarded as a totally ridiculous move. None of them could bear any kind of transport. Trains, boats, planes, cars—they were all demonic inventions designed to upset your stomach and make you feel sick. The birds had thrown up for almost the entire journey and the plants had nearly been poisoned by their own chlorophyll, which had curdled like off milk.

"Come on, everyone into the workroom!" ordered Dragomira. "I have to go out—my granddaughter is going to school today. Come, my Lunatrixes, I could do with some help, please."

Two eccentric creatures in blue dungarees hobbled in as fast as they could. One was plump with a downy head and the other was spindly with a lemon-yellow tuft of hair but they shared certain distinctive features: they were short—two and a half feet tall—with pudgy faces and huge blue eyes full of kindness.

"The orders given by Your Graciousness are an everlasting pleasure. You can be assured of our support and our loyalty," they said gravely.

Dragomira went over to the huge double-bass case leaning upright against the wall at the far end of the room and opened it. There was nothing inside. She placed her palm flat against the wooden back, murmured a few mysterious-sounding words and the back of the case immediately opened like a door. Dragomira bent down and walked in to reach a spiral staircase which led to her attic and workroom. Obediently following her, the two Lunatrixes each picked up a plant and led the way for the other creatures, which also entered the strange passageway. When everyone was in the workroom, Dragomira went back out through the case and closed it carefully behind her.

2

The Pollock Clan

"**H**I DAD, HI MUM!"

Marie and Pavel Pollock were sitting at the table in the functional kitchen. When they heard their daughter come in, they both looked up from their steaming cups of tea at the same time and stared at her in amazement.

"Yes, I know," sighed Oksa. "I'm unrecognizable."

"Well… yes, you are, apart from your adorable little face," said her father, looking at her with curiosity. "It's hard to believe that this is the intrepid ninja warrior I know and love, although I must admit the change of style is delightful. Drastic, but delightful."

"It's certainly drastic, you can say that again," muttered Oksa.

Her parents couldn't help chuckling at her irritated expression. She looked at them reproachfully and snapped: "My life has been turned upside down and you think it's funny? Have you seen *how ridiculous I look*!"

"You look like a real English schoolgirl," replied her mum lightly, sipping her tea. "And, to my mind, it really suits you!"

Oksa gazed down at herself again doubtfully and grunted. Who'd have thought that she'd ever be caught wearing a pleated skirt, a white blouse and a blazer *in public*? Certainly not her.

"If I'd been told that I'd have to wear a school uniform, I'd have refused to come to England," she muttered, crossly loosening the green and black tie displaying her new school colours.

"Oh, please, Oksa," sighed her mum, studying her with attractive hazel eyes. "It's just for school. You can wear your jeans and clumpy trainers outside as much as you like."

"Fine!" said Oksa, resigned, throwing both hands up in the air. "I won't say another word. But I'll never forget that you sacrificed me on the altar of your career. And for parents who claim they love their only daughter, that's pretty low. Don't complain if I end up suffering from serious psychological after-effects."

Her parents smiled at each other, well accustomed to Oksa's fiery outbursts. Marie Pollock stood up, put her arms around her daughter and they stood there for a long moment, hugging tightly. Although Oksa thought she was a bit too old for demonstrations of affection, deep down she had to admit she really enjoyed hugs like this, so she happily buried her face in her mum's mane of chestnut hair.

"What about me?" Pavel Pollock butted in, pretending to be put out. "No one cares about me. They never have. No one ever gives me a big kiss on my lovely unshaven cheek. No one cuddles me. I'm left all alone in my corner, like a sad, smelly dog!"

Her father's pronounced features always wore a solemn expression. His ash-grey hair and grey eyes made him look a little less dejected, but those who knew him well knew that his worries ran deep. Even his smile seemed sad. Marie Pollock summed up her husband's charms perfectly when she affectionately referred to his strangely appealing whipped-dog expression. To which he'd usually reply, "That's what shouldering life's painful burden has done to me," revealing his biggest asset—a robust sense of humour, inherited from his mother Dragomira, which he employed all the time, although no one knew whether he did it in jest or out of desperation.

"Oh! The great Russian tragedian, Pavel Pollock, is making a come-back," joked Oksa's mum with a merry laugh. "Aren't I lucky to have you two around!"

Oksa looked affectionately at her parents. She loved their witty repartee, which both touched and amused her. The alarm on Pavel's mobile broke in, noisily announcing that it was 7.30 a.m. Time to go.

"Baba, we're just waiting for you now," Oksa shouted up the stairs leading to the third floor of the house.

Dragomira Pollock came out onto the landing, immediately prompting cries of admiration. This remarkably imposing woman was respectfully called Baba Pollock by her immediate circle. She had a very straight, almost stiff bearing, but her face, far from being haughty, was always animated, and her piercing dark-blue eyes were enhanced by flushed cheeks and a broad forehead. Her blonde hair, threaded with silver and braided around her head, added a subtle Slavic touch to her arresting appearance. Yet this morning it was not these qualities that sent her family into raptures but her outfit, which was stunning.

"I'm ready, my darlings!" she said, walking downstairs regally. Her long purple dress was patterned with hinds embroidered in black pearls, and it floated around her like the petals of a flower.

"Wow, Baba, you look amazing!" exclaimed Oksa in delight, throwing herself into her arms and giving her a hug.

In her enthusiasm she didn't pay any attention to the happy cries coming from Dragomira's earrings. Intricately worked in the shape of perches, they carried two tiny golden birds, about an inch high, who were swinging on them and whispering shrilly about their feats as fighter pilots.

"Oh! I forgot something... give me a minute, I'll be right back."

As soon as she said this, Dragomira turned round and ran back upstairs to her apartment, double-locking the door behind her.

16

3

THE REUNION

Gazing into her mirror, Dragomira began scolding her reflection, wagging an admonishing forefinger.

"I can't take you two anywhere! You're supposed to be quiet, my Ptitchkins, you promised! Otherwise I'll never take you out of your cage again. Do you understand?"

"Yes, Your Graciousness, we get it! Message received loud and clear. Radio silence!" sang the tiny golden birds at the top of their voices, rubbing against Dragomira's neck to earn her forgiveness.

She gently patted their little heads and they continued swinging enthusiastically on their golden perches—this time, silently.

"Ahem, Your Graciousness, Your Graciousness…"

Nearby, the creatures in blue dungarees were wringing their hands in distress and coughing softly to attract her attention.

"What's the matter, my Lunatrixes?" she asked, turning round.

"The Abominari has snapped its nerves," one of them told her, his eyes impossibly round.

Dragomira went over to the double-bass case and went inside. She hastily climbed the staircase leading to her workroom, which was strictly private. A creature just over a foot tall was standing in front of the skylight, scratching angrily at the glass. It whirled round, growling and glaring evilly at everyone within reach. The Abominari had stumpy legs, long arms and a skeletal body, and its head was covered in a greyish skin which gave off

17

a nauseating stench. An iridescent white substance was dripping from its wide mouth, which revealed two sharp, protruding fangs.

"The Abominari has performed bitings on the Goranov plant," explained one of the Lunatrixes. "We did attempt to initiate preventative measures but our limbs sustained stinging scratches."

The two Lunatrixes held out their badly scratched arms as evidence of the violent encounter. When she saw this, Dragomira exploded with anger—anger which doubled in intensity when she saw the poor Goranov, which had been attacked and was writhing in pain. Sap was slowly oozing from one of its stems and pooling on the earth of its pot.

"ABOMINARI!" shouted Dragomira. "This is intolerable, you've gone too far! What on earth is the matter with you?"

The creature leapt onto some boxes and growled, revealing its pointed fangs and filthy claws.

"Curse you! Curse you all! You're not my mistress, old lady, you are nothing to me! You won't be so full of yourself when my Master comes to get me…"

"No, of course not," replied Dragomira with cool indifference. "Let me remind you that you've been saying the same thing for fifty years or more and your so-called Master still hasn't come."

The Abominari gave an angry growl.

"You are nothing to me, do you hear? You're just a stinking pile of garbage! A dirty speck of blowfly excrement!"

At these words, all the creatures huddling in the four corners of the workroom shuddered with indignation. Dragomira walked over to the boxes on top of which the insolent Abominari was arrogantly perched. But as soon as she came close, the creature leapt down onto the floor and pounced on one of the Lunatrixes, seizing him from behind and tightly squeezing his neck as if to strangle him.

"I warn you, old lady, if you touch me I'll kill him, then I'll tear you and your pathetic menagerie to shreds!" the Abominari spat at Dragomira.

Unimpressed, she gazed up at the ceiling with a vexed expression. She took a slim iridescent cylinder about six inches long from the folds of her dress and coolly pointed it at the threatening Abominari. In a weary voice, she said: "Get Set Croakettes!"

Then she blew softly into the cylinder. A flurry of green sparks immediately sputtered from one end with a loud crackle. Two small live frogs with translucent wings appeared and flew at the Abominari, grabbing it firmly beneath its puny arms and lifting it almost three feet into the air. They shook the creature to make it release its hostage and the Lunatrix tumbled heavily onto the parquet floor. Dragomira marched over to the Abominari and seized it by the scruff of the neck, holding her arms out in front of her to avoid being clawed or bitten. When she opened a cage to imprison it, though, the aggressive creature took its chance and viciously scratched her forearms.

"I'll deal with you later," she warned imperiously as she double-locked the cage. Then, addressing the Lunatrixes, she held out a small pot and said softly: "My Lunatrixes, I must go out now. Please put this ointment on the Goranov, it should ease its pain. I won't be long."

"Our obedience is never in doubt and your return our greatest desire," they replied, still shaken by the attack.

Just before leaving her apartment, Dragomira readjusted her crown of hair braids. "That's better," she concluded, before heading back downstairs. "But I really am going to have to do something about that Abominari."

※

"Is everything okay, Dragomira?" asked Marie Pollock a few seconds later. "You look annoyed. Oh! Have you hurt yourself?"

Dragomira looked down at the two bloody stripes on her forearms. She'd been so preoccupied with that insufferable Abominari's malevolent behaviour that she hadn't even realized she'd been scratched.

"Oh, it's nothing, Marie. I had a fight with a pair of scissors when I was unpacking my boxes and I'm afraid I came off worst," she fibbed with a grin. "But it's probably time to go now, isn't it?"

The little group set off for St Proximus, the French school which Oksa was about to see for the first time in a few minutes. She was going to be in Year 8 and, despite her seemingly laid-back attitude, she was feeling a bit apprehensive: everything was so new! Starting with her... Oksa often dreamt of being a heroic adventurer or an invincible ninja warrior, but high on the list of things she hated most in the world, along with leeks, the colour pink and creepy-crawlies, was drawing attention to herself. And new kids, as everyone knows, rarely go unnoticed in lessons. Nervously she put her hand in the pocket of her grey blazer and touched the talisman given to her by Dragomira the evening before—a small flat leather pouch containing seeds with relaxing properties—and remembered her advice: "If you feel tense in body and mind, hold this and gently stroke it. It will make you feel more at peace with the world, the sky will seem clearer and your path more sure."

As she recalled these comforting words, fat raindrops softly began splashing on the London pavements that were bringing her closer to school with every step.

"Yeah, right! The sky isn't likely to seem clearer today," she grumbled to herself.

❋

"OKSA!" She turned round. A boy accompanied by his parents was running towards her, his dark-blue eyes shining with joy.

"Gus! Gosh! Is that really you?" she asked with a laugh.

"Save your sarcasm for yourself," he replied, looking her up and down. "Have you looked in the mirror lately? I'm finding it hard to believe my eyes—Oksa Pollock in a pleated skirt!" he added, sniggering.

"Yeah, and Gustave Bellanger in a suit and tie!" said Oksa in the same tone. "Stylish or what?! Actually, you look rather *classy*. Not bad at all."

"I'll take that as a compliment," said Gus, flicking back his long dark hair, "and try to forget that these shirt collars are super-tight."

"You could begin by loosening your tie. You might not look so flushed," teased Oksa, watching him out of the corner of her eye.

After Gus had taken this good advice, the two friends picked up the bags they'd dumped on the pavement in the excitement of their reunion and everyone continued walking to the school, chatting.

"So how are you after all this time?" asked Gus, his face glowing. "It's been a whole week since we've seen each other."

"Great!" replied Oksa, looking just as happy. "I'm now the proud owner of a pleated skirt—have you any idea how long I've dreamt of that? And have you seen these ultra-cool grey ankle socks? I wonder how I've managed to live without them all this time," she continued lightly. "Other than that, the house is a complete tip. You have to open thirty boxes to find anything you need. But that's fine. I love the neighbourhood."

"Me too… I can't get over the fact that we're here. We left France so fast! This place is incredible. It feels like we've travelled thousands of miles and ended up on the other side of world."

As soon as Pavel Pollock had mentioned his plans, Gus's father, Pierre Bellanger, had jumped at the chance to go into partnership with him and they were about to open up a world-class French restaurant. The Bellangers had been the first to cross the Channel a few days earlier, and had taken up residence a few streets away, right next to the colourful streets of Chinatown.

"I hope we're in the same class," continued Gus.

"You can say that again," said Oksa. "If we're not, I'll make a scene. Or have hysterics. I'll roll around on the floor, foaming at the mouth with my eyes bulging and I'll bite the calves of anyone who comes near me."

"I can't wait to see that!" laughed Gus. "You obviously haven't changed a bit, despite the uniform of a model student. Or, at least, not for the better."

21

At these words, Oksa pounced on him with a roar and pretended to strangle him.

"Ungrateful so-and-so. After all I've done for you. You'll never understand girls," she growled, shaking him like a pear tree.

"And you're off your rocker, you loony," replied Gus, crying with laughter. "Off your rocker and totally OTT."

"I can't help that, it's genetic," objected Oksa, shrugging in resignation. "You know full well that the Pollocks are over-the-top by nature. It's all down to our Russian blood. Anyway, I reserve the right to make a scene and have hysterics. All I want is for us to be in the same class! Is that too much to ask?"

4

St Proximus College

THE HEAVY WOODEN DOUBLE DOORS OF THE ENORMOUS entrance were wide open. Under the magnificent stone arch leading into the paved courtyard, two bowler-hatted porters greeted the crowds of schoolchildren and their families. Gus and Oksa made their way hesitantly under the porch, attracting quite a few glances between them. A group of girls seemed particularly interested in Gus, elbowing each other and making remarks. Oksa couldn't help noticing, once more, that wherever Gus went, girls stopped talking and stared at him, probably fascinated by his good looks. The boy blushed in embarrassment and ran his hand through his hair. The two friends kept walking, reluctantly leaving their families with the parents gathered at the back of the courtyard.

"Great, Cave-Girl is still here," muttered a schoolboy loud enough to be heard by the two friends.

"Who?" asked Oksa, turning to look at him.

The boy who'd just spoken gazed at her intently. Blond curls framed a face animated by big brown eyes.

"Hi! I'm Merlin Poicassé," he continued enthusiastically, holding out his hand formally. "How are you? Are you new?"

"Yes," replied Oksa, instinctively holding out her hand too. "We've just arrived in London. I'm Oksa Pollock."

"I'm Gustave Bellanger. But you can call me Gus."

"Well, Gus. She's Cave-Girl," he said, jutting his chin discreetly towards a remarkably large girl with a bad-tempered expression. "Her real name is Hilda Richard and all I'd say is that no one who's had any contact at all with that girl is likely to forget the experience in a hurry."

"Why's that?" asked Gus.

Merlin sighed, looking serious.

"She's all about ambushes, bruises and humiliation, if you get what I mean? Well, that's life… Welcome to St Proximus!"

"I warn you, Gus," said Oksa through gritted teeth, "if you're not in my class and I have to be with that girl, I swear I'll have a fit, a real one."

"Ah, that's the roll call," said Merlin briskly, suddenly standing up straighter. "Let's go nearer."

❋

Surrounded by the schoolteachers, Lucien Bontempi, the Headmaster of St Proximus, was perched on a small platform, tapping the microphone in front of him. His chubby cheeks and bulky figure gave him the appearance of a roly-poly clown, an impression enhanced by his apple-green tie and the orange handkerchief in the breast pocket of his jacket. However, as soon as he began giving his short speech, everyone realized that his firm, authoritative tone was in marked contrast to his affable figure.

"Next we'll come to what you've all been waiting for: class allocation. As is customary at London's French school, the three classes in every year are named after chemical elements: Mercury, Hydrogen and Carbon. We'll begin the roll call with the youngest: Year 7."

The names were read out one by one at regular intervals and the uniformed schoolchildren gradually formed lines. But at the end of the second list, Mr Bontempi's voice suddenly faltered.

"Williams, Alexandre," he called.

The Headmaster beckoned to a young boy who came over, accompanied by a very pale woman dressed all in black. Visibly upset, the

24

Headmaster placed his hand on the boy's head, leant over and whispered a few words into his ear.

"Is that his son?" murmured Oksa to Merlin.

"No," he replied. "That's the son of the maths teacher who was found dead in the Thames two weeks ago."

"Oh!" exclaimed Oksa, upset. "How awful—was it suicide?"

"No, he was murdered," continued Merlin in a confidential tone. "A terrible murder. It was in all the papers."

"Poor boy," said Oksa, swallowing with difficulty.

Suppressing a shudder, she concentrated again on the roll call of students.

"Now, the Year 8 Hydrogen class with Dr McGraw," shouted Mr Bontempi, inviting a tall, thin man to come and stand by his side. "Will the following students please step forward: Beck, Zelda... Bellanger, Gustave..." Gus shouted "Here!" and, giving Oksa one last look and a smile, he went over to the group gradually forming in front of Dr McGraw. Oksa's heart was beating fit to burst. Her eyelids fluttered nervously over her large grey eyes and she felt as if the heartbeats thumping against her chest were echoing off the walls of the courtyard like the names as they were read out one by one by the Headmaster. She felt terribly alone. She looked around for her parents. They were only a few yards away. Her father was making encouraging signs to her, clenching his fists. Feeling better, she gave him a little wave. At his side, Marie and Dragomira were grinning widely. Oksa's eyes were suddenly drawn to a movement on her gran's skirt: for a nanosecond, she thought she saw the embroidered hinds leaping as they frantically chased each other! Her eyes had to be playing tricks on her because of the stress. How she hated feeling stressed. *I can't start seeing things now... please let this be over soon, let me be in Hydrogen! Please say Pollock, P-O-L-L-O-C-K, say it now,*" she thought to herself, closing her eyes and crossing her fingers so hard that she almost dislocated the joints.

The alphabet was completely mixed up in her head, she was hearing names all over the place. She even thought that the letter P had already been read out.

"Prollock, Oksa," said the Headmaster finally, looking around for her in the courtyard.

Dr McGraw leant over to murmur something in his ear.

The Headmaster began again:

"Sorry… Pollock! Pollock, Oksa, please," he announced, placing a great deal of emphasis on the *Po*.

This time Oksa's heart exploded into a thousand sparks. She managed to splutter "Here", then, feeling weak with relief, she rushed over to join Gus, darting a joyful look at her parents.

"St Proximus, here we come."

※

Following Dr McGraw into one of the school's lofty corridors, the students in Hydrogen walked along with upturned faces and eyes wide with amazement. "Wow," murmured Oksa, "this place is unreal!"

Housed in a former seventeenth-century monastery, the school had a highly distinctive atmosphere. The stately entrance hall was adorned with faded coats of arms engraved with Latin inscriptions which Oksa had difficulty deciphering. There were classrooms all along the cloister and on the two arcaded floors giving on to the courtyard. The slender granite colonnades had been preserved, as had the stained-glass arched windows, which gave the daylight a colourful, opaque quality.

"You said it," agreed Gus in a low voice. "And look! They're keeping a close eye on us." He glanced up to point out the many statues lining the high passageways. The students had the strange, unsettling sensation of being unable to escape from their fierce, unwavering vigilance.

"No talking, please!" ordered Dr McGraw sternly. "Do we have some volunteers for an hour's detention on the very first day?"

Their enthusiasm dampened, the class walked upstairs and entered a bright room with anatomical charts on the walls. The double desks were made of dark wood and smelt of polish.

"Sit down!" shouted Dr McGraw imperiously.

"Wherever we like, sir?" asked a student.

"Wherever you like. As long as it's within these four walls, obviously," replied their teacher sarcastically. "You can leave your things at the foot of your desks for now. Later, I'll show you the lockers where you can keep anything you might find useful: snacks, sports gear, books, lucky charms, comforters, etc.," he added with a little sardonic laugh. "We'll be spending the morning together, and I'll explain school procedures and tell you about your timetable and your teachers. I'm Dr McGraw; I'll be taking you for maths and physical sciences, and I'll also be your form teacher. But let me make it quite clear that I haven't got any time for childish nonsense. You're no longer in Year 7; you have to take responsibility for who you are and what you do. I'm only prepared to listen to you if you have something valid and important to say, do you understand? I expect you to be highly disciplined and to work as hard as you can. Neither I nor this school will tolerate laziness or mediocrity. You're only allowed to be mediocre if that's the very best you can do. Your pinnacle of achievement, your finest effort. We expect you to do your best and nothing less. Understand?"

A polite murmur ran through the class. Sitting beside Gus, Oksa made herself as small as possible. She desperately hoped that she never had to ask Dr McGraw for anything. If she had a problem, she'd find someone else to give her some advice. At that precise moment she wasn't feeling too good, partly because of Dr McGraw's speech, which made her feel uncomfortably pressurized. But it wasn't just that she was overawed. That man was really making her feel ill.

"Now I've introduced myself, it's your turn," he continued in an icy tone, more likely to encourage them to run for the hills than have a cosy little chat. "Tell us briefly who you are, what subjects you're good at, your passions if you have any and anything else you'd like your classmates and me to know about you. But don't get carried away and please don't feel obliged to tell us your life story… young man, will you begin, please?"

Gus squirmed in his chair, not looking best pleased at being the lucky one to start. "My name is Gustave Bellanger," he said hesitantly. "I moved to London with my parents a few days ago. Maths is pretty much my forte. I really like manga and video games. I've done karate for six years and I also play the guitar."

"Maths is your forte, is it? That's good to hear," remarked Dr McGraw. "Your turn, young man."

Waiting for her turn as the other students spoke, Oksa studied their teacher while his attention was occupied by the introductions. A beanpole of a man, Dr McGraw was stylish and sombre in appearance, with slicked-back dark hair that showed off his finely lined face and inky black eyes to good advantage. His thin, slightly pursed lips looked as though they had been soldered together. He wore a plain black suit and a charcoal-grey shirt buttoned up to the base of his neck, where it was grazed by his prominent Adam's apple which kept jumping up and down with every inflexion of his voice. One other detail caught Oksa's attention: on the middle finger of his right hand the teacher wore a superb twisted silver ring with an amazing slate-grey stone which seemed to shimmer with a shifting light. It was an imposing ring which looked far too heavy for a hand so thin it was almost skeletal.

"Your turn, young lady, we're listening."

Dr McGraw stared right at her as he spoke these words in a low voice. Meeting his harsh, inquisitive gaze, Oksa felt sick, as if a pain were growing inside her and cutting off her air. She took a deep breath, the way her mum had taught her to help her relax, but she realized in astonishment that her ribcage had locked the moment she began to breathe in. For a fraction of a second her face contorted in an expression of fear.

"My name is Oksa Pollock—"

She again attempted to breathe, trying to draw some air into her lungs. A trickle of oxygen managed to get through.

"My name is Oksa Pollock and I like astrono—"

Out of air! Panicking, Oksa tried to take another breath. No! She mustn't let her feelings get the better of her. Bravely she drew another breath, trying to act as though nothing was wrong, but it was no good. She had an enormous bubble of air trapped in her chest. A bubble too large to be dislodged. Feeling panicky, Oksa loosened her tie.

"Yes, Miss Pollock, I think we know who you are now. We're listening," added Dr McGraw, clearly growing more impatient.

Oksa could barely hear his voice, which sounded as if it was muffled by cotton wool. The girl was suffocating, unable to breathe, her heart racing like a bolting horse. Then an even more intense, unbearable wave of pain hit her, which felt like a violent punch to the stomach. After resisting it for a few seconds, her body and mind succumbed to the pain and panic. Oksa looked round in the hope that someone would come to her help. No use—everyone was looking at her, but none of the students seemed to realize how distressed she was. And if they had, what could they have done? She had no strength left to fight it—she clutched Gus's arm and crashed to the floor.

5

A Terrible Day

Ever since she was a little girl, Oksa had been in the habit of visiting her gran after school in the evening. Her parents were very busy with work and Dragomira was always there. Oksa could count on her. They'd chat about one thing or another—what had happened during the day and sometimes about more serious matters, such as Oksa's worries, disappointments or triumphs. That evening had been unusual: when she'd come home after that terrible day—one of the worst she'd ever had—the house had been dead silent, much to her annoyance.

"Mum? Dad? Are you here?" she'd called, already feeling disappointed.

With a sigh, she'd thrown her bag at the bottom of the stairs. Of course they weren't here; they were at the restaurant, busy getting things ready. She was in Dragomira's apartment now, though, and it felt so welcoming, despite being messy and old-fashioned. She'd been waiting for this moment all day. As usual, Dragomira immediately bombarded her with questions: "So how did it go? Tell me everything!"

She'd prepared a delicious afternoon snack with all Oksa's favourites: fresh raspberries with little biscuits and spiced tea, a special home-made recipe. Now that she was here with her Baba, Oksa could relax at long last. She flopped into the small, threadbare pink armchair, the one she liked best, and curled up into a ball. Opposite, a vast wall was lined from floor to ceiling with shelves laden with jars, cans, boxes and books which it had taken Dragomira all day to arrange.

"It went well, Baba, very well," she said, feigning an enthusiasm she was far from feeling.

"You look awful, Dushka! You seem worn out. Have they been working you so hard on the very first day?" Then, changing the subject completely: "Are you hungry?"

"I'm starving," replied Oksa, biting greedily into a delicious chocolate biscuit.

"Eat up and tell me everything, even with your mouth full. I can't wait to hear all about it!"

"Well… inside, the school is totally amazing, it's an incredible place, you'd love it. Our form teacher is Dr McGraw, who also takes us for maths and physical sciences. He's *very* strict, you need to watch your step with him. He's not exactly a bundle of laughs."

There was a tense silence. Dragomira waited for her to go on. "And?"

"Well, apart from that, being in the same class as Gus is a dream come true! I'm over the moon, as you can imagine… Otherwise, nothing much else to report," she added, trying her hardest not to let on that she was upset. "Gus and I met a really nice boy. His name is Merlin. He's lived in London for five years and I think he's probably very brainy. The other students seem pretty cool, except for one girl who has a face like a pit bull terrier. She looks as if she hasn't got two brain cells to rub together."

"Come with me," said Dragomira, studying her carefully, not at all convinced by Oksa's outward cheerfulness. She took her by the hand and led her to a gorgeous red velvet sofa, which she hastily cleared of everything heaped on it.

"Hang on a moment…"

She went to the back of the apartment where there was a massive, cluttered set of shelves and a large work surface made of polished wood, where she indulged her passion for botany and medicinal plants—Dragomira had been a herbalist for some thirty years. With a small key hanging from one of her bracelets she unlocked a bookcase with opaque panes of glass. Instead of books, it contained hundreds of phials lined up on the shelves. Dragomira picked one and locked the door.

"Here's something that'll do you good, my darling. A special oil for 'difficult days'."

"But the day hasn't been difficult, Baba."

"Hush… not another word."

Oksa obeyed and let her gran massage her temples comfortingly as she stared at the fragrant coils of incense burning in every corner of the living room, which was filled wall-to-wall with knick-knacks, consoles, pedestal tables and sofas upholstered in old gold or crimson velvet. The coils drifted gently towards the stucco ceiling roses, as unpleasant thoughts circled around Oksa's head. Dragomira couldn't be more wrong: the day hadn't been difficult. No. It had been just terrible! And her memories of it, which were still very raw, continued to torment her. Unable to fight them, she was relentlessly taken back in time to the classroom, two hours earlier…

❊

When she'd regained consciousness, she was lying on the classroom floor, her forehead covered in sweat and her blood hammering furiously through her veins. She felt as though she'd hit herself on her chair when she fell, because her stomach was hurting badly. Several faces were leaning over her. A worried-looking Gus was crouched beside her. Merlin, his forehead furrowed and his cheeks scarlet, was murmuring, "Don't worry, don't worry about a thing," and the pretty girl with a penetrating gaze he'd sat next to, Zelda, had also knelt down, but was at a loss what to do to make Oksa feel better.

Dr McGraw, on the other hand, looked annoyed. "You're easily upset, Miss Pollock, very easily upset," he remarked coldly.

To prove the teacher and his unsympathetic words wrong, she made a huge effort and struggled to her feet, seething with anger, shame and frustration.

"Sir, sir, should we call an ambulance?" asked one boy in a frightened voice.

Dr McGraw looked at him contemptuously then replied in a curt, mocking tone:

"Why not the special response unit from the Department of Health while you're at it? But perhaps we should ask Miss Pollock? Should we take you to the infirmary, Miss Pollock, or do you think you're in a fit state to endure this *exhausting morning* right through to the end?"

Amazed, Gus glared reproachfully at their teacher, but the man ignored him. With the help of her classmates, Oksa sat down again as best she could, trying to ignore the pain in her stomach and the anger darkening her heart.

"Anyone else planning to collapse? Yes? No? Any volunteers?" asked Dr McGraw, his voice sharp as a knife. To his great surprise, someone raised their hand. "Miss Pollock?" Dr McGraw looked thrown by this sudden, and obviously unexpected, turn of events. Devoid of all sarcasm, his voice was virtually shaking. Perhaps through remorse at being so harsh…

"I'd like to finish what I was saying, sir."

Just as Oksa said these words in a monotonous but clear and determined voice, a gust of wind cold enough to raise goose pimples swept through the classroom and the half-open windows banged violently shut. Everyone jumped. Except for McGraw, who hadn't taken his eyes off Oksa.

"My name is Oksa Pollock," continued the girl, not permitting any interruption, "and I've just arrived in London. My favourite subjects are science and maths. I like astronomy and rollerblading and I've done karate for six years, like Gus. There, I'm done, sir."

All the students looked at her, some in amazement, others in admiration. But what none of them could see was the profound exhilaration she was feeling deep inside and which was acting like a bumper dose of vitamins.

"Thank you, young lady," drawled Dr McGraw in a flat voice. "Shall we continue now? We've wasted enough time."

❋

When the bell rang for break, Oksa felt immediately relieved. At last she could escape from this classroom. Not a moment too soon! Any longer and she'd have begun screaming at the top of her lungs. This had never happened to her before—it wasn't like her at all. Gus found his friend crouched against the statue of a winged angel in the school courtyard and knelt down in front of her. Seeing how sad she looked, he wanted to put his arms around her and give her a hug, but he didn't dare.

"What happened?" he said. "I thought you were having a heart attack! You went stiff as a poker, then you fell down. You scared the living daylights out of me."

"I've never felt so ill in my life. Everything was spinning, I couldn't breathe."

"Were you in pain? Were you scared of speaking in front of the class?"

Oksa didn't reply. Puzzled, Gus watched her out of the corner of his eye, not knowing what to say to make her feel better. He thought for a moment then said: "Don't worry about it! Don't think about it any more, it's ancient history!"

"Yes, you're right," replied Oksa. "You're right, of course…"

❋

In the darkness of her room, Oksa was lying on her bed, staring at the phosphorescent stars stuck to the ceiling, which were glowing with a milky light. She was trying and failing to get to sleep. Her headache had vanished—Dragomira's massage had been very effective—and she could barely feel the pain in her stomach now. Gus had called her during the evening to check up on her. It had given them the chance to tell each other again how glad they were to be in the same class. It was such a relief! The call had done her good, she was so glad she had a friend like Gus. But what a strange day it had been, all the same… she really hoped they wouldn't all be like that. It was almost midnight and sleep was the last thing on her mind. She turned on her beside lamp and, sitting up in bed, looked around, thoughtfully. Her desk was littered with the contents of a box that she hadn't had time to put away: trinkets and toys she no longer used but couldn't bear to part with. Her gaze fell on her Poupette doll with red hair, which had been one of her favourites a few years ago. The happy times of childhood were long gone now; she sighed and shrugged sadly. Her half-closed eyes lingered on the doll before closing. She thought back over the most unpleasant events of the day. The butterflies she'd felt at going back to school. The anxiety, which still churned her stomach and made her feel sick. She reopened her eyes and immediately widened them in surprise: the doll's long hair was standing up on its little plastic head as though magnetized by some mysterious force! Oksa blinked to convince herself she wasn't dreaming. Then she leapt out of bed, sending her duvet flying. With her hand stretched out in front of her, she just had time to see a small fireball fly from her palm, heading straight for the doll's head.

"*What on earth is going on?*" she thought frantically.

Before her horrified eyes, the synthetic hair began to crackle with flames. Instinctively she grabbed the doll with both hands—a very bad idea which she immediately regretted as the scalding plastic burned her fingers. Stifling a cry of pain, she dropped the doll and—another bad idea—began to blow on the hair, which only made it burn more fiercely. The flames soon reached the wood-panelled wall against which the desk had been placed, emitting alarming, acrid smoke. Her heart thumping painfully in her chest, Oksa's only option was to grab the vase of flowers put there that morning by her gran and throw it on the fire to douse the flames. Startled by what had just happened, she fell back onto her bed, panting. She felt terribly ill and her stomach was hurting again. She writhed in pain, overcome by feelings of nausea, which soon turned to a violent dizziness. She closed her eyes and slipped into a state of unconsciousness, allowing her to blank out reality.

❋

"Oh no…" she groaned, covering her head with her pillow. Oksa had just woken up and the first thing she noticed was her little doll, which had been the biggest casualty of that strange night. It was missing an eye, its foam body was ripped open and, what was worse, its fire-red hair was now fire-damaged hair.

"What have I done? What have I done?! I burned my Poupette doll!" wailed Oksa, wringing her hands, knowing full well what had actually happened.

Because now she'd woken up, it was obvious she hadn't dreamt it. This wasn't a figment of her imagination or her mind playing tricks: something had really happened, something all too real. The poor balding, charred doll lay on the desk, her smile twisted by the melting plastic. Oksa gazed at her toy for ages, feeling terribly ashamed that it had met with such an unhappy end. Ashamed. Terrified. Excited. Filled with wonder. Mainly filled with wonder, if she were completely honest.

6

DIFFICULT DAYBREAK

K NOCK, KNOCK, KNOCK.
"Oksa, are you going to have breakfast with me?"

Oksa jumped: her gran had just knocked three times on her bedroom door. The grand opening of the restaurant was taking place in a few days and her parents had worked very late; they must still be asleep.

"I'm just coming, Baba."

She rushed over to the mirror on the door of her wardrobe—one of the few unscathed pieces of furniture in the room—and examined herself carefully, certain that she must have turned into a monster overnight. She ran her fingers over her face, checking everything. Nothing had changed—her slate-grey eyes, her cheeks with their prominent high cheekbones, her well-defined lips, her slightly uneven teeth, her dimples, which appeared when she smiled or pouted, and her bobbed hair looked the same as they had the night before. Except she felt more tired than ever. Still... She quickly pulled on her pleated skirt and blouse and popped into the bathroom to run a quick comb through her hair and splash some cold water on her face.

❋

She was heading for the kitchen when a sudden thought made her do a U-turn: the state of her room! She couldn't possibly let anyone see the burnt wall or the charred doll. She anxiously searched for her thick black felt-tip, which must have landed somewhere in the room when she'd swept everything off the desk with the back of her hand to stop it going up in flames. She eventually found the pen beneath the wardrobe and made a sign on a piece of cardboard, which she stuck to her bedroom door:

WORK IN PROGRESS
No entry under any circumstances
at the risk of MAJORLY serious reprisals!!!

Oksa didn't say a word during breakfast. She was in a state of complete shock. How was she, Oksa Pollock, capable of producing these incredible phenomena? She would never even have dared to dream it. It was mind-blowing.

"Dushka," said Dragomira, tightening the knot of her granddaughter's tie, "I don't want to sound like a prophet of doom or anything, but you look terrible. Did you sleep badly? Are you worried about something? Perhaps you're sickening for something?"

"I didn't sleep very well, Baba."

"Don't move a muscle, I've got just what you need."

Dragomira pushed back her chair and rushed upstairs to her apartment. She came down a few minutes later with a small bottle.

"Take this."

"What is it? Another of your odd concoctions?" asked Oksa, intrigued as always by her gran's eccentric behaviour.

"It's Elixir of Betony," replied Dragomira, as she filtered the contents of the bottle through a tiny sieve, humming softly. "This is excellent for getting rid of those ugly circles under your eyes," she said at last, handing her a brimming cup. "Drink this and you'll be on top form until tonight, believe me!"

At the thought of that, Oksa gulped the liquid down in one. "Eugh, yuck. That must be the most disgusting thing I've ever drunk," she said, pulling a face.

"Come on, finish your breakfast quickly, otherwise you'll be late."

"I'm never late, Baba, you know that," replied Oksa.

Oksa was never late for the simple reason that she could run incredibly fast. She merely had to imagine she was a gazelle trying to escape from a hunter or a magical character with fantastic abilities and her legs would increase in strength and speed. Her favourite role was that of a fierce ninja warrior with superhuman powers. She'd imagine that she'd acquired remarkable powers while she was sleeping, either invisibility, exceptional sight or hearing, or Herculean strength—it varied. These powers, inspired by books and films, were often prompted by everyday life: an annoying problem, an obstacle, an argument, anything could make Oksa imagine that she had a "supernatural" gift. This ability might not be enough to solve all the world's problems but it was a valuable tool which helped her to overcome difficulties and to daydream. Nothing more than that. She didn't inhabit those dangerous virtual worlds which tempted their temporary inhabitants to lose touch with reality. Not at all. Oksa was a sensible girl who could tell the difference between fantasy and reality. But this morning, things were completely different from the night before... a fantasy had become part of *real life*—her burnt fingers were a painful reminder of that. Oksa had desperately wanted to be able to do what she'd done last night on many occasions. Okay, she was only a beginner, but still she had to admit it was amazing. She only hoped that it wouldn't all disappear as quickly as it had come—a worry that made her feel light-headed and sick and gave her palpitations. But for the time being, Oksa the fire-throwing ninja had to meet an important challenge: to run to school at least as fast as the speed of sound if she didn't want to be late for the first time in her life.

When she got there, slightly out of breath, the other students were just starting to go to their classrooms. Phew... she'd done it! Oksa went looking for the Marco Polo room, where she had her first lesson of the day: history and geography with Miss Heartbreak. Walking through the cloister, she saw some Year 9 students heading for a classroom at the other end to hers. When she drew level with them, one of them shouldered her violently.

"Ouch!" she couldn't help crying out.

"Why don't you look where you're going, loser?" said the boy who'd bumped into her.

"You're the one who barged into me!" retorted Oksa indignantly.

"Why don't you go back to nursery school if you can't walk in a straight line! You'd better watch your step, you moron," he grunted, shoving her again and sending her reeling into a column.

He swaggered past, sniggering with his friends. Oksa watched him walk away. Very dark-haired and quite well-built, he was a good head taller than she. And about thirty pounds heavier. He turned round to give her a brooding look full of hatred, which surprised her. She shrugged and made her way to her classroom. "Hey, you almost missed the start of the lesson," exclaimed Gus, welcoming his friend. "That would have been a first in the famous Oksa's life story. I could have said: '*I was there!*'"

"Hi Gus! It was less of a first, more of a—" She broke off, rubbing her shoulder.

"What's the matter? Did you fall over?"

"You could say that—I fell over a lout of a Year 9 who bumped into me. That Neanderthal really hurt me."

"I hope he said sorry?"

"Yeah, right! Not a bit of it! He also called me a moron and laughed at me, the creep."

"Oh well, forget it, he's not worth it," advised Gus.

"You're right... but, still, it's really sore."

※

Miss Heartbreak came into the classroom and began her lesson. Petite and slender, she was a charming, sweet-natured woman who smiled a lot. The complete opposite of Dr McGraw, whose icy severity made the students shiver, Miss Heartbreak had a keen, friendly gaze which hinted at an underlying gentleness. Oksa was captivated by this first history lesson. When the bell rang for the end of the two-hour period, she wasn't the only one to sigh with disappointment, which made their teacher smile.

"We'll be seeing each other again tomorrow, I believe, from ten to eleven, this time for geography. In the meantime, have a very good day!" she said pleasantly to the students.

And it was a good day for Oksa. At break, the students were already starting to form small groups. Merlin Poicassé immediately came over to Oksa to ask how she was feeling. As for Gus, after seeing Zelda Beck sitting alone on a bench, he'd asked her if she'd like to join the trio, inviting her to share a packet of chocolate crêpes large enough to feed the whole class. Zelda smiled and gratefully accepted the invitation.

"I feel a bit lost. I don't know anyone; my parents and I only moved here a month ago."

"Same goes for Gus and me!" exclaimed Oksa. "Don't you think it's odd to be in England at a school where everyone speaks French? It feels like we're still in France. I'm finding it hard to believe I've changed country. Except when I see double-decker buses and taxis."

"Yes, that's how I feel too," replied Zelda. "It's very touristy, but I can't help being delighted when I see a red bus or when I walk past a real English *bobby*!"

"We'll get used to it," said Gus.

"That's for sure," said Merlin reassuringly. "And the day you can really enjoy their fluorescent pink jelly is the day you'll have stopped being an expat and have become a real English kid!"

"How long have you been in London?" asked Oksa.

"This is the start of my fifth year... and I still can't bear jelly!"

They all burst out laughing, delighted at their growing camaraderie. Oksa glanced at Gus, who smiled back. There's nothing like good friends to make you feel better.

7

A MAGNIFICENT DISCOVERY

ON SEVERAL OCCASIONS DURING THE DAY, OKSA HAD wanted to talk to Gus about her mind-blowing experiments of the night before. She'd almost dragged him to one side at lunch break, but the crowded, noisy cafeteria wasn't the ideal place for this kind of revelation, so the two friends went to lesson after lesson all day without getting the chance to talk in private, even for a minute. Which wasn't such a bad idea after all. Oksa needed to check up on a couple of little things. Well… little things… a figure of speech… As was so often the case, her parents weren't back when she arrived home, which was annoying, so she spent part of the evening with Dragomira. Baba Pollock was delighted to see that her granddaughter was on much better form.

"That elixir you gave me this morning was wonderful, Baba. I felt brilliant all day!"

"I know, Dushka, I know."

She was longing to tell Dragomira her secret. She was bound to understand. Dragomira always understood everything. But what was happening to her was *a bit* strange… No, for the time being, it would be better for everyone if she kept quiet. For a minute, she toyed with the idea of giving them a demonstration and shivered at the thought of her father's reaction. She knew him—he'd scream in shock and terror. She wouldn't be allowed to leave the house, he'd be afraid for her all the

42

time. Bottom line—it would be sheer hell. She cut short her afternoon snack with her gran, her supper with her parents and Gus's call to wish her a good weekend, then shut herself away in her room. Fortunately everyone had obeyed the sign and no one appeared to have entered while she was away. Phew! It would have been really tricky to explain what had happened.

Suddenly—as she'd been in the habit of doing for ages—she assumed the ninja position, her hands upright in front of her, one leg bent at a right angle, the other stretched back, then she turned her head slowly, eyes narrowed as if on the lookout for an enemy or some kind of danger.

"Yaahhaa!" she growled, looking fierce.

She finished her inspection and, just as suddenly, adopted a more ordinary pose.

"Nothing to report, venerable Oksa-san," she concluded to herself. "Now let's move on to more serious matters."

Brimming with energy, she sat on the edge of her bed and stared at the clothes draped over the back of her desk chair. She concentrated, eager to see whether what she thought might happen would. A few seconds later, the clothes were tossed into the air by an invisible force. Oksa cried out in a mixture of surprise and triumph. She then decided to focus her attention on her desk: the pencils standing innocently in a pot lost no time in shooting upwards like missiles, embedding themselves in the ceiling like large nails. Oksa stifled another cry of amazement. When she focused on them, the unpacked removal boxes imploded, scattering their contents across the room. Nothing escaped her destructive power, and in a few seconds all her hard work tidying up the day before had been undone.

"This is incredible!" she murmured, overturning knick-knacks by sheer force of will. After searching under her bed and rummaging around in the few boxes that still hadn't been unpacked, she remembered where she'd put the little figurines of cartoon characters which she wanted to use for a new experiment: they were in a box on top of her cupboard, which was filled to overflowing with clutter. She pushed her desk chair over and clambered onto it. Even when she stood on tiptoe and stretched out her arms, though, she was still a good four inches too short.

"That box is beginning to annoy me," she grumbled. "Come on, Oksa, flex your muscles and GET HOLD OF IT!"

Suddenly she felt herself growing taller, or rather rising, until her hand was within easy reach of the box. But the power of the ninjas or her muscles had nothing to do with it. Oksa was simply floating above her chair! She kicked her feet and felt nothing but empty space beneath her.

"What's going on?" she exclaimed, before crashing to the floor.

The box of figurines toppled over as she fell and the contents rained down on top of her.

"Wow! This is completely unreal," she said, rubbing her bottom.

She climbed back onto the chair and tried to get another box, which was just as hard to reach. She held out her arms and focused on her objective. The same thing happened: it was as if her feet were being pushed *from underneath*.

"Amazing!" she just had time to say, before she crashed to the floor again.

Despite landing painfully on her bottom every time she fell, she repeated the experiment about ten times to try and understand what was happening. Euphoric and bedraggled, her cheeks flaming, she finally collapsed onto her bed.

"I must think about this… this is crazy."

But she was so worked up she couldn't concentrate.

"I've got an idea!"

She sprang up and stood in front of her mirror.

"I'll work it out."

She tried to remember her state of mind when she'd wanted to get the box. The strain on her arms, the stretching, the muscles tensing, her fierce desire to touch that stupid box. No, not desire. It wasn't a desire.

44

It was more a feeling of exasperation and impatience. Yes, it was *very* annoying not to be able to get that bloody box, it had almost made her lose her temper. She had to reach it at all costs, it was the only thing that mattered. She closed her eyes and imagined floating like she'd just done. A few seconds later she felt her feet resting on something other than the floor. She cautiously opened her eyes to look in the mirror: she was standing upright, intact, still the same Oksa. But she was suspended about three feet above the ground.

8

A WORRYING SECRET

IN LONDON, AS IN PARIS, THE FIRST THING GUS DID WHEN he woke up was to switch off his computer. He couldn't finish his day without playing a video game for at least an hour. And when he started dozing off, more often than not in front of his computer, he'd burrow under his duvet, virtually comatose, and fall asleep immediately, the screen casting an opaline light over the walls of his room.

This Saturday in London felt really odd. It was the first time Gus had moved house and what he was feeling today was light years away from what he'd feared. There'd been nothing terrible about this change of scene, which was actually proving to be quite exciting. After a week, everything felt so familiar! Having dreaded the move to the point of making himself sick, he couldn't get over how happy he was. Of course, if he was honest with himself, the fact that the Pollocks—and particularly Oksa—were here made it much easier to adapt. But, as his mum said: any type of happiness is good happiness.

※

He decided to go downstairs for breakfast. His parents were already up and they each planted a wet kiss on his cheeks.

"You're so affectionate," he remarked, pretending to wipe his cheeks with his pyjama sleeve.

Pierre Bellanger, nicknamed "The Viking" by his friends, was a bulky man who always dressed in black. Long strands of greying blond hair hung over his forehead, partly obscuring his plump face. Jeanne had an oval, Madonna-like face framed by short black hair. She was much shorter than her husband, with a slender figure and a lively expression in her brown eyes. Discovering at the age of thirty that they couldn't have children had been a terrible shock for them both. Jeanne had struggled with depression, while Pierre had buried himself in his work, only coming home to sink into a restless sleep. One spring day, they realized they had a choice: either they let cruel reality get the better of them or they did something about it. The next day they began the adoption process. After several trips to China, during which they met Marie—who would become Mrs Pollock, the wife of their best friend, Pavel—their hopes gradually began to materialize. Two years later they went over to an orphanage to fetch Gus, their little miracle, and bring him home to France. He was just over a year old and all they knew about him was that his biological mum had been a young Shanghai girl who'd fallen in love with a Dutch student. By the time she'd realized she was pregnant, the young man had already gone back to his own country and she didn't have the courage to terminate the pregnancy or tell her family, who still lived in the countryside. When the baby was born she abandoned him at the orphanage, since she was unable to take care of him herself. It was love at first sight for Jeanne and Pierre Bellanger, the minute they saw the toddler playing on his own in his cot. And the feeling had been mutual—as soon as Gus had seen them at the orphanage, he'd tottered towards Jeanne and Pierre, babbling "Mama, mama". The orphanage staff had been dumbfounded. Quite a few people wanting to adopt had come through their doors, yet this was the first time they'd ever seen such a young child warm so quickly to strangers.

*

Jeanne and Pierre watched their son eat his breakfast. He was a handsome boy with slanting blue Eurasian eyes, dead straight, sleek black hair and long, tapering hands. They'd lost count of the number of girls who'd fallen for him since nursery school. Still, more often than not, it was Oksa who noticed that kind of thing; Gus just blushed and looked embarrassed when his friend pointed out some new crush.

"Honestly, Gus, are you blind?"

"What? Why me?" he asked, sincerely at a loss.

Most of the time, Oksa preferred not to answer and would just shrug and sigh. Why Gus? Very simply because he had a fantastic physique, good looks and a shy nature which made him irresistible to girls. But for Oksa, who knew him better than anyone else, he had some really special qualities: he was loyal, considerate, modest, kind, intelligent... The list was long, but what Gus was to her could be summed up in three words: her best friend.

✳

Two streets away, in the small house on Bigtoe Square, Oksa was hopping up and down beside the phone impatiently, chewing her nails. Every thirty seconds she started to dial Gus's number, which she now knew by heart, then broke off before the last digit. She was dying to speak to him about her amazing discovery, and yet something was stopping her. She didn't doubt him for a second, but what she desperately wanted to tell him was pretty mind-blowing even for her. So, glued to the spot by the phone, shaking with contradictory emotions, she tried to face facts: it was too soon to talk about... *that*. She just wasn't ready.

When Pavel came out of his bedroom, he found her lying on the floor by the phone, looking agitated and trying to concentrate on a sample menu her mother had scribbled on a scrap of paper the night before when she'd come in from the restaurant.

"What are you doing there, darling?" he asked in concern.

Oksa jumped.

"Er… nothing," she stammered. "I was just waiting for someone to bother to get up and have breakfast with me," she said as flippantly as possible. "I've been hanging around in this draughty hall for forty-eight and a half minutes!"

"It's all your mum's fault," replied Pavel, defending himself, his eyes sparkling roguishly. "You know what I'm like—if it were up to me, I'd be out of bed at the crack of dawn!"

Oksa burst out laughing at this outrageous assertion.

"Yeah right—only if you believe that dawn is around 10 a.m.!"

Pavel gave a sigh, which was meant to sound pathetic but which merely made Oksa giggle.

"What's going on? You're very cheerful this morning!"

Marie Pollock had just drowsily appeared at the top of the stairs.

"My daughter is the cheerful one," replied Pavel. "She's cheerfully persecuting me."

"You poor thing," said Marie, winking at her daughter.

All three sat down in the kitchen to enjoy a hearty breakfast and the mood continued to be light-hearted—outwardly, at least, because the thoughts running through Oksa's mind were as heavy as lead. Molten lead. Even while she was devouring thick slices of buttered bread, she was in turmoil. On several occasions she almost opened the floodgates and told them her secret. Should she get up and make a solemn announcement? Or slip the information into the conversation casually, naturally? Or even better: give them a demonstration! Send that tea towel by the sink flying into the air? Add a little creative chaos to the perfect rows of spice pots on the shelves? The idea was tempting but Oksa couldn't do it. She couldn't do anything. Or say anything. To anyone. Not yet.

*

I'm going to have a bath, Mum," said Oksa.

"Okay, darling."

Lying in the hot water, gazing at the tiled wall as it gradually misted up, Oksa tried to make sense of her muddled thoughts. She felt exhausted and at the same time brimming with energy. How complicated everything was… something fantastic was happening to her, she knew that. She'd always dreamt of being able to do what was now well within her capabilities. But it also terrified her. She rested her head against the rim of the bath and shut her eyes. Then she heard a strange noise, initially very faint, sounding a long way off, but coming closer and swelling until it mounted an assault on Oksa's eardrums. She sat bolt upright in fright, trembling as she realized the horrific nature of the noise, which she could now hear clearly: it was the strange, terrifying sound of women screaming. She stiffened, listening intently, wondering whether she should come out of the bathroom or stay put. But after a few seconds she realized that the screams weren't coming from somewhere inside the house or from outside. No—the screams were coming from *her*. They whirled through her mind and swept over her from head to toe, paralysing her with horror. Then, just as suddenly, they fell silent and vanished. Startled, Oksa looked round and, feeling slightly reassured, she sank down into the hot water until only her face was showing. Her heart had only just stopped racing when she noticed a golden shimmer on the steamy tiled wall. She moved her hand under the water to see if the reflections were coming from the bath, but this had no effect on the remarkable colour of the shimmering patch, which remained unchanged. Oksa closed her eyes and when she opened them again the brightness had gone.

"*Perhaps I should try to get more sleep,*" she thought to herself. "What if I'm starting to see things now?" It had all seemed so real, though!

"You all right in there, Oksa? You still alive?"

Pavel Pollock was on the other side of the door asking how she was. As usual. Every time she took a bath—and this had been since she was old enough to do so alone—he'd call out to her every three minutes or so to check that she was all right.

"Yes, Dad, I'm just drowning myself," she replied in a mock-serious tone. "And I plugged in the hairdryer because I want to dry my hair in the bath. Oh, and I forgot, I used bleach instead of bubble bath."

"Fine, make fun of a poor man concerned about the well-being of his darling little girl!"

"Oh, it's a hard life being a darling little girl," muttered Oksa with a smile.

"Okay, call me if you need anything."

"No problem, Dad, don't worry."

"I'm not worried."

Oksa couldn't help smiling. "The legendary Russian OTT-ness," she murmured, sinking beneath the water.

✻

She climbed out of the bath a few minutes later. Wrapping herself in her dressing gown, she noticed a large star-shaped bruise on her stomach around her belly button. Oksa wondered when she could have got such a bad bruise. It hurt a bit but, given its size and colour, it wasn't too bad. Perhaps it had been when she collapsed after feeling so ill, on her first day at school? It looked as if she'd been punched and that was exactly how she'd felt just before her fall.

Weird! She looked closer. What an odd shape! *"I'll have to show it to Baba, she's bound to have some ointment for it,"* she thought. She got dressed and went upstairs to see her gran, who greeted her wearing a long midnight-blue velvet housecoat embroidered with brightly coloured Russian motifs.

"You look amazing, Baba!"

"Thank you, Dushka. How are you?"

"I'm fine. I wanted to see you because I have a large bruise on my stomach. I was sure you'd have some cream or oil to put on it."

"Show me."

Oksa lifted up her T-shirt. Seeing the bruise, Dragomira put her hand over her mouth in amazement.

"How long have you had that? Why didn't you show me before? Has anyone else seen it?" she gasped breathlessly.

"Hang on a minute, Baba, that's a lot of questions for a tiny bruise! No, I haven't had it long, I've only just noticed it, but I fell over three days ago, so I might have hurt myself then. Er… what was your last question?"

Dragomira didn't say anything, which was totally out of character as she was normally so chatty. She seemed stunned and euphoric at the same time. She looked at her granddaughter, her eyes shining, muttering incomprehensible words which, Oksa thought, were probably Russian.

"Baba? Have you got some cream then?" she repeated.

Dragomira roused herself, still looking incredulous, and stammered: "Yes, yes, of course, Dushka."

✻

Once Oksa had gone back downstairs, Dragomira went up to her workroom. The two Lunatrixes, who were brushing the shelves with tiny feather dusters, greeted their mistress deferentially. Dragomira patted their rumpled little heads absent-mindedly and sat down at her desk. She switched on her computer, opened her email programme and tapped feverishly on the keyboard:

Leomido, something incredible has just happened: it's the Mark. There's no doubt about it. Come as soon as possible! I'll contact our friends.

From: your affectionate sister.

She clicked "High Priority" then "Send", her heart racing and her hands shaking. Her face lit up in a smile and a strange light flickered in her eyes. She couldn't help giving a sigh, which sounded like a cross between a groan and a whoop of delight.

"Is something vexatious tormenting Your Graciousness?" asked the Lunatrixes, rushing to her side.

By way of reply, Dragomira began to dance round the table in the middle of the workroom. Floating vertically three feet above the floor, she spun round with her arms in the air, clapping and singing at the top of her lungs. The frizzy-haired potato-like creature clambered onto the table and waddled heavily, running its fingers through its luxuriant mane, while another creature lethargically undulated its fat, wrinkled body. The plants moved their leaves in rhythm, except for the Goranov, which seemed frightened by this sudden frantic activity. Apart from Baba Pollock, none of them knew what had caused this outburst. Still, none of them thought twice about joining in cheerfully with their mistress. The whole workroom was celebrating.

"My valiant creatures, my dear Lunatrixes, the Mark has reappeared!"

"The Mark has reappeared? The Mark has reappeared? But what does that mean?" asked the golden-crested wrinkled creature. The others looked up at the ceiling and sighed wearily.

"I'll explain it to you, Incompetent," offered the frizzy Getorix. "I'll explain…"

"It's an extreme gloriousness!" exclaimed one of the two Lunatrixes. "Is hope possible? That is the crux of the matter, isn't it, Your Graciousness?"

"I don't know," replied Dragomira, looking thoughtful again. "I don't know yet… but I have some very important things to attend to now, so please don't disturb me."

The creatures immediately went back to their snug niches hollowed out of the walls of Dragomira's workroom. She sat down at her computer and got on with writing emails, sending messages to her godfather, Abakum, and other close friends scattered all over Europe. Once she'd finished, she descended the narrow spiral staircase and went out through the double-bass case, closing it carefully behind her. Then, her mind seething with excitement, she stretched out on the red sofa, her head resting on three soft cushions, and became lost in thought.

9

CONFRONTATIONS

I T WAS MONDAY MORNING, AND OKSA AND GUS WERE racing to school on their rollerblades. Oksa was still feeling confused. It felt like she was suffocating; her secret took up a great deal of room and seemed to grow bigger with every passing hour. On many occasions she'd found herself heading for the phone or computer and she'd very nearly given into the temptation of telling Gus everything.

"*I'm going to explode*," she thought mournfully on Sunday evening as she flopped onto her bed.

Fortunately, she'd slept like a log after drinking a special potion prepared by Dragomira: Fairy Gold Elixir made from parsley, wine, honey and Incompetent slime, her gran had told her. Incompetent slime? Probably a Dragomiran joke…

Today she had to cope with two hours of lessons with Dr McGraw, physical sciences at nine in the morning and maths at eleven. What a dreadful start to the week! To cheer herself up, she told herself that she'd be able to relax for the rest of the day afterwards. Until tomorrow. McGraw was a real pain.

✳

As soon as they got to school, the two friends put their rollerblades in their lockers. Merlin was waiting for them, along with a group of girls who were gazing ardently at Gus, giggling nervously and nudging each other.

"Stupid idiots," muttered Oksa, glaring at them.

Usually she found this sort of behaviour entertaining. But today—why?—she felt exasperated.

"What?" asked Gus, as impervious to the simpering girls as usual.

"Hi!" interrupted Merlin, walking over. "I was on the bus and saw you shooting past."

"Oh, Oksa was born with wheels on her feet," replied Gus, with an amused glance at her.

Merlin whistled in admiration. Oksa turned round, feeling her face go red.

"It's probably time to go in now," she said hastily, adjusting her pleated skirt.

The first hour, Dr Bento's English lesson, went very quickly—too quickly for the liking of all the Year 8 students in Hydrogen. And at nine o'clock they dragged their feet towards the science room. Gus was the first to enter and to greet Dr McGraw, who was banging a nail into the wall.

"Sit down, please, and no talking! If that's possible, of course," he said by way of a welcome, without turning round.

As they all took their seats, he finished hanging a small picture showing the holographic image of a strange, dark spiral, which puzzled quite a few of the students. After making sure the picture was suspended securely from the nail, Dr McGraw turned round and coldly fixed each of the students in turn with his dark gaze, as if trying to unmask the person responsible for a foul murder. The man seemed perpetually suspicious of everyone, although no one knew why. Then, after this frosty inspection, he turned his back on them and began writing the day's instructions on the board. Suddenly the heavy silence was broken by the clatter of a pencil falling onto the floor. Dr McGraw froze. Without even looking round, he snapped: "Miss Beck! Do you need help controlling your unusually lively pencil this morning or do you think you can manage unaided?"

"Sorry, sir," mumbled poor Zelda, bending down to pick up her pencil. A few of the students exchanged surprised looks. Others nervously lowered their heads. Oksa gave Zelda a little smile to cheer her up and the girl tossed back her long chestnut hair and gave her a despairing look in return, her large brown eyes misting over.

"Take out your notebooks," ordered their teacher, "and copy down this exercise."

Still facing the board, he went on writing. Two minutes later he broke off again. He turned round to glare at Zelda, who'd been so flustered that she'd accidentally let her bag slip off the back of her chair.

"Since you're determined to go on disrupting my lesson, Miss Beck, allow me to disrupt your timetable by giving you two hours' detention."

"But, sir, I didn't do it on purpose!" said Zelda, tears in her eyes.

"Oh please! Don't think you can get round me by whining and turning on the waterworks—that kind of soft behaviour just leaves me cold."

"Naturally..." murmured Oksa.

Dr McGraw turned to her.

"Does Miss Pollock have something she'd like to share with us?"

Startled, Oksa paused, then took a deep breath and said bravely:

"I just think two hours' detention for a bag falling on the floor is a bit harsh."

There was a long, uncomfortable silence before their teacher replied, during which all the students sat very still.

"Miss Pollock, thank you for your heroic speech, but I can do without your opinion," he said curtly. "Those two hours' detention are well deserved and it isn't your place to question them. Now shall we continue with the lesson? This interruption has gone on far too long."

He turned round and continued writing on the board with barely suppressed irritation.

"*Really, he's going too far,*" thought Oksa. She felt angry and frustrated at this glacial man's severity. And to think she had the means to make him

56

pay... she could make the board fall on his head or send all the pages of the book on his desk flying—she had no end of choice. The idea soon became irresistible. A few seconds later, the felt-tip that their teacher was holding literally flew out of his hand and hit the ceiling before tumbling to the ground. Was it by accident or design? Whatever the case, the sharp little noise made by the falling pen was bound to irritate Dr McGraw. Everyone held their breath. Exultantly, Oksa squirmed on her chair, making the four metal legs screech against the polished wood floor. Gus glanced at her in alarm, just as their teacher stiffened dangerously. Then a guttural, frightening roar erupted.

"MISS POLLOCK!"

Oksa's heart looped the loop in her chest. Dr McGraw still had his back to the class, but no one needed to see his face to know that he was really furious.

"Miss Pollock!" he thundered. "Get out of this classroom *now*!"

Oksa's smile vanished and she looked panic-stricken. Her blood ran cold and her ears felt blocked by mounting pressure. All the students looked at her in surprise. None of them knew why their teacher was picking on her. Trying not to show her growing distress, she proudly strutted out of the classroom without a glance at the terrible Dr McGraw, who impassively watched her leave.

❋

Once outside, though, her bravado disappeared. She was both furious and frightened at being sent out. She wandered along the corridor for a moment, looking into classrooms through the windows occupying the upper half of the walls. Dr McGraw had sent her out, but she didn't know where to go. Just because she'd made her wretched chair scrape along the floor...

"It was a bit extreme," she said to herself, shocked by what she regarded as a real abuse of power.

She continued walking down the corridor, nervously biting one nail. As she was walking past the bathroom, she came face to face with a student coming out of the boys' toilets. Horror of horrors! It was the Year 9 bully who'd barged into her.

"Now you're lurking round the boys' toilets, are you, you snotty little brat?" he hissed right in her face, prowling around her like a lion circling his prey. She froze, unable to move.

Then, violently and unexpectedly, he pushed her inside.

Oksa fled into the cubicle at the back and cowered there, even though she knew it didn't offer much protection. She was at the Neanderthal's mercy, caught like a mouse in a trap. But what did he want with her? Why was he picking on her? It didn't take him long to find her.

"Ah, there you are! Not so high and mighty now, are you?" he yelled, glaring at her, his dark eyes as piercing as poisoned arrows. "You got sent out of class, did you? Her Ladyship thinks she's the genius of the century, but she's just a pathetic loser!"

"I don't even know you! I've never done anything to you. Why won't you leave me alone," she said, trying to defend herself.

"Why should I?" he replied nastily.

Alarmed, Oksa shrank back in the cramped space. She began to tremble and her vision blurred—she couldn't remember ever being so afraid in her life. At the same time she was furious at finding herself in this absurd situation.

"I don't want to see you hanging around me again. It really gets on my nerves having snotty little kids like you under my feet," spluttered the Neanderthal with his fat, slobbery mouth. "I'm going to lock you in the toilet because that's the best place for pathetic brats who think they're better than anyone else."

These monstrously unfair words made Oksa bite her lower lip so hard that she could taste the metallic tang of blood in her mouth. The Neanderthal grabbed her arms and pulled her viciously out of the cubicle. Oksa moaned. The knot of terror which had formed in the pit of her stomach was gradually turning into a surge of anger that was making her head spin. She wasn't going to give up without a fight! Suddenly, one of the double doors banged violently against the wall. She couldn't help jumping. But she was even more surprised when all the doors began banging so hard that little flakes of plaster began falling off the walls. The noise was terrible. Eyes wide, she watched the doors hitting the partitions. Suddenly, the Neanderthal gave her a hard shove from behind. She whirled round. He didn't seem to realize how odd the situation was—or how dangerous. She glared at him, desperately longing to flatten him like a pancake, while holding a hand out in front of her to stop him coming any closer. There was a low rumble and the Neanderthal's body suddenly began to writhe strangely. Oksa wasn't sure what was happening but she watched the awful outcome: as if being attacked by an invisible force, the Neanderthal was literally lifted into the air and thrown against the washbasins over twelve feet behind them. He landed heavily against the wall tiles, which cracked under the impact, and lay sprawled on the ground, dazed and groaning in pain, with blood flowing from his nose. Oksa ran over to him in a panic, her eyes wide and frightened.

"I didn't do anything! I didn't touch you—it wasn't me!" she cried, wringing her hands. "I swear it wasn't me, I swear!"

The Neanderthal struggled to his feet as best he could, rubbing his head and glaring murderously at Oksa. His trousers were riding low, revealing a pasty roll of flesh. He ran his hand roughly over his black crew cut and pulled up his trousers. Then, just as he was lumbering towards Oksa, brandishing a threatening fist, the door suddenly opened. Mr Bontempi had just burst into the toilets and was surveying them sternly.

10

A Stormy Temper

"WHAT IS THE MEANING OF ALL THIS NOISE?" roared Mr Bontempi. "The whole school can hear you!"

"Sorry, sir," said the Neanderthal. "The door was jammed, I couldn't close it and a draught slammed all the doors."

"Hmmm," muttered the Headmaster, giving the place the once-over. "What are you doing in the boys' toilet, Miss Pollock?" he asked, noticing Oksa, who was trying to make herself as small as possible. "You should be in class!"

Then his attention wandered back to the Neanderthal, who was dabbing his nose with a hand towel. He looked back and forth between him and Oksa.

"What's going on? Have you two been fighting?" he demanded, half-suspicious, half-worried.

Oksa, bemused and bewildered, couldn't bring herself to say a thing. "I'm the most dangerous girl in the world, don't come near me, I can't control my power!" was all she could have said at that precise moment. The Neanderthal threw her a hate-filled look, paused for a few seconds, which filled her with black terror, and replied with a little laugh:

"Fighting? Oh no, sir! Dr Lemaire gave me permission to leave the class because I had a nosebleed. I met Oksa Pollock in the corridor and she came with me to the toilet to help me clean myself up."

Oksa was stunned at the Neanderthal's lie. There hadn't been a grain of truth in what that bully had said, except for her name. But how on earth did he know her name? And why was he telling Mr Bontempi this nonsense? Some of the connections in his brain must have been damaged in the "accident", that was the only explanation. Why else would he conceal the truth? This was his golden opportunity to get her into trouble. Unless this was just a dry run, and he was lying to cover *himself*...

"Is this true, Miss Pollock? You weren't fighting?"

"No, sir," replied Oksa, looking outwardly self-assured, although her heart was thudding painfully in her chest. "I wouldn't be able to fight such a strong boy!" she added with a grimace, carefully avoiding eye contact with the boy in question.

She cursed herself inwardly for seeming such a wimp. Of course she could fight. She'd just proved it.

"It's certainly hard to see you as a boxer," agreed Mr Bontempi, immediately contradicting Oksa's thoughts. "Okay, Mortimer, you should go to the infirmary."

"That won't be necessary, sir," replied the Neanderthal. "I'm going back to class. I feel much better."

With this, he turned on his heels and walked stiffly out of the toilets without sparing a look for Oksa, who was making herself appear smaller than ever. Once he'd gone, Mr Bontempi continued to question her.

"What about you, Miss Pollock, what were you doing in the corridor? Were you going to the toilet too?"

"No, sir. I'd been... I'd been sent out of Mc... Dr McGraw's class," stammered Oksa, too upset to tell him anything other than the truth.

"Sent out? Good Lord. Why?" replied Mr Bontempi, frowning.

"I don't know, sir," replied Oksa in a very small voice.

"What do you mean, you don't know?"

"He just told me to get out of the class, sir."

"I'm very surprised to hear it," he muttered through clenched teeth.

He looked at her closely: she seemed too harmless to cause someone of McGraw's calibre to send her out of the class. Frankly, he wondered what on earth could have necessitated such harsh measures. A Year 8 student, and a new girl to boot.

"Come with me."

The Headmaster placed his hand firmly on Oksa's shoulder. When she realized that they were going back to the science room, she became even more desperate.

"Oh no, for pity's sake, please don't," she couldn't help saying.

Mr Bontempi must have had particularly good hearing because he caught these words, even though she only whispered them.

"Why 'for pity's sake', Miss Pollock? Is Dr McGraw really that scary?"

"No, sir," she lied, mentally slapping her forehead.

As she walked along the colonnaded corridors with the Headmaster, she felt as if she were treading on hot coals. Waves of anger and fear washed over her, spreading like poison through her veins. Her unfortunate adventure in the toilets had deeply shaken her and she really didn't want McGraw to make things worse. Enough was enough. Suddenly the Headmaster paused. Resting against the stone balustrade around the gallery, he leant out towards the courtyard. Looking up at the sky, he murmured:

"Good Lord, it looks like we're going to have one hell of a storm."

Dark, heavy clouds were massing, blackening the sky. There was hardly any daylight left. Even though it was barely ten o'clock in the morning, it was as if night was falling. Lights came on in the classrooms, partially illuminating the corridors. A long shiver ran up Oksa's spine as torrential rain began to fall.

The Headmaster and Oksa had arrived at the door of the science room, as she'd feared. Mr Bontempi walked straight in after knocking twice on the door. The students stood up, making their chairs scrape over the wooden floor, just as she'd done earlier. "*Oh dear, McGraw won't like that at all… that's not going to help my case*," thought Oksa, trying very hard to become invisible. Perhaps her new talents would stretch to that?

"Headmaster, what can I—"

"Dr McGraw, I met this student wandering aimlessly in the corridors and I wanted to make sure that she found her way back to her classroom," interrupted Mr Bontempi, saying nothing about the episode in the boys' toilets.

"Miss Pollock wasn't lost, Headmaster, I sent her out of the class," snapped McGraw.

"Sorry?" asked Mr Bontempi. "I didn't hear what you said, this rain is making such a racket."

McGraw repeated what he'd just said, straining his voice to drown out the noise of the pouring rain outside. He looked very pale and was clearly finding it hard to control his anger.

"So what did Miss Pollock do to deserve being sent out?" asked Mr Bontempi casually.

"Let's drop it now, sir," muttered McGraw through gritted teeth, white with rage. "Go back to your seat, Miss Pollock."

And for the first time since the Headmaster had burst in, McGraw's eyes met Oksa's. It was a dark, sinister look that hit the girl like a punch in the stomach. She felt her brain freeze, then explode. The pain was so bad that it felt as if her skull was being relentlessly stabbed by sharp splinters. Suddenly there was a deafening clap of thunder, followed by a brilliant flash of lightning that slashed across the dark sky. All the lights went out and screams rang out from the classrooms.

"Good gracious!" exclaimed Mr Bontempi. "The fuses have blown, that's all we need!"

Oksa was deafened by the violent crack of thunder. Taking advantage of the darkness into which the whole school had now been plunged, she ran out of the classroom, whose open door was banging against the wall. A strong draught was blowing through the three-storey colonnaded galleries giving onto the courtyard and panicked students were running in all directions. Oksa went over to the balustrade and looked up at the sky with a mixture of fright and fascination. Terrifying streaks of lightning were penetrating the leaden clouds one after the other, intermittently lighting up the courtyard and the stone statues.

"It's the Flood!" cried one student beside her.

"The end of the world!" added another, before running for shelter in a classroom.

Oksa couldn't tear her eyes away from this cataclysmic sight. The violence of the elements matched her inner feelings, and even though she was terrified, she felt in perfect harmony with this dark sky, ripped apart by lightning.

"I've never seen such a bad storm," said someone at her side.

Oksa turned her head and recognized Merlin.

"It's dreadful!" he shouted, to make himself heard. "Stand back, it might be dangerous."

The storm didn't last for long. A few minutes later the rain stopped and the clouds dispersed to reveal a clear blue sky. The students, excited by the interruption, went back to their classrooms and the lessons continued in comparative peace and quiet. Oksa slumped onto her chair, knowing that she had been granted three reprieves—by the Neanderthal, by Bontempi and by McGraw—and vowed that she wouldn't move a muscle until the end of the lesson.

During the break, there were two main topics of conversation. First, the storm, which had left behind some very visible traces—the drenched courtyard was strewn with broken tiles that had been dislodged by the violent downpour, and puddles of water had formed on the unevenly paved ground. The second talking point was none other than Oksa. Many of the students had seen her coming back from the toilets escorted by the Headmaster and rumours were rife.

64

"Well," said Gus, "that's the second time you've scared the living day-lights out of me! No one understood what happened. And the upshot of it all was that you got the blame. It's so unfair! And for someone who hates drawing attention to yourself, you didn't do yourself any favours."

"I know, I'm gutted. What a mess," replied Oksa miserably.

"Why?" said Merlin, looking insistently at Oksa. "You deserve to be carried around on our shoulders for standing up to McGraw!"

"Well done, Oksa!" another student congratulated her, having just joined the group. "You dared to say what we were all thinking. McGraw is going too far."

"He'll calm down eventually, you know," said Zelda comfortingly. "The Headmaster didn't look very happy with him. Particularly as you didn't do anything wrong."

"Nor did you," Oksa rightly pointed out.

She almost added that McGraw had also been rather clumsy in letting his felt-tip "escape" from his grasp. But, as her conscience wasn't particularly clear on that score, she chose to keep quiet about the incident.

"It's really crap," added Merlin, looking outraged.

Gus watched Oksa sadly out of the corner of his eye as she huddled into an even smaller ball on the bench.

✳

She kept herself to herself as much as possible for the rest of the day and concentrated on her lessons, including Dr McGraw's before lunch. This was made easier by the fact that he behaved as though Oksa didn't exist for the whole hour. He didn't meet her eyes once. He didn't make a single hurtful remark to anyone. Disconcerted but relieved, they all made the most of this temporary respite, diligently immersing themselves in their strange teacher's lesson.

"Mr Poicassé and Miss Pollock, please stay behind to put the equipment away," he announced when the bell rang.

Although Merlin was silently delighted, Oksa looked at Gus in irritation. This unpleasant day seemed to be going on for ever.

"Chin up!" murmured Gus. "Meet you in the cafeteria, okay?"

"Okay," muttered Oksa.

She began to collect the test tubes scattered over the work surfaces. While she did this, Merlin rinsed the pipettes, glancing covertly at her.

"You know what Einstein thought?" he said suddenly.

"No," replied Oksa, pleased at this diversion.

"Well, it's pretty amazing. He's mainly known for his theory of relativity but the man was a true visionary. For example, it didn't take him long to realize that we could use solar energy."

"I totally agree with you!" boomed Dr McGraw's voice.

Oksa froze and Merlin looked shaken. Neither of them had heard the teacher come in.

"What do you like so much about Einstein?" continued McGraw, his eyes shining.

The mere mention of the famous scientist seemed to have transformed the stiff McGraw into an attentive, enthusiastic man, eager to hear what the boy had to say.

"I'm particularly interested in his work on light," replied Merlin blushing, startled and uneasy at the interest he'd aroused.

McGraw studied him for a second, then encouraged him to continue.

"What do you know of Einstein's works?"

Merlin hesitated, then let himself be swayed by the gleam of curiosity in their teacher's eyes.

"I know he demonstrated that light can be compared to a wave or a current of particles…"

"I can see that this subject interests you. I too am fascinated by the famous scientist and the photoelectric effect. I worked on it for the CIA, you know, and I can tell you that Einstein's theories lend themselves to countless applications, particularly in the military sphere."

Carried away by his enthusiasm, he gestured expansively with his hand, hitting a bottle filled with bluish liquid standing on his desk and propelling it into the air. Knowing she was making a terrible mistake, Oksa couldn't help reacting: the bottle froze, suspended six feet above the floor, staying perfectly vertical, then regained its former position on the desk. The work of one and a half seconds and, look, no hands! Oksa bit her lip, horrified by what she'd just done. Merlin went on cleaning his pipettes—so there was nothing to fear there. But as far as McGraw was concerned—oh dear! The man was gazing at her impassively. Totally impassively. He'd seen everything, Oksa just knew it. And yet he stood there, looking unruffled, as if there was nothing unusual about what she'd just done *in front of his very eyes*!

"We'll talk about Einstein again another time, if you like," he said finally. "It's high time you rejoined your classmates."

Oksa didn't need telling twice. Disconcerted, she picked up her bag and ran out, her stomach churning, with Merlin hard on her heels.

11

The Statues' Den

OKSA KNEW THAT GUS WAS TRYING TO DO EVERYTHING in his power to have a private chat with her. "What happened? You look really peculiar," he'd whispered to her when she'd got to the cafeteria. But as soon as lunch was over she fled, mumbling vaguely that she had to go to the loo. Rubbish! She'd just been, only ten minutes ago. Far from being taken in, Gus tried to stop her. Too late. She made her escape.

On their first day at school, making the most of his years as a pupil at St Proximus, Merlin had acted as a guide, showing Gus, Oksa and Zelda around the school's maze of corridors. One place had particularly struck Oksa: the storage space for broken statues, which the small group immediately named "the Statues' Den". Desperate to escape Gus's questions, Oksa struggled to find it. But as soon as she walked in, she thought to herself that she'd picked the perfect spot to be alone. The strange, enclosed atmosphere of the former monk's cell suited her state of mind perfectly. Inside, sitting with her back against the bust of an unknown saint, she spent almost an hour in the darkness, which was barely penetrated by the light filtering in through the opaque stained-glass windows.

Since that unfortunate incident with the terrible McGraw, she felt extremely confused and racked by doubt. When she'd made the felt-tip fly out of his hands, she knew she'd acted foolishly. And yet she'd really enjoyed annoying him! She'd felt an inner power which had fascinated her. What had happened next, on the other hand, felt completely differen

Because now she could replay the events in her head as they'd happened, she realized how reckless she'd been and dreaded the consequences. None of it had been premeditated. She'd acted instinctively—whatever was inside her had become uncontrollable. And that was the worst thing of all.

"What have I done?" she muttered in despair.

Oksa felt even more at a loss when it came to the "Neanderthal affair". Even if that bully had made her furiously angry, she'd never meant to hurt him. Not at all. She might have a vivid imagination, but she knew the difference between dream and reality. It was very tempting to use her powers, and so very easy, but she knew they were subject to the constraints and demands of the real world. However, when she'd been confronted by the Neanderthal, it had felt as though there was no longer any difference between the two. When he was terrorizing her in the toilets, she would have loved to have given him an ultra-powerful punch in the stomach and sent him flying. She would have really loved it—but only virtually speaking. And yet it had happened *for real*, even though she hadn't done anything! How could she have managed it? And what about him? How had he ended up in that state? She hadn't even touched him. She pictured the boy's bloody nose and his body crumpled against the tiled wall. It had been such a violent attack—he could have been killed! Could she have killed him? The thought made her shiver.

❋

Still sitting on the ground feeling vexed, with her elbows on her knees, Oksa took a deep breath. A ray of reddish light was slanting through the grimy stained-glass windows and filling the strange room with a dusty light. It came to rest on a tiny, clogged-up washbasin which Oksa found she was staring at defiantly. Just for fun, and because she was curious, she focused all her attention on the small tap. She couldn't see it clearly from her vantage point, but it looked rusty and broken. A strange longing

hy shouldn't she turn it on by force of will alone? It was a
ss exercise, but so comforting to think that she could do
g, she resolutely gathered her thoughts along with the
energy. The tap didn't take long to yield... a few seconds
ter, a trickle of water formed an astonishing vortex in the air and twisted
in graceful spirals to splash delicately at Oksa's feet. She stretched out
her hand towards the stream of water, which was now performing a
complex arabesque. It spurted softly onto her palm, lightly splashing her
blazer sleeve. This was all beyond belief and yet nothing was more real.

12

DISTURBING THEORIES

"OKSA, WAIT FOR ME!"

Gus was trying to catch up with his friend, who'd sped off on her rollerblades as soon as the last lesson had finished, losing him for the umpteenth time that day. Feeling guilty, Oksa pretended not to hear him, although she did stop trying so hard to outdistance him. Speeding along, she glanced behind to see if he was still following her. She knew she was being cruel, petty and contradictory. She wasn't acting like a true friend. She really regretted it, although she didn't feel able to do anything about it.

She kept going until she reached St James's Park, where she sat down under a weeping willow and watched the ducks on the river peacefully flowing past. They were lucky. No McGraw to ruin their lives, no Neanderthal to mar the landscape.

"Oh, there you are!" she exclaimed, catching sight of Gus who, a few minutes later, came towards her, looking annoyed.

"Yes, here I am and don't tell me you're glad to see me, because I won't believe you," he replied cuttingly. "Thanks a million! Nice of you to wait for me."

"Sorry, I didn't mean to upset you. I feel a bit odd today."

"So I've noticed," he added, unable to help smiling indulgently at her. "I only hope you're not forgetting who your best friend is!"

He sat down next to her and gave her a gentle shove.

"I thought you might come here."

For a while they watched the squirrels leaping about on the grass and the children throwing them peanuts.

"Do you remember when we came to this park last year on the school trip?" asked Gus. "If anyone had told me that, a year later, I'd be living really close to here…"

Then he added sadly:

"I feel as if we never see each other these days… lucky we're in the same class; just think what it'd be like if we weren't."

Oksa felt ashamed. She hadn't treated her friend very well today. Feeling a bit embarrassed, she waited for him to go on.

"You okay?" he asked, without looking at her, fiddling with a piece of grass.

"No, not really," she admitted, "my feelings are all over the place."

"There's nothing strange about that," declared Gus. "We've had a lot of changes in a short period of time, everything is new: the country, the house, the school—it's just a reaction."

"It's not that, Gus…"

A few minutes went by in uneasy silence.

"Fine," Gus said finally, glancing sidelong at his friend. "It seems like I'm going to have to worm it out of you if I want to get to the bottom of this."

Oksa felt as if she couldn't escape from her own thoughts. Her secret was beginning to take up a lot of space and she was dying to tell him. So why was she hesitating?

"Gus!" she said, feeling on edge. "I am your friend, aren't I? And whatever happens, I'll always be your friend, won't I?"

"Er, yes, of course!"

"You swear it?"

"I swear it."

Oksa took a deep breath, feeling excited by what she was about to do.

"See that pine cone over there, near the bench?"

"Yes," replied Gus, intrigued.

"Watch closely."

The pine cone rose from the ground, hesitantly at first, then more stead-ily, and then flung itself some thirty feet away, where a squirrel pounced on it. Gus cried out in amazement, looking back and forth between the pine cone and Oksa. But the demonstration had only just begun. The pine cone rose vertically into the air, as if lifted by an invisible hand. The squirrel was jumping up and down to catch it and Oksa couldn't resist driving the poor creature to distraction by making the fruit it craved shoot from the ground into the lowest branches of a tall tree. Then she decided to focus on a huge pile of dead leaves—a rising whirlwind immediately sent the leaves flying, provoking the outraged shouts of the park gardeners.

"Don't tell me you just did that?" exclaimed Gus in a choked voice.

"Why? Did you think I didn't? Look!"

This time she targeted Gus's bag, which began floating almost two feet above the ground. Gus sprang to his feet, snatched his bag out of the air and looked around uneasily before muttering:

"How are you doing this?"

"I don't know, Gus."

"Fine," he said sceptically, "you want me to believe that you've some-how succeeded in defying the laws of gravity and you have no idea how you're doing it, is that it?"

"I just will it to happen, that's all."

"You know, I'd like to be able to do this kind of thing too. But there's no point me just willing it, I'm pretty sure that wouldn't be enough. You'll have to be a little more convincing than that!"

"Like this?" said Oksa, rising above the ground like a Hindu yogi.

Gus watched her in astonishment and grabbed her hand, pulling her sharply down to the ground.

"Are you mad? What if someone sees you?"

Oksa's face clouded.

"I'd rather they didn't."

"But how has this happened?"

"I haven't the slightest idea, Gus."

It was such a relief to be able to talk to someone and she began telling him everything that had happened over the past six days. The experiments in her room. The trick she'd played on McGraw. The duel with Mortimer-the-Neanderthal. Gus listened attentively until the end without interrupting. When she'd finished, he leant back against the tree trunk and whistled through his teeth:

"That's totally amazing! I'd never have believed this sort of thing could happen *in real life*!"

He looked at her again and this time he met her eyes, which were shining with elation.

"But you must be very careful, you understand? You could get yourself into serious trouble. Do you feel as if you're not *exactly* the same as everyone else?"

Oksa nodded vigorously.

"You know what they did with people like you not so long ago? They burned them alive or hung them from trees until their corpses rotted away to nothing."

"Oh Gus, don't get carried away, this *is* the twenty-first century! In any case, thanks for making me feel better, you're such a pal."

"I'm just saying it because I know you. You do have a tendency to go over the top."

Oksa had to agree with him. Gus had always been the voice of reason, ever since they were little kids. "*Be careful, Oksa! You shouldn't... Be sensible... Hell's bells! Oksa, no...*" How many times had he stood between her and danger? It was very annoying, but she had to admit that he was always right.

※

When Oksa and Gus decided to leave the park, it was just after six o'clock—time to go home for their tea. The two friends headed for the exit, reassured by their renewed bond; but as she put on her rollerblades, Oksa's mood suddenly seemed to darken.

"You okay?" asked Gus anxiously.

"I didn't want to tell you, but there's something else…"

"What do you mean, something else?"

Oksa hesitated.

"He isn't who he seems."

"Who isn't?"

"McGraw. It's hard to explain," she mumbled, not daring to look at him. "He isn't a maths or physical-sciences teacher. That's just a *cover*," she whispered.

"Are you crazy?"

"Hear me out, please," begged Oksa, looking tense. "I've thought a lot about this and everything adds up, you'll see. Firstly: McGraw knew who I was before he met me, I'm sure he did. Do you remember when Bontempi gave the roll call in the courtyard: he mispronounced my name and McGraw jumped in to correct him. That's odd, isn't it? Secondly: he sent me out of the class. Officially because of the noise I made with my chair. But wasn't it really because I sent his felt-tip flying?"

Gus stared at her with an intrigued expression. He felt unsettled by Oksa's theories.

"Thirdly: something totally… conclusive happened."

Gus's expression became more enquiring.

"What did you do?" he asked softly.

"I swear I didn't do it on purpose!"

"Oksa, what did you do?" he repeated.

She told him about the incident of the "rescued bottle" without omitting the slightest detail. Gus put his head in his hands.

"You're completely mad!"

"I couldn't help myself—it was an instinctive reaction. And he just stood there, staring at me, without batting an eyelid! That guy isn't what he seems, Gus. I think he may be there because he's looking for something. Or someone. I'm not imagining things."

"No, that's not your style," interrupted Gus with an edge of sarcasm. "We all know and love the legendary restraint of the Pollocks. So what conclusion have you come to about all this?"

"If you remember, he said he worked for the CIA. So, looking at things objectively, imagine what supernatural powers like mine could mean for someone in the CIA, KGB or any other secret service. McGraw knew I had these powers *before I did*, he knows me better than I know myself. He knows everything! I'd stake my life on it. I don't know how he's done it and why exactly he's there, but I'm sure it has something to do with me. You're bound to think I'm being paranoid, but I'm scared, Gus."

"Scared? Why?"

"I don't know. All I know is that I'm not normal. Do you remember that story about the crickets?" she asked suddenly, out of the blue.

"Crickets? What are you talking about?"

"We talked about them not so long ago," explained Oksa. "Scientists want to study the microscopic worms that live in crickets' brains—"

"Oh yes," interrupted Gus, "I remember! Crickets throw themselves into water and then they die, because they can't swim. For years people thought they were committing suicide, which didn't make sense, because animals don't commit suicide. It was a mystery for ages. Then they discovered that it was because of worms that burrow into their brains. When it's time for them to reproduce, they guide the crickets to the water, the crickets dive in and drown because they can't swim. Then the worms tear through the shell of the drowned crickets and reproduce in the water. But what has this got to do with McGraw and you?"

"Maybe he wants to clone me or experiment on me—perhaps even dissect my brain to see how I can do these things. Like the scientists did with those worms to find out how they manage to make the crickets head for water, even though it's against their nature. Just think what these abilities could be used for."

76

Gus looked at her out of the corner of his eye, disconcerted by his friend's theory and troubled by the conviction in her words. Oksa was gazing into space, spinning the wheels of her rollerblades with her fingers, but she was as tightly strung as a bow and terribly hot and bothered—she would have paid good money for some ice-cold lemonade! They stood there, side by side, in a confused silence which dragged on for several minutes before it was broken by Gus.

"Your theory does stand up to scrutiny. But if that's really the case, we're in a real mess."

"I think it's crucial we find out more about McGraw, don't you?" asked Oksa hopefully.

"Agreed," confirmed Gus. "But you mustn't panic. You have to keep a cool head and not let him provoke you. If you're right, he'll do anything he can to make you give yourself away again. In the meantime, we'll try to find out where he comes from and what he's doing here. You know you can count on me," he said.

He stood up and held out his hand to help Oksa up. He was burning to ask one last question.

"Have you said anything about this to anyone?"

"You must be crazy!" burst out Oksa angrily. "Who would you like me to tell?"

"I don't know. Your parents or your gran," he retorted, concealing his deep sense of relief and pleasure at being the only one in the know.

"No," replied Oksa, horrified at the idea. "I can't tell *anyone*!"

Gus wasn't sure what to make of her reply, but after thinking about it for a few seconds he decided it meant that Oksa was giving him special treatment.

"Don't worry," he said reassuringly, "you're not on your own."

After seeing his friend safely home, Gus needed some time to think. He threw himself down on his bed, his heart pounding and his nerves jangling.

What an astonishing revelation! He felt exhilarated and a little freaked out. Oksa was like his sister. No, better than a sister, more than a sister— his alter ego. The person who knew him best, after his parents. Just as he knew exactly who she was. Or had done until today… Because what she'd shown him went way beyond anything he could have imagined. And yet he hadn't dreamt it. Was Oksa a witch? A supernatural being? A fairy? It beggared belief, but he was in no doubt: she was a little of all these things.

13

AN ENJOYABLE EVENING

IMMEDIATELY AFTER SAYING GOODBYE TO GUS, Oksa went up to her room. Once she closed the door behind her, she felt every muscle and nerve in her body relax and the tension subside. It was so quiet here that she knew nothing bad could happen to her and that she was completely safe from the world and its dangers. She then moved on to the evening's top priority: swapping her pleated skirt and blazer for threadbare jeans and a bright orange T-shirt.

She ran her fingers through her hair, lay down on her bed for a few minutes and then, unable to stay still any longer, she got up again. She was just about to head upstairs to Dragomira's apartment when she heard the front door bang: her mum had just come in from work. Oksa rushed downstairs to see her. It was so nice when she was at home.

"Hello darling! Did you have a good day?"

"Ugh, a killer of a day. But don't worry, as you can see, I survived! I was just going up to see Baba."

"Wouldn't you like to have a bite to eat with me instead? I know you have your little habits," acknowledged her mum, gazing at her daughter. "But your gran is busy with your father and some friends, and they mustn't be disturbed."

"Oh! Baba's Band? In that case, they'll be chatting for ages. Not my idea of fun, thanks."

When the Pollocks lived in Paris, Dragomira liked to have friends over to her apartment regularly and they'd talk for hours, drinking tea as black as coffee—a custom which she seemed keen on continuing here in London.

"Yes, there's a large Baba's Band this evening," replied Marie Pollock, laughing. "But that's nothing to do with us. Come on, I've made some *piroshki* filled with meat, just the way you like them. It's my turn to spend some time with you for a change!"

Sitting at the kitchen table, mum and daughter devoured half a dozen of the little Russian pastries fresh from the oven, then attacked a sausage, before polishing off the Camembert. Oksa was enjoying sharing some moments of intimacy—and pigging out—with her mum; she wouldn't have swapped these precious hours for the world. Brimming with happiness, she kept glancing over at her mum with sparkling eyes and Marie smiled back radiantly in reply.

"How's the restaurant going?" asked Oksa, after talking about school for ages.

Marie had always worked with Pavel. In Paris, her husband had done the cooking while she'd managed an army of waiters and run the restaurant with great panache. "*An iron hand in a velvet glove!*" said Pavel, who admired his wife's flair more than anyone. Now they were opening their own restaurant, Oksa knew her parents would have to work even harder. And deep down, she was sorry that was the case. Evenings spent as a family were going to be very few and far between...

"The work's almost finished, but your father is convinced that nothing will be ready in time for the opening, you know what he's like. The workmen are going flat out, but he's always breathing down their necks. I really feel sorry for them! Fortunately Pierre's there and he's much less hyper... I'm glad they've become partners. Your dad's such a worrier—it should do him good. Even if I'm starting to lose hope of ever seeing him relax... but we just have to put up with it and accept him how he is. After all, that's why we love him, isn't it?"

Oksa nodded energetically.

"What about your lessons?" said Marie, changing the subject. "Do you want to show me what you've been doing?"

Enjoying all this attention, Oksa rushed off to find her schoolbooks. They'd unpacked all the boxes, so now they had to get used to the new house, which was so English with its cosy rooms, temperamental plumbing and sash windows, and so unlike their Parisian apartment. Oksa had very mixed feelings about it all: everything was here, the furniture, the objects and the people she loved. But it was all in a new city—an unfamiliar and so far rather hostile environment. At least, where school was concerned. The house on Bigtoe Square was actually very nice and London was incredible, Oksa loved it. All those parks and museums—it was really amazing! So was the British way of life, which was a natural combination of laid-back attitudes and politeness, eccentricity and sophistication. She liked it all, but she still needed some time to feel really at home.

When she came back to the living room, her mum was sitting on a chaise longue by the fireplace, so she paused for a moment to watch her unnoticed. Marie Pollock was a tall woman with a creamy complexion. Willowy yet strong, she had a positive, calm temperament. Although on first impression she seemed easy-going and unruffled, she actually had boundless energy and was very resilient. She always wore understated clothes in solid colours, which reflected her discreet nature. Tonight she looked attractive in a bluish-grey silk dress, with her hair gathered in a loose bun. But Oksa noticed her worried expression and the lines creasing her forehead. Tiredness, probably... Admittedly, all traces of the recent move had disappeared in a few days. No one would have thought that the Pollocks had just arrived; Marie must have worked flat out to achieve this. The few years she'd spent in China had left their mark on her character and her tastes. She'd created a look for this room which was unexpectedly Oriental in character. Despite being built on the same model, all the neighbouring houses boasted motifs like lace, floral prints and leather or taffeta upholstered chairs. But the Pollocks' home was completely different. Near the fireplace stood the grey stone statue of a mandarin who appeared to rule the roost, and there was a bamboo mat on the floor beneath the red lacquer coffee table on which stood a vase holding a large bunch of anemones. Hanging from the ceiling, an enormous yellow oiled-paper lantern shed a golden light over the walls, which were decorated with masks from Peking opera, examples of calligraphy and photos of Oksa. The décor of the two lower floors and the floor reserved for Dragomira and her baroque world formed a sharp contrast with the outside appearance of the house. Oksa loved these contrasts; they suited her family down to the ground. Not to mention her life at present... She sat down on a chaise longue upholstered in black brocade near the window and opposite her mum, who was listening carefully as she talked about her lessons. After doing her maths and English exercises, Oksa went over and curled up next to her mum. Nestling in the crook of her shoulder, she affectionately played with a long strand of her mum's hair and drank in her perfume, the one she'd always worn, with its base notes of white gentian. After a few minutes, worn out by this difficult day and comforted by her mum's warmth, she fell asleep with clenched fists.

When she reopened her eyes, Oksa realized she was still lying on the chaise longue in the living room. The only light was filtering in through the windows from the street lights around the square. Oksa was covered with a cosy quilt embroidered with lotus flowers, her head resting on a cushion.

"Mum?"

There was no answer. Oksa got up, feeling a little groggy from dozing off. She turned on a lamp and looked at the clock: nine o'clock. She'd only been asleep for an hour. Should she go to bed or did she feel up to doing something else? She didn't really know. Having nothing better to do, she launched a small fireball at the hearth to rekindle the fire, which had gone out.

"Yes!" she said, punching the air in triumph.

Then she noticed a large sheet of paper on the table in front of her. A note from her mum.

Darling, you fell asleep. I didn't have the heart to wake you. I'm popping over to the restaurant for a while to help Pierre. Sleep well, sweetheart, I love you. Mum.

Feeling a little dazed, Oksa gathered together her school things and went up to her room. She put on pyjama bottoms and a T-shirt, then brushed her teeth, although she still didn't want to go to bed right away.

"I know, I'll go and kiss Baba goodnight."

She hadn't seen her gran since the night before, when she'd put that ointment on her stomach. Instinctively, she lifted up the bottom of her T-shirt to see what had happened to her bruise.

"Ooh! What's *that*?"

The ointment had worked quite well because the bruise was no longer black and blue with hints of yellow and brown, as it had been a few hours ago. But there was still a strangely distinct outline around her belly button which formed a perfect eight-pointed star about two inches high. The lines were so even that they looked as though they'd been drawn with a purple felt-tip using a ruler. The skin was slightly puffy but it didn't hurt any more. Intrigued and slightly worried, Oksa headed for the stairs and went up to see Dragomira.

14

SUMMIT MEETING

OKSA STOPPED ON THE LANDING AND LISTENED. IT SOUNDED as if a lot of voices were discussing something very serious. Although they were speaking softly, some of them weren't managing to keep their voices as low as the others, because the odd worried word could be heard through the closed door. "*Strange kind of reunion,*" Oksa thought. "*They don't seem to be having much fun in there.*" She moved even closer and decided to take a peek through the keyhole. She recognized Dragomira from the back with her braids coiled around her head. Her father was sitting stiffly in his chair to one side. Opposite him, a woman with brown hair whom she didn't know was watching Pavel closely, frowning. She heard a voice that she recognized as Leomido, Dragomira's brother.

"But you must admit we have to ask ourselves the question, my friends."

She was dying to go in, if only to hug her great-uncle, whom she adored.

"Don't you realize what you're asking of me?" rang out her father's voice. "A few weeks ago, when this *problem*—so to speak—arose, I did my utmost to plan our escape under the best possible circumstances, you must give me that, Dragomira. But, make no mistake, that was just to protect my family. I've never made any secret of my opposition to the possibility of going back."

Oksa had never heard him sound so serious. And yet he certainly knew a thing or two about playing the tragedian! What was going on? What were they talking about? What was all this about an escape?

"We all have families, we've all become Outsiders," continued Pavel Pollock in a choked voice.

"That's true," replied a woman's voice. "But none of us have ever forgotten who we were or where we came from. Pavel, you're Dragomira's son, you know what that means."

"Furthermore," added Dragomira, "we've just had to leave again in a frantic rush. But you know very well it's merely another reprieve. We'll never be safe. Anywhere."

Oksa couldn't hear what followed. Startled and unsettled by what had just been said, her mind was spinning. Immediately the cogs of her imagination began turning: her father and her gran were leading a conspiracy! A secret society. A gang of spies. Of course! Spies from the East, naturally. Or worse: members of the powerful Russian mafia. *"Oh please no, not the Russian mafia,"* she thought, chewing her lip, as she pictured bloody battles between rival gangs. Her curiosity aroused, she put her eye up to the keyhole again. Suddenly, she saw something go past—something… *"Aahh! What was that?"* she exclaimed, instinctively pressing her hand to her mouth to stifle her scream. She jumped back in shock and rubbed her eyes, convinced she was seeing things. *"I'm hallucinating! I must be dreaming! Yes, that's it, I'm dreaming."* She pinched the back of her hand hard to check and grimaced in pain. No, she was definitely awake. Which meant that what she'd just seen had been all too real. She'd only caught a fleeting glimpse of it, but it was totally mind-boggling. She sat down on the first step of the landing and, with her hands over her eyes, tried to recall the *thing* she'd seen. A plump creature with a small, flat nose and sticking-out ears, a disproportionately large mouth and huge round eyes. Its only human aspect had been its blue dungarees. Oksa took a deep breath and decided to take another look through the keyhole. She had to accept that she hadn't been seeing things because the creature was still there, just as she'd seen it, near Dragomira, holding in its hand a tray laden with glasses.

She was about to run away as fast as her legs could carry her when there was a massive thunderclap just above the building. A sudden gust of wind mingled with rain rushed in through the open windows and all the lights began to sizzle, winking on and off fitfully and making the light flicker. Suddenly the bulbs went out with a sharp crack. The room was plunged into shadow, but none of its occupants seemed to react to this odd phenomenon—or to the appearance of an orange octopus-like creature which immediately took over from the malfunctioning lights. Stationed in one corner of the living room, fluttering just below the ceiling, this odd mollusc gently waved its bright tentacles, allowing everyone to see as though it were broad daylight. Too amazed to run away, Oksa concentrated on the keyhole.

"Ahem, ahem, Your Graciousness, there is a piece of information which needs to be communicated," said the creature in a small, rasping voice.

Oksa frowned sceptically. "*Your Graciousness?*" she wondered. "*But what on earth does that mean? They're all crazy!*" The strange creature was trying to attract Dragomira's attention by coughing so hard that it was almost choking. Baba Pollock turned to it and, seizing its protruding ears, pulled hard. It stopped coughing immediately and bowed:

"Your Graciousness must be respectfully thanked for the rescue of her Lunatrix from suffocation. But you should receive the knowledge that someone has placed their eye in the keyhole."

Dragomira and Pavel gazed at each other for a couple of seconds without saying a word. Then, looking mortified, Pavel nodded slightly and Dragomira got up to open the door. Oksa had descended several steps after hearing—and understanding—the creature's warning, but it was too late to hide.

"Oksa, grandchild, come here!"

Dragomira called, her voice trembling with emotion.

"Baba, I didn't mean to! I didn't see or hear anything, I swear it! I just wanted to say goodnight."

"I know, Dushka, I know. Don't be afraid. Do you want to come in and say hello to a few old friends?"

Dragomira held out her hand invitingly. Oksa went back upstairs and her gran hugged her tighter than usual. Pavel, who'd joined them on the landing, kissed Oksa nervously. His eyes were bright and he looked very troubled. This was nothing unusual for him, but he did seem particularly agitated.

"Are you okay, Dad?"

"I'm fine, sweetheart, I'm fine," he said hurriedly.

The three of them walked into the apartment. The feverish mood in the room was heightened by the subdued lighting and the obvious concern on the faces of the other people in there, who were watching Oksa. They all stood up when she came in.

"Leomido! I knew it was you!" Oksa rushed over to her great-uncle, who flung his arms around her in a hug.

"How are you, my lovely? You've grown!"

It was about six months since Oksa had seen him. She might have grown, but Leomido looked exactly the same: tall and lean with fine features, clear blue eyes and a radiant smile brightened by exceptionally white teeth. Looking very distinguished, he was wearing a black velvet frock coat with garnet pinstripes over impeccably cut woollen trousers. His shock of white hair was tied back with a large plum-coloured bow.

"How elegant you look!" exclaimed Oksa.

Leomido Fortensky was Dragomira's eldest brother. He'd been a renowned orchestral conductor and now lived on the rugged Welsh coast. His wife had died before Oksa was born and his two children, Cameron and Galina, lived in London. Seeing him here in his sister's apartment was quite an occasion, because Leomido rarely left home.

"Good evening, my dear Oksa!"

"Abakum!"

Delighted to see the person who'd just greeted her, Oksa threw herself into his arms. Abakum was Dragomira's godfather. He'd also left France and a few weeks earlier had moved for good to the country house he'd owned for years, an ancient, superbly renovated farmhouse about thirty

87

miles from London. A sturdily built man, he was very tall, despite a stoop, with a short, neatly trimmed beard and an animated expression. He radiated an aura of great wisdom. However, despite being naturally unobtrusive, his charismatic presence meant that he always attracted attention wherever he went, although no one could exactly say why. He'd watched over Dragomira since she was born. Both of them had worked together in the herbalist's shop she'd run in Paris and he'd proved as much an expert as she in the field of botany.

As soon as she hugged Abakum, Oksa was again beset by the terrible sound of women screaming which she'd heard before in the bathroom. She felt the blood drain from her face and she paused for a moment, glancing at Abakum in surprise and fear. But the old man also seemed to be suffering from severe discomfort. His face was distorted and he nervously clamped his hands over his ears. A few seconds later, the screams faded away.

"Abakum, are you ill?" asked Dragomira hastily.

"Thank you for asking, Dragomira," he replied, regaining his composure. "I have a bad earache which causes stabbing pains I could well do without," he added, without taking his eyes off Oksa.

"Earache?" asked Dragomira in astonishment. "Where did you pick that up, my dear friend?"

"God knows," said Abakum with a mysterious smile. "But we mustn't let ourselves be distracted by these little inconveniences. Please Dragomira, why don't you introduce our friends."

"Oksa, I'd like to introduce Mercedica de La Fuente, an old friend from Spain."

"Good evening, Oksa," replied the Spanish lady with a little nod. "It's a great honour to meet you."

Mercedica was tall and thin. She had an oval face framed by dark hair so black it was almost blue, gathered in an enormous, complicated bun. She was wearing a poppy-red suit with a high collar which made her look very imperious. With eyes as dark as her hair, she studied Oksa with intense curiosity.

"Tugdual?"

Abakum had just called to a fourth guest, whom Oksa hadn't noticed. Sitting nonchalantly in an armchair at the back of the living room, his long legs hanging over one of the arms, the young man who'd been called stood up and came over. About fifteen years old, he was the strangest person in a group which was already very eccentric. He was dressed entirely in black in an overtly Goth style: skirt over trousers, and a tight-fitting shirt hung with heavy silver chains, crosses and charms. His eyes, lost in his pale, emaciated face, covered with piercings, were heavily circled with deep mauve make-up and partly hidden by a long strand of jet-black hair. This gave him an expression of despair mingled with hostility. There was something so unusual about this gloomy youth that Oksa couldn't take her eyes off him.

"Hi there," he said, with icy intensity, before sitting down again.

Oksa felt herself blushing foolishly, embarrassed at meeting this strange young man in her pyjama bottoms and T-shirt—a totally incongruous thought, given the circumstances, but the more she tried to banish it, the more embarrassed she felt.

"Tugdual is the grandson of our very dear friends Naftali and Brune Knut," explained Dragomira, rescuing her from her awkwardness. "He's staying with Abakum for a while."

Everyone looked intently at Oksa. However, despite the smiles on everyone's faces, she began to feel uncomfortable. She could think of better things than being the focal point in a group, even one so familiar. And there was another, more worrying, problem: she'd just stepped right into something way beyond her. "*This is no laughing matter*," she thought to herself. The moment that odd creature had seen her, an inexorable chain of events had been set in motion. She couldn't turn the clock back now.

"Well, I'd better leave you all to it," she said politely, trying to make her escape, although she knew it was futile. "See you tomorrow, Baba?"

"Oksa, I think you should stay for a moment," said her father looking troubled. "There are some things we've got to tell you."

15

EDEFIA

"THINGS TO TELL ME? ME? IS THIS SERIOUS?" SAID OKSA in alarm.

"I don't know whether it's serious," replied her father, "but, in any case, it's very important."

"Can I ask a question first?" she replied hesitantly.

"We're listening," said Dragomira encouragingly, her forehead creased with worry.

"I know I shouldn't have done, but I saw… *something* in your apartment, Baba."

Dragomira stood up and went into the kitchen, returning a few seconds later with the creature that Oksa had glimpsed through the keyhole. The girl gave a cry of surprise and took a step backwards.

"Oksa, I'd like you to meet my Lunatrix. Don't be afraid," added Dragomira seeing Oksa's instinctive movement. "He's completely harmless."

"A very good evening to you, granddaughter of my Gracious," said the creature bowing to Oksa.

"What is—what is this *thing*, Dad?" stammered Oksa, turning to her father.

"It's your gran's Lunatrix, sweetheart."

"Her WHAT?"

"Her Lunatrix, a sort of steward if you like. Dragomira has two

90

Lunatrixes in her service, one male and one female. They do housework and all kinds of chores," explained Pavel, with the hint of a smile.

"Cool! Where did you find them, Baba?" exclaimed Oksa, unable to take her eyes off the creature.

"It's a long story, Dushka. Why don't you come and sit by us?"

Oksa sat down beside her father on the red velvet sofa, opposite her gran and her guests. The Lunatrix came over and offered them something to drink. Full of curiosity, Oksa accepted the glass he held out, so she could take a closer look, although she didn't dare to touch him.

"This creature is amazing! Is he an extra-terrestrial?"

"No, he isn't," replied her father.

"Did you bring him over from Russia then? Is he a creature from the steppes?"

"We do not draw our origins from extra-terra or the steppes, grand-daughter of my Gracious, that belief is completely erroneous," explained the Lunatrix, frantically shaking his large round head.

Dragomira paused for a few seconds before speaking. She looked at all her guests as if silently consulting them. They all lowered their eyelids as a sign of approval. Dragomira took a deep breath and continued:

"Dushka, my Lunatrixes don't come from outer space or from Russia but, like all of us here, from a distant country. Your father, Tugdual and you were born here. On this Earth. However, the eldest among us were born in Edefia."

"Edefia? I've never heard of it! Where is it?"

"Edefia is our country," replied Dragomira, "a country located some-where on Earth, although there is no record of it anywhere."

"Wait, Baba... a parallel world? Is that what you mean?" exclaimed Oksa, amazed and fascinated.

Leomido and Abakum smiled. "Yes and no," replied Dragomira, trying to find the right words. "It's a land protected by a mantle of light which makes it invisible to Outsiders."

"Outsiders?" Oksa immediately broke in.

"Outsiders, as opposed to Insiders, are people who live outside this land. Imagine Edefia as a sort of giant biosphere which no one can see."

"Yes, I can imagine that. You can imagine anything," breathed Oksa. "But believing it is a little harder."

"That's perfectly natural," continued Dragomira, sympathetically. "You're bound to need some time to take this in, but I'll explain it to you as clearly as possible. Edefia has existed as long as the Earth, but it's a land protected by a solar mantle which cannot be seen by Outsiders. Why? Our findings suggest that the light inside moves faster than ordinary light. In Edefia, the barrier is impenetrable but visible because our eyes have genetically adapted to the amazing speed of the light which lends it a colour that none of us have ever encountered Outside. An unknown colour."

"How can there be an unknown colour?" repeated Oksa in amazement. "All the colours are supposed to exist, aren't they?"

Dragomira didn't reply and looked down, clearly unsettled by the story she'd just begun.

"But what you're telling me is crazy, Baba! Totally crazy!" remarked Oksa, rubbing her hand across her forehead. "I hope you're not winding me up..."

Everyone around her maintained a solemn silence, which allayed her doubts. Her father tightened his grip on her hand and Oksa turned to him.

"Dad?"

"Your gran is telling the truth," said Pavel with difficulty. "Apart from Marie, who is a genuine Outsider and knows nothing of our origins, we all have a little of Edefia inside us. Even if some of us weren't born there, we belong to that community which we decided to name the Runaways."

"The Runaways?" asked Oksa in amazement.

"The Runaways are exiles from Edefia, darling. A name which perfectly sums up who we are, whether we like it or not, don't you think?" asked her father bitterly. "It took me a while to accept the part of Edefia which exists within me. For years, I wanted to turn my back on my origins and I'm not even sure that I've managed to accept them now. For a long time, I refused to be different. But I had to face facts in the end: I was never like other boys, just as I'm not exactly like other men."

"I'm not like everyone else either!" exclaimed Oksa.

All eyes turned to focus on her. Carried away by curiosity, she'd forgotten she'd promised herself to be discreet. She gnawed her lip, reproaching herself for her carelessness.

"Does that mean you are able to do some rather unusual things, Dushka?" asked Dragomira hastily.

"Er, rather unusual; yes, you could put it like that…"

She immediately rested her elbows on her knees and put her face between her hands, feeling breathless. They were all hanging on her every word, staring at her. Abakum gave her an encouraging look.

"Well, I can float above the ground, not very high but it's amazing. I love it!" she began. "And I can move objects just by concentrating."

"The Magnetus! Excellent!" exclaimed Dragomira.

"I can also throw little fireballs, but I don't know how I do it, they just fly from the palm of my hand—"

She broke off, unsettled by such an enthralled audience.

"What else?" asked Pavel gently.

"I can also make hair stand on end at a distance," she added, recalling her very first magic experiment.

Her eyes were shining with excitement, but the people who knew her better than anyone else in that room—her father and Dragomira—could see that she had mixed feelings. The two vertical lines between her eyes were the most obvious sign. Her conscience was being put to the test by countless memories. Should she tell them about McGraw? The Neanderthal? Although she longed to do so, her instinct screamed *"NO! Don't do that!"*

"I'd really like to be told a bit more about Edefia now," she said finally, in a firm voice to brush aside any remaining doubts.

Dragomira made herself comfortable in her armchair and took a long breath.

"Of course, darling girl, of course. To start with, I'd say that Edefia could be described as an immense solar-power station about the size of Ireland, divided into five regions. In our land, protected by the mantle and respected by the Insiders, animal, vegetable and human life could evolve abundantly and harmoniously in ideal conditions. Our civilization was founded on a sense of equilibrium which governed everyone's way of life. Our people were split into four tribes, all of them different but interconnected: the Sylvabuls, the Firmhands, the Long-Gulches and the Ageless Fairies."

"The Ageless Fairies?" broke in Oksa, her eyes open wide.

"Mysterious creatures, as you might imagine, very mysterious… The Ageless Ones lived on the Island of the Fairies, a region which was theirs alone. I lived in Thousandeye City, in the Glass Column, which was built on the exact spot marking the convergence of Edefia's four cardinal points. This crystal residence was reserved for the Gracious and her family, and also the High Enclave."

"What is the High Enclave?" asked Oksa, stopping her. "And the Gracious?"

"The High Enclave? Well, you could say it's like our government. And as for the Gracious—"

"That's what the extra-terrestrial… er… the Lunatrix called you!" exclaimed Oksa, glancing over at the little creature who was quietly sitting cross-legged against the double-bass case at the back of the room.

"The Gracious is the queen of Edefia," continued Dragomira, gazing intently at her granddaughter. "She can draw on all types of power. She's the only one who can communicate with the Ageless Fairies. She's the one who works with them to protect the rainfall and the beneficial effects of the sun's ultra-fertile rays, which make Edefia what it is. Or was: a land of plenty whose resources allowed us to live in harmony, equality and prosperity. The Gracious is the woman who protects and preserves our sense of equilibrium. She wields the fabulous power of light, heat and water—the origin of all animal, mineral and vegetable life."

Dragomira fell silent for a moment, her eyes unfocused and her nostrils quivering with each uneven breath. "It's been so long since I've spoken about all this," she said quietly.

No one in the room moved a muscle or said a word, out of respect for Baba Pollock. Oksa, awed by this atmosphere, looked in turn at each of the people involved in this strange reunion. Leomido and Abakum were like mirror images of each other with clasped hands resting on their laps and their troubled faces filled with nostalgia. Elegant Mercedica was shaking her head and scraping her red lacquered fingernails across the back of her right hand. But Pavel seemed to be the most deeply affected of all. He was sitting beside Oksa, so she could only see his solemn profile and the pulse beating rapidly at his temple. He was swallowing with difficulty, his features looked strained and he seemed to have a lump in his throat. Only enigmatic Tugdual seemed unaffected by what was going on around him. Still slumped in his armchair, he was concentrating on his iPod, which was emitting a rhythmical chirruping which drifted above the silence.

"So Baba… you're a Gracious?" ventured Oksa, in a very small voice.

She felt her father stiffen beside her when Dragomira nodded. This silent, intense, endorsement had just sealed her family's fate.

"You remember the mark on your stomach yesterday?" continued Dragomira in a voice choked with emotion.

"My bruise? Oh yes, I wanted to show you that!"

"I know, Dushka, I know. The bruise has disappeared, hasn't it? And you now have a mark shaped like an eight-pointed star around your belly button," added the elderly lady.

Oksa was amazed and instinctively put her hand on her stomach. She was eaten up with curiosity combined with an urgent feeling of anxiety. What did that mean?

"How do you know, Baba?"

"Because I had the same mark over fifty years ago. Like my mother and others before us, I felt honoured to receive it. But it disappeared when I became one of the Runaways. You've inherited it, Oksa."

"What does that mean, Baba? What does that mean?"

Oksa's voice was shaking and she was finding it hard to think straight because of her growing excitement and apprehension. Finding it hard to catch her breath and feeling tight-chested, she looked at her gran.

"Quite simply, the bearer of that mark is the next Gracious," replied Dragomira breathlessly. "And that's you, Oksa, you! YOU ARE EDEFIA'S FUTURE GRACIOUS! OUR LAST HOPE."

16

THE SECRET-NEVER-
TO-BE-TOLD

D RAGOMIRA HAD BROKEN OFF, CHEEKS FLUSHED AND
tears welling, as if she couldn't quite believe what she'd just said.
The silence grew heavier. All eyes were on Oksa, who felt bewildered.
Her head was spinning. She was a… queen? The queen of an invisible
land inhabited by people with supernatural powers? It beggared belief;
and yet the thought that all this might be true was intensely exhilarating.
Her? Oksa? It was insane. Totally insane!

"But why are you here? What happened?" she asked breathlessly.

"We had to flee," replied Dragomira, her large blue eyes shining with
tears. "I had not long turned thirteen. My mother, Malorane, was the
ruler at that time and I had been designated by the Mark as the next
Gracious. I was supposed to begin my training soon…"

"What do you mean your training?" asked Oksa, interrupting her.

"You don't just suddenly become a ruler, particularly at that age! You
have to learn the ropes and the reigning Gracious is in charge of that: she
rules until the new Gracious is ready. Apart from her many innate gifts, the
most important thing for an apprentice Gracious to learn is self-control."

Dragomira broke off and took her hand.

"You must also learn to channel and control your powers. At the
moment, they're all over the place—you have no idea how to use them

or what their consequences might be. Like all Graciouses, you have to be initiated. In Edefia, this training begins with an official ceremony during which the future Gracious receives a Cloak. Made by the Fairies, it brings vast powers, the most important of which is the opening of Edefia's Portal, which leads to the Outside. That is, or rather was, the Secret-Never-To-Be-Told. Unfortunately, though, my mother, Malorane, was very foolish. Her carelessness allowed someone to know the Secret when she was supposed to be its sole guardian. As soon as the Secret was revealed…"

Dragomira suddenly stopped, a lump in her throat. She seemed distressed by her resurfacing memories. Back bowed, features drawn and eyes brimming with tears, Baba Pollock rose heavily from her armchair, took down two large pictures from the wall and, with a wave of her hand, extinguished all the lights, plunging the room into darkness.

"What is she doing?" murmured Oksa in awe.

"Turn round and you'll be able to *watch* what happened," replied her father.

Dragomira went back to her seat and stared at the space she'd just cleared on the wall opposite her. As if Dragomira's eyes were a projector, images as sharp as on a TV screen appeared. Oksa cried out.

"I don't believe it! This is amazing!"

"Your gran has the gift of Camereye—she can project her memories or thoughts so that we can see them," explained Leomido quietly.

"What I'm going to show you," said Dragomira, in a voice choked with emotion, "is my most terrible memory, a memory which still haunts me. But watch, sweetheart, watch what happened…"

A huge circular room appeared on the wall, surrounded by translucent pillars covered with scarlet Virginia creepers. A dazzling light fell from the glass ceiling and filtered through the windows. At the centre of the room, a bowl laden with enormous fruit gleamed on a low table which seemed to be carved from a diamond. At the far end of this amazing room, they could see a tall woman standing in front of a riot of outsize plants and flowers. Her figure was regal and slender and her long black hair tumbled down her back. Suddenly they heard a loud noise and violent shouting. The projected image trembled then turned in all directions. Oksa realized she was seeing what had happened in Edefia through Dragomira's eyes. *This was a live broadcast of her gran's memory!*

The tall woman came rushing back into the centre of the room, her voluminous yellow dress floating around her, and went over to Dragomira.

"Mother, what is it? What's happening?"

They now had a closer view of the tall woman who logically had to be the Gracious Malorane, Dragomira's mother. Although very beautiful, she was also very pale and there was a look of panic in her eyes.

"Stay there, child, don't be afraid!"

The door banged open and several men came storming in, shoving past anyone who futilely stood in their way.

"We're here to see Malorane!" bellowed one of them, throwing a guard against the wall simply by stretching out his hand.

"OCIOUS!" cried Malorane.

A tall, thick-set man stood out from the group. He was wearing widely pleated baggy trousers and the upper part of his body was protected by some sort of light armour made of supple leather. The air of confidence and coldness in his eyes was unsettling. Malorane, visibly demoralized by the sudden appearance of these men, gave the young Dragomira a look filled with deep sadness, then walked over to the man who had just entered.

"Ocious, so it's you—you, the First Servant of the High Enclave, who is at the head of this conspiracy! Traitor!"

"Why do you speak to me of betrayal?" thundered Ocious. "Don't forget, Your Graciousness, that it was *solely* as a result of your carelessness that I learnt the Secret-Never-To-Be-Told!"

"My carelessness is one thing, certainly," retorted Malorane. "But if you hadn't used trickery to steal that secret, we wouldn't be here. My biggest mistake *was* my foolishness, but the blind faith I willingly placed in you against the unanimous advice of the High Enclave coupled with your overweening ambition are also what has led to our ruin. Look what you've done!"

Casting out her arm, she indicated the balcony from where a restless din was coming.

"Your betrayal caused my Sovereign Hourglass to explode!" continued Malorane, even louder. "The impact was felt as far away as the borders of Edefia and we're already beginning to see the consequences of your behaviour. But unfortunately I won't be the only one to be punished. Have you seen how much the light has faded? And how the temperature has dropped? The people are in a panic. Never before has such a state of chaos occurred in the history of Edefia!"

"Yes! And you can pride yourself on being the cause of it, Your Graciousness," hissed Ocious, glaring at the queen defiantly. "My purpose is not to bring about Edefia's decline, quite the reverse. I want to make our land the centre of the world! I know you can open the Portal. I want to pass through it to the Outside!"

"NEVER! DO YOU HEAR ME?" yelled Malorane.

"Your stubbornness is clear proof of that fanatical selfishness and blindness which none of the Insiders will accept for much longer," growled the man.

"None of the Insiders?" broke in Malorane, sounding irritated. "Have the courage to speak for yourself, Ocious! You're the one who wants to leave, not the people! You're the one who betrayed me, not the people!"

"Your Graciousness, you're wrong, I'm far from being the only one," snarled Ocious. "You'd be surprised to see who has joined my ranks. But today is a great day; you will open the Portal for me and my allies, either of your own free will or by force. You don't have a choice."

"Open the Portal for you? Of my own free will or by force? But Ocious, it can't be done by free will. I know what you want to do on the Outside, because all you're interested in is power. I didn't want to accept

100

it, I thought naïvely that everyone could change for the better and that it was unfair to make you take responsibility for mistakes made by your ancestors. Despite all opposition, I gave you a chance, which has cost me very dearly. Allowing you to leave would definitely put Edefia, and the Outside, in danger. Our powers were not given to us to subjugate people who don't possess any: that is a principle we've always respected. Anyway, now that the Secret-Never-To-Be-Told is no longer a secret, who says that the Portal can still be opened? That power may have died when my hourglass exploded. Do you want me to tell you the oath I took in the Cloak Chamber, like all the other Graciouses before me?" asked Malorane with a glacial expression.

> *Only you the Gracious*
> *Will keep this secret*
> *No one else but you shall know it*
> *Because there is in mankind*
> *On the Inside as on the Outside*
> *Both good and evil*
> *If the Secret be revealed*
> *You will lay down your life.*

Ocious shuddered and looked rattled by these words, which Malorane had virtually spat at him. He seemed lost in thought for a few seconds, then he recovered:

"You're bluffing, Your Graciousness. You're trying to trick me, so I shall use force to make you submit. And if you don't do it, she will," he concluded savagely, striding over to young Dragomira.

"NO! Dragomira won't be of any use to you today. Until she has entered the Cloak Chamber, she cannot open the Portal. She doesn't have the power. Only the Cloak can give her that."

Ocious stopped short, looking fazed. Then an evil smile spread across his face:

"I'll leave you to think about it until nightfall. Once that deadline has passed, if you still refuse to co-operate, there will be terrible consequences. For you and your loved ones. After all, what's a few more hours' wait for the first Edefian man to pass through the Portal?"

Then the wall went blank.

17

THE GREAT CHAOS

WHEN THE IMAGE REAPPEARED ON THE WALL, THE atmosphere in the large room where Malorane and Dragomira were being held prisoner was oppressive. A man sat in an armchair, his back to the window and the balcony, watching the mother's and daughter's every move. The Camereye changed angle slightly to show two young men in their early twenties climbing over the windowsill and motioning them to keep quiet by placing an index finger on their lips. One was slightly round-shouldered, the other very thin. They blew into a type of blowpipe and the guard immediately collapsed.

"Abakum! Leomido!" said Malorane in a hushed voice, standing up. "I thought you'd never come back. Have you found anything out?"

The face of the round-shouldered youth darkened.

"It's more serious than we thought, Your Graciousness. Ocious has many supporters who have infiltrated the tribes and the High Enclave. Traitors have rallied to his cause all over Edefia."

"He's going to abduct Dragomira, Mother," said Leomido. "Tonight!"

"What?" spluttered Malorane. "But I told him she wasn't ready. He knows she can't open the Portal until she's received the Cloak in the Chamber, and not before."

"That's why he wants to get his hands on her," explained Abakum. "All he can think about is the moment when she is enthroned. Then he'll be able to force her to open the Portal and pass through it to the Outside."

"I don't want to go with Ocious!" rang out little Dragomira's voice. "I'll never open the Portal for him, NEVER!"

She turned to look at her mother. Malorane's face appeared in the Camereye.

"The Cloak Chamber has disappeared," whispered the queen, blanching.

The Camereye spun round. The two young men looked at her in amazement.

"As soon as the Secret-Never-To-Be-Told was revealed, the Oath was broken and the Chamber vanished. I lied to Ocious, making him believe that he had to wait until Dragomira entered the Chamber. I was trying to play for time."

"But then… will the Portal remain closed?" spluttered Abakum.

"Dragomira cannot open the Portal, but Ocious doesn't know that. However, there is one last possibility," replied Malorane gravely, her voice shaking.

Abakum stared at her with a horrified expression.

"At what cost, Your Graciousness?"

"We must save Dragomira," replied Malorane, sidestepping Abakum's question. "That's more important than anything. She must pass through to the Outside. The future of Edefia depends on her."

"But I don't want to!" raged Dragomira.

Malorane turned to look at her with tears in her eyes.

"You must, daughter. You must escape Ocious at all costs!"

Then, addressing the two young men:

"Take her away. Quickly!"

Abakum picked up Dragomira. He barely had time to climb over the balcony again with her on his back before several men rushed into the room. The Camereye showed Malorane rising more than six feet above the floor with her arms outstretched. She began to spin at breakneck speed, creating an unbelievable wind which sent everything nearby flying. The fruit on the table took flight and exploded against the walls or hit Ocious's men, who were staggering and holding on to the walls and columns to keep their balance. Then Dragomira was carried away by the young man while the battle continued to rage in the large room. Two floors down, they slipped through a very narrow opening to emerge into a dark corridor where several people were waiting for them.

"Where's Malorane?" asked one of them.

"She stayed upstairs with Leomido," replied her young protector. "I hope they'll be able to join us. But there isn't a minute to lose."

And, tightly holding hands, they ran along that parallel corridor which echoed with terrible cries. The walls must have been made of one-way mirrors because no one seemed to see them, while they could watch a pitched battle being fought: men thrown into the air crashed against the transparent walls, others rose above the floor striking their adversaries violently with their outstretched arms or legs. But worst of all were Ocious's men, who could be spotted by their leather armour. Armed with plain tubes which looked like the blowpipes carried by Dragomira's protectors, they launched substances which seemed to be lethal since their targets immediately collapsed holding their throats, overcome before they could even try to defend themselves.

"What are they?" asked Oksa in an undertone.

"Black Globuses," whispered Pavel in her ear, not realizing that Oksa was none the wiser for his answer.

Suddenly the small group arrived at a closed door embedded in the glass wall.

"The corridor stops here, we'll be out in the open after this," said Abakum, his hand on the doorknob, ready to open the door. "They mustn't spot Dragomira, let's go!"

They dashed forward. The place was in such confusion that no one seemed to notice them. Suddenly the Camereye dropped towards the floor: young Dragomira had probably fallen over. When the image righted itself, they were looking straight at a man stretched out on the ground, writhing in pain. His right arm seemed to be decaying very fast.

His skin began to turn green, then broke out in blisters of whitish dust. The man, who was obviously in agonizing pain, gave a terrible groan. Young Dragomira was then literally snatched up from the floor by her protector and the frantic race continued.

They jostled their way down the many flights of stairs through the tall tower, which was in total chaos. Men and women were lying all over the place, dead or afflicted by horrific wounds, their cries echoing in corridors strewn with bodies. Suddenly they heard a yell: a huge man in a leather helmet was blocking their way, brandishing one of those mysterious little tubes like a weapon.

"YOU'RE A TRAITOR!" shouted Abakum.

"Give me Dragomira!" retorted the man. "We won't harm her. Quite the reverse, in fact. We just need her to open the Portal. Give her to me and you'll all be safe."

"Dragomira cannot open the Portal, she hasn't received that power!"

At that, the man charged straight at them. One of Dragomira's protectors tried to stand in the way and was hit full on by a substance ejected by the Felon's black blowpipe. The blood seemed to have spurted on Dragomira because the images projected on the wall suddenly turned red. She gave a piercing scream and wiped away the blood from her eyes with her hand. As for the Felon, he appeared to have been hit by something which had overpowered him: he was spinning round at top speed, like a raging tornado swept along by its own momentum. However, their way was still blocked by his accomplices.

"We're done for."

"No. There's still a way out."

The young protector pointed to the small alcove overhanging the floors they had yet to negotiate.

"Go on, Your Graciousness, jump! Your father is down there!"

Young Dragomira obeyed without a second's hesitation, followed by several others. The Camereye showed a leap into the void and a gentle descent, as if Dragomira were floating.

"Father! Are you hurt?"

A slim man with a gentle expression looked at the girl, then at the man who had carried her.

"Dragomira, my child! Abakum! Where are my wife and son?"

"We're here, Waldo."

The Camereye spun round: Malorane and Leomido were there. Both of them were drenched in perspiration, their hair was unkempt and their torn clothes were stained with soot and blood.

"Leomido and I tried—" panted Malorane breathlessly. "But Ocious planned his attack carefully, thirty or so Firmhands and Long-Gulches have rallied to his cause. They have mineral weapons that we cannot ward off. We don't know how to defend ourselves. We must flee. Dragomira must pass through to the Outside."

Waldo held out some rustic-looking clothes which they hurriedly put on.

"Don't forget this!" said Waldo, throwing them several straw hats. "Malorane, Dragomira, these two are for you."

He handed each of them a hat trimmed with a thick veil like those worn by beekeepers. After securely adjusting their bags over their shoulders, they headed towards a sort of sled harnessed with two giant hens which were pawing the ground with impatience—or nervousness, because the vehicle was laden with beehives which were buzzing furiously.

"We must separate, otherwise the Felons will notice us," said Abakum. "Our Gracious's family will leave with me on the Gargantuhen carriage," he added indicating the two massive hens.

"Meet us at Lake Saga before sunset," said Malorane. "Take care of yourselves, my dear friends. By the time it is dark, it will be too late. Good luck to you all!"

She bid an emotional farewell to each of the group members who then disappeared into the crowd. Only five people were left standing beside the sled: Malorane, her husband Waldo, Abakum, Leomido and Dragomira, whose presence was indicated by what she was seeing around her. In particular, the noise of fighting could be heard drawing dangerously near.

"Quick, hurry up! There isn't a minute to lose!" exclaimed Waldo.

The image projected on the wall suddenly became more opaque; Dragomira had probably put on her beekeeper's hat to hide her face. Her gaze rested one last time on the magnificent, translucent column-like building which she'd just left. The upper floors were on fire; long flames could be seen escaping from the balcony where Malorane had been standing earlier. The vehicle left the courtyard and pulled out into a street filled with perfectly ordinary-looking people as well as much more unusual creatures. Suddenly the sled jolted slightly, the giant hens flapped their gigantic wings and the vehicle took flight.

"Stop! Go no further!"

Three stern-looking men dressed like soldiers were standing suspended in the air in front of their strange vehicle. In one hand they held the same type of blowpipe as the Felons in the glass tower. Two of them had these weapons trained on Abakum and Leomido, who were wearing the brim of their hats low to hide part of their faces.

"Be careful," muttered Malorane. "They're bound to be Felons in Ocious's pay."

"Who are you? Where you going? What are you transporting?" boomed the man who seemed be in charge.

Abakum gave a little cough before replying confidently:

"We're Sylvabuls from Green-Mantle. My name is Per Boeg and this is my mother and my two apprentices. We're on our way home because we've sold all our honey. You can see the hives in the sled…"

The soldiers came over and the Camereye then showed Malorane discreetly kicking the hives, which immediately emitted a very unsettling buzzing noise. The men hastily backed away.

"The bees are a little agitated at the moment," explained Per Boeg, alias Abakum.

"We have orders to check the identity of all the people travelling through this sector," said the first soldier firmly.

Malorane jumped up and opened one of the hives, shouting:

"Dragomira! Protect yourself!"

The scene erupted in confusion. The bees swarmed onto one of the soldiers and entirely covered his face. The man danced around frantically and began to scream. But the bees immediately flew into his mouth, quickly silencing him. A few seconds later he crashed to the ground a few yards below. During this time, Leomido had grabbed a harness strap with which he began violently whipping the second Felon, leaving a long, deep gash on his face and head which immediately started bleeding heavily. The blow was so mighty that his armour and leather helmet parted company as though slashed by the claws of a bear, and the man hurtled down in turn before he had time to react. Making the most of the confusion, Malorane had attacked the third Felon simply by blowing into her blowpipe. A yellowish substance spread over his ribcage and, acting like acid, ate through the man's leather armour, then his skin, reaching his lungs and dissolving them in a matter of seconds. The Felon—or what was left of him—also tumbled into the void.

Abakum pulled lightly on the reins and the large hens took off again. Dragomira removed her hat and the view immediately cleared.

"Such a cool head, Your Graciousness!" murmured Abakum in a shaky voice.

"My thanks to you, bees," replied Malorane.

"It's an honour to be of service to you, Your Graciousness," buzzed the latter loudly, making the hives shake dangerously.

"We're getting close!" reported Leomido.

The Camereye focused on the horizon. The sky looked strange—it was an unusual hue, an indefinable, mysterious colour.

"That must be Edefia's frontier," whispered Oksa, who understood now what her gran meant by an "*unknown colour*", never encountered on Earth.

When they arrived at the edge of a dense forest clustered around the gleaming waters of a lake, the giant hens began their descent and landed the sled on the ground.

"Look! Naftali is here already!" said Dragomira, running towards an immense tree whose trunk had to be at least 130 feet in diameter.

A man with emerald eyes came over with ten other people they'd seen fighting then fleeing the tower.

"We were concerned when we left Thousandeye City. Ocious was there—he recognized me when some Felons tried to stop us," said Naftali. "We must hurry, they can't be far behind."

Dragomira's attention was caught by a red bird which was drawing closer.

"There's your Phoenix," announced Malorane, sounding exhausted. "It rose from the ashes of mine when the Mark appeared on your stomach."

She looked drained and her face was frighteningly pale.

"I'm the cause of everything that is happening to us, child. Because of my irresponsibility, Edefia faces a terrible evil which is dragging us into Chaos. The power which governs the Cloak Chamber has been shattered because, by revealing the Secret-Never-To-Be-Told, I destroyed the essence of our land: balance and respect for all forms of life."

From her neck she took a fine chain from which hung a striking antiquated gem.

"This Medallion belongs to the Graciouses. Keep it with you at all times and protect it as if your life depended on it," she whispered in Dragomira's ear, putting the chain around her neck. "The Portal will open thanks to the union of the Ageless Fairies and the soul of former Graciouses. But by offering you their power, they will be condemned to wander. You're the one who must find the strength to save them and the wisdom to undo the curse. If, by your courage and by the choices you make, you manage to find the solution, the Chamber will forgive my mistakes. Above all, never forget what I told you: the answer lies within you. You bear the Hope of Edefia."

"But Mother, I want to stay with you!" sobbed the girl.

"Trust me!" begged Malorane. "And never forget…"

The Phoenix was now very close. It landed at Dragomira's feet and she crouched down to stroke its gorgeous plumage. Suddenly she looked round and the Camereye followed her gaze: scores of men were flying towards the gigantic tree at top speed.

"Go, Dragomira! GO NOW!" ordered Malorane.

The Phoenix started singing a deep, poignant song which pierced the heart of every person there. An arch of light appeared against the mysteriously coloured surface and began to shine in the approaching twilight.

"Go on! GO THROUGH THE PORTAL! WHATEVER YOU DO, DON'T LOSE DRAGOMIRA! You others, quickly, cover them," yelled Malorane at the top of her lungs.

"Mother, I don't want to, NO! Come with us!" yelled Dragomira.

Abakum and Leomido seized Dragomira and together they raced towards the arch of light. Naftali flew past them and suddenly disappeared when he reached the arch, while one of their friends collapsed, hit by the Felons. Others passed through the bright arch and disappeared. The Camereye spun round to see Waldo, who was attempting to stand between them to prevent the Felons from pursuing his daughter. Suddenly he froze in mid-movement and rolled heavily onto the ground. Dragomira gave a heart-rending cry. Further away, Malorane was fighting hand-to-hand with Ocious. She appeared to have a head wound because they could see blood flowing down the side of her face. Suddenly she rose above the ground and violently kicked the leader of the Felons, then crashed down on top of him with all her weight. Exhausted, dazed by their attacks on each other, they ended up kneeling face to face beside Waldo's bloody body. It seemed obvious to the spectators of the Camereye that the two enemies had just mounted a lethal attack on each other: their figures collapsed and disappeared in the tall grass.

"Mother!" yelled Dragomira.

The arch was now very close.

"HOLD TIGHT!" shouted Leomido.

And the wall on which Dragomira's memories were being projected showed nothing except a sort of black vortex, spinning at top speed like a hideous helter-skelter. When the descent finally came to an end, Dragomira's shaky gaze turned to show a desolate, arid landscape. It must have been extremely cold, because Leomido's teeth were chattering.

"Where are we?" rang out Dragomira's terrified voice.

"All I know, Young Gracious," replied Abakum, "is that we are on the Outside. Where? I don't know."

The wall screen blurred over and the images were obliterated by the tears brimming in Dragomira's eyes.

18

CONFUSION

OKSA GAZED AT THE COLOURED PATCHES OF LIGHT ON the walls thrown by the sunbeams filtering through the leaded glass windows of the classroom. She'd certainly had the shortest, most intense and most amazing night of her whole life and, even though she was tired, she felt wide awake. By turns euphoric and anxious, she was being besieged by thousands of conflicting emotions that made her tense and over-emotional. This study hour was a real bonus! Bent over her geography book, Oksa could let her mind wander without anyone accusing her of daydreaming or being lazy. She couldn't stop thinking about the Inside and Edefia. She was drawn to that land in a deep, almost visceral way. The only person she couldn't fool was Gus. Her friend kept glancing at her impatiently after she'd told him she had something *extremely important* to tell him. They finally managed to contrive some time alone together, just after lunch. To do so, they had to resort to trickery and hide out in the first-floor storeroom—the Statues' Den was already occupied by students quicker than they. So it was among the brooms and floorcloths that she gave him a detailed and breathless account of the night's revelations.

"THIS IS FAN-TAS-TIC!" exclaimed Gus, open-mouthed with amazement. "What an incredible story!"

For almost an hour, Oksa had talked nonstop. Then, exhausted and relieved at confiding her big secret, she looked at Gus in feverish excitement.

"Wow! How do you feel?" he asked, running his hand through his hair. "What difference does... *all that...* make to you?"

"I'm not sure," admitted Oksa, her wide grey eyes shining with elation. "The fact that I now know my powers are hereditary counts for a lot. It makes me feel better. But at the same time, it's so strange to find all this out and I keep thinking that if I hadn't shown that mark to Baba, no one would have told me anything. I would never have been any the wiser and I'd have spent my whole life in the dark!"

Gus looked at her, surprised to see her face cloud over so suddenly. With her jaw set, Oksa continued:

"Just think, Gus, they've kept it to themselves all these years. They could have spoken to me about it... what's more, they've never said anything about it to my mother, imagine that."

"There may not have been any point in telling her," suggested Gus, trying to reason with her.

"But Gus, that's not the problem!" shouted Oksa, losing her temper. "It's a matter of *trust*! It's still important to know where we come from and why we're like we are, isn't it?"

Gus lowered his eyes as Oksa's words hit home. Suddenly realizing how tactless she'd been, Oksa bit her lip.

"I'm sorry, Gus, I didn't mean that, I'm such an idiot," she said quietly, her voice trembling.

"It's fine, don't worry," said Gus bravely. "See, you were just like me and you didn't even know it... I understand what you're going through. When my parents told me where I came from, I was only seven or so, and it made me happy and angry at the same time. Happy because at last I understood why I was different. I'd realized for years that I looked nothing like my father or mother. Anyway other people had no problem pointing that out. When I learnt who my biological parents were and what had happened, it was as though an enormous weight had been lifted. My differences were no longer a mystery and I felt almost proud, even though it was always hard for me to talk about it. When things weren't good, I'd think about it all and I'd tell myself that it was an interesting story, that I was lucky and that I ought to prove myself worthy."

"So why were you so angry?" asked Oksa, listening closely to what Gus was saying.

"Because I felt as though I'd wasted so much time. I was furious with my parents for waiting so long to tell me, because it was such a relief to understand and know about it all. I could have felt like that so much sooner! That's what drove me crazy. I didn't cope very well over the next few months, as you might remember—we were in Year 3."

"Yes," admitted Oksa. "You withdrew totally into your shell. You were even more uncommunicative than usual."

"I was bottling up all that anger," continued Gus. "You know me, I'm not the demonstrative type. But this was worse, it was all pent up inside me. I felt like it was killing me! One day, I was sitting on my bed playing a video game. I'll never forget it. My dad sat down opposite me; he took the console from my hands, looked me straight in the eyes and began talking to me. Then I understood that there's never a *right time* to learn things like that. Whether you find out at five, ten or fifteen, it turns your life upside down, it hurts, and it changes everything. That's what's happening to you."

Oksa gave him a long look. It was unusual for Gus to talk about himself so much; in fact, he looked more surprised than she was. He ran his hand through his hair for the umpteenth time and in embarrassment began twisting a paperclip he'd found lying on a shelf.

"Anyway, your story trumps anything anyone could have made up," he remarked. "I'd so love to see what this Edefia is like. I hope you won't forget your old pal from the Outside and that you'll invite me over when you're the Supreme Queen... er... what should I call you, anyway?"

"Yaaahhoooo! Call me Oksa-the-fearsome-ninja-Gracious!" shouted Oksa to let off steam.

She'd risen three feet above the floor and had assumed a kung-fu attack position, raising her leg to one side, as she'd seen Malorane do during her gran's Camereye session. But the storeroom wasn't really suitable for that kind of activity and she sent all the bottles of cleaning products in her way crashing to the ground. Gus burst out laughing.

"Not a very well-controlled attack, if I may say so, Oksa-san! There's still room for improvement…"

Coming out of their bolt-hole, they were unpleasantly surprised to find themselves face to face with a few of the students from their class, including the dreaded Hilda Richard—Cave-Girl—and her sidekick, Axel Nolan, who seized their opportunity to launch an attack:

"Look who we have here: Miss Super-Smart and Mister Faithful-Little-Doggie-Woggie, hiding behind the dustbins together! Isn't that a little bit stinky for a romantic chat? What do you think, Axel?" chortled Cave-Girl, suddenly pinning Oksa against the wall. "Huh, not half as stinky as them!" replied Axel with a snigger.

Oksa was seething inside. Grimacing contemptuously, she took a few steps forward to stand right in front of Hilda, as if about to smash her fist in her face. Although she was dying to make arrogant Cave-Girl eat her words, she managed to control herself after a fashion.

"Hey, losers!" said Merlin Poicassé, who'd just witnessed the scene. "Isn't it time you learnt to read? You probably didn't see what's written on the door: it says 'Cleaning equipment' not 'Dustbins'. Although you must be familiar with the dustbin store, because I should think it's pretty much a home from home, isn't it?"

"Shut your face! Stop acting like you're top of the class!"

"He isn't acting," retorted Oksa. "He *is* top of the class."

"Drop it, Oksa," said Merlin, embarrassed.

The two girls looked him up and down scornfully and walked off, laughing like hyenas.

"Great. Now everyone will know where we were in a matter of minutes," muttered Oksa, her fists clenched.

Beetroot-red, Gus looked at her in embarrassment.

"That's for sure, with those two," said Merlin wryly. "You can count on them to spread the news all over the school. But what on earth possessed you to hide away in that storeroom?"

"We needed to talk," replied Oksa defensively. "The Den was taken."

"Yes, that's the problem with good hideouts! Er... I don't mean to pry but... what was so important that you had to hide in there to discuss it?"

Disconcerted, Oksa turned to Gus for support. But he was busy studying the granite floor and couldn't tear his eyes away from the stone slabs.

"Um, just family stuff, that's all..."

"It must have been pretty intense—you were in there for ages," insisted Merlin.

"It's complicated," answered Oksa. "We should probably make a move, shouldn't we?"

"I'm just popping to my locker. I'll be back in a minute. Will you wait for me?" he asked, hurrying off.

Gus finally looked up from the floor.

"Thanks a million for helping me out of that tight spot!" Oksa said venomously. "You were a great help."

"You managed fine on your own!" retorted Gus, smiling.

Oksa growled, baring her teeth at him, before smiling back.

"Anyway, I think we've just seen two fine specimens of Felons, don't you agree?"

"You mean the hyena and the vulture?" he asked.

"Too right! Hey, that would make a cool book title, *The Hyena and the Vulture: A Heroic Adventure* by Gracious Oksa and Daring Gus. Not bad, is it?"

Having made up, they quietly resumed their chat about the secrets revealed in the storeroom for a little longer. Gus listened closely to everything that Oksa had to say, simmering with excitement. Then the bell rang and they went back to their classroom with Merlin, feeling even closer to each other than before because of the secret that Gus swore to keep at all costs.

"Will you give it a rest! I'm not crazy. Anyway, if I did tell anyone they'd think I was insane. They'd put me in a straitjacket and lock me up in an asylum."

The two classmates found it hard to concentrate during the afternoon. They only listened to their lessons with half an ear, but fortunately no one noticed. Overcome by all these mixed emotions, Oksa felt agitated and, ignoring the warnings of her conscience, she couldn't help practising Magnetus on her books a few times, an activity which she could now perform unobtrusively.

"Stop sniggering, you'll get us noticed," she muttered to her friend.

"What? You've got a cheek! I'm the one who's going to get us noticed?" hissed Gus indignantly in an undertone, trying hard not to laugh. "What a nerve!"

⁂

As soon as she walked through the door, Oksa sensed that something strange was going on in the house. She could hear the sound of the TV and her father and Dragomira's low voices. Silently she put her bag down and took off her shoes, then positioned herself by the half-open glazed door to the living room.

"Pavel!" shouted Dragomira as the signature tune of the BBC news rang out. "Come on, it's about to start."

"Good evening," announced the presenter. "Tonight's headlines: the body of Peter Carter, the famous American investigative journalist, was discovered this morning in a London hotel. Scotland Yard detectives believe the circumstances are suspicious, since the cause of death appears to have been the complete disintegration of the victim's lungs. Tiny quantities of an as yet unknown substance have been found. At the present time, the origin of this substance is a mystery, but investigators should soon learn more from the results of analyses

currently under way. Politics: the Polish Prime Minister is on a visit to the UK..."

The voice on the TV suddenly stopped and there was silence. Oksa's heart was beating fit to burst. She tried as best she could to hold her breath and almost suffocated. When Dragomira began speaking, she finally allowed herself to breathe again.

"My God!" Baba Pollock struggled to say, sounding choked. "Peter Carter murdered! In London! It can't be true—"

"What on earth can have happened?" asked Pavel.

"I have no idea... Pavel, my dear Pavel, I'm very much afraid it might have been one of us."

"What do you mean?" he asked coldly.

"I know you'll find it hard to accept, but did you see how Carter died?"

"He was hit by a Pulmonis," he replied gravely.

"Yes. Which means it must have been one of us who did it!"

"I know, Mum," replied Pavel slowly, sounding resigned. "I'm sorry that he's dead but Carter caused us a great many problems and he was liable to go on doing so since he was in London. Although it's a terrible thing to admit, the man or woman who did this saved us from great danger."

Oksa's blood ran cold with horror. Her family was behind a man's murder! But *why*? She leant against the wall, her back perspiring and her heart racing. She recalled one of the violent images from the Camereye: Malorane dispatching a terrible substance which had dissolved the lungs of one of the Felons. Peter Carter had died in exactly the same way! This was a nightmare. She was going to wake up. She had to wake up. But instead, she remained rooted to the spot outside the living room, wide awake and more than anything horrified by what she was hearing. Her body still pressed against the wall, she inched back very slowly to the staircase and crept silently upstairs to her room where she threw herself onto her bed, her mind seething. Dragomira had actually said: "It must have been one of us who did it." But why had her family killed that journalist? It was awful.

19

UPHEAVAL AT THE POLLOCKS'

OKSA COULDN'T BELIEVE THE ATMOSPHERE AT HOME AS the week went by: everyone seemed to have slipped back into their usual routine as if nothing had happened, despite the fact that her life had been turned upside down. Learning that her own family came from an unknown land and that one of its members was a cold-blooded murderer was a really big deal, but everyone was acting as though everything was normal. Oksa felt totally abandoned. Her father was only interested in the building work being done at the restaurant, which was due to open soon. He was very anxious, but no more so than usual. Marie wouldn't let him out of her sight, patiently fulfilling her role as private therapist to her highly stressed husband. They were both spending most of their time at the restaurant and not even bothering to take turns with her as they'd been so careful to do in Paris. Oksa had barely seen them for more than two hours running over the past few days. Her bitterness was eating away at her heart like poison.

One evening, she'd gone upstairs to see her gran as usual, but no one seemed to be there. The official version was that Dragomira was staying with her godfather Abakum for a few days. But Oksa knew for a fact that she'd come back at least two days ago—a certainty which really bugged her. It would be the last straw if her Baba was starting to neglect her as well! On Saturday evening she finally decided to rap at the door after pressing her ear to it and hearing the Lunatrix humming in the apartment.

"Oohh, granddaughter of my Gracious, your visit is unexpected but my delight at the seeing of you is a comfort," said the creature, opening the door.

"Who's that, my Lunatrix? If it's Oksa, show her in, please."

That was Dragomira, sounding weak and hoarse. The Lunatrix bowed low to Oksa and stepped back to let her pass. Baba Pollock was lying on a sofa under a thick tartan quilt. Her head was resting on some brightly coloured cushions which formed a striking contrast with the pallor of her gaunt face. Her long plaited hair hung carelessly down to the floor and her eyes were half-closed.

"Come in, Dushka!"

Oksa rushed over to her gran and put her arms tenderly around her. They stayed like that for a moment, enjoying being together after their time apart.

"You don't look too good, Baba. Are you ill?"

Dragomira looked at her with boundless kindness.

"Yes, I'm ill. But it's nothing serious, so don't worry. I just need to rest."

Immediately after saying this, she closed her eyes a little more and her head rolled slightly to the side. Oksa was convinced that her gran's condition was linked to the death of that journalist. The burden of guilt? The nagging sensation of remorse? She found it hard to imagine her gentle gran as a murderer. But who would guess that the exiled queen of a deposed empire lurked beneath the exterior of this somewhat eccentric elderly herbalist? So why not a manic acid killer? It wasn't beyond the realms of possibility... The only thing Oksa could be certain of was that Dragomira knew much more about this affair than anyone else. "It must have been one of us who did it," she'd said. Who? Her father? Abakum? Leomido? It was hard to believe. But during the past week, Oksa's life had been filled *only* with things that were hard to believe.

"I must rest, darling," repeated Dragomira in a weary voice.

But before rising to her feet, Oksa couldn't help asking:

"What's wrong with you, Baba? Tell me, please!"

Dragomira hesitated for a second. She turned her head, then said in a hoarse whisper:

"I'm an old lady and all those memories are very upsetting. You know, it was very painful seeing those images of chaos and hearing my mother's words again. I need a little time to get used to the idea that you've just inherited all this. But things will be fine. I'll be back on my feet in no time, don't worry."

"Baba, can I ask you a question?"

Dragomira nodded silently.

"What's going to happen? I mean… now that I have this mark?"

"We'll talk about it later, Dushka."

"I do hope so! Can I just say hello to Leomido and Abakum?" insisted Oksa, reluctant to give up hope of learning anything more. "They're still here, aren't they?"

"Yes, we're still here. Hello Oksa."

Oksa turned round: the two men were there, near the enormous double-bass case at the back of the room.

"We'll come and eat with you and your parents, if we're invited," announced Leomido after kissing her hello. "But now you must let your grandmother rest."

Oksa stood up reluctantly, kissed Dragomira again and left the apartment.

But halfway down the staircase, she changed her mind and ran back up the few steps to the landing. She tapped on the door again. Leomido opened it.

"But I've got some questions for you," she said briskly. "We haven't had a chance to speak since last Sunday!"

"Later, Oksa, later," replied her great-uncle, sounding preoccupied and looking so vague that she wasn't sure that he was actually seeing her.

Oksa went back downstairs to her room, muttering angrily to herself.

"They tell me tons of really important stuff and when I want to know more, they've all gone AWOL. I've got loads of questions. But they shut

the door in my face and leave me to my own devices. I'M SICK OF IT!"
she protested rebelliously, kicking her school bag violently across the floor.

She sensed someone behind her and turned round: her father was
leaning against the door frame, looking at her anxiously.

"Dad?"

Pavel Pollock's only answer was to rub his face wearily with his hand
and turn on his heel.

"DAD!"

Oksa followed him. But when she saw him in the living room, slumped
in an armchair, his head in his hands and his body huddled over, she
turned round and ran back to her room. There she exploded. Glowering
with rage and without moving from her bed, she swept everything off
her desk, then attacked her posters on the walls, shredding them into
long strips of paper by the sheer force of her gaze. When everything
was broken, ripped to pieces or torn apart, she turned her fury on the
pieces of debris and willed them into the air, where they drifted limply.
Then she broke down, her heart aching with sadness and resentment.

When she reopened her eyes, her father was sitting on the floor next
to her, his back against the wall.

"A rather bold new style of décor, if I may say so," he said with a thin
smile, looking at the mess floating around him.

"Oh Dad!"

Oksa threw herself into his arms and buried her face against his
shoulder.

"Dad, I don't know what to think any more... I'm so confused."

"This is all very sudden, sweetheart. I hate the fact that you had to
learn about our history like this, without being prepared. Frankly, I wish
it hadn't happened this way. I would have preferred to wait; but the harm
is done now," he added as if talking to himself.

"It's not just that, Dad," said Oksa, looking at him intently.

But, fixing Oksa with his sad, blue eyes, he ignored what she'd just
said and kept talking:

"Just be patient for a while. We're all pretty confused ourselves, and we're not sure how to proceed. We don't even all agree! We just need to take time to think things over so we don't make any mistakes," he said sensibly, putting his arm round Oksa's shoulders.

"I don't understand: what do you have to agree about?"

"I can't tell you anything more when we're not seeing things clearly ourselves."

"Okay, fine, don't complain when you've totally traumatized your only daughter!" she retorted, laying it on thick to lighten the atmosphere. "Because I'm warning you: later on, when I'm a complete neurotic head case, I'll tell the leading psychiatric specialists who are examining me that it all stems from my adolescence. I'll explain how I had a terrible psychological shock and that I was badly neglected by my family, so there!"

Her father hesitated for a second, then gave a loud snort of laughter which was so contagious that Oksa burst out laughing too, glancing at him sidelong as he tousled her hair affectionately.

"So if I understand correctly, I'm to keep all my questions to myself until you deign to bestow your precious attention on me," resumed Oksa more provocatively. "After all, I'm only a teenager who has to do as she's told by the grown-ups, who are *so* wise and *so* reasonable..."

Her father looked at her again, not even trying to hide his embarrassment and helplessness. A sudden surge of pity made Oksa decide to leave it be for the time being.

"I'm not promising anything, but I will try," she said, twisting the bottom of her T-shirt around her finger. "Oh, I almost forgot to tell you—Leomido and Abakum are joining us for dinner."

"That's excellent news!" exclaimed her father, happy that they had reached a truce. "Come on, let's prepare a feast worthy of the name. And, er, it might be a good idea to tidy up your room a little before your mother sees it, don't you think?"

So they both got down on all fours to pick up everything that Oksa had thrown or smashed during her last, furious Magnetus. Pavel Pollock noticed the large burn mark on the wall but preferred not to mention it, merely sticking a poster back over it as best he could. After all, there was no point adding fuel to the flames.

20

(Un)controlled Slip-Ups

MARIE POLLOCK DIDN'T NEED TO KNOW ALL THE details of the matter in hand to sense that something had happened. The only difference between her and everyone else in the house was that she didn't know what. It had all started at the beginning of the week when Dragomira's friends had arrived. It hadn't escaped her attention that Pavel and Oksa had come back downstairs well after midnight on Monday. She'd almost stepped in and read the Riot Act to her husband for keeping their daughter up so late on a school night, but she hadn't had the heart to do it when she saw Pavel's expression the next morning. He'd looked so worried. She'd tried to find out what had gone on as tactfully as she could, but Pavel, who could retreat into an impenetrable silence when he wanted, wouldn't breathe a word. That evening, the atmosphere over dinner was strange—highly charged and subdued at the same time. Leomido and Abakum had joined the little family. Although they were usually excellent company, they seemed preoccupied. Perhaps Dragomira's condition was affecting them more than she had realized, Marie thought. Anyway the fact that Leomido was still there was clear proof: over the past ten years, he'd never stayed longer than two days. And he'd been here almost a week this time...

"Isn't Dragomira coming down?" asked Marie.

"No, my dear Marie, she still feels a little weak," replied Leomido looking kindly at her.

"I hope you aren't hiding anything serious from me," added Marie with a slight smile.

"No, don't worry, darling," replied Pavel in his turn. "Everything's fine, she's just a bit dizzy at the moment. It will pass."

"*They've certainly got some nerve!*" Oksa thought unhappily. She fidgeted on her chair, glaring at her father. Abakum and Pavel sat up very straight, looking stern and frowning.

"But what's up with you all this evening?" asked Marie in concern.

"We're tired, dear Marie, very tired," replied Leomido, trying and failing to soften his tone.

Oksa, on the other hand, wasn't at all tired. She was seething with anger, agitation and impatience, which made her a bundle of nerves. The short discussion with her father had done her good, but had come nowhere near satisfying her. She was finding it hard to hide her frustration at all these unanswered questions. What had happened to Malorane? Why didn't she leave at the same time as the others? What was all that about the Phoenix? Had someone already attempted to go back to Edefia? Did they know where it was? And how many of them had fled? Who had killed the journalist? Why did they refuse to answer her questions? Why were they lying to her mother? WHY? There was nothing but *whys* and not one *because*. Her father was watching her out of the corner of his eye and the feeling of being watched made Oksa furious. She looked at her mother, who was putting the finishing touches to the salad. She had her back to them and was leaning forward slightly over the work surface, her shoulders moving up and down to the rhythm of her arms as she stirred the vinaigrette. "*All the same, they could have told her. It's really shitty keeping her in the dark like this,*" thought Oksa.

Suddenly the urge was too strong: IT WAS TIME TO ACT. Although she didn't realize it, deep down she was longing to provoke her father and make him pay for his distant behaviour towards her during this strange week. Blinded by frustration, she stared straight in front of her unthinkingly. Every single piece of cutlery ended up standing on end in the middle of the table and then began turning in a circle. Although Oksa hadn't laid a finger on them, of course; she just tapped on the table as if beating time for this strange dance. The three men hastily put the knives and forks back beside the plates, just before Marie came back to her seat. But Oksa was far from finished. She decided to try something new. The Magnetus was good fun, but now she was going to get serious. Her mother gave her the idea for her next target; she'd just got up again to light the perfumed candles on the occasional table by the entrance to the kitchen. She lit the first candle with the lighter. Oksa took care of the second as though it were the most natural thing in the world: without moving from her chair, she simply opened the palm of her hand to send a tiny ball of fire straight towards the wick of the candle. Her mother stood there astonished in front of the candlestick, the lighter in her hand and her forehead wrinkled.

"What were you saying about tiredness, Leomido? I think it must be catching…"

Oksa, on the contrary, was overflowing with energy. The three candles were now lit. About ten flames escaped from them and, like demented fireflies, began to flit about randomly above the guests' heads. But anarchy wasn't to her taste so she decided to remedy it: the fireflies gathered in a group just below the ceiling and, on Oksa's order, went into a nosedive towards Pavel's and Marie's heads before making an emergency stop a few inches from their hair. Opposite them, Abakum and Leomido couldn't help exchanging alarmed looks while trying to hide their growing panic.

Leomido kicked Oksa in the shins and Abakum took her hand to try and reason with her. To no avail, because Oksa smiled back at them with a mixture of satisfaction and mockery—her expression saying "I'm-a-teenager-and-I'll-do-what-I-want-when-I-want"—while continuing to orchestrate the dancing sparks in the air with her fingertips. Her attention inevitably drawn by the lights—and by the fact that Abakum and Leomido kept glancing at the top of her head—Marie looked up. Everyone held their breath, preparing for the worst. She looked down and didn't move an inch, her eyes on her plate. Then she blinked as if to erase what she'd just seen, passed her hand over her eyes and continued eating. Abakum made the most of this unexpected lull to create a distraction and start chatting about a topical subject which was of absolutely no interest to Oksa, who was busy working out what she could do next. She felt totally hyper, game for anything. Glancing around, she found what she was looking for: the tap. That was something new! What came after fire? Water. There was nothing like staying with the elements; how cool was that and how innovative! She stared at the sink tap twirling her index finger in discreet circles. After a few seconds, a trickle of water came out of the tap, and quickly grew heavier, gushing out in large spurts which splashed Leomido and Pavel, who were nearest the sink. Marie cried out and Pavel jumped up to turn it off, which proved relatively difficult because the water was really pouring out by now. Soaked from head to foot, his hair and shirt dripping, he glared at his daughter.

"Oksa, stop it right now! THAT'S ENOUGH!" he roared, beside himself with anger.

Marie looked at him in astonishment.

"Really Pavel, she didn't do anything! It was just a leak..."

Oksa gave a satisfied grin: it was panic stations all round, particularly in the case of her father. A direct hit! "*After all these years, you'd think he would have told her,*" she thought angrily. Taking no notice of her father's warning, she decided to go out with a bang. The bread basket became her final flourish. Sitting in the middle of the table, it amazed everyone by rising eighteen inches into the air and emptying its contents onto Pavel's plate.

"WHAT IS GOING ON HERE?"

21

PAYING THE PRICE

MARIE HAD JUMPED BACK FROM THE TABLE, overturning her chair.

"Do you want to tell me what's going on here?" she yelled. "This isn't funny. Do you see me laughing?"

Leomido smiled at her distantly, despite the growing feeling that this was just the start of their problems.

"Marie, would you come with me, please?" said Pavel despondently, his face deathly pale.

He took her firmly by the arm and drew her into the living room. Leomido and Abakum looked at Oksa gravely, their silence rebuking her more effectively than any tongue-lashing could have done.

"I'm... sorry..." she murmured, biting the inside of her lip and feeling a little ashamed.

"So are we, Oksa, so are we," said Abakum, stressing the dual meaning of these words, which Oksa wasn't sure how to interpret.

Looking dejected, Abakum got up from the table heavily and walked out of the kitchen, followed immediately by Leomido, leaving the girl alone with her responsibilities.

When Oksa went back up to her room, her parents were still talking it over in the living room, and the snatches of conversation which reached her ears did little to reassure her: the discussion was developing into a heated argument. Oksa sat down in front of her computer and started writing an email:

Gus, I've really screwed up. I think my mother knows now. Dad's talking to her and it's not going well at all—they're arguing. I did some things in front of her, I'm such a moron. I'll try to find out more. I'll keep you posted. See you tomorrow. From: Oksa-the-Prize-Idiot.

Although she should perhaps have learnt her lesson from her last attempt at spying outside Dragomira's door, she sat down on the floor in the corridor facing the living-room door. It was closed, but Oksa could hear perfectly what was being said inside because their voices were so loud.

"Our daughter is heir to the power of Edefia, she has the Mark…"

"Sure! And I'm Tinker Bell!" replied Marie with a hysterical cackle.

"Marie, why would I lie to you? I'm not capable of it. Oksa has powers, she already knows how to use some of them, but she has incredible potential! Our daughter is phenomenally strong, stronger than anyone I know."

"Stop it! You're driving me crazy with your insane stories, your *Edifia*, and everything."

"Edefia."

"And even if I did believe you, how come you're only telling me this now? How long have we been married? I'll tell you since you seem to be finding it hard to remember: EIGHTEEN YEARS!"

"Come with me," her husband said with a deep sigh. "I want to show you something. We're going up to see Dragomira, you'll understand better."

The door opened, but they were so wrapped up in their conversation that neither of them noticed Oksa sitting huddled miserably in a corner in the corridor, which only upset her more. Dragomira, who was waiting for them on the second-floor landing, ushered them inside. Oksa followed them upstairs and sat down on the top step. A few minutes later,

Marie gave a bloodcurdling scream. *"Oh dear! Mum must have seen the Lunatrix,"* thought Oksa. The conversation continued inside the apartment, sounding just as venomous as before.

"You've seen too many films, the lot of you! You need to stop this right now and come back down to earth."

Oksa couldn't help murmuring sadly, "But we are on Earth, Mum."

❋

The first thing Oksa noticed when she opened her eyes was that she was in her own bed. Virtually as soon as she woke up, all kinds of questions sprang to mind. Had she fallen asleep on Dragomira's landing? Who'd carried her back to her room? How had things turned out between her parents? Had Pavel managed to explain everything to her mum? When she went down to the kitchen for breakfast, there was a much more important question she had to ask:

"Where's Mum?" she asked, her voice faltering.

Everyone was there: her father, Dragomira—who'd finally left her apartment—Leomido and Abakum. Which made Marie's absence even more noticeable.

"Your Mum has gone to visit her sister," replied Pavel, his face haggard with tiredness and worry.

All four looked at her with a mixture of pity and severity.

"Is she angry with me?" she asked abruptly.

"No, it's not you she's angry with," said her father, looking away and sliding a piece of paper folded in four towards her.

Oksa unfolded it and read:

Oksa, my darling daughter, I'm going to stay with your Aunt Geneviève for a few days. I need some peace and quiet to think things over. I'll be back soon. Never forget that I love you. Mum.

"Oksa, what you did was serious," continued Dragomira straight away. "It was a cruel thing to do to your mum and to all of us."

"I know, Baba, I'm sorry!" cried Oksa, with tears in her eyes. "I'm such a moron, I'm sorry!"

"We know you're sorry," replied Leomido, sounding irritated. "But the harm has been done. Your mum has had a nasty shock. All this has hit her very hard."

"It hit me very hard too," retorted Oksa. "If you'd told us sooner, it might have been easier to deal with."

Although the four of them flinched at this scathing remark, they didn't answer back: there was more than a grain of truth in what Oksa had said.

"What was going through your mind? Why did you act like that?" asked Abakum, looking at Oksa with kindness, in marked contrast to the three other adults, who were still very tight-lipped.

Oksa hesitated before replying. She chewed a nail noisily with her head tilted to one side, then exploded:

"I find out some extraordinary things and then everyone goes AWOL and refuses to answer my questions! The house is like a graveyard, no one speaks to me, it's like I'm landed with this *huge thing* which I have to deal with all on my own. On top of that, I can do loads of stuff I want to show you… but you couldn't care less, you haven't even asked to see what I can do! You don't realize that ALL THIS IS CHANGING MY LIFE! No, you adults continue whispering in corners without sparing a thought for Mum or me. You have no idea how angry I was… it was taking up so much space inside, I couldn't breathe. I could have smashed everything without moving from my chair, just by looking around. When Mum asked if you were hiding anything from her, I didn't have the strength to stop it: it began all on its own, I couldn't stop myself."

"And how do you feel now?" asked Abakum very gently.

"Now? You really want me to tell you how I feel?"

"Yes," replied Abakum simply.

"Well, see the rain falling outside?"

They all turned to look at the window. Heavy rain was pelting on the square. At the same time, the windows rattled at a clap of thunder.

"I feel like the weather today: I feel like I'm drowning in tears," said Oksa, her voice trembling. "I feel miserable. Miserable and furious. I'm so furious I could explode."

The four adults glanced at each other uncomfortably. They all knew that Oksa's fragile state of mind was directly caused by their detachment and lack of consideration. And they appeared to be deeply sorry for it. They only had to look at her to see how she was struggling to control her feelings in her over-emotional state and there wasn't anything they could do to make her feel better. The harm had been done, as Leomido had said. Oksa's face was drawn and frighteningly pale. Her eyes were brimming with tears and she'd bitten all her nails down to the quick. Her father and loved ones suddenly realized that she'd been showing clear signs of depression for days now in the form of violent mood swings—veering from laughter to tears and from wild enthusiasm to black despair. But they were most surprised at her rage—a terrible seething rage which was completely out of character for Oksa. Pavel went over to his daughter, knelt down in front of her and put his hands on her shoulders.

"We're sorry," he told her as gently as he could. "But please, don't be angry. You're right, we have ignored your questions, but we'll explain what you need to know in good time. It's still too soon…"

"TOO SOON!" exclaimed Oksa, beside herself with rage again. "But you've already told me too much! You have no right to leave me standing here on my own as though it's all beyond me!"

With these words, she leapt to her feet in a fury and, with her fists on the table, glared at them with blazing eyes. Their silence and lack of reaction made her blood boil and she felt rage coursing through her veins and making her head spin. She'd had this feeling before when confronting the Neanderthal in the boys' toilet and during that terrible storm a few days after school started. She looked down, trying to calm herself. No use. Alarmed, she saw the bowl of hot chocolate in front of her take off from the table and hurl itself against the wall, splattering Dragomira on its way. The bowl shattered on impact, leaving a brown trail of chocolaty milk down the wall.

"NOW LOOK WHAT YOU MADE ME DO!" yelled Oksa.

She whirled round and bolted out of the kitchen, her heart beating frantically as the mounting pressure became unbearable. Her father rushed after her, catching up with her in the hall, where a large mirror was about to suffer the same fate as the bowl.

"Have you decided to break everything in this house?" hissed Pavel angrily, grabbing her arm.

"Leave me alone, Dad. All of you just leave me alone!" shouted Oksa, struggling desperately to extricate herself from her father's vice-like grip.

She managed to pull free so suddenly that she lost her balance and fell over, which made her even angrier.

"Now look here," thundered her father, "you have to calm down and listen to me! We are *all* going through a very difficult time and we're *all* struggling to understand things. What's happening is very complicated for us *all* and you'd better believe it. So please don't make things worse."

"Too complicated to speak to a kid, is that what you mean? Then you should never have told me everything you did. Everything that has happened to Mum is your fault! I HATE YOU!"

Oksa was screaming at the top of her voice. She was so angry she couldn't breathe and she was shaking from head to foot. Leomido and Abakum were watching her sorrowfully from the kitchen, distraught at her anguish. Dragomira had shut her eyes and was standing there rigid, her face ashen. Pavel held out his hand to Oksa to help her up. She ignored it, stood up and charged up to her room, doing her utmost not to burst out sobbing. After furiously sticking her no-entry sign on the door, she threw herself onto her bed, her emotions in turmoil.

❋

She couldn't help jumping when she saw the Lunatrix in front of her. The small creature was waiting quietly near her bed, his arms hanging limply either side of his podgy body.

"Fear must be dismissed from your mind, granddaughter of my Gracious," he said in a shrill voice. "The domestic staff of my Gracious did not premeditate to cause alarm."

Oksa sat up, unable to tear her eyes away from the creature.

"I… I'm not afraid," she stammered, "I'm just surprised. Er… can I help you?"

The Lunatrix shook his head so wildly that Oksa was impressed.

"The Lunatrix of my Gracious has received words in his ear which have been exchanged by the guests of this dwelling… the granddaughter of my Gracious has experienced the combustion of her heart, which was crammed with rage. This made a flood of magic and none of the Runaways have been able to build dams to contain the energy produced by this anger."

"I really messed up, didn't I?"

"Mistakes are filled with humanity and the granddaughter of my Gracious now possesses the knowledge that she harbours parts of great variety within her heart. So she must conduct her life henceforth with this compositeness of Outside and Inside. The mistake cannot be put right but she must still encounter acceptance: the granddaughter of my Gracious no longer has the ignorance of new-born babes, she has entered the vigorous age of adolescence where acts come into contact with the payment of their price."

"In other words, I must take responsibility for my actions," muttered Oksa.

"The granddaughter of my Gracious has taken enlightened receipt of the Lunatrix's words."

Then, leaving Oksa deep in thought, the small creature bowed formally and backed away until he reached the door of the room and disappeared.

22

FILE UNDER "TOP SECRET"

REALIZING THAT HE WAS ALSO UPSET, PAVEL POLLOCK waited a good hour before going to comfort his daughter. He sat down on the edge of her bed and very gently stroked her hair.

"I'm really sorry, Dad, please forgive me."

"It's fine, it's all forgotten."

"I hope I didn't hurt Baba with the bowl," she continued.

"Oh, she only had a few little pieces of china embedded in her face last time I saw her. In fact, she looked amazingly like a porcupine…"

"Oh Dad, stop it. It's not funny!" replied Oksa, trying not to laugh.

He looked at her affectionately, his eyes sad despite his relief at being able to tease her again. Neither of them said anything for a moment, then Oksa broke the silence:

"Are you going to get divorced?" she asked, staring at the wall opposite.

"Divorced? Of course not, Oksa!" cried her father. "There's no question of that. Don't worry about your mother. She's had a nasty shock but she's pretty tough. Anyway she loves you, there's no doubt about that. Everything will be okay, you'll see."

"Do you really think so?" asked Oksa, looking up.

"I'm sure of it. And I apologize on behalf of all of us for not paying you enough attention. We're going to be more on the ball from now on, I give you my solemn promise," he added, raising his right hand and pretending to spit on the floor. "But before you go back to school tomorrow, you must promise not to use your gifts *in public*. You possess a power greater than you can even imagine. I understand how you might be tempted to take advantage of it, but it'll only put you in danger."

"I think I understand," said Oksa quietly.

"I'll give you an example which should make you realize what risks we all run if anyone slips up. And this is a valuable lesson for us all, anyway, not just for you. Do you remember Tugdual?"

"Yes," she replied, biting the inside of her cheek at the thought of their first meeting. "He was that boy in Baba's apartment who was sort of out of it and didn't say a word all evening."

"Yes, that's him," replied her father. "He's the grandson of Naftali and Brune, Runaways from the Firmhand tribe who are your gran's friends. When Tugdual was a child, everyone thought, wrongly, he was very shy and introverted because he was so silent and taciturn. But you can't judge a book by its cover. In actual fact, Tugdual's sullen expression and silence masked the fact that he was having a really bad time and I'll explain why. His grandparents had decided to keep quiet about their origins. Their children knew nothing about Edefia for many years and, as a result, neither did their grandchildren. Now, as it happens, the Firmhands' metabolism causes young boys to slough their skin when they reach adolescence: at a given point, scabs form over the entire surface of their body and then fall off to be replaced by an entirely new skin."

"Like snakes!" noted Oksa, stunned.

"Yes, it's quite symbolic… but, more than anything else, it's quite scary. When it happened to their son, Naftali and Brune skilfully managed to pass off this unavoidable phase in the life of a Firmhand—even a Firmhand who doesn't know he's one—as some kind of allergic reaction caused by him eating something exotic. Things proved to be much more complicated for Tugdual, because no one knew that, since the age of thirteen, the boy had belonged to a group involved in witchcraft, black magic and so on, the way certain teenagers of that age tend to do. With his friends, he performed occult rites during which he concocted

138

beverages supposed to give various powers. All of this would have been relatively harmless if not for the fact that, at the same time, Tugdual was beginning to realize that he had certain gifts: levitation, telekinesis and ultra-keen sight."

"Did he discover all this on his own? Like me?" asked Oksa, interrupting him.

"Yes. And he didn't tell anyone for two years. He attributed these powers to the beverages that he'd been making with his friends. Although he was much younger than they were, he soon became the group's supreme leader due to his gifts. He had no idea that the beverages had nothing to do with it."

"Let me guess," broke in Oksa. "I'm sure those drinks contained some really gross ingredients."

"You're right," admitted her father. "From what I know, Tugdual and his friends—his followers, I should say, because he became the leader of a real sect—drank pints of blood from sacrificed hens and goats, mixed with pounds of squashed woodlice, toad hearts, crushed rats' livers and various dubious herbs."

"Stop it, Dad," begged Oksa, feeling sick. "I think I get the picture."

"As you can imagine, there was nothing magical about these potions. But Tugdual was sure that he was slowly turning into an exceptional magician. Using and abusing his natural gifts during these secret ceremonies, he acquired a terrible power over his friends, who worshipped him. He made them do exactly what he wanted—morbid things like collecting earth from freshly closed graves or obtaining hairs from corpses waiting to be autopsied at the medical examiner's office, that kind of thing. He wasn't daunted by any experiment. With the advantage of his gifts, he indulged in all kinds of sordid wrongdoings. Tugdual's 'slough' began the day after a pretty revolting evening during which he'd planned to sacrifice a black cat. After sprinkling the poor creature with one of his foul potions, it scratched him badly on his forearm—which only served him right, if you want my opinion. When he woke up the next morning, his entire body was covered with scabs and his skin was falling off in strips. Tugdual assumed there was a connection between the cat's scratch and the state he was in. He became so terrified that he entered a deep state of paranoid delirium—don't forget he was only fifteen. His parents were just as panic-stricken and were about to rush him to A&E. Fortunately, before doing so, they told Naftali and Brune, who firmly dissuaded them. In the days after, the whole family found out about their origins and everyone tried their best to cope with the shock. At the same time, they hastily arranged a move to Sweden. As for Tugdual, he soon acquired a new skin. However, he'd been violently disturbed by the things he'd imagined during those long unhealthy months, although he did admit that the truth had its attractions. Being a Firmhand from Edefia is much more exciting than being a macabre pseudo-magician obsessed by death and corpses. Despite that, he was still very shocked, especially as he remembered drinking all those blood-based concoctions *for nothing*! These shocks, combined with his natural predilection for the forces of darkness, meant that Tugdual became a danger to himself, while his family found it difficult to understand him. His parents were totally out of their depth. A month ago, the boy was entrusted to Abakum's care since he has the skill and the instruments to treat that kind of illness. Tugdual isn't a bad person deep down, otherwise Abakum wouldn't have taken charge of him. I'm sure, as we all are, that he's on the mend."

Oksa gave a long whistle between her teeth and nodded, looking worried.

"That's a terrible story… but what's it got to do with me, Dad?"

"What it has to do with you, scatterbrain," replied her father, pretending to be exasperated, "is that it shows you must never abuse your power. Particularly when it's a question of powers which should be filed under 'Top Secret'. This story has a valuable lesson for you to learn. Trust us and listen to our warnings. Okay?"

"Okay," replied Oksa, gazing into the distance.

But the next day, racing to school on her rollerblades, her mind full of these stories and images, she began fantasizing that she was flying, without having to worry about onlookers—Outsiders who wouldn't understand. Suddenly she realized that, with the speed from her rollerblades and her ability to float above the ground, she had taken off. She'd been levitating about a foot above the pavement while rollerblading.

"Wow, this is amazing! But I'd better come back down to earth before I get myself into trouble," she resolved sensibly, looking around.

Unfortunately, it wasn't long before she forgot that resolution. The Year 9 Neanderthal was standing at the school entrance with a gang of boys who looked just about as friendly as he was.

"Great start to the week," grumbled Oksa. "First Mum, then a row and a fit of hysterics, and now the Neanderthal! The whole shebang…"

She sat down on the bench on the other side of the street to remove her rollerblades and used the time to try and come up with an emergency plan which would get her safely into the courtyard.

"Well, well, if it isn't my favourite loser!" exclaimed the Neanderthal, blocking her way as she tried to sneak in with a group of students.

Her attempt to slip in unnoticed had been a complete flop.

"You give me the creeps, you know," said the boy with a grimace, blasting hot breath in her face.

"You give me the creeps too," muttered Oksa, switching to Plan B.

Saying this, she fixed her large grey eyes on him with such intensity that he couldn't help shuddering. Oksa smiled inwardly and dropped her steely gaze until it came to rest on the Neanderthal's tie, which immediately began to tighten very slowly around his thick neck. The boy looked at Oksa in amazement and tried to slip a finger between his skin and the fabric, which was strangling him. The veins in his neck and temples began to bulge as he panicked and his breathing became shallow and laboured. With his eyes watering, he continued to pull desperately at his collar. But the tie tightened relentlessly, responding only to Oksa's will. Satisfied at last, she released the pressure.

"You *really* give me the creeps," she repeated, glancing one last time at his scarlet face.

Then she walked into the courtyard with her head held high.

23

NOTHING VENTURED, NOTHING GAINED

G US WAS LEANING AGAINST HIS OPEN LOCKER, DEEP IN conversation with a very pretty girl whom Oksa didn't know. He was so engrossed that he didn't notice his friend putting away her rollerblades in the locker next to his. Feeling hurt, Oksa went straight to the classroom. Gus joined her a few minutes later.

"Hi there! You okay? I rang your bell as I went by, but your father told me you'd already left… where were you?"

"I arrived just after you, but you were *busy*," replied Oksa, in a tone heavy with reproach, not looking up from her desk.

"Huh," he sighed, shrugging with studied casualness. "So how are things with your parents?"

"I think they're getting divorced," said Oksa quietly. "Mum's gone."

"WHAT?"

They couldn't continue their conversation. Dr Bento came in and the lesson was starting. Oksa paid very little attention during the next hour. Everything was getting on top of her and she felt totally isolated. And, to cap it all, Gus was so intent on chatting up other girls that he didn't even notice her. Was he abandoning her? The traitor. And then there was awful McGraw, who kept picking on her… things weren't going well for Oksa-san. The break was too noisy and crowded to talk about something as private as a family crisis. Gus and Oksa tried to get some time on their own, but their friends made that impossible. When the bell rang for lunch, they raced to the cafeteria and Oksa managed to give him a broad outline of what had happened.

"I'm so angry with myself, Gus, you have no idea—and I'm so angry with all of them too! Especially my dad."

During lunch, Gus realized how depressed Oksa really was. He'd never seen her like this, her eyes brimming with tears and her voice choked with emotion. She suddenly looked so... vulnerable. It was as if her protective shell had been stripped away by her sadness and the deep feelings of guilt she was describing in veiled terms. Gus longed to comfort her and help her get back to her bubbly, vivacious self, but he didn't know how. How had she managed to help him when he was going through some difficult times a few years ago? That was a hard question to answer. All he knew was that she was better at comforting her friends than he was. "*I'm so pathetic, such a dead loss, I can't even help my best friend,*" he thought, beating himself up inside. He watched her, opposite, helping herself to some of that strange dish of meat served with mint sauce. Their eyes met and Gus realized immediately that she was feeling better. That was Oksa all over! Any obstacles or ordeals she found in her way only served to make her stronger. And there he was, wallowing in his hang-ups, while Oksa was making signs at him which he couldn't interpret. He looked at her and mouthed "*what?*", to which she replied just as silently by rolling her eyes towards the far end of the cafeteria. Finally he realized what she was trying to show him: Mr Bontempi and Dr McGraw were sitting at the same table. A few minutes later, Gus and Oksa were outside, having ditched their trays. And their friends...

"Did you see that?" said Oksa. "McGraw is eating lunch with Bontempi!"

"Yes, it is rather unusual," acknowledged Gus. "What are you thinking?"

"How about raiding Bontempi's office?" suggested Oksa. "He must have files on all the teachers and we're bound to find some info on McGraw."

"Wait a minute—you want to get into the Headmaster's office and go through his files?" exclaimed Gus in a low voice, looking round in the fear that someone might overhear this compromising conversation. "You're not frightened of anything, are you?"

"Oh Gus, nothing ventured, nothing gained! Where do you think we're going to find info? By going direct to McGraw? 'Excuse me, my dear Dr McGraw, could you tell us where you come from, who you are and if you're working for the secret services?'" said Oksa defiantly. "No, frankly Gus, we don't have a choice. But you don't have to come with me if you don't want to…"

For a few seconds, Gus was tempted by this much more sensible alternative. But, blinded by his friendship for Oksa, he agreed to go with her, all the while telling himself that this was probably the one thing he'd regret most for the rest of his life.

"I've thought it over and I think you should keep watch in the corridor," explained Oksa. "I'll go into his office. At this hour, everyone's eating. The teachers and monitors were all in the cafeteria, I counted them, so we should be left in peace."

"We *should*," muttered Gus who, despite cursing himself, was looking forward to such a dangerous yet exciting expedition. "What if someone comes?"

"You warn me!" said Oksa briskly. "That's why you're keeping watch, isn't it? All you need to do is cough or whistle, whatever you want."

"What if they ask me why I'm standing in the teachers' corridor?"

Oksa scratched her head, narrowing her eyes. Suddenly she walked over to a corner of the courtyard, unhesitatingly stepped over the low fence around the rose bed and snapped off a magnificent white rose, which she brandished like a trophy in Gus's face.

"Just say you were looking for the staffroom so you could leave this rose in Miss Heartbreak's locker, because she's your favourite teacher."

"WHAT?!" cried Gus, beetroot-red. "I could never say that!"

"Have you got any better ideas?" asked Oksa.

"Not yet, but you can bet your life I'll think of something!" retorted Gus.

"Fine! In any case, hold on to the rose, it may come in useful," said Oksa grinning. "Come on, we'd better get a move on."

The two friends went up to the first floor. The staffroom was just opposite Mr Bontempi's office, which suited Gus, who was mentally preparing himself to justify his presence there.

"Damn! It's locked," cursed Oksa. "I'm going to try to open it."

"How?" asked Gus, hoping this pitfall would put a halt to her plan. His hopes were dashed after a nanosecond.

"With this," replied Oksa, waving her index finger mischievously under her friend's nose.

She turned round to concentrate on the door. Then, barely an inch away from the lock which was barring their entry, she began moving her index finger very slowly in anti-clockwise circles. The mechanism seemed to respond, at first imperceptibly, but Oksa sensed she had it beaten. She hadn't doubted it for a minute. After two minutes, she put her hand on the door handle, pressed down and... the door opened. She stifled a cry of satisfaction but punched the air in a sign of victory for Gus's benefit. He managed only a weak smile, running his hand through his hair—a clear sign that he had mixed feelings. Oksa disappeared inside the office and closed the door behind her.

"Bento, Heartbreak, Martino... Ah here's McGraw!" murmured Oksa.

Leaning over one of the drawers in Mr Bontempi's filing cabinet, she took out a brown file and leafed through it. "*What an idiot! I didn't bring anything to take notes,*" she said to herself.

She looked around—on the immaculately tidy dark wooden desk stood several piles of neatly stacked papers, a telephone, a lamp, a computer and a notepad, but not a single pencil. Against the left-hand wall was a shelf laden with books and against the right-hand one was a unit holding a fax, a printer and... a photocopier."

"Yay!" exclaimed Oksa in a hushed voice. "Just what I need."

She switched on the machine and began photocopying the ten or so sheets of paper in McGraw's file without reading them—she'd have time to do that later. The photocopier must have been an old model, because the first copy wrested a loud grating noise from the machine. And a frantic groan from Oksa…

"Hang in there, Oksa," she told herself quietly to keep her spirits up.

She placed the sheets on the glass, pressing on the lid with all her might and holding her breath, which unfortunately did nothing to muffle the photocopier's complaints. Between two copies she managed to hear Gus, who seemed be in the grip of a violent coughing fit. The signal? The SIGNAL!

24

OPERATION McGRAW

AS SOON AS OKSA BEGAN MAKING THE FIRST COPY, GUS had a feeling of foreboding. What Oksa thought of as a shushing sound sounded to Gus more like the roar of a jet at take-off. As the corridor was quite dark, the bluish flashes from the photocopier filtered under and around the door frame, projecting bright stripes onto the walls. Gus gritted his teeth and wrung his hands in misery, glancing up and down the corridor, terrified he might see someone coming. Suddenly he saw the light go on at one end: someone was climbing the stairs! With a little luck, the unwelcome intruder would stop at the first floor. But what if they didn't? Gus felt icy perspiration trickling down his back and beading his forehead. His legs grew heavy, rooting him to the spot, and his mouth suddenly went dry. Without waiting to find out if the person who'd switched on the light in the staircase was coming up to the first floor, he started to cough. Because his throat was so tight and dry, this cough soon turned into a loud, irritating coughing fit. "*Oh damn!*" he panicked. "*This stupid cough is going to bring the whole school running! Oksa, Oksa, what have you got us into now?*"

Jake, one of the monitors, had just appeared at the end of the corridor. Gus felt all his blood drain away. Inside Mr Bontempi's office, the bluish flashes and the roaring of the photocopier had stopped. Gus vaguely heard the click of the lock: Oksa had probably locked herself inside. He'd expected her to come out when he warned her, but apparently she had other plans. Unless she was trapped inside and counting on him to get her out of this tight spot? *"But what can I possibly do?"* he wondered in a panic. *"She was insane to take me with her!"*

Fortunately Jake was nowhere near the most feared monitor in the school—which didn't stop Gus being caught off guard when he called out.

"What are you doing there?"

"Er… I was waiting for Dr McGraw, um no, Miss Heartbreak… I wanted to ask her something about our history lesson," he managed to splutter out in a monotone.

"I rather think you wanted to give her that, didn't you?" teased the monitor, glancing at the rose Gus was holding.

"This? Er no," replied Gus, feeling like a right idiot.

"Whatever, you can't stay here anyway. You can ask her during your next lesson with her, okay? Go back to the courtyard now."

"Okay!" said Gus, still unsure about going back downstairs on his own.

But he could hear the sound of voices, including those of Miss Heartbreak and McGraw, coming from the staircase. Nightmare! Struggling with his conscience, Gus had no choice but to walk back along the corridor and obediently, if reluctantly, go downstairs to the courtyard.

※

Inside Mr Bontempi's office, Oksa had heard Gus's entire conversation. Realizing that her friend was trapped, she turned off the photocopier and quickly put McGraw's file back, pleased nonetheless that she'd been able to copy all of it. She rolled up the sheets of paper and stuffed them in the waistband of her skirt beneath her shirt. There were other voices in the corridor now, so she couldn't get out that way. With her heart pounding, she quickly ran through her possibilities: hide under Mr Bontempi's desk and risk being trapped there all afternoon a couple of inches from the Headmaster's knees; shoot out of there and bolt away so quickly that no one would have time to recognize her; or take the only remaining way out: the window. Behind her, she heard the Headmaster's voice coming nearer. The door of the office was about to be opened. Ignoring the voice of caution, she opened the window, pulled the curtain behind her and knelt on the windowsill, partially shutting both sides of the window again. One of the countless gargoyles was sticking out in front of her, providing an additional surface. But when she looked down, she suddenly remembered she was on the first floor. *"Wow, this is high! A new challenge for Oksa-san!"* She shut her eyes and concentrated on the empty space below her, driven by her need to escape this trap of her own making. After two seconds of total self-absorption, she confidently stretched out her left foot and moved it up and down slightly, as if she were testing the terrain. The empty space felt solid. PHEW! *"It works!"* she told herself without losing focus. She put her foot down as if she were treading on firm ground and decided to step forward with her other foot. This was more hazardous and the consequences much more serious if Oksa failed, because she was in danger of crashing to the ground thirty feet below. This thought insidiously crossed her mind, making her wobble.

"No! Don't even think about it," she told herself.

Bravely she looked down one last time to make sure there was no one there. No, the coast was clear, the students were still in the cafeteria but not for long, it was now or never. Focusing on her descent, Oksa put her right foot forward and, since she didn't feel as though she was falling, imagined floating like a feather until she finally landed on the flagstones, a few minutes before the students streamed out into the courtyard.

❋

"You gave me the fright of my life," Gus whispered in Oksa's ear. "I thought I was going to have a heart attack. Are you okay? How did you get down?"

With her arms pressed to her sides, Oksa flapped her hands as if she were fluttering.

"From up there?" continued Gus, stunned, gazing up at the first floor.

"You bet!" nodded Oksa with a radiant smile. "And look what I've got here," she continued, briefly showing him the roll of paper stuck in her waistband.

Gus whistled through his teeth in admiration.

"What are you two up to?" asked Merlin, coming over. "An airborne escape, eh?" he added, gazing intently at Oksa. "St Proximus must look pretty cool from the sky, wouldn't you agree?"

"Why did he say that to me?" Oksa whispered to Gus. "Do you think he saw me?"

"Sshhh," breathed Gus, "I don't even want to think about it. Come on, it's time to go."

"I'll see you in a bit, I just need to put something in my locker," said Oksa, made uncomfortable by the roll of papers sticking to her stomach and unsettled by Merlin's ambiguous words.

During Dr Lemaire's lesson she sank into a soothing reverie. She'd had to concentrate so hard during her free fall that it had left her feeling both hyper and drained of energy. But the teacher's calm voice eased these two extremes and put the young student in a more reasonable state of mind. As for Gus, he had suffered a few minutes of black terror, convinced he'd find Oksa smashed to a pulp on the flagstones of the courtyard.

Like all lessons before those given by Dr McGraw, this one flew past much too quickly. An hour later, with a great deal of sighing, the students made their way to the science room. Despite her best efforts and her good resolutions, it only took Oksa a quarter of an hour to attract attention:

"Miss Pollock!" bellowed Dr McGraw. "If it's not too much to ask, would you do us the great honour of coming back down to planet Earth? We know you're an expert in astronomy, but even if it's a real disappointment for you, let me remind you that we're in a maths lesson! Come and sit at this empty desk in the front row, so it'll be easier for you to stay with us."

Oksa blushed to the roots of her hair and obeyed. She'd been totally absorbed in her own thoughts. Just before McGraw had interrupted her musings, she'd been wondering what she would find in his file. What a crazy day… She looked despondently at the desk which McGraw had pointed out, a couple of inches from his table and the rostrum; it was such a popular seat that no one ever wanted to sit there! She had only just sat down when the classroom door opened to reveal Mr Bontempi. They all stood up.

"Dr McGraw, can you spare a moment, please?"

"Of course, Headmaster," said Dr McGraw. "Mr Poicassé, you will look after the class while I'm gone."

"Yes, sir," said Merlin, looking worried.

After McGraw's departure, it didn't take the Year 8 Hydrogen students more than ten seconds to start whispering. At first, Merlin tried to reason with his classmates, stressing the dire consequences which would befall him, but they were more interested in letting off steam than listening to his arguments. There was a cheerful hubbub as some of them threw balls of paper at each other and others decided to run races around the desks. When Axel Nolan knocked over McGraw's satchel on the rostrum, she unwittingly placed an idea in Oksa's mind, which was working overtime: that school bag was bound to contain personal papers or other interesting things about their teacher. Taking advantage of the confusion, she stood up and went over to pick it up. Trying not to draw attention to herself, she risked peeking inside. She noticed his wallet immediately. She dipped her hand in and took it, amazed at her own daring. This type of thing was just not done, but her investigation was too important to let principles stand in the way. She went back to her seat, huddled over so that her body acted as a screen and opened the wallet. She had to be quick! A few seconds later she stood up and again went over to pick up the satchel, which was still lying on the floor, and put the wallet back. The room was in such an uproar she was sure no one had noticed anything. But to justify being near her teacher's desk, she set about coming to Merlin's aid. Two precautions were better than one...

"Watch out, McGraw's coming back!" she yelled loudly.

Everyone hurriedly returned to their seats. McGraw came in soon after and when he opened the door the Year 8 Hydrogen students were the image of a studious class, above all suspicion.

25

THE MYSTERIOUS LIST

"**O**RTHON-MCGRAW, BORN 1960 IN MILWAUKEE, Wisconsin, in the United States."

Gus was sitting on Oksa's bed. At last! The afternoon had dragged on interminably and, as soon as lessons were over, they'd raced back in record time to the novice spy's home on their rollerblades. Breathlessly they had rushed into Oksa's room and spread the photocopies of McGraw's file all around them so they could study their booty carefully.

"That means he's forty-nine," mused Oksa. "Look, this lists his personal details: he lives at 12 Franklin Roosevelt Street, that's appropriate for an American! He's married and has a fifteen-year-old son. That must be who I saw in the photo."

"There's a photo?" asked Gus, interrupting her.

"Yes, in his wallet, there was the photo of a woman with a young boy. They were standing in front of what looked like the Capitol in Washington. So what else is on this sheet? Oh look! Here's what he told Merlin—he was a researcher for a scientific laboratory attached to the CIA for ten years. He collaborated with NASA, working on the photoelectric effect and light waves. Wow! Take a look at this list of degrees—McGraw is a real brainbox!"

Oksa held out the long list to Gus and continued to leaf through the documents spread out on the bed. Suddenly she cried out in a shrill voice:

"Look at this! McGraw was an official representative for the American government for two years. Didn't I tell you he's a secret agent?"

Gus sighed noisily.

"But Oksa," he remarked as tactfully as possible, "not everyone who works for a government is necessarily a secret agent."

"Perhaps not *necessarily*, but it could be a good cover, don't you think?"

"It is a bit strange that a man like him should be teaching maths and physical sciences in a school. I agree with you on that," confirmed Gus, holding McGraw's curriculum vitae.

"Going from NASA to physical sciences is a bit *spaced out...*" added Oksa.

Gus began laughing.

"NASA... *spaced out...* Congrats, very funny! I see your brain is working overtime."

They continued to analyse the ten sheets of paper photocopied by Oksa for quite a while. The young spy was a little disappointed because the documents were mainly administrative in nature and not very interesting. Only one was a little more personal: McGraw's application letter, written in a beautiful flowing hand, which outlined his reasons for wanting the job.

"Listen to this: he applied to St Proximus 'for personal reasons'. Personal reasons, Gus! And he said that he was particularly keen to rediscover 'the exhilaration of teaching younger generations'! Honestly, give me a break," said Oksa angrily.

"It is a bit much," agreed Gus, frowning.

"A bit suspicious, you mean!" added Oksa excitedly. Gus took the letter and read it carefully. He had to agree—it did confirm Oksa's suspicions. He put it down and lay back on her bed, stretching out his arms and legs, then looked at his friend sitting cross-legged, scrutinizing each of the sheets that she'd photocopied at such risk to herself. She was incredible, so strong and determined. And yet he knew how hard she was finding things at the moment. He felt a surge of admiration and concern. As long as she didn't flip out…

Oksa felt exultant. She might not have learnt as much as she would have liked but the fact that she'd pulled off such a daring exploit gave her a feeling of intense satisfaction. Sneaking into Bontempi's office and going through McGraw's file! Looking inside his wallet without him being any the wiser! The work of a true pro, even though it had given her palpitations and brought her out in a cold sweat more than once, particularly when she'd made her amazing, death-defying descent from the first floor.

"And were you able to see what there was in his wallet? Anything interesting?" asked Gus, still stretched out on the bed, never taking his eyes off his friend.

"No," continued Oksa, without looking up, "not really. Everything you usually find in a wallet: credit card, driving licence, receipts, scribbled phone numbers, nothing really exciting. There was also a card with an odd phrase written on it: "If you think you're stronger than me, you'll have to prove it.""

"Strange…"

The two friends fell silent for a moment. Gus nodded, engrossed in what Oksa had just told him. Oksa, on the other hand, was finding it hard to relax from the tension that had been tying her stomach in knots all day. She would never have thought she was capable of doing anything like that. It was easy to imagine it or daydream about doing it! She loved pushing the boundaries like this, but at the same time she was alarmed by what she'd done. She thought about the unknown risks she'd taken for what was after all a pretty mediocre result and about what would have happened if McGraw or Bontempi had noticed anything. No, better not to think about that, unless she *really* wanted to scare herself silly. As usual, she was more afraid afterwards than she had been during. Which was something that could become a problem…

"Anyway, it was a masterstroke!" said Gus breaking the silence.

"All the same I was a little scared," admitted Oksa, ignoring Gus's compliment.

"Oh, Oksa! It's true that sneaking into the Headmaster's office and photocopying teachers' files isn't strictly legit, I won't disagree with you. But the circumstances are exceptional. McGraw isn't on the level and we can now prove it. You didn't do anything really wrong, you just photocopied a file and looked inside someone's wallet, it's no big deal. You didn't steal anything!"

"Well—" breathed Oksa, miserably studying her badly bitten nails.

"Wait… don't tell me you took something from his wallet?" cried Gus suddenly, sitting bolt upright on the bed.

"This," admitted Oksa, taking from her pocket a piece of paper folded in eight, the corners dog-eared with use.

"Oh no," groaned Gus, rubbing his forehead wearily. "You're insane! What's on that piece of paper then?" he continued, his curiosity getting the better of his concern.

Oksa carefully unfolded it, smoothing it out with the palm of her hand, and they both studied it intently to find out what it contained:

G.L. 19/04/54 Kagoshima (Jap.) 10/67+08/68
G.F. 09/06/60 London (Engl.) 09/73+05/74+01/75
J.K. 12/12/64 Plzeň (Czech.) 04/77+02/78
H.K. 01/12/67 Mänttä (Finl.) 11/79+10/80
A.P. 07/05/79 Mýrdalsjökull (Icel.) 01/91+06/92
C.W. 16/03/88 Houston (USA) 12/99+05/01+10/01
Z.E. 29/04/96 Amsterdam (Neth.) 07/08
O.P. 29/09/96 Paris (Fr.) 05/09

The two friends looked at each other in confusion, then again tried to decipher the mysterious document so they could understand the meaning of the letters and numbers.

"It's like a list," said Gus. "With initials and dates."

He carried on carefully reading the sheet of paper. Suddenly he exclaimed:

"Hey, that's odd! There's my mother's date of birth! And beside it, the town where she was born!"

Oksa narrowed her eyes in amazement and found the line Gus was pointing to.

"There—look! '*J.K. 12/12/64 Plzeň (Czech.) 04/77+02/78*'."

"Do you know your mother's maiden name?" asked Oksa, increasingly intrigued.

"Kallo," breathed Gus, suddenly looking very drawn. "With a K. Before marrying my father, she was called Jeanne Kallo and she was born on 12th December 1964 in Plzeň in Czechoslovakia. How come my mother's name is on a list drawn up by McGraw?"

"And above all *why*?" added Oksa, breathlessly.

Silently they exchanged a look of concern and amazement.

"Look!" he said pointing to the last line. '*O.P. 29/09/96 Paris (Fr.) 05/09*'. That's you…"

He groaned as he watched the blood drain from Oksa's face.

"You're bang on," she whispered, looking stunned.

"If the numbers afterwards represent dates, as far as you're concerned, that would correspond to May 2009…"

"Which would mean that McGraw already knew about me then. He came to St Proximus because of me, I was right!"

"It looks like it, I'm afraid," muttered Gus.

Oksa shivered. She felt a certain satisfaction at coming up with what had today proved a watertight theory. But facing the facts sent shivers up her spine. Breathing heavily, her head swimming with fear, she fell back on the bed and stared at the ceiling.

26

FAMILY TROUBLES

OKSA HADN'T SEEN HER MUM OR HER GRAN FOR TWO weeks. Marie Pollock was still holed up with her sister and Dragomira was convalescing with Abakum in the countryside. This left Oksa and her father alone in the house on Bigtoe Square, which suddenly felt far too large for the two of them. The situation had forced Pavel to reorganize his schedule and he was spending less time in the restaurant: he had to put his family before his career. Anxious to do the right thing, Pavel was getting up before Oksa and making hearty breakfasts, and he was always there to lavish attention on her when she got in from school. They spent all their evenings together. Although it was still only late summer, Pavel would build a roaring fire in the hearth and they'd enjoy each other's company until bedtime. Taking a keen interest in her homework, he rediscovered the pleasure of sharing in his daughter's daily life. Oksa had decided to buckle down to her studies, which was her way of showing her parents that they could be proud of her, despite the mistakes she'd made. And her hard work was beginning to pay off: her first marks had been excellent and Oksa was receiving well-deserved praise.

"A mind sharp as a sword blade and the speed of a vigorous body—the perfect ninja!" Gus had exclaimed, punching her on the shoulder.

"A sharp mind, I'm not so sure about that," Oksa had retorted. "Look at the tight spots I keep getting into!"

She was obviously thinking about her new powers. As her father had predicted, they could easily get her noticed, which wasn't all that clever, as she'd quickly realized. She hadn't been able to refrain from reoffending a few times, though, particularly with the girl who, in her opinion, was getting too close to Gus. "*Much too pretty for her own good*," she grumbled to herself. When she'd again caught her friend deep in conversation with that *schemer*, she hadn't been able to stop herself from making a button pop off her blouse, from a safe distance. The poor girl dashed off to escape prying eyes, which had earned Oksa a horrified grimace from Gus.

"Why did you do that? You're horrible!"

"That girl gets on my nerves. Always hanging around…"

"Hanging around? Oksa, don't tell me that's why you did it? That's really *pathetic*! Anyway, what if I like her hanging around?"

Those words, added to the events of the last few days, had given Oksa serious food for thought. That evening, curled on the sofa in front of the crackling flames, she'd talked to her father in a way she'd never been able to do before and their closeness made her feel so much better. She did however keep a few secrets to herself, particularly the unsettling "McGraw File", as she now called it. She had tried to talk to him one day about her pseudo-teacher and how keen he was to torment his students, but without even knowing the details her father had smiled, saying that he didn't know anyone who hadn't encountered an odd or question-able teacher at least once at school. Telling her not to overdramatize, he'd encouraged her to hang in there and put on a brave face about this awkward situation.

"Awkward?! I'd like to see you handle it," she'd grumbled, while deep down she was still sure that McGraw wasn't who he claimed to be.

Her father had also insisted that she tell him about her magic experi-ments and she'd even been able to give him several dazzling demonstra-tions. Impressed and anxious, he had admired them gravely and had repeated his warnings, with just cause. And even if she didn't always enjoy hearing them, she knew he was right.

"You're very gifted, Oksa. But please be careful. You know, I personally always avoided using those *gifts*. I'm not saying I never wanted to, but I was too afraid someone might ask questions."

"You restrain yourself, is that what you mean?"

"Not really. But I absolutely don't want anyone to find out about it, it's more to do with an instinct for self-preservation. It's not quite the same for you, it's better and, at the same time, it's worse, because you're a Gracious."

Pavel looked at his daughter sadly with a small, weary smile, which made his face appear even more lined.

"Dad? You discovered your powers when you were in Russia, didn't you? That's where you were born, isn't it?"

"Yes, it was called the Soviet Union back then. Strictly speaking, I was born in Siberia. When your gran, Leomido and Abakum were ejected from Edefia, they found themselves in a place which had nothing in common with what they'd always known. Siberia was a terrifying place for Insiders. Coming straight from a temperate, luxuriant and fertile land to cold, hostile Siberia was an appalling contrast, I can tell you. Your gran was terrified. Just imagine: until then, she'd been living happily with her parents in a land of harmony and plenty. And in the space of a few hours, she'd faced chaos, flight, abandonment and then Siberia. You must have heard of Siberia, darling, haven't you?"

"The country where they had the gulags? The place where there were so many prison camps?"

Pavel looked at her in surprise and amusement.

"That's not the first thing I would have remembered about it, but I see things differently from you—Siberia is where I was born. You're not wrong though and it's not a complete coincidence that they put the gulags there. You can go hundreds of miles without spotting a living soul, apart from animals and the spirits of nature. Nature reigns supreme there—a magnificent though very cruel ruler with the power of life and death. Abakum, young Dragomira and Leomido wandered for several days, frozen to the marrow. On Edefia, the temperature never fell below twenty degrees and it never snowed, so you can imagine what a shock it was for them. Abakum kept them fed with roots, berries and fish he caught in the rivers. And Leomido kept them warm by using his Fireballistico—the power of fire, which was vital for survival in those lands. A few days later, they met a very powerful shaman who lived in a small isolated village on the edge of a forest. Winter was fast approaching and Metchkov, the shaman, gave them shelter and protected them during the bitter icy months until the thaw, when he could show them the way to a large city. Abakum and he were very similar and quickly became as close as brothers. Both were capable of hearing, understanding and communicating with the natural world. In their company, Dragomira became an exceptionally gifted student. When spring came, only Leomido decided to leave. He travelled across Europe as far as Britain, where he became the great conductor you know. Twelve years later, I was born in the same small Siberian village.

"So... your father was the shaman Metchkov?"

Pavel laughed gently.

"No, not Metchkov, he was over 100 years old! My father was his grandson. Life was hard but we were very happy together until I was eight. Then everything fell apart. My father was killed by the KGB and political conditions had become so difficult that we were forced to flee our small village and leave Siberia. Abakum came with us— he'd given Malorane his word to protect Dragomira and even though she was now a wife and mother, he always kept his promise. We had many problems leaving the Soviet Union. It was during the Cold War and the country had become a vast prison for its inhabitants. You risked your life trying to leave. Your grandmother and Abakum made frequent use of their powers at that time, which was a great help to us. But, without Leomido, I don't think we'd ever have succeeded. He was on a world tour with his orchestra and it was during his visit to

St Petersburg—which was called Leningrad then—that we managed to leave the country illegally."

"How?" asked Oksa, thrilled by her father's story.

"Well, would you believe he passed us off as members of his orchestra. It was extremely dangerous for him and he was brave to do it, because he could have lost everything: not only his freedom but his life too. The real problem was deciding what to do with me, because how do you justify the presence of an eight-year-old child in an orchestra? Well, the answer was simply to sacrifice a cello and shut me inside one of the cases! The KGB carefully examined the double-bass cases, which were large enough to hide a man, but, luckily, not the cello cases, which were smaller. We had a narrow escape, though—thanks to Leomido. He'd become such a well-integrated Runaway."

"So had you!" remarked Oksa.

"Yes, we had too but, still, we were living in a rather *peculiar* environment. For the first eight years of my life, I was surrounded by people like your gran and Abakum who'd never made a secret of their powers, as well as a father, grandfather and great-grandfather who were all remarkable shamans. On top of that, we lived a relatively isolated life in a small Siberian village, so you can imagine the way I viewed the world. My native village was my whole universe—those were the days! I would have liked them to last for ever—because I wasn't all that impressed by what I found out about mankind after that. My integration into society wasn't easy, I can tell you. It was even worse for your gran and Abakum: they'd been living in a remote area for twenty-one years! All the same, they did amazingly well and I'm full of admiration for them; they fitted into that new world with incredible ease, blending in by a process of imitation, like chameleons. They did a lot of people-watching and copied what they saw. But I could see from the inside how hard it was for them. I think Leomido had realized very early on that he had to leave our small circle if he wanted to live successfully as an Outsider. He quickly abandoned all hope of returning to Edefia, unlike your gran and Abakum, who in some ways continued to live as before—just taken down a notch or two. The three of us were experiencing things the other way round: magic, extraordinary powers and strange creatures had always been part of our daily lives, the villagers accepted and respected us just as we were. It was all *normal*! I'd been convinced that the whole world was like us. But as soon as we left, we had to be careful and it was crucial to camouflage ourselves. I had no idea how ordinary Outsiders lived."

"You'd never seen normal people?" asked Oksa, interrupting him. "Er, sorry Dad, I don't mean that you aren't normal…"

"No, I know what you mean, don't worry. By 'ordinary Outsiders', I mean those who couldn't accept how different we were. From now on our gifts had to become a secret which could never be revealed. Anyway, I quickly learnt this to my cost."

"How?" broke in Oksa.

"Leomido had arranged for us to live in Switzerland in a small, peaceful town in the mountains. Dragomira lost no time at all in enrolling me in school."

"Was this was the first time you'd gone to school?"

"No, we'd had a school in our Siberian village. And my parents had taught me a great many things."

"And how did you manage with the language? You spoke Russian, didn't you?"

"Ah, you're so practical, sweetheart! Yes, I spoke Russian since it was my mother tongue. But also French, English, German, Chinese, Spanish, Swedish…"

"WHAT? You're making fun of me, Dad!" exclaimed Oksa.

"Not at all," protested her father. "We Insiders have the power of Poluslingua."

"Which is what?"

"The ability to become fluent in the language of whatever country we're in in just a few hours. It's sort of an ultra-fast immersion in a language, if you like. In Edefia, no one knew about that gift, but those of

164

us who left discovered it and immediately put it to good use, as you can imagine. And there's no doubt that this skill has done wonders for our integration. You might have noticed that Mercedica and Leomido have no accent when they've never lived in France—and even less learnt the language. And yet, after a few hours with us, they can speak French like you and me. Or Russian like your gran and Abakum. Or Finnish with Tugdual. That's Poluslingua!"

"Then I'll soon be able to speak English as well as the Queen of England, won't I?" asked Oksa hopefully.

"Perhaps," smiled her father.

"Amazing! I'll be getting wicked marks! But you haven't told me what happened in Switzerland."

"Oh, Switzerland…"

After a few long minutes lost in thought, Pavel continued.

"It was awful; I spent my time trying not to overstep the mark. But after a few days, my true nature got the upper hand."

Pavel fell silent, upset by the memories he'd buried for so long.

"Well? What happened, Dad?" asked Oksa, impatiently.

"What happened? It was a bit of a catastrophe," he replied. "I performed several Magnetuses at the bakery I hated."

"Why did you do that?"

"Anger, Oksa, anger… that's something you're familiar with, isn't it?" he remarked casually. "This baker was a spiteful woman who wasn't very tolerant of foreigners. She made the big mistake of saying something which particularly upset me, then all the loaves of bread took off like rockets and crashed into the ceiling while the cakes dropped down on her like bombs. She didn't really understand what was going on, but the next day Leomido came to get us, so it was my fault that we had to leave Switzerland as a matter of urgency."

"Like Tugdual's family," remarked Oksa. "And like us too, isn't that true?"

"Why do you say that?" asked her father, taken aback.

"We had to leave France," explained Oksa unable to restrain herself, her heart pounding. "We ran away because of that journalist who died."

Pavel Pollock scrubbed his hand over his forehead, his face white as a sheet. He looked helplessly at his daughter, then shut his eyes with a deep sigh.

27

EXPLANATIONS

"THAT JOURNALIST, PETER CARTER—HE DIED BECAUSE of us, didn't he?" pressed Oksa.

She felt some remorse when she saw how upset her father was at this question, but all the guilt in the world couldn't overcome her need to know. With a resigned expression, her father said:

"Yes. Peter Carter died because of us."

"But that's horrible!" shouted Oksa furiously, staring at her father in alarm. "Why? Who did it? Which one of you?"

Pavel Pollock flinched.

"Which one of us? Why do you ask me that, Oksa?" he said in amazement. "And anyway, how do you know? Who told you?"

"I overheard you and Baba," replied Oksa miserably.

"Oh Oksa, one day your annoying habit of listening at doors will land you in big trouble. Fine, since you heard us, I may as well tell you everything—but, I warn you, it may be a bit of a let-down, because I don't know very much. You really are the most infuriating daughter a father could have!"

He sighed noisily before continuing.

"It all began with one of us, Petrus, a Runaway who found himself ejected into the United States. He'd decided to make a living as an art thief, a career which, thanks to his gifts, soon took off in a big way. For years he travelled the world 'visiting' scores of museums, galleries and private collections. But one day his luck changed and he was caught red-handed. In his haste to escape, he used his powers to get out of the apartment of a wealthy collector he was robbing, which was on the forty-seventh floor. The police officers who'd come to arrest him panicked and fired at him, killing him instantly. At his house they found hundreds of pictures, some of them priceless, whose disappearance had mystified the most experienced detectives. And with good reason. How could they have imagined what was going on? The problem was that a journalist, Peter Carter, had already been on his trail for a few months. He'd met Petrus at an art sale and had been intrigued by him. He'd begun to follow him, slowly becoming convinced that he was an extra-terrestrial. When Petrus was killed, Peter Carter continued his investigation and discovered things which enabled him to get closer to us."

"What sort of things?" asked Oksa, fascinated.

"Oh, souvenirs from our land which Petrus had kept very carefully, particularly a notebook containing names, dates, information about Edefia and newspaper articles about Leomido."

"Oh no!" said Oksa.

"Yes, exactly," agreed her father. "Carter arrived at some conclusions which weren't altogether unfounded. And that's when our problems started. He investigated Leomido, then your gran and our family. Shortly afterwards, he contacted us asking us to pay him to keep quiet."

"Really!" exclaimed Oksa. "What a lowlife. I hope you didn't give in to him."

"What choice did we have? He was threatening to reveal everything. Imagine what a disaster that would have been. We paid, once, twice, three times…"

"And then, off to London, is that it?"

"Too right! Because of that man, we had to disappear as a matter of urgency and in the utmost secrecy, without leaving a trace. And it wasn't easy, I can tell you."

"Now I understand why you were in such a rush," breathed Oksa. "But the guy is still dead."

"Yes, and that's very worrying," added her father. "Carter was an unscrupulous predator and I can't say I'm sorry he's dead. But we should never take delight in a man's death."

Oksa narrowed her eyes, vaguely suspicious.

"Dad?"

"Yes, Oksa?"

"Who killed him? Who killed Carter? Do you know? Why did Baba say it had to be one of you?"

Pavel Pollock's gaze grew troubled and he gave an annoyed scowl.

"Carter was killed by a Pulmonis, a substance which can only be made by the Runaways," he explained. "But all I can tell you is that neither I nor your gran are responsible for his death."

"That's a relief!" exclaimed Oksa. "Oh Dad! You don't know how worried I was—this business had me imagining all kinds of crazy things. But do you think it could be Abakum or Leomido?"

"No, neither of them could do that. None of us is capable of it. That's what makes it even more mysterious. It's as if whoever did this wanted to protect us."

Pavel Pollock stood up and went to pour himself a fizzy drink, which he downed in one gulp, trembling, then slammed the glass on the mantelpiece so hard he almost broke it. Oksa jumped and stared at her father in concern. But before she could ask any more questions, he gave her such a grave look that she changed her mind about continuing her cross-examination.

"We've had to run away a great deal, you know," he continued. "Edefia, Siberia, Switzerland, France—"

"How did you get to France?" broke in Oksa, listening intently.

"That's partly down to Malorane, believe it or not. You remember when Dragomira told you about the powers of the Gracious?" asked her father.

"The one that made it possible to escape from Edefia?"

"Indeed, the Graciouses do possess that enviable power: to open the Portal and leave. But Malorane was familiar with France because there's another power that only Graciouses have—the legendary power of Dreamflying."

"Dreamflying?" asked Oksa, interrupting him.

"Dreamflying involves travelling by thought alone while your body stays put. The mind or consciousness undergoes some kind of transformation, if you like. Malorane was an inquisitive woman, so she Dreamflew frequently to see how the Outsiders lived. Unlike most of the previous Graciouses, she preferred to know what was happening on the Outside, instead of shutting her eyes and pretending that Edefia was alone in the universe. Afterwards, she'd put on public Camereye shows of her travels. She Dreamflew several times in France, a country which she liked a lot and she'd hold special screenings just for Dragomira to 'show' her France the way other mums tell their children bedtime stories. That's why we set off for that country which has become so dear to my heart. It's an odd story, isn't it?"

"An odd story? You mean am-az-ing, surely!" replied Oksa enthusiastically. "But you have to admit it isn't the most unbelievable thing ever—I can tell you at least a hundred more bizarre things I've heard over the past few days, if you like!"

"I don't know what you mean," said Pavel, playing the innocent. "*E.T. phone home*," he added, rolling his eyes, his little finger in his ear. "No, nothing weird here."

Oksa burst out laughing, exhaling with a loud whoosh. Then, looking serious again:

"Dad, something else has occurred to me."

"What's that, sweetheart?"

"If the Graciouses have the power to Dreamfly, does that mean I can too?"

She looked at her father in excitement. Pavel gave a deep sigh, stretched his long legs out in front of him and paused for a couple of seconds before replying.

"It's perfectly true. You do possess that power. But you could only use it if you had entered the Cloak Chamber. The Cloak activates the power."

Oksa felt a little disappointed; she would so love to Dreamfly! Seeing her vexed expression, Pavel hugged her tightly.

"You know, it's something I'd love to do too. And I don't think I'm the only one. But there are many other powers we're going to teach you. At least, your gran and Leomido will for the most part. Abakum will also be a very good teacher for you; he's very strong, the strongest of us all."

"Stronger than the Gracious?" asked Oksa.

They were interrupted by the telephone ringing. It was Marie Pollock. Every evening she called to talk to her daughter for a while. Her voice sounded strained, emotional and choked, but Oksa tried not to notice how deeply this whole affair seemed to have upset her. It was all because of her. It broke her heart to hear how sad her mum was, so she tried to take her mind off things by telling her about her day, as if she were at home, as if she were sitting opposite her at the kitchen table in front of a plate of steaming *piroshki*. And when she sensed Marie was smiling at the other end of the phone, she felt better.

"Eighteen out of twenty in maths, what do you say to that, Mum?"

"Not bad," Marie replied, feigning indifference.

"Mum! Let me remind you that it was with frightful McGraw, the fearsome dictator of St Proximus!"

"Ah well, given those extreme conditions, I accept and acknowledge your excellence, my darling daughter."

"You should have seen his face when he gave me back my paper. It was a scream!"

"I'm proud of you, sweetheart. Are you okay otherwise? Is your dad okay?"

They chatted like this for a few minutes, as they did every evening, then wished each other goodnight, blowing kisses down the phone. Oksa asked if she wanted to speak to her dad, but when he took the handset, Marie had already hung up.

"Why does she do that every time?" asked Oksa angrily, a lump in her throat.

That evening, more than usual, it would have been nice to hear them talk to each other. Talk normally.

"Is she that angry with you? But why?" she continued, her cheeks flushed with frustration and her heart near to breaking.

"You were also angry with me, if you remember," replied her father sadly. "Things will sort themselves out, you'll see."

"Do you think so?"

"I'm sure of it!"

Oksa rested her head on her father's shoulder and closed her eyes, as if making a wish.

"So long as she's here for my birthday."

"Don't you worry about that, I don't think she'd miss that for the world."

After a brief pause, he continued:

"Would you like a bit of light relief?"

"You bet!" exclaimed Oksa, suddenly interested. "What did you have in mind?"

By way of an answer, Pavel took her hand and led her up to Dragomira's apartment.

28

An Incredible Discussion

As soon as the door opened, the Lunatrix planted himself in front of them and gave a comical—but sincere—bow, performing flourishes with his long arms and frantically bending his plump body.

"Oh, granddaughter and son of my Gracious, your presence in this hovel is welcome!"

"Hovel?" asked Oksa in surprise.

"You know, Oksa," said her father, "the Lunatrixes read absolutely everything they can lay their hands on: newspapers, dictionaries and Dragomira's books, of course. Not to mention directions on bottles of cleaning products, food ingredients, clothes labels—nothing escapes their notice. They're compulsive readers who use the words they come across in a highly individual way. Our friend the Lunatrix must have read that word; it appealed to him and now he's using it. In a rather ludicrous manner, perhaps, but the Lunatrixes are ludicrous creatures," explained Pavel.

"Oh, son of my Gracious, you are so magnanimous!" exclaimed the creature, obviously beside himself with joy at being described this way. "The son of my Gracious pays a compliment which engulfs my heart in delight!"

"See what I mean?" said Pavel to his daughter with a wink.

"He's ad-or-a-ble!" murmured Oksa, articulating every syllable.

"Have you come visiting up to this floor to make a request, son and granddaughter of my Gracious? It is with delight that the Lunatrixa and I will provide assistance, you can count on our fervour for ever," broke in the Lunatrix, quivering.

"Oh—talking about the Lunatrixa, where is she?" asked Pavel.

"In the side of this room, son of my Gracious; she is performing the application of a salve to relieve the stress of the Goranov plant, which has been jittering since my Gracious has been in the countryside for convalescing. Would it give you pleasure to have sight of her?"

Pavel nodded. Oksa took advantage of the Lunatrix's absence to express her enthusiasm, speaking softly to avoid being heard:

"You bet I'd like to 'have sight of her'! And the Goranov? What's that?"

Her father didn't have time to reply, as the Lunatrix was on his way back followed by the Lunatrixa, an equally incredible creature. Looking out of all proportion, the female was as long as her companion was wide, with her legs accounting for two-thirds of her body. Apart from the fine lemon-yellow hair on top of her head, her face was exactly like her companion's: rumpled brown skin, small, squashed nose, ears sticking out at right angles to her head, two large, round teeth protruding from her mouth, if you could call it a mouth—it was more like a long, curved slit that split her face from ear to ear. Both were wearing dark-coloured, perfectly ironed dungarees sporting a cheerful smiley. As soon as she saw Oksa, the Lunatrixa ran towards her. But, flustered by this encounter and hampered by her two long legs, which were as spindly as broom handles, she stumbled and fell flat on the carpet. The plant she was holding in her hands flew into the air and was caught by Oksa, startled at this surprising sight.

"Oooh, granddaughter of my Gracious," cried the clumsy Lunatrixa. "How ridiculous I am to make a fall like this! My legs are madly absurd, can you ever forgive me?" she wailed, rubbing her back.

Oksa turned to her father, who looked as though he didn't know whether to laugh at the creature or feel sorry for her.

"Are they like this all the time, Dad?" she asked, smiling.

"Yes!"

Pavel really began laughing this time.

"Hey! What's going on?" exclaimed Oksa suddenly.

It seemed as if the plant she was holding had just woken up. Delicate round, flat leaves of a beautiful glossy green were growing out from a slender stem about sixteen inches tall. The plant looked as if it was swaying, its foliage shook as if it were trembling and it gave a cry of alarm.

"But it's *alive*!" cried Oksa, open-mouthed.

"Plants are generally alive, Oksa," remarked her father, stifling his laughter.

"Yes, but not to this extent."

"Alive, alive... I'm not so sure about that," the plant protested angrily all of a sudden, calling Oksa to witness and turning all its leaves towards her. "That Lunatrixa has lost her head."

"No, Goranov, my head has not encountered any loss, it is my balance which is suffering a deficiency," said the Lunatrixa, correcting it.

"But you must be mad to make me perform a loop the loop! You want me dead, is that it?"

"The loop the loop is going to extremes, Goranov, you performed a perfectly executed gliding flight," retorted the Lunatrixa.

"Loop the loop or gliding flight, same difference!" yelled the Goranov, all its leaves trembling. "You wanted to murder me, you serial *killeress*..."

And with these words, all its leaves collapsed down the length of its stem.

"It's just fainted," Pavel explained to Oksa, who was crying with laughter. "But don't worry, this happens quite a lot."

"They're amazing, I love these creatures!" said Oksa, holding out her hand to help the Lunatrixa up.

She looked at Oksa gratefully and accepted her help. Suddenly, they heard the phone ring. Oksa put the still unconscious Goranov on the floor, and rushed off:

"I'll go. That must be Gus. See you soon, Lunatrixes!"

And she raced cheerfully downstairs at breakneck speed.

※

"Definitely see you tomorrow then?"

The week was over and Oksa, surrounded on the pavement by her friends, was reminding Gus, Merlin and Zelda one last time before they all went home. They were getting to know and like each other better and were becoming a close-knit group.

"Oksa, do you mind if I bring a friend?" asked Zelda. "Her name is Zoe, she's in Year 8 Oxygen. We're in the same dance class and she's really cool. I invited her to a sleepover at my house this weekend and I don't want to leave her on her own, or miss your birthday."

"No problem," exclaimed Oksa. "I reckon my father is making a cake big enough for at least thirty, that's just like him. There'll be plenty for one extra."

"Thanks, that's great," Zelda went on. "Zoe needs some friends, she got here a few weeks ago. Her parents died last year and her gran was looking after her, but then she died too, it's really sad... now she lives with her great-uncle."

"All the more reason for her to come and have some fun with us! It'll do her good. See you tomorrow."

"See you tomorrow, Oksa!"

※

Leaning out of her window that evening, Oksa watched the comings and goings in the square. She felt sadness pressing down on her. Night had fallen, but the sky was clear and she made the most of her solitude to think things over in peace and quiet. Although it wasn't easy: her thoughts were jumbled together in her head like laundry in the drum of a washing machine. *During the spin cycle.* The transition from being an ordinary girl to being the heir to the power of an unknown and fabulous land hadn't been painless or uneventful. Oksa felt full of extraordinary feelings. Her brand-new gifts were becoming stronger and this gave her a heady sensation of power which was hard to resist. And it was exactly her inability to stand firm which had caused her so many problems and had led to her overwhelming unhappiness today. At the same time, an uncomfortable feeling was stealthily taking hold of her. She had the disagreeable impression that her life had reached a mysterious, and dangerous, turning point. She was longing to know more about Edefia and to see this famous land. But at the same time, where would it all lead? She didn't know. To the best and worst of things, probably. The appearance of that Mark had turned her life, or rather her future, upside down. Would she become an astrophysicist, as she'd dreamt of doing since she'd discovered that the sky held such riches? Would she get married? Would she have children? Or would she lead the Runaways to Edefia and become their queen? All she knew today was that she was missing her mum terribly and that she was scared stiff that her parents would get divorced. She'd give everything she owned to go back to normal. But would that ever be possible? She saw a falling star which left behind a sparkling silvery trail, and made a wish. A wish as far out of reach as the stars in the sky.

These gloomy thoughts were suddenly interrupted by a brainwave. There was someone in this house who could answer her questions! She quickly ran up to the third floor and knocked softly at the door. Dragomira's Lunatrixa opened it, a wide smile splitting her round face.

"Oohh, granddaughter of my Gracious, a visit lavish with abundance, what a delight!"

"Good evening. How are you?" asked Oksa, slightly taken aback to find herself in private conversation with this odd little creature.

"Very excellent, as always. This is a reliability which we keep to, we Lunatrixes. We have work to do, Her Graciousness has given us responsibility, we must be reliable, it is of voluminous importance!"

"You're right," agreed Oksa, trying to keep a straight face. "And what news of Dragomira... do you by any chance know when she'll be back? And... my mother?"

"I have the knowledge of this information but I can tell you nothing. My lips are not stitched together with thread and yet I must keep silent. But do not be melancholy, they both have true love for you and their return is in proximity, that is fixed," replied the Lunatrixa, gazing at Oksa with wide, kind eyes. "Would you wish an enchanting beverage?"

Oksa accepted happily. She stayed for a while with the creature, who was totally lovable. She felt a little ashamed of taking advantage of her kindness, but she needed to find out things so badly.

"Tell me, Lunatrixa, why did my gran never go back to Edefia?"

The Lunatrixa looked at her in amazement.

"Why? You have asked me about why? I plunge into total astonishment. You do not have the understanding?"

"Tell me, please, it's so complicated for me," insisted Oksa with pleading eyes.

"Well... I have fright in replying to you, but I shall nonetheless deliver the explanation. Two gravely important things put that return in impediment: the curse struck the Portal with closure. But the seriousness is removed since you are the future Gracious. Thanks to the alliance of the Two Graciouses, return again experiences a possibility. The second thing, on the other hand, inscribes a lasting sadness in our hearts: that is ignorance. Edefia is somewhere but who knows where?"

"You mean that no one knows where Edefia is? Not even approximately? In the North? In the South? Someone must have a clue, don't they?" asked Oksa angrily.

"Only one person had the Landmark: Gracious Malorane. The Cloak Chamber is the giver of the Landmark and Gracious Malorane is the one who paid the last visit to the Chamber. But her life has been engulfed by the loss of the Secret-Never-To-Be-Told. However, may I formulate a thought to the granddaughter of my Gracious? A thought which is my conviction?"

"Yes, of course!" said Oksa impatiently.

"I knew the foresightedness of Gracious Malorane, she without fail has entrusted the Landmark to someone, my hope in this certitude is vast."

"You think my gran?…"

"That is my hope. Our Gracious treads the path towards the solution. Hope will no longer be barren."

The Lunatrixa wiped her wide eyes, which were gleaming with pinkish tears, then sniffed very noisily. Oksa gently stroked her large, rumpled head.

"I must go," she said, dropping a kiss on top of her head. "Thank you for this information, Lunatrixa. See you soon!"

29

HAPPY BIRTHDAY, OKSA!

"BE PATIENT A LITTLE LONGER, WE'RE ALMOST THERE," murmured Pavel, guiding Oksa.

Every year, for his daughter's birthday, he planned some kind of memorable surprise. The ritual was always the same: he came to fetch Oksa, blindfolded her and then took her somewhere unexpected. When they reached their destination, the blindfold was taken off and the mystery solved. For her twelfth birthday, he'd simply taken her to the top of the Eiffel Tower—an amazing surprise which she wouldn't forget in a hurry. Pavel never did things by halves. This year, Oksa had an inkling what was waiting for her: ever since they'd arrived in London, her parents had categorically refused to let her see the restaurant, which seemed rather suspicious. All she knew was that the date of the opening had been set for 29th September, the day of her thirteenth birthday. "A lucky date for two red-letter days in my life," Pavel had told her solemnly. So, although she had a hunch about where he was taking her, Oksa let him lead her along, spontaneously sharing his impatience and delight.

"We're here… get ready for a surprise, my brave Oksa-san," Pavel whispered in her ear, untying the blindfold.

Oksa blinked at the extraordinary shopfront opposite, which was covered with ivy, wisteria and climbing roses. Above the entrance, a streamer floating in the wind informed all the passers-by that it was Oksa's birthday.

"Oh Dad, this is brilliant!"

"Welcome to the *French Garden*, darling! But wait. You haven't seen anything yet…"

Pavel took her hand and led her inside. As soon as he opened the door, Oksa felt as if she'd entered a different world: a fantastic garden stretched out before her, an idyllic plant world filled with a riot of unexpected vegetation. The girl took a few steps forward, fascinated.

"Is this grass?" she exclaimed, kneeling down to touch the floor.

"Yes," replied Pavel gravely, his eyes shining.

Oksa continued to look around, feeling impressed. There were plants everywhere, banks of flowers, clumps of shrubs and even an oak tree in the middle of the room. Beneath the warmth of giant reflective lamps, rushes and reeds rustled quietly around a pool filled with goldfish. Low box or hawthorn hedges preserved the intimacy of each table, while roomy leather chairs allowed diners to eat in comfort. The mezzanine overhanging part of the first floor was just as magical, with canvas deck-chairs facing a wall of water.

"You've recreated a garden… inside a house?! That's super-cool!"

"It's all thanks to my origins. The Sylvabul blood running through my veins gave me the power of Greenthumb, which I used to good effect."

"It's magnificent, Dad!"

"I know. Hey, come over here for a moment."

Pavel led her towards an arbour covered with dark roses which concealed another equally fantastic room with a glass ceiling. Standing on the daisy-dotted grass, all the guests began singing at the top of their voices around the table, which held a gigantic three-chocolate cake, the largest Oksa had ever seen. Everyone rushed over to hug her warmly. The Bellangers and her school friends were there, Gus standing right next to her, bellowing "Happy Birthday". Then music started playing and some of the guests began dancing. The party was a great success and the cake to die for—Pavel had seen to that. Everything was just perfect. Everything or almost: Marie Pollock was the only one who wasn't there. On the verge of tears, Oksa kept watching the door in the desperate hope that her mother would appear. Pavel could sense his daughter's heart sinking lower and lower as time went by. She was doing her utmost to put on a cheerful, light-hearted front, but she felt terribly sad.

Dragomira had arrived that morning. As soon as she'd come through the door with their faithful family friend, Abakum, Oksa had thrown herself into her arms. She'd been too polite to mention how ill her gran looked, but her joy at seeing her again hadn't prevented her from noticing Dragomira's drawn features and the dark bags under her sunken, tear-filled eyes. But at least her Baba was here!

As for Oksa's younger guests, they'd taken over the deckchairs and were pigging out on sweets while examining their friend's haul of gifts: an astronomical telescope, a webcam, a bag printed with the effigy of a manga heroine, a green plastic inflatable armchair, the latest CD by her favourite band and some perfumed soap. The last gift had been from Zoe, Zelda's friend. When Oksa had seen her, she hadn't been able to hold back her amazement: this was the girl who kept hanging round Gus! The most annoying girl she'd ever met. The one she'd decided to call the Schemer. At first she'd been wary of her and a little annoyed that she was at her birthday party, and she'd thought that Zelda was being manipulated. That girl probably wasn't interested in anything except getting as close as she could to Gus—which didn't please Oksa at all. After watching her for a while, she realized it wasn't that simple and this annoyed her even more. No one was immune to Zoe's charm. She was pretty, she moved with the grace of a dancer and her skin was as delicate as porcelain. Even worse: there was an aura of sadness about her which set her apart from the others and which everyone found deeply moving. There was something touching about her large, sad, shy eyes. Oksa sensed she was a tortured spirit, and found her intriguing. Feeling irritated, she couldn't help scrutinizing Zoe's reaction to Gus—and vice versa—rather tactlessly in fact, since her friend lost no time in coming over:

"You'd make a very bad spy."

"What do you mean?" retorted Oksa, pretending she didn't understand.

"Why are you watching us like that?"

"That girl really annoys me," said Oksa, as if this was a perfectly normal thing to say.

"She annoys you because she's talking to me and because I like her, is that it?"

"Whatever," she sighed, by way of an answer.

"Do I sulk when Merlin chats to you?" asked Gus bitterly.

Taken aback by this remark, Oksa gaped at him, then quickly turned on her heel, which didn't stop Gus following her, grumbling under his breath:

"I don't say a thing when you're both sniggering. Nothing at all. Anyway, if you really want to know, I don't give a damn!"

Feeling cut to the quick, Oksa flopped down into a deckchair to chat with Zelda. Gus was so pig-headed! Suddenly she saw her friend was looking at something. She turned round and her eyes brightened.

"MUM!"

Marie Pollock had just arrived. Forgetting her problems, her heart bursting with joy, Oksa rushed over to her and they showered each other with kisses.

"Darling, I missed you so much!"

"Oh you came, thank you, Mum!"

"No, Oksa, I didn't come," said her mum, correcting her. "I came *back*."

Oksa nestled against her and hugged her, thinking that she'd never felt anything so good. Then, grabbing her hand and with her arm tightly around her waist, she shouted proudly.

"Hey everyone, this is my mum!"

Marie looked around at them all gathered there and stammered, with a lump in her throat:

"I'm terribly late…"

"It doesn't matter, Mum," replied Oksa.

Everyone greeted her warmly, aware that she was the most eagerly awaited guest of the afternoon. Dragomira, Abakum and Pavel had risen to their feet. Marie walked over to them a little hesitantly, then threw herself into her husband's arms, murmuring what were probably loving words in Pavel's ear, to judge by the radiant look on his face. Then it was Dragomira's and Abakum's turn to hug her, much to Oksa's delight as she watched in relief. What a wonderful birthday! The best ever.

30

Some Unusual Gifts

T HE PREVAILING MOOD WAS AS BRIGHT AND WARM AS the late-afternoon sun. After Marie's return, the guests soon made themselves scarce, leaving the Pollocks and Abakum to enjoy their reunion. They all walked briskly and cheerfully back to Bigtoe Square and, to set the seal on this new-found harmony, Dragomira decided to show Oksa and Marie her strictly private workroom for the first time—a highly symbolic gesture for Baba Pollock.

"Wow!" cried Oksa in amazement, as she walked into the double-bass case which led to the secret room hidden under the eaves. "This beats everything! Is there a code? How does it work?"

"No, there isn't a code," replied her gran, climbing the narrow spiral staircase. "But no one can break into the case, it only obeys three people: my two trusty Lunatrixes, who look after the creatures living under this roof, and me. All we have to do is put our hand on the back of the case for it to open."

"So it's digitally activated?" asked Oksa in delight. "But that's really high-tech!"

"What did you expect, Dushka? We're a highly evolved people! This method of opening doors is as old as the hills... at any rate, what I mean is that we've been using it in Edefia since the dawn of time."

"Gosh," remarked Oksa thoughtfully, "did you have the same set-up in the Paris apartment?"

"Yes, in the attic, just above your room... Well, here we are," proclaimed Dragomira. "Oksa, Marie, welcome to my strictly private workroom."

"Oh my God," breathed Marie, her hand over her mouth.

"Aaah, wow! I see..." exclaimed Oksa stopping short on the landing.

And what she saw would have silenced anyone. Before her eyes, various weird and wonderful occupants were sleeping peacefully in alcoves hollowed out of the wall. There was some kind of large long-haired potato, little frogs with folded wings, a deeply creased dwarf walrus, a tiny hen cocooned in a ball of cotton wool... but what Oksa found stranger than anything was knowing that these odd neighbours had always led a secret existence in a magic lair a couple of yards above her room!

"Come in, come in," said Dragomira. "Don't be afraid: my creatures sleep like logs."

Oksa stepped forward and took a closer look at this workroom, which was bathed in a pleasant natural light filtering through huge glass skylights. Like the other rooms which Baba Pollock inhabited, this one was in an indescribable muddle—which was Dragomira to a T. An alcove carpeted with overlapping rugs contained a greyish-blue sofa and a small piece of furniture painted bronze. The octopus which Oksa had seen the evening when everything had been revealed to her was lying on a wrought-iron console table, creating a pleasing pattern by waving its eleven light-tipped tentacles in the air. The walls were hung with heavy silk fabrics which muffled the smallest noise and made the whole room feel enclosed but very comfortable. The Lunatrixes were standing in a corner of the room, totally immobile too, like little statues.

"This is unbelievable," whispered Marie in Oksa's ear.

"Come in and make yourselves at home!" said Dragomira, inviting them to sit down on a long plum-coloured velvet love seat.

Marie took her husband's hand, while Oksa curled up against her, leaning her head on her shoulder. The three of them formed a moving tableau after these tough weeks of separation. Abakum, standing back slightly, looked at them with great emotion.

Dragomira took a small packet from her pocket and handed it to Oksa, who ripped it open.

"What's this, Baba? A bracelet? It's fab. It's so soft!"

"This is a Curbita-Flatulo, sweetheart," explained Dragomira.

Oksa looked at it incredulously.

"We think you might have had some difficulty controlling your abilities."

"To say the least!" broke in Marie Pollock, her hazel eyes fixed on Oksa. "To be honest, what your gran told me shocked me to the core. At first, I refused to believe it, then I was totally terrified by what was happening. I always knew that the Pollocks were a little odd when I married your father—but not that odd! And you didn't spare me either, my little witch!"

She made no attempt to hide her sadness, which surprised Oksa. The girl had never seen such a serious expression on her face. She usually only looked at Oksa's father that way.

"Don't worry, Mum," she murmured.

"Oh, I'm not worried, I'm *petrified*!"

A heavy silence filled the workroom. The Lunatrixes turned a surprising greenish colour and discreetly tried to leave. Unfortunately, their uneasiness only accentuated their natural clumsiness: both of them tripped over a cushion lying on the floor and fell flat on their faces.

"Ohhh, great disappointment," wailed the Lunatrix, promptly helping his companion to get up. "Discretion meets with burning failure!"

They turned their backs with a groan and decided not to move another muscle. Marie looked at Oksa with a mixture of amusement and resignation, and continued:

"Tell me, Oksa, the other evening in the kitchen, did I get a complete overview of everything you can do?"

Oh dear! Oksa looked at Dragomira, then her father, wondering how to reply. Pavel nodded at her encouragingly.

"You can tell me the truth, you know," said Marie reassuringly. "No more secrets, okay?"

"Well, Mum," said Oksa, mustering all her courage, "I can shift objects and move them from a distance, start a fire, rise above the floor and float through the air..."

"Really? Float through the air?" asked Marie Pollock, rubbing her forehead in dismay. "I didn't know that—it's probably just as well you didn't give us a demonstration of the rest. I think I might have screamed loud enough to bring all of London running!"

"Er," said Oksa hesitantly, "there's another thing too, but I'm not sure..."

All four of them stared at her intently.

"Tell us, Oksa," entreated her father.

"I think I can throw punches without using my hands. I do mean 'I think', though."

"Punches?" asked her mother in alarm. "Without using your hands?"

"The power of Knock-Bong. But that's fantastic!" exclaimed Dragomira as Pavel frowned, visibly less convinced than his mother of the advantages of this gift.

"The problem is that I can't really control what I feel inside me. I want certain things to happen and they do all by themselves, without any magic words or a wand! I have to watch myself all the time because I get the feeling that this stuff is super-powerful," explained Oksa.

"It is, actually," confirmed Dragomira. "Which is why I've given you that Curbita-Flatulo. It's a very useful present, as you'll find out. Watch it carefully."

Marie moved closer to look at the bracelet with her daughter. About half an inch thick, it was covered in silky-soft reddish-brown fur with blue stripes. In the middle, it had a tiny bear's head with sparkling brown eyes. When her mother put it around Oksa's wrist and looked for the clasp, the bracelet began moving as if it were alive.

"Ooh! What's going on?" shrieked Oksa.

The tiny claws at each end had just entwined to encircle her wrist and the bracelet creature undulated slightly to curl into a comfortable position. Once it was settled, it blinked and gave a smile of satisfaction. Marie stifled a cry—which Oksa failed to do.

"This is totally un-bel-iev-ab-le! I've never seen anything like it. But how does it work? And what does it do?"

"The Curbita-Flatulo is a creature, Dushka," replied Dragomira. "A small being from Edefia. As you'll see, it's harmless. Its only concern is your well-being. The gifts you've just discovered can be activated not only by your thoughts but also by anger or frustration—and emotions can be hard to control."

"Oh, I know," admitted Oksa, remembering her discussion with Gus a few days ago. "I'm really bad at controlling myself."

"It may sometimes prove impossible. And there's no point in having power if you can't control it. From what you tell us, you've already failed to keep your gifts in check, haven't you?"

"Yes… at school," replied Oksa, looking ashamed.

This last piece of information was immediately greeted by a flurry of concerned looks, which didn't escape her notice. She decided to keep quiet about the McGraw episode and the visit to Bontempi's office, which remained right at the top of the "Top Secret" list. Best not to make matters worse…

"There's a Year 9 student who's picking on me," she continued, choosing her words carefully. "As soon as he sees me, he feels compelled to shove me and call me names. The other day, he trapped me in the toilets."

"What?" cried her father. "And you didn't tell us?"

"No," replied Oksa miserably. "But you mustn't worry, I wasn't hurt! He was the one who…"

She faltered, while everyone hung on her every word.

"He was the one who?… What do you mean?" continued her father, encouraging her to go on.

"Well, I panicked," admitted Oksa. "To be honest, I was frightened to death. And suddenly that Neanderthal was hurled backwards against the wall! He was bent double as if he'd been punched. I just held out my arms to prevent him from getting near me, but I didn't touch him. I'm sure I didn't. But I know it's coming from me, it's crazy," she concluded in a small voice, seeing her parents' dismayed looks.

The silence lasted for a moment, broken only by Dragomira's fingers drumming on the armrest of the chair. Abakum cleared his throat, while Marie sat there without moving a muscle. Oksa was on tenterhooks. She should have kept quiet. And she was certainly glad she hadn't been stupid enough to tell them about the levitation in the courtyard at St Proximus.

"Hmmm… you won't be surprised to know that you don't get any praise for that," remarked her father, his forehead creased with worry. "Not from me or from any of us, isn't that right?" he continued, looking at his wife, Dragomira and Abakum in turn with an expression designed to discourage them from disagreeing with his point of view. "Violence is never the answer."

"But Dad, I had to defend myself!" retorted Oksa, her cheeks on fire.

"There are other ways of defending yourself," snapped her father, raising his voice. "First of all, it isn't normal for an older boy to act like that, especially at school. Why didn't you say anything to us? Do you have so little faith in us?"

"Oh Dad, don't make such a song and dance about it," grumbled Oksa, flushed with shame.

"I'm not making a song and dance about it," her father continued sternly, "on the contrary, I think I'm being very reasonable. You should have told your teachers or the Headmaster about this. Anyway, that's what I'm going to do myself first thing on Monday morning."

"No! Please don't do that."

Taken aback by the vehemence of her entreaty, Pavel Pollock paused for a second before asking:

"Why?"

"I'm old enough to defend myself," she grumbled.

"I understand why you might have behaved as you did because I'm not such a rabid pacifist as your father," said Marie, glancing rebelliously at her husband. "I think, in this society, everyone should defend themselves with whatever weapons they possess. But the problem is that your weapons aren't very conventional. You're taking a big risk using them. And that is why I'm so concerned. Not because of Edefia or because of your remarkable origins—I can accept that. The reason I'm so worried is because your powers are all over the place. What if someone realizes you aren't like everyone else. What would happen then? I'd rather not think about it, and yet it's a crucial question. I hate knowing you're in permanent danger, darling. On the other hand, and here I agree with Pavel, it isn't normal for an older boy to hassle you and follow you into the toilets or anywhere else. We won't tell Mr Bontempi on Monday. But if it happens again, I want you to tell us immediately and we'll do something about it. I hope we can count on you."

"Yes," mumbled Oksa, eyes lowered.

"You must realize, sweetheart," added Dragomira, "that what you did was also very foolish when it comes to all of us. It's *vital* no one knows. No one must even guess that we're... how shall I put it... a little *different*. I hope you understand what we're all saying to you, despite being so stubborn. Right, shall we say the matter's closed now?"

Everyone agreed, Oksa a little more eagerly than anyone else. The image of dissected crickets on a laboratory table surrounded by secret agents who all looked like McGraw came unbidden to her mind and made her shudder. Abakum began speaking.

"That's what the Curbita-Flatulo is for, sweetheart. It'll help you control your moods and emotions by applying pressure to your wrist."

"A stress reliever, that's great!" exclaimed Oksa.

"However, if you persist in doing what you were thinking of doing, despite its attempts to stop you, the Curbita-Flatulo will show its displeasure. I'd rather you were forewarned: quite frankly, it's not very pleasant.

And one very important thing," continued Abakum, "you must feed it every morning. That's extremely important. It's essential you don't forget."

"Or else?" asked Marie Pollock, sounding slightly worried.

"Or else, the Curbita-Flatulo will be like a bear with a sore head. And when it's in that kind of mood, it feels sorry for itself and, although its job is to encourage discretion, I'd say that its displeasure won't go unnoticed—far from it, in fact! So one granule a day, no more and certainly no less, okay?" said Abakum firmly, handing Oksa a small round tin. "This contains enough food for a month. And I have a present for you too. The key accessory for any self-respecting Insider. Here you are, my dear Oksa, this is your Granok-Shooter."

31

THE LOWDOWN ON GRANOKOLOGY

FROM THE INSIDE POCKET OF HIS JACKET, ABAKUM DREW a small tube about six inches long and an inch in diameter.

"What is that?" asked Oksa. "A flute?"

Everyone began laughing, particularly the Lunatrixes, who rolled around on the ground.

"Oh, oh, granddaughter of our Gracious, a flute! How comical! Your humour expands our zygomatic bones, oh, oh!"

"Those two are completely mental!" remarked Oksa, spluttering with laughter.

Then, growing more serious again:

"But isn't that the sort of blowpipe I saw on Baba's Camereye?"

"Exactly," answered Abakum. "To be more precise, this is a Granok-Shooter. YOUR Granok-Shooter, my dear. Everyone in Edefia has one. I made your gran's Granok-Shooter many years ago and now it's your turn to have one."

Abakum held out the precious tube with a smile. As soon as she grasped it, a strong gust of wind made the walls creak and stripped the leaves from the trees in the square. A bright flash haloed Oksa with an intense light, which she just had time to glimpse before it disappeared. Dragomira and Abakum looked at each other in amazement.

"What was that?" asked Oksa.

"Recognition, darling," replied Abakum, sounding more emotional than he would have liked. "Your Granok-Shooter recognized you and, through it, the Ageless Ones greeted you."

"Oh yes, the Ageless Fairies!" blurted Oksa, filled with wonder.

Dragomira smiled, but it was Marie who spoke next, sounding upset:

"My Goodness… Fairies… You've really decided not to spare me anything, haven't you!"

Oksa turned her Granok-Shooter round cautiously, examining it from every angle. It was a strange, magnificent object with a slight shimmer. Its mouthpiece was engraved with floral motifs which perfectly complemented Oksa's name, written in rose-gold letters at the other end.

"It's made from an alloy of meerschaum and amber," explained Abakum, getting a grip on his emotions. "There are minuscule compartments inside designed to hold different kinds of granules, called Granoks, which can be animal, vegetable or mineral in origin, depending on their function. The Granok-Shooter allows us to store them and use them when we need them. Granokology has always existed, but great progress has been made over the past two centuries. On their Dreamflights, the Graciouses observed that the Outside was making great leaps forward in science, technology and space travel. As Outside technology advanced, the Graciouses began to fear that our land might be discovered one day and they decided to implement a huge Granokology development programme at the end of the nineteenth century, a programme which hinged upon the design of defensive Granoks. Just in case… Since weapons were banned in Edefia, Granoks had always seemed like a good compromise between our values and our expertise. There are a great many Granoks, all very different from each other, ranging from so-called 'recreational' Granoks like the Laughing-Rill to more aggressive Granoks like the Dozident, for example."

"The Laughing-Rill?" asked Oksa, stopping him.

"Yes, the Laughing-Rill, which makes the person who receives it laugh so much that they lose control of their bladder. The Dozident, on the other hand, can plunge someone into a deep sleep."

"For ever?"

"That depends on the dose and your adversary's constitution," explained Abakum. "But yes, the sleep can last for ever."

"Are there any other aggressive Granoks?" asked Oksa, fascinated. "Which is the most dangerous?"

"Oh, without going into detail, I'd say that the Stuffarax is one of the most dangerous Granoks. It releases insects in the throat of the person who receives it and chokes them."

"Killing them?"

"That can happen, yes."

"That's fiendish!" exclaimed Oksa. "Who makes the Granoks?"

"As you know, your gran and I were herbalists. But, first and foremost, we're experts in Granokology; we know how to make most of the existing Granoks. In Edefia I belonged to a very select brotherhood of official suppliers, which kept a very low profile. But one of our number joined the Felons and secretly made substances against which none of us had any defence during the Great Chaos."

"The Black Globuses?"

"You know a thing or two, don't you, young lady?" remarked Abakum, staring at her intently.

His face darkening suddenly, he continued.

"Those Granoks belonged to the most dangerous category, because they were based on chemical products banned for use due to their toxicity and, as a result, their monstrous potential for destruction and death. But the Felons surprised us by their mastery of the Black Globuses and by the large stocks they'd managed to accumulate in the utmost secrecy. All this clearly proved that they'd been planning the attack for quite a few months—such treachery. The Black Globus which caused the worst injuries was the Putrefactio, produced from rock dust from the Peak Ridge mountains. This simply rots any limb it comes into contact with."

"That's what I saw on the Camereye!" exclaimed Oksa. "That man who was groaning on the floor while his arm decomposed; it was disgusting."

"Yes, the Putrefactio is a terrible weapon," agreed Abakum, nodding gravely. "Since we've been on the Outside, though, I've managed to perfect a few substances even more powerful than the Putrefactio, such as the Crucimaphila, which can only be used by your gran, who is a Gracious."

"What does that Granok do?" asked Oksa, seeing that Abakum was in two minds about continuing his description.

"It kills, my dear. This is a lethal Granok. It absorbs your enemy in a black light which kills him."

"Wow, that's radical! What about me, can I use it? I'm also a Gracious!"

"Yes, you can," replied Dragomira, taken aback by Oksa's enthusiasm. "But before you can handle Granoks as dangerous as that, you must learn a great many things. Granokology is a thrilling but complex science which leaves nothing to chance. And there are also the powers, not only those you already know, but others you don't. You have to be initiated. Abakum, Leomido and I will be your teachers, if you like."

"You bet I do! But there's something else—"

She stopped herself. She was burning to ask a question. A crucial question. But should she ask it? Did she *really* need to know?

"Something else?" encouraged her gran.

"What's the use of knowing all this?" she risked saying. "I love being able to do all these things, it's unreal! But if I have to hide it, it sort of makes me wonder *why* I have to learn it?"

She looked at her parents with concern. But, contrary to what she'd feared, they appeared calm and resigned. It seemed as though everyone had been expecting that question. Her gran was the one to speak:

"My dear granddaughter, we need you. I've shown you why we had to flee Edefia and, deep down, we all want to return to our lost land and restore the equilibrium which has been shattered. Our people

196

are suffering, they need help. We've made a great many attempts, but without the Mark they've been futile. Since the Chaos, you are, to our knowledge, the first person to bear it. And you've become the last link in the chain which will make it possible to lift the curse and restore the Cloak Chamber. That's why our hope is stronger than ever."

"But… what's in the Cloak Chamber? What's so important?" asked Oksa.

Dragomira's eyes clouded.

"No one, except the Graciouses who've entered it, can know. So apart from the Secret-Never-To-Be-Told—or rather, the Secret-Which-Is-No-Longer-A-Secret—I don't know. I can't answer your question, because the doors of the Chamber were closed to me for ever after Ocious's attack and our escape to the Outside. But I do know that the Cloak bestows supreme power. A power that only the Gracious may receive, and no one else, even if they use the utmost violence."

"But Ocious did seize the power, didn't he!" exclaimed Oksa excitedly.

"Yes, he did, but it's a power which wasn't intended for him. And I fear that this usurpation has caused a dangerous imbalance which may bring about the ruin of Edefia."

"If it hasn't already," added Abakum sombrely.

"Then we must go there!" said Oksa passionately. "We must save Edefia!"

"It's not that simple." Pavel looked dejected.

"But I have the Mark!"

"You aren't ready…"

"You mean I'm just a beginner!" retorted the girl.

"Not in the sense you mean," answered Dragomira calmly. "You are a beginner, when it comes down to it, and it would be foolish to embark on this venture before we're ready. We don't know what we're likely to find in Edefia. All we know is what we left behind: a land governed by chaos and bloodshed. Who knows what has become of it with the Felons and Ocious in power?"

Everyone around the table fell silent, thinking gravely about what she'd just said. After a few minutes Oksa looked up and said:

"Fine. When do I begin this apprenticeship?"

Dragomira gazed at her gratefully.

"Are you okay with this?" asked Oksa, turning to her parents.

Marie and Pavel Pollock nodded, looking emotional.

"Are you *really* okay? Are you sure? I can't believe it!"

"We're okay with it, darling," replied her father, despite his obvious anxiety. "Although I have to say I have very conflicted feelings… Ever since you were born, I've always been afraid that this might happen. I understand the hopes harboured by my dear mother and everyone else who once lived in Edefia, but I'd much rather you didn't get mixed up in all of this. Unfortunately, you're the Gracious. You're the key."

"Oh Dad, aren't you being a little overdramatic?"

"Not in the least," retorted her father suddenly. "You are the Last Hope. What else can I do except face facts? Let's just say that I'm okay with it, with serious reservations. That's just the way it is. All I want now is for you to learn to live with your powers and, most importantly, be taught how to control them. If you're sensible from now on, you can go to your great-uncle Leomido's house during the next school holiday and you can begin—how should I put it—your first practical training course."

"Yay! Thank you, thank you! You're the best parents ever!" cried Oksa, throwing her arms round her mother's neck, then her father's.

"Mmm, did you hear that, darling?" said Marie turning to her husband, her eyes brimming with tears. "We're the best!"

"This is a birthday laden with success! Glorious birthday, beautiful granddaughter of our Old Gracious!" exclaimed the Lunatrixes, throwing themselves flat on their stomachs in front of Oksa.

"I'm not entirely sure I like being called 'Old Gracious'," said Dragomira. "But I think you can start calling my dear granddaughter 'Young Gracious'. That's what she is from now on."

32

SUSPICION

THE END OF TERM WAS DRAWING NEARER. MOTIVATED by the prospect of starting her apprenticeship as a Gracious, Oksa applied herself seriously to her work. She concentrated twice as hard in class, earning constant praise from the teachers—except McGraw, who didn't think anyone was or ever could be up to scratch. That morning he lived up to his grim reputation, handing back the maths homework papers. The lesson turned into something resembling a game of darts, which their pitiless teacher played with vast enjoyment.

"Miss Beck, twelve out of twenty. It would seem that a basic knowledge of geometry will always be beyond you. Miss Pollock, eighteen out of twenty: tolerable. If you could spare me the trouble of deciphering your appalling scrawl, I'd be very grateful. Mr Bellanger, fifteen out of twenty. Sitting next to Miss Pollock seems to have paid off..."

And so on. Dr McGraw treated them all the same when it came to making unkind comments. Except for Merlin who, because of his interest in Einstein, was miraculously spared the volley of barbed remarks.

"That teacher is mental. Eighteen out of twenty, when you didn't make a single mistake, what a nerve!" said Merlin crossly during break. "And he dared to say it was tolerable! He's a total nut job. What did he write on it this time?"

"'Execrable writing. Must take more care,' like last time—a bit unimaginative," replied Oksa shrugging. "I'm trying to take no notice."

"It's lucky you're so laid-back about it," said Gus. "I can't take it that lightly. Did you hear what he said to me? He was implying I copy from you! That really annoys me, it annoys me *bigtime*!"

"Don't worry, he's out of his tiny mind. Everyone knows you don't copy. There wouldn't be any point!" added Oksa, nudging him in the ribs.

"That's all very well," muttered Gus. "But what if he puts that on my report card, how will that look?"

"But fifteen out of twenty is a good mark. In any case, it's much better than mine," added Zelda, looking upset. "My parents are going to be furious, I'd prefer to be in your shoes, Gus—or in Merlin's."

"Oh! If you think it's easy being in the good books of a man like that, you can think again," retorted Merlin crossly. "I'd rather do without it, I can tell you. Even if I had to put up with his snide remarks every lesson."

"I hate McGraw," grunted Gus. "I loathe and detest the man!"

"In any case, I pity his wife and children," said Merlin.

"Oh right! Do you really think a psychopath like that has a wife and kids?" said Zelda. "Where would he have found a wife anyway?"

"In the *Addams Family*, perhaps," suggested Merlin.

"Hey, look Oksa, isn't that your pal over there, the Neanderthal in Year 9?" remarked Gus.

Oksa turned round to look. It was him. Sitting on the edge of the stone fountain in the middle of the courtyard, he was sending some really dirty looks her way. A girl sitting next to him said something to him while looking at Oksa and they both sniggered stupidly.

"Go on then, laugh, moron, laugh," murmured Oksa.

She felt the Curbita-Flatulo tighten round her wrist. This had happened several times since Dragomira had given it to her—practically always in McGraw's presence, since he had the exceptional knack of making her feel totally stressed and exasperated. On several occasions she'd almost used the Magnetus and Knock-Bong powers, which she found easier to control now. She'd fantasized about hurling McGraw to the other end of the classroom, though the observant little bracelet creature dissuaded her every time. But the Neanderthal's mocking, scornful gaze—in addition to the return of the maths papers with their liberal dose of sarcasm—was the last straw. Suddenly a light bulb came on in Oksa's mind.

"Gus, watch! I haven't yet shown you what Baba taught me, I'm sure you'll find it amusing," she murmured, drawing her friend slightly away from the others.

Saying this, she took her bottle of water from her bag and poured a little in her palm. Then she rubbed her palms together as if modelling clay. After a few seconds, she discreetly showed Gus what she'd just made: a ball of water, a superb, silvery ball of water, which shivered on the palm of her hand like a large drop of mercury.

"That's amazing!" said Gus.

"Wait! You'll love this."

Oksa raised her arms as if she was going to scratch her head and, looking innocent, threw the ball of water towards the fountain. The ball curved in a perfect arc to land on the Neanderthal's head, causing him to jump up as if on a spring. The Curbita-Flatulo increased its pressure around Oksa's wrist and, given the urgency of the situation, progressed to the next stage. There was absolutely no doubt that Oksa was going to do it again. It scratched the delicate skin in very specific areas and Oksa immediately experienced a sensation of pins and needles which made her go slightly numb and temporarily distracted her attention. But it was futile: the time for revenge had definitely come. Even more determined, Oksa had just made another ball and was about to throw it.

"Ouch!" she cried, at the same time as she threw the second ball.

The Curbita-Flatulo had just pricked her wrist painfully. But her cry was drowned out by sudden peals of laughter. The Neanderthal had just been hit in the face by the ball and was dancing about madly, yelling:

"Who did that? WHO DID THAT? I'll smash his face in!"

"It was the fountain, Mortimer, it was just spray," his classmate said, offering him some paper tissues.

But Neanderthals don't calm down so easily. His only answer was to kick the edge of the fountain violently, hurting his foot and making himself look even more stupid. After glaring at the angelic statue on top of the fountain, he whirled round in a rage and made a dash for the toilet, water trickling down his face.

❊

Everyone was concentrating on the action in the centre of the courtyard. Everyone except Zoe, Zelda's friend, whom Gus liked so much. Oksa saw that her eyes were bright with curiosity. Unless it was suspicion... what if Zoe had guessed what had happened? But no, that was impossible. Still Oksa began to regret what she'd done. And it wasn't as if she hadn't been warned! What an idiot she was. Mechanically she stroked her Curbita-Flatulo beneath the sleeve of her sweater and gave Zoe an embarrassed smile.

"It looks like it might be better to stay away from that fountain!"

"Yes, the mechanism must have gone wrong, it is a very old fountain," replied Zoe, smiling back.

She nodded her head, her long fringe of strawberry-blonde hair bobbing up and down. Her expression was so sincere that Oksa regretted misinterpreting Zoe's gaze. She was a shy girl, who seemed to find it difficult to relate to others and just wanted to make friends. She was always with Zelda and everyone in the group had accepted her. Particularly Gus. Oksa had made a considerable effort not to show her antagonism once Zoe had become friendlier with him. Despite her efforts, Oksa didn't feel at ease when Zoe was there. She always looked at her so oddly! It was all very well Oksa telling herself that she hadn't had an easy life and that she needed lots of friends; she couldn't make herself feel closer to her or even speak to her naturally. And she was cross with herself for not having Zelda's generosity or her other friends' open-mindedness. She thought about the soap that Zoe had given her for her birthday—a really nice perfumed soap in the shape of a tortoise which she'd passed on to her mum because she was allergic to the glycerine in most soaps. The same as she was kind of allergic to that girl…

Gus broke into her thoughts, whispering in her ear:

"You almost got yourself noticed this time! So what's your Curbita-Flatulo doing?"

"It's pretending to be a vampire, that's what it's doing," replied Oksa, gritting her teeth. "Look, I'm bleeding to death!"

She pulled back the sleeve of her sweater to show Gus her wrist, which was covered with fairly deep, bleeding scratches.

"You must admit you deserved it!" retorted Gus. "You seem to forget that if you go looking for trouble, you'll end up finding it."

"His Lordship seems to be playing the philosopher," said Oksa ironically, pretending to make a new ball of water. "Maybe His Lordship wants to give me a lesson in ethics?"

"Don't even think of throwing *that* at me, or I swear I'll throw you in the fountain fully dressed!" cried Gus, pointing a threatening finger at her.

Saying that, he shook his long hair over his eyes so that she wouldn't notice they were shining with delight.

33

IF YOU GO
LOOKING FOR TROUBLE…

WHEN OKSA KNOCKED ON DRAGOMIRA'S DOOR IT WAS
opened by the Lunatrixa, who was wearing a striped apron over
her dungarees and seemed hard at work.

"Ooooh, my Young Gracious, how welcome she is! Have you the
desire to make the division of our afternoon snack?"

"Lunatrixa! Would you please let her in?"

Dragomira had come over to welcome Oksa. She put both hands on
her granddaughter's shoulders, gave her a resounding kiss on her cheek
and led her inside the apartment. She was back on the form she'd lost
some time ago when the Mark had been revealed on Oksa's stomach and
was her old beaming self, resplendent in a long, full, turquoise dress as
she bustled around her granddaughter.

"I've made you some of those sweet cheese crêpes you're so fond of!"

"Oh, thank you, Baba, I love those. But, tell me, what's the Lunatrixa
making?"

The Lunatrixa was perched on a small chair in front of the ironing
table and was pressing the iron down with all her might on a small packet
wrapped in aluminium foil.

"A cheese and ham toastie, Dushka," replied Dragomira, sounding
disconcertingly matter-of-fact. "A 'Lunatrixa-style' toastie, cooked with
the iron."

"Unbelievable!"

"Oh, you know, the Lunatrixes are endlessly resourceful."

Dragomira served Oksa a cup of her favourite tea, flavoured with cardamom.

"So? What news do you have?"

Oksa took a mouthful of tea. To tell or not to tell, that was the question...

"Well, Baba; I got eighteen out of twenty in maths and seventeen in history. Not bad, is it?"

"Not bad at all. Almost perfect, well done!"

However, Dragomira was staring at Oksa's crudely bandaged wrist, and particularly the Curbita-Flatulo, which had dull eyes and looked bad-tempered and sullen.

"Apart from those excellent marks, you wouldn't be hiding anything from me, would you? Do you have a completely clear conscience?" asked Dragomira, slipping her finger under the Curbita-Flatulo's tiny chin to try and cheer it up.

"Okay, I give in—but promise not to say anything to Mum, please Baba?" begged Oksa.

"Is it that bad then?" asked Dragomira, frowning.

"Promise?"

"Fine, I promise not to say anything to your mother—not that I won't tell you off, if you deserve it!"

"Er, I think I probably do deserve it—I drenched the Neanderthal," admitted Oksa looking at her gran with a mixture of delight and shame.

"You drenched the Neanderthal? And?" asked Dragomira, her clear gaze darkening.

"The Curbita-Flatulo did everything it could to warn me and make me stop, but I didn't want to obey it. The Neanderthal started it, again, by openly making fun of me! I made a ball of water. That's all."

Looking helpless and disheartened, Dragomira rubbed her forehead wearily and gave a deep sigh.

"Is that *really* all?"

"Yes… well, I'm not sure," said Oksa hesitantly, biting her lower lip. "I have a feeling that Zoe realized I had something to do with it."

"Zoe? The girl who came to your birthday party with your friend Zelda?"

"Yes, that's her."

"What makes you think she might have realized it was you?"

"I don't know, it was just a feeling. Maybe it was the way she looked at me."

"You know, that certainly seems to be her way," said Dragomira, as if thinking aloud. "On your birthday, I noticed she was watching everything very closely and with a great deal of curiosity. But to come back to what we were saying, what you did was not something to be proud of, you understand. I won't say anything to your parents, firstly because I've just promised not to and secondly because I really want you to go to stay with Leomido to begin your apprenticeship. But I don't know if you realize—"

"I do, I do. I'm sorry, Baba!" exploded Oksa feverishly. "I'm really sorry."

Dragomira looked at her sternly, but not as severely as she would have liked.

"Liar," she said, her eyes betraying a certain amusement, "you aren't sorry at all! You might have felt sorry for that poor Curbita-Flatulo which is trying to make you see reason. Now all we can do is make it feel better."

She stood up and selected a small bluish phial from the hundreds inside the glazed cupboard and dampened her index finger with the oily liquid it contained.

"What's that?" asked Oksa.

"A special salve made from Incompetent crest," Dragomira replied mysteriously, gently massaging the sulky bracelet's tiny head.

"Incompetent crest?" repeated Oksa.

"It's the only thing that can make your Curbita-Flatulo feel better," continued Dragomira, without answering Oksa's question. "When you disregard its warnings, it feels defeated, which is hard for it to bear, believe it or not. It's as if it has failed in its mission."

Its eyes half-closed, the Curbita-Flatulo began purring with pleasure, smiling blissfully. That salve was terrific—if only Oksa could have some for McGraw… although, massaging their vile teacher's head, yuck!

"What about your friend Gus? What does he think about all this?"

"Oh, Baba!" protested Oksa.

No one apart from the Pollock family and the Runaways from Edefia was supposed to know about the events of the past few weeks, Gus no more than anyone else.

"Oh, Oksa Pollock, please. Don't go trying to tell me you haven't told him anything. Not me!" said Dragomira ironically, her blue eyes fixed intently on her granddaughter.

"You always know everything, it's so annoying," wailed Oksa, abandoning all pretence. "How do you do it?"

"Trade secret, darling, trade secret. Do me a little favour, will you?"

"Anything!"

"Go and get your parents, please."

A very unpleasant feeling of fear kept Oksa rooted to the spot—probably the delayed effect of her guilt.

"Don't be afraid," said Dragomira reassuringly, with a slightly mocking smile. "Go and get them."

A few minutes later, all four were sitting in Dragomira's apartment in front of the fire. Oksa felt seriously worried. Despite her gran's comforting words, was she going to pay dearly for the afternoon's excesses? Her father began speaking:

"Darling, we've received your results, you've worked very hard."

"Congratulations for our Young Gracious!" echoed the Lunatrixes, who were enjoying their iron-cooked toastie.

"It's no big surprise," continued Pavel Pollock, "but that doesn't mean we're not very proud of you. Your teachers' comments are very good, except those of Dr McGraw. And I have to say we're at a bit of a loss about that: you haven't scored less than eighteen and all he can talk about is sloppy handwriting or some such thing, it's really odd."

"McGraw? He's crazy, he isn't even a teacher—he's a psychopath!" blurted out Oksa, as disastrously spontaneous as usual.

"A psychopath is he? Don't you think you're being a little extreme?" remarked her mother. "Come to think of it, he does seem a bit strange. But why do you say he's not even a teacher?"

"Because he's a secret agent with the CIA," muttered Oksa, immediately regretting her words.

The ensuing silence did little to put the girl at ease. Her mother gave an amused smile, which soon faded and was replaced by a worried scowl. She glanced quickly at her husband and Dragomira, who also looked visibly concerned.

"What makes you say that?" she whispered in a monotone.

At that precise minute, Oksa wished she was a million miles away from her gran's apartment. Why had she said that? *"I may be getting good marks but when it comes to engaging my brain before opening my mouth, I'm a dead loss,"* she thought to herself angrily. Her head was buzzing. If she explained her theory, she'd have to tell them everything from the beginning—in other words, the fainting fit on the first day at school, the 'non-existent fall' of the bottle, how suspicious McGraw seemed to be about her, the theory about worms remotely guiding the brains of crickets, the evidence that she and Gus had collected. And mentioning the evidence related to McGraw also meant mentioning the visit to Bontempi's office, vertical levitation in the courtyard in broad daylight and going through a wallet which didn't belong to her. She could kiss her holiday with Leomido goodbye. So, full of remorse, she heard herself saying casually:

"It was just a joke. My friends and I like making things up... we have a blast imagining that McGraw is a secret agent."

The three adults immediately appeared relieved. Oksa sighed inwardly while looking at them with an innocent expression.

"So we're right in thinking you've been well behaved, are we?" continued her mother. "No using Magnetus? No Knock-Bongs? No flying in public? See?" she whispered, her eyes sparkling. "I'm speaking like a true Runaway!"

Oksa smiled uneasily and glanced anxiously at Dragomira. Honestly, this discussion was sheer torture.

"Nothing to report from my end," replied her gran, sounding strained. "I'll just add one minor thing: Gus knows. But that certainly isn't headline news, is it?"

Pavel and Marie Pollock nodded, smiling, to Oksa's great surprise. So they knew! What a turn-up—this was the best news she'd had all year. Well, no… not all year… but certainly all day, no contest.

"Good, so have we come to a decision about this girl?" continued Dragomira, enjoying Oksa's renewed anxiety.

"You mean my daughter? My wonderful, totally brilliant and highly talented daughter?" asked Pavel Pollock, acting as though Oksa wasn't there. "What do you reckon, Marie? We'll have to think it over, don't you agree?"

"Dad…" groaned Oksa, squirming in her chair.

"I need time to think," continued Marie, playing along with her husband. "But I promise to give you my answer before six months is up."

"Mum…" Oksa groaned even louder.

"Darling," said her father, putting her out of her misery. "We agree, you can stay with Leomido during half-term. Dragomira will go with you, because we've got a great deal of work to do in the restaurant. But you can also take a guest, someone you're very fond of and from whom, it seems, you have no secrets…"

"Gus?" exclaimed Oksa, beside herself with joy. "Oohhh, thank you, Dad! Thank you, Mum!"

"We need to sort out one or two little things with Jeanne and Pierre Bellanger and in a week's time, all three of you can leave for Wales.

"That's brilliant—I'm thrilled!"

34

Destination Wales

THE THREE OF THEM DIDN'T GO UNNOTICED AT THE airport—far from it. Dragomira was the main focus of attention with her striking travel clothes: a crimson suit with a fitted coat of purple velvet, the whole outfit crowned by a matching hat. She was dragging an enormous brown leather suitcase on wheels behind her and over her shoulder she wore a bag which she hugged tightly to her side. Gus and Oksa might have been less conspicuous, but they were much more excited than the eccentric, yet calm, Dragomira. Oksa felt as if she were fizzing—large bubbles of happiness were popping all over her body. After the conflicts and tensions of the past few weeks, she couldn't deny she was desperate for a change of scene. This short trip would do her the world of good. Gus's feelings were much more conflicted. There was no doubt he was delighted to be visiting Leomido with his best friend and to have the good fortune to witness what was likely to be an amazing "apprenticeship". But, at the same time, he hated having a secret which he couldn't share with his parents and this was weighing heavily on his conscience.

The Bellangers and Pollocks headed for the departure lounge, which was the scene of some emotional displays of affection, during which Pavel Pollock sighed long and hard. At last, the plane took off.

"We could almost have flown there, that would have been cool!" said Oksa once they were above the clouds.

"You don't say!" replied Gus. "Especially if we wanted to be mistaken for UFOs and pursued by the Air Force…"

"Oh, you—you're so down to earth, aren't you?" retorted Oksa ironically, nudging him in the ribs.

"I can see my granddaughter hasn't hidden anything at all from you, my dear Gus," remarked Dragomira.

"Everything I know, he knows," said Oksa proudly.

"Er, yes, that's true," muttered Gus, who didn't know if Dragomira thought this was a good or a bad thing.

❈

A few hours later, they were sitting by a crackling fire in a vast hearth. Leomido had picked them up from the airport in his car and driven them back to his home, some thirty miles away in the middle of the Welsh countryside. This was no ordinary house, but a former church built four centuries ago, then converted into a monastery. He'd bought it before it had collapsed into ruins and had turned it into a magnificent, comfortable home which would have resembled a manor house more than a religious site, were it not for the small cemetery extending along the back of the property. Situated in one of the winding lanes along the coastline of the Celtic Sea, a couple of miles from a small, peaceful village, the incredible building was set in vast grounds sheltered by heather-covered valleys. The furthest hill led down to a small sandy inlet. Oksa hadn't been here for two years, which felt like a lifetime. Leomido's property looked even more beautiful than she remembered, with its small lake, its rolling hills and the wind rippling through the long grass.

"This place is totally unreal! Do you really live here?" asked Gus enthusiastically.

He couldn't help looking open-mouthed at the stone walls hung with modern art and the enormous black crystal chandelier suspended above the huge room. Comfortably ensconced in an immense worn leather armchair, Leomido smiled.

"Yes, Gus, I *really* live here. Ever since my dear wife died, twelve years ago. This place brings me peace, I feel free here, and no one disturbs me."

"Don't you ever get lonely?" continued Gus, gazing at him in fascination. "This house is huge."

"Ten rooms, plus this room, which used to be the chancel of the church... but no, actually, I don't get lonely," replied Leomido.

"Well, it's really kind of you to train me, Leomido," said Oksa. "Thank you so much."

"Oh, you're welcome, my dear," he said, tapping his chin with his fingertips. "I just hope I'm not too rusty; it's a very long time since I taught anyone. A very long time... since Edefia, to tell you the truth."

Everyone could hear the nostalgia tinged with regret in those last few words. The large living room fell silent for a few seconds. Oksa and Gus made no secret of their impatience to find out more—which Leomido soon realized.

"As you know," he began in a slightly hoarse voice, "Dragomira, Abakum and I were ejected from Edefia in October 1952 and arrived in Siberia. We immediately realized that the differences between the Inside and the Outside were far greater than anything we could have imagined or discovered through Malorane's Dreamflights. In the first few months, the drastic change was unbearable. Siberia was too harsh for me from every point of view. I watched my little sister Dragomira suffering in silence and making a heroic effort to cope with the shock of our escape, while Abakum was putting all his energy into helping us to adapt to our new living conditions. I didn't let my feelings show, I wanted my sister to be able to lean on me as our mother had asked. But I failed to keep my promise."

"Stop it, Leomido," interrupted Dragomira, frowning. "You mustn't blame yourself like this after all these years. I didn't turn out so badly, did I?"

"Not at all. You've made a great success of your life. But that's no thanks to me," replied her brother gravely.

"Anyway," Oksa butted in, "it's still down to you that Baba and Abakum were able to leave Russia."

"That's right, Dushka!" cried Dragomira. "Thanks for reminding that stubborn individual who never wants to take credit for anything he does. But do go on, Leomido, please."

"Eight months after the Great Chaos, during the summer of 1953, I travelled across Europe and settled in England. It was with considerable sadness that I soon realized my memories of my country of origin were fast receding. I could see my mother Malorane's face less and less sharply in my mind's eye and these memory losses concerned and upset me. I didn't find it hard to adapt to England. A few months after settling in London, I was hired by a prestigious orchestra and I married my beloved Lisa. My professional career took off, while Edefia faded from my thoughts and my memory. But not from my heart... All this was very unsettling and I was consumed by nostalgia, I missed Abakum and Dragomira terribly. In 1955, when Cameron, my first child, was born, I really started thinking seriously about the need to pass down our heritage, because even if I didn't see myself revealing my origins—I wasn't ready for that—it seemed vitally important to leave behind some trace of what we are. It took a few more years before I was able to talk about it, first to my wife, then to my children. It wasn't easy, I can tell you. When I was finally reunited with my dear Dragomira and Abakum, I found it much easier to come to terms with my past and I now feel ready to teach you everything I know, my dear."

"Thank you, Leomido," murmured Oksa, moved by her great-uncle's story.

She wondered if her father had benefited from this training too. Obviously not: didn't Leomido say that he hadn't taught anyone since Edefia? She was about to ask her great-uncle why, when she noticed a now familiar silhouette.

"Have you got some Lunatrixes?"

"I do indeed, a couple and their child. They're busy in the kitchen, preparing a feast for us."

"Aha!" exclaimed Gus. "At last I'm going to see these famous Lunatrixes with my own eyes."

"I hope they're as good at cooking as Baba's," said his friend.

"Yes, you'll see, they're first-class cooks! But coming back to your question a while ago about being lonely, Gus, the reason I don't feel alone is because *I'm not alone*. This house may be isolated, but that's just as well, both for me and mainly for my creatures. That way, they can live their lives without having to hide and with no fear of being seen."

"Creatures? What creatures, Leomido?" exclaimed Oksa and Gus.

"Follow me."

35

A Vegetable Plot with Strange Inhabitants

"I hope you brought your Boximinus, Dragomira?" asked Leomido.

"Of course I did. And I have to say there's a revolution going on in there!" replied his sister, tapping the bag she was still hugging to her side.

The four of them left the magnificent room and entered a corridor lined with stained-glass windows on one side and massive metal-studded doors on the other. At the very end, they came into a windowless room filled with compartments of all sizes, cosily padded inside, then into another room cluttered with gardening equipment and jars of grain. At the back of the room, they glimpsed the wall of flat stones bordering a small garden.

"Where have they gone?" said Leomido. "Ah, perhaps they're in the vegetable plot."

He pushed open the door and his two young guests were greeted by a totally unexpected sight: the small plot of land was inhabited by all kinds of creatures, each stranger than the last. Real live talking creatures! Creatures which were *very* alive and *very* talkative. Some were busy doing odd gardening jobs, others were polishing the leaves of the fidgeting plants while chatting to them while others were simply enjoying the sunshine, stretched out on enormous pumpkins.

"Come here, come here!" said Leomido. "My dear creatures, allow me to introduce you to the girl I told you about, Oksa, my great-niece. And this is her friend, Gus."

The creatures stopped what they were doing and gathered in front of Oksa and Gus, who were both rooted to the spot in amazement at this sight.

"Hello, Young Gracious! Hello, young friend of our Young Gracious! Hello, Old Gracious!"

"That's not very polite," cried Leomido indignantly. "Please forgive them, Dragomira. I'm terribly sorry."

Dragomira laughed heartily, not in the least annoyed.

"Don't worry, that's what my creatures call me too."

"Oksa, Gus, may I introduce my small companions. Getorixes! Would you both like to come over here?"

Two creatures about a foot high stepped forward and bowed their large heads in greeting to the two friends. Which meant they actually bent over double, since their bodies seemed to be formed of nothing but this large head; they looked like brown potatoes covered with a voluminous tuft of tangled hair, from which emerged two long arms dragging on the floor and two incredibly long feet.

"I'd better warn you right now," said Leomido. "The Getorixes like to joke around and they love driving some of their comrades mad. Like the Incompetent, for example."

"Hey, Incompetent! Fire, fire, send for the fire brigade! Your crest is burning!" one Getorix started yelling while the other imitated the siren of the fire engine.

"Huh? What? What's going on? Where's the fire?" shouted the butt of their jokes.

The other creatures began laughing in stifled guffaws.

"Don't worry, Incompetent," said Leomido comfortingly, taking the small creature by the hand.

Oksa and Gus bent down to examine the creature called the Incompetent. A little bigger than the Getorixes, it looked terribly awkward. Its flabby,

216

yellowish body bristled with a crest running the length of its back and ended in a defenceless walrus head which had no tusks. It gazed at the two friends lazily with large, gentle eyes.

"The Incompetent has a brain which is, how should I put it… a little soft," explained Leomido.

"Soft in the head, soft in the head!" yelled both over-excited Getorixes.

"It's a little slower than the others," continued Leomido. "But it's an extremely sweet-natured, useful creature, as you'll soon see."

"Every creature has its uses, is that what you mean?" asked Oksa, stroking the downy body of the Incompetent, which was smiling blissfully.

"Exactly right," said Leomido. "Squoracle, come here please!"

A reddish-brown hen no bigger than a canary came over to Leomido's young guests and addressed them in a shrill tone, waggling its little tuft frantically:

"You! You come from the south-east, a land much milder than this freezing country lashed by the west winds. I know it! I know it! Because I can sense it! Is it warmer where you come from? I'm sure of it! I'm certain of it! Winter won't be long in coming now. For pity's sake, why won't they take me to the tropics? Why don't they stop telling me 'when hens have teeth!' Because I do have teeth! Why do they leave me here with chattering teeth? Why aren't I allowed to join my migratory cousins?"

"Why don't you take a good look at yourself. You don't look anything like a swallow, my dear. You don't even know how to fly!" said a strange grinning frog which had a magnificent pair of dragonfly-like wings on its pustule-covered body.

Oksa and Gus looked at each other, taken aback, but fighting the giggles. Leomido picked up the hen and settled it comfortably inside his fleece-lined jacket.

"I have to say that the Squoracle is very prone to hysteria, my dears, a hysteria which is often caused by its sensitivity to the cold. And also by the Croakettes' wicked sense of humour," explained Leomido, casting an amused look at the four flying frogs which were bobbing up and down in the air.

"It must have been unhappy when you were in Siberia," remarked Oksa.

A long groan came from Leomido's jacket.

"A name to avoid, if you don't mind, Oksa," continued Leomido in a low voice. "It's something of a 'chilling' memory for our poor Squoracle, which spent a few years confined to the edge of the hearth in Dragomira and Abakum's forest cabin. But if you disregard its phobia of the cold, this little creature plays a very interesting role as a revealer of the truth, because it looks beyond appearances. On Edefia, the Squoracle was used as a lie detector and also as a kind of meter to gauge how much work everyone did."

"That's amazing!" exclaimed Gus, thrilled by these introductions.

"I totally agree, my boy."

"Hey, there are the Lunatrixes." cried Oksa suddenly. "Look Gus!"

Two Lunatrixes resembling the ones Oksa already knew had just walked into the vegetable plot. They had a smaller one with them, which was immediately greeted by cries of enthusiasm from the three guests.

"That child is gorgeous!" exclaimed Dragomira.

"May I hold him? Please Leomido?" implored Oksa. "He's so adorable!"

"Blue-eyed boy, blue-eyed boy!" chanted the Getorixes.

"Who are you?" asked the Incompetent looking at Gus, whose hand it had been obediently holding for a good ten minutes.

Oksa bent over to pick up the chubby little Lunatrix with his rumpled, coppery skin. He smiled at Oksa with big eyes fringed with woolly lashes, looking delighted.

"I think it's time to let you out, my friends," said Dragomira, talking to the box whose boisterous movements she was finding it harder and harder to control.

She undid the leather strap securely fastened round the box and carefully opened the lid.

"One by one, please, no pushing!"

Oksa and Gus leant over and saw the same creatures as the ones in front of them but tiny, as if they'd been reduced to miniature versions.

They stared wide-eyed and gaping.

"This is a Boximinus, children," explained Dragomira, seeing their intrigued expressions. "When we had to flee Edefia, Abakum—who must have more foresight than any man I know—collected various specimens which he reduced in size using this amazing invention. The main purpose of the Boximinus was to save space and we used it to store foodstuffs or bulky archives. But only Abakum knew it could be used for living things. Which was lucky, because this way we were able to bring a large number of plants and creatures from Edefia with us to the Outside. Certain varieties of plant didn't survive the journey through the Portal or the shock caused by the drop in temperature when we arrived in Siberia. But, in the main, they're all here."

One by one she brought out the small-scale creatures, which resumed their original size as soon as they were out of the box.

"What a revolutionary invention," Gus murmured to Oksa.

"You're telling me!"

Dragomira's Lunatrixes bumped their prominent stomachs with Leomido's Lunatrixes, a clear sign they were glad to see each other again. The Getorixes raced over to the grass, where they rolled around happily, until they looked like a great ball of tangled hair. As for Leomido's Incompetent, it nonchalantly made its way over to Dragomira's one.

"You look like someone I know," it said feebly, looking at its mirror image.

"I think I've seen you somewhere before," replied its alter ego, its funny-looking eyes rolling languidly in their sockets.

A Squoracle fluttered out of the Boximinus and immediately joined the one keeping warm inside its master's jacket, while some octopus-like creatures with flies' heads intertwined their many legs.

"Hey, I've seen one of those things before," exclaimed Oksa.

"They're Polypharuses, children, phosphorescent Polypharuses, brighter than a flashlight," explained Leomido. "We used them frequently for public lighting or as interior lamps. Would you believe that, when they reach adulthood, the light they produce is so intense that you can go blind if you look at it for more than a few seconds."

"That's so cool! And what's that?" Oksa pointed to the last specimen, a completely hideous skeletal cockroach-like creature. Bound and gagged, it was writhing at the bottom of the Boximinus.

"That's an Abominari," said Dragomira, sounding upset.

"Strange name," remarked Gus. "And why is it tied up?"

By way of an answer, Dragomira took it from the box and removed the rope tightly binding it. As soon as it was free, it leapt to its feet and stood there, yelling.

"You'll pay dearly for this, you old bag! If you come near me again, I'll tear your rotting body to shreds after I've drained its antiquated blood and ripped out its mouldering guts, which will be no more than you deserve!"

Beside itself with rage, the Abominari threatened Dragomira with its long, dirty, razor-sharp claws as it delivered this unpleasant verbal attack.

"What's the matter with it?" asked Oksa.

"What's the matter with me?" hissed the Abominari. "WHAT'S THE MATTER WITH ME? That decrepit, disgusting old shrew has no respect for what I am."

"And what are you?" ventured Oksa, frowning.

"WHAT AM I? You ask what I am? You're as stupid as that washed-out old hag! You deserve to be disembowelled on the spot. I'm the faithful Abominari of Ocious, the one true master of Edefia."

36

AN UNCONTROLLABLE REBEL

ALL THE CREATURES, WITHOUT EXCEPTION, SHUDDERED and cast scandalized looks at the vile Abominari, who was furiously belching out insults in the middle of the vegetable plot.

"Has it been like this for a long time?" asked Leomido, looking concerned.

"A few weeks," replied Dragomira. "Since we've been in England, I'd say. It doesn't seem to respond to any kind of treatment any more."

"Not even the Psychosfortis?"

"No, not even the Psychosfortis. I've run out of ideas. It attacks the other creatures, it scratches or bites me as soon as I go near it, forcing me to use an immobilizing Granok or a Knock-Bong on it so that I can handle it."

Leomido looked at Dragomira with a worried expression, then at the Abominari, which was growling through its pointed teeth, ready to do battle with anyone who came near it.

"But why is it talking about Ocious, Baba?" asked Oksa.

"The Abominaris are to the Firmhands what the Lunatrixes are to the Gracious's family," replied Dragomira, tight-lipped with annoyance. "Ocious was actually the Abominari's master. Just before being ejected from Edefia, we were chased by that Felon's son. He was hard on our heels and the Abominari clung on to my dress, seconds before we passed through the Portal. We were in such a panic that I didn't notice. Once we were on the Outside, we took it in and cared for it like any other creature, although it has always made life difficult for us. It has never accepted me and only acknowledges its master's supremacy, even after all these years. Staunch loyalty, wouldn't you say? For years it was no trouble, particularly thanks to the Psychosfortis, a treatment developed by Abakum to mellow… how shall I put it… its malevolent tendencies. But for some time it has become uncontrollable, and I have to confess that I'm at my wits' end."

"My Master is coming to get me, old lady," said the Abominari, slyly edging nearer to her with its claws unsheathed. "And before I see him again, I'm going to gouge out your eyes and crack open your rancid head!"

"Oh! You're beginning to annoy me with all your threats," snapped Dragomira in irritation.

She turned the palm of her hand towards the spiteful Abominari, which was instantly hurled backwards a good twenty yards. With a dull smack, its slimy body hit the low stone wall bordering the cemetery.

Oksa gave a cry and murmured proudly to Gus:

"That's exactly what I did to that idiot Neanderthal."

Leomido went over to the unconscious Abominari, picked it up and carried it inside the house. A few seconds later, he came back on his own.

"I've put it in solitary confinement," he explained gravely. "It's in a locked room, from which it can't escape. It's really out of control, it's very strange. But let's go on with our introductions, shall we?" he continued, more cheerfully. "Where were we?"

"Have you got many creatures like that?" asked Oksa, a little shaken by the obnoxious creature's performance.

"Like the Abominari? No, luckily it's one of a kind. But as far as the others go, there are about ten species, accounting for around twenty creatures in total. You see, Gus, I'm far from living alone," remarked Leomido with a wink.

"That's for sure. You certainly can't be bored! What about the plants? Are they just as unusual?" asked Gus, seeing Dragomira take some tiny plants from the Boximinus.

As soon as they had resumed their original size Baba Pollock placed them beside their fellow species, where they celebrated their reunion with a great deal of rustling leaves and joyful sighs.

"Yes, more or less," replied Leomido. "Every plant has its significance, but that's nothing new. In that respect, it's the same on the Outside as it is on the Inside. The only difference is that plants from Edefia have distinctive personalities, as well as a language and a mode of communication which humans can understand. And vice versa. Oh, Dragomira! Did you manage to bring your Goranov with you? Well done, you're so good with them. I find it hard to put mine in the vegetable plot sometimes, you know? It gets so stressed."

"I've brought you some Incompetent crest salve which should help. Apply it to its leaves and let me know how you get on."

For the benefit of the young guests, she added:

"The Goranov is the plant of the Ageless Fairies. Its sap is like mercury. Mixed with a person's DNA, it can produce a unique substance which we use in the manufacture of Granok-Shooters. This is a very tricky and extremely complex process, and Abakum was the only person authorized to carry it out in Edefia. Your Granok-Shooter, Oksa, contains some drops of this sap mixed with a few of your hairs which I got from your comb. But the Goranov has two weak points: it's terribly fearful and prone to stress."

The two friends went over to the plants, weaving their way between the creatures which were enjoying some noisy reunions. The Goranovs were in mid-discussion:

"Such a frightening journey! I thought I was going to die... by plane, can you believe it! By PLANE! They don't spare me anything..."

"I know what you mean. I was on one once and I had an attack of chlorophyllic hypertension. I thought I was going to burst my veins! Just thinking about it..."

All the plant's leaves began to shake in a worrying manner, as if a very strong wind had just got up. Then, suddenly, it crumpled in a heap. Oksa exclaimed and put her hand over her mouth. She'd seen this happen before, but it still surprised her.

"Help!" shouted the other Goranov. "Help us!"

And all its foliage collapsed down the length of its stem too. Gus and Oksa were amazed.

"It's autumn!" cried the Squoracles immediately, poking their little heads out of Leomido's jacket. "Watch out, the leaves are falling, it's autumn! Everyone run for shelter!"

"What now? What's all this about autumn?" interrupted the Incompetents. "Every day there's something new, how are we supposed to keep up with it all?"

Oksa snorted with such infectious laughter that Gus, Dragomira and Leomido couldn't help laughing too.

"They're totally irresistible. I adore them, Baba, I AD-ORE them!"

"This is unreal... totally unreal," added Gus, unable to tear his eyes away from the two unconscious plants.

"Ahem, ahem."

"I think the Lunatrixes are trying to tell us something," remarked Leomido, pointing to the plump creatures.

"The meal has successfully concluded preparation. The invitation to sit down on the table is one of immediate promptitude, if your will be in favour," the Lunatrixes explained to Leomido.

"They speak exactly the same as your Lunatrixes, Dragomira," noted Gus.

"They do, don't they?" she said, smiling. "Let's go back inside and have something to eat."

✺

"That was the most fantastic day of my life," said Oksa with a yawn.

Stretched out on a sofa opposite a roaring fire in the huge hearth, Oksa ran over the events of the day with Gus, who was yawning as much as she. The meal had been delicious—apart from the leek dish, a Welsh speciality which Oksa hated—and everyone had remained in a fine mood. Mesmerized by the dancing flames, the two friends were struggling to stay awake.

"All the same," murmured Gus drowsily, "a salve made from Incompetent crest—yuck."

"That's not the strangest thing we've seen today, you must admit," remarked Oksa, just as sleepily.

"Incompetent crest…"

Gus's sentence petered out in a succession of low snores, which Oksa soon echoed. In the small room at the back of Leomido's house, the weird and wonderful creatures had also fallen asleep in their padded compartments after discussing the exciting events of the day.

37

VERTIFLYING ON THE AGENDA

THE PALE SUN FILTERED THROUGH THE WINDOW. OKSA opened her eyes and gave a long stretch. Where was she? Oh yes... at Leomido's house, in the sweet little room that she'd stumbled back to last night, more asleep than awake. The soft crackling of a log burning to nothing in the hearth roused her properly. She got up, drew the curtains and opened the window. The view was stunning—nothing like the one from her city bedroom. All she could see here was lush greenery stretching into the distance. She could hear birds singing and the sound of the sea a little further away, like background music. It was so beautiful.

"Hello, Young Gracious! Has sleep made its refreshment?"

Oksa leant over and saw Leomido's and Dragomira's Lunatrixas in the vegetable plot, a lettuce in each hand.

"Fantastic, thanks," she replied, waving to them.

She felt great, actually, so she decided to pay Gus a visit. If she could trust her hazy memories of the night before, he was in the room next door to hers. She pressed her ear against the door and knocked.

"Er... it's open," rang out her friend's voice.

She pushed open the door in exuberant high spirits. Gus was awake and rubbing his eyes.

"Were your dreams filled with Incompetent crests then?" she said, jumping on his bed like a cat.

"Hiya, Oksa. I slept like a log."

226

"A log which snored like a bear," said Oksa. "Even with stone walls three feet thick, I could hear you."

"Huh, whatever," muttered Gus, suppressing a smile.

They got up, put on thick bathrobes and went down to the kitchen. The Lunatrixes were making breakfast and bickering, it appeared, over the best way to make good toast. Leomido and Dragomira, looking very aristocratic in long silk damask housecoats, were drinking cups of steaming tea.

"Wow, the height of class!" exclaimed Oksa, pretending to curtsey. "My humble respects of the morning to you, my Lord and Lady."

"Hello, youngsters! Did you sleep well?" asked Dragomira.

"Really well," replied Gus with another yawn. "It's amazing here. Thanks for inviting me."

The two friends set about their breakfast with ravenous appetites.

"Shall we talk about our timetable for today?" suggested Leomido. "That is, if our dear Lunatrixes would be so kind as to lower their voices…"

The creatures didn't need telling twice. There was an immediate silence and Leomido continued speaking.

"My dear Oksa, you're here to learn certain things. You've had an overview of the world of the Runaways from Edefia, which is also your land, by heritage and by birthright. You must now hone your skills so that you can control them all the time, without being governed or led astray by impulses like anger, fear and so on. You have to realize that control and mastery are the keys to power."

While speaking, Leomido was carefully buttering a slice of toast and Oksa's attention was suddenly caught by the huge ring her great-uncle wore on his right hand. A superb silver ring set with a strange grey stone, which intrigued her. "*I've seen that stone before*," she thought. But her train of thought was interrupted by Dragomira, who carried on where Leomido had left off.

"My dear granddaughter, you should know that Leomido is extremely talented. In Edefia, he was a respected teacher, an expert. No Leomido,

227

don't blush, it's true! He'll take the lion's share in helping you with your powers."

"I suggest we compile a short list, so I can see what you can already do," said her teacher. "Gus, you'll be coming with us, won't you?"

"Just try to stop me, Mr Fortensky!" exclaimed Gus, immediately jumping up from the table.

"Oh, please, we're one big family now, so for pity's sake call me Leomido, not Mr Fortensky."

⁂

Half an hour later, the four of them were at the bottom of a small valley, not far from Leomido's house. Gus and Dragomira were sitting on the ground on a car rug, watching Oksa float vertically above Leomido's head. Gus particularly liked her kung-fu attack position, right leg outstretched and hands pressed together, while Dragomira had a slight preference for the horizontal position, the so-called "heavenly board".

"Not bad, Oksa, not bad. But do you think you could go a bit higher?"

"I've never done that," replied Oksa nervously, landing back on the ground. "This is the first time I've done this outside. I've only ever done it in my bedroom before and I never went higher than the ceiling."

Gus rolled his eyes at that barefaced lie, as if to say: "*You wouldn't by any chance be forgetting a certain descent from the first floor of St Proximus, would you?*"

"I don't want to die," she murmured, avoiding her friend's scandalized gaze.

"My dear girl," retorted Leomido calmly, "just remember that it's mind over matter: if you think about falling, you'll fall. If you think about flying, you'll fly. That's the first rule of Vertiflying."

"Vertiflying… I know how to Vertifly, that sounds so cool! But I'm still scared," remarked Oksa, scuffing the ground with her heel.

"If it'll make you feel any better, I'll go with you, but I'm sure you don't need me to. Come on, let's get cracking! Concentrate."

Leomido smiled and held her two hands. Oksa gripped them, closed her eyes, the tension showing in her face. Then, reopening her eyes, she locked her gaze on her guide and began to rise. Leomido kept pace with her without letting go and they both continued to rise vertically through the air. When they were the equivalent of five floors up, by Gus's reckoning—five floors!—Oksa stopped, and Leomido let go of first one hand, then the other. Oksa shuddered. Her body wobbled slightly, worried by all that empty space beneath her.

"Don't let your concentration waver, Oksa, I'm here," whispered Leomido. "Nothing can happen to you. I'm going to take your hands again and you can bring us back down."

A few seconds later they were back safely on the ground.

"Did you see that, Gus?" whispered Oksa, her eyes shining with exhilaration. "Didn't I go high?"

"Ever so high!"

"Do you want try on your own?" asked Leomido.

Oksa hesitated for a fraction of a second, then set off. She started by rising about six feet, her legs shaky and her breath coming in short gasps.

"Go on, Oksa, you can do it!" shouted Gus encouragingly, cupping his hands around his mouth.

Determined to ascend on her own, she took a deep breath and, concentrating hard, quickly gained height. Leomido was right—it wasn't difficult. Perched at a height of more than 130 feet, she ventured a backflip but fumbled the landing, because the empty space didn't provide all that firm a foothold. Gus shuddered and Dragomira put her hand over her mouth to stifle a cry of alarm. Only Leomido stayed calm, with unshaken confidence.

"You're a fast learner, which is good," he said casually, when she landed on the ground again. "But let me show you something now. Although height is good, it's even better if you add speed."

The old man—who was almost eighty—stood absolutely still with his arms at his sides, then took off like a rocket until he was no more than a tiny figure over 600 feet in the air.

"Whoa! Did you see that? Unreal!"

Eyes wide with amazement, Oksa looked up at her great-uncle who waved to them. As quickly as he'd shot up, he plummeted down head first, singing a famous opera aria at the top of his lungs. He stopped level with Oksa's face, dropped a light kiss on her cheek, then floated horizontally down to the ground, still singing.

"You'll have to work flat out if you want to do that one day," said Gus, slapping Oksa vigorously on the back.

"I'm totally hooked," remarked Oksa, astounded by what she'd just seen. "I want to try it too. I can do it, I'm sure I can."

"Of course you can!" exclaimed Leomido.

Surprising even herself, Oksa shot as fast as lightning into the sky, which was clouding over. Then she reappeared, a tiny speck quickly growing larger as she approached the ground head first, like Leomido. But Oksa's yell was also growing louder... and it was not so much a yell as a downright *scream*—which prompted Leomido and Dragomira to shoot off at such staggering speed that Gus only reacted when he recognized Dragomira's red dress in the air. In a flash, her great-uncle and her gran had reached Oksa and had escorted her down onto solid ground, holding her securely under her arms. Both looked annoyed.

"Hey!" shouted Oksa, pulling roughly out of their grasp. "I was doing fine. You don't trust me, do you?"

"Don't take it the wrong way," replied Leomido gravely. "It usually takes weeks of training before you can Vertifly at that speed—it's very hard to master. It wasn't a lack of trust, we were just afraid you were in free fall."

"*In free fall*? Are you kidding, Leomido? I was having a whale of a time!"

And to prove what she said was true—just in case anyone doubted her—she shot off again at incredible speed. Her powerful take-off took her so high that she disappeared into the clouds. This magnificent flight was followed by a flawless landing which, this time, earned her a round of applause.

"Well, that was a very productive first day, congratulations Young Vertiflier!" said Leomido with a broad smile.

"I was on fire, wasn't I?" beamed Oksa.

"You're amazing!" said Gus, admiringly. "And Dragomira you were totally awesome too. I didn't know you could fly so well."

"I'm a little rusty," replied Dragomira, stretching. "But thanks for the compliment, Gus. Well, I don't know about you, but I'm starving. And I think we're being called, anyway…"

The two male Lunatrixes, hanging from the small chain attached to the bell in one of the house's towers, were ringing to summon them in for dinner, while the Lunatrixas were signalling to them by vigorously waving tea towels. In the setting sun, Leomido, Dragomira, Gus and Oksa walked back to the house, shoulder to shoulder, physically exhausted but buzzing with exhilaration.

38

A QUESTION OF WILLPOWER

"Today, Oksa, I suggest we look at the Magnetus in a little more detail," Leomido told his great-niece. "With it, you can animate objects from a distance, using inner spirit and attraction."

"What do you mean by 'inner spirit'?" asked Oksa in surprise.

"Your mind is what makes things move," her great-uncle replied. "The spirit is born within and moves through you. Relayed through your eyes, it's as though this spirit assumes solid form. It can then carry or move objects just as your hands would."

"Oh of course," said the young apprentice, pretending to sound casual. "Naturally."

"I believe you've already tried this, so it shouldn't pose too much of a problem."

"Problem? What problem? No problem!"

In perfect agreement, teacher and student headed for the same place as the day before, the practice ground sheltered by rolling hills overgrown with heather. Leomido had brought all kinds of implements in a large bag. Seeing that some of the creatures were accompanying them too, Oksa was for a moment perplexed.

"You don't want me to practise on living creatures, do you? That won't be possible, Leomido, I couldn't. I'm totally against animal experimentation, I warn you right now!" she said forcibly.

"Animal experimentation? Good lord, there's absolutely no question of that," he said, with a laugh. "The creatures are simply there to help you and nothing can be done without their agreement. You'll begin with objects and I'll make your task more complicated as you progress. Let's get an idea of what you can do, my dear."

Leomido dotted various objects around on the heather and told Oksa to make them move. There wasn't actually anything difficult about it—she had already put her technique to the test on numerous occasions. The young apprentice simply had to focus all the attention she could muster on the object she wanted to move, as if all the strength and movement came from her eyes. Her will did the rest. None of the objects, whether heavy, bulky, soft or tiny, could withstand her Magnetus.

Delighted, Gus watched her every move.

"Do you have the wish for a collaboration with my body, my Young Gracious?" offered the Lunatrix. "My will is in full agreement!"

Oksa hesitated, but seeing the entreaty in the eyes of the adorable creature, she couldn't resist. Soon after, the Lunatrix found himself suspended in the air, circling Gus, who was crying with laughter.

"My lightness! My lightness!" exclaimed the small creature.

"Hey, Zeppelin, can you hear me? This is Earth speaking," said the Getorix. "It's true, isn't it? Don't you think it looks like a Zeppelin with its big paunch?"

Oksa turned to glare at the bushy-haired, mischievous creature, making its shaggy head of hair stand on end. The Getorix was drawn upwards as if an invisible hand were lifting it up by the hair until it found itself level with the Lunatrix. It put its long arms around the neck of the household steward and straddled his back.

"Giddy up, you old nag, giddy up!" it bawled, its enormous mess of tangled hair falling over its eyes. The Lunatrix tried to unseat this unwelcome rider, a difficult task because Oksa kept them suspended in the air.

"I reveal my inadequacy!" screamed the Lunatrix, which was obviously furious at the excess weight. "Will this Getorix please remove itself from my spine! Young Gracious, evict him so I can float with peace."

No sooner said than done: the Getorix was dispatched *pronto* into Gus's arms and the Lunatrix regretfully landed on the ground. Leomido gave a long whistle of admiration at Oksa's new feat.

"Do you like flying, Lunatrix?" Oksa asked the little creature, who was full of wonderment at the experience he had just had.

"Oooh, Young Gracious, that is a certainty! Vertiflying is my most exotic desire."

"Your desire is not the only exotic thing," said the Getorix, sniggering.

"No, you're not the only one with that desire, Lunatrix!" insisted the Squoracles, which were shivering and nestling in a ski cap. "It is also ours. Why is exoticism refused to us? Why? Why won't someone tell us!"

"Come here and let me put my arms around you," said Oksa, beckoning to the small steward.

"Oooh, Young Gracious!" was all the Lunatrix, purple from head to toe, could mumble.

"Hold tight, okay?"

And they took off like a rocket, accompanied by two loud cries, one from the deliriously happy Lunatrix and one from Oksa, the great Vertiflier.

❁

Escorted by the elated creatures, Gus and Dragomira had already gone back to the house a while ago, when Leomido decided to train Oksa in a completely different subject.

"My dear, I'd like to check on something," he said mysteriously. "See those clouds above the hills in the distance?"

"Yes, I see them," replied Oksa, intrigued. "Surely you don't want me to bring them closer, do you?"

Leomido didn't reply immediately, for the simple reason that he wasn't exactly sure what he wanted Oksa to do. He gazed at her affectionately, then turned to look at the clouds.

"Do you think you could have any kind of effect on them?" he asked her finally.

"No, Leomido, of course not!" exclaimed Oksa.

"Why?"

Oksa was baffled and began to doubt her great-uncle's sanity.

"Why? Because they're clouds. How am I supposed to make clouds do anything? That's impossible!"

"Think, dear girl," Leomido said gently. "Think."

Irritated, she gazed at the clouds. They were a dazzling white and looked as soft as huge balls of cotton wool.

"To tell the truth, Leomido…" she ventured.

But her great-uncle had stretched out on the heather with his hands crossed under his head and seemed to have fallen asleep.

"Brilliant," grumbled Oksa, disconcerted. "Thanks a million for your help."

Suddenly she remembered something with almost blinding clarity: the violent storm which had broken after her disastrous mishap in the boys' toilets—had that been caused by HER? She sat up, her mind spinning at this insane idea. The terrible weather had reflected the waves of anger and fear washing over her. And she remembered perfectly how amazed she'd been.

"It's not possible," she whispered, walking away from her sleeping great-uncle. "I can't believe it!"

When the white clouds turned an unsettling leaden colour, Oksa understood perfectly what Leomido had meant. The light faded as a thick blanket of purple-streaked clouds covered the sky. The clouds, swollen with rain, grew even blacker and raced towards Oksa with a rumble of thunder. The wind, which had only been a light breeze till then, began to blow more violently, moaning as if carrying distant screams to her ears.

"Oh no, not that," she murmured instinctively, putting her hands over her ears. But it was no use, she realized. They were the same awful screams she'd heard before and which made the hairs on her arms stand on end. They pierced her brain like lightning bolts, sounding even more heart-rending than before. And when she heard her name chanted by distant women's voices, she thought she was completely losing her mind. The voices might have seemed a long way off, but she sensed they weren't and that they were trapped inside her. What a nightmare. She stood there looking at the dark clouds as heavy rain lashed the rounded hilltop on which she stood.

※

The shower barely lasted a minute. The sky brightened and in no time was as clear and blue as it had been, just as if there hadn't been a violent downpour on that precise spot a few seconds ago. Dazed and drenched, Oksa turned round and found herself face to face with Leomido, who was wiping his face with a large handkerchief. She looked at him in alarm.

"Leomido! I think… I think I understand," she whispered, her heart thumping.

"Oksa… my dear girl… I think I understand too," he said with great emotion.

And when his great-niece looked at him enquiringly, he added in a shaky voice:

"You're a powerful Gracious, Oksa. Certainly the greatest of them all."

When they neared the house, Dragomira and Gus raced to meet them, towels in hand.

"My goodness, don't tell me you were caught in that terrible shower!" exclaimed Dragomira.

Still in shock, Leomido and Oksa didn't reply and merely wrapped the towels around them.

"Come into the warm quickly before you catch your death of cold," said Dragomira.

Sitting by the fire after changing into dry clothes, Oksa needed time to recover from her strange experience. She couldn't ignore the intrigued look her gran had given Leomido and his reaction: an imperceptible nod. The silent answer to the question Dragomira had just murmured, "*Was that caused by Oksa?*" Yes, it was. The Lunatrixes brought her a steaming hot toddy which she drank with a grimace and only then did she see that Gus was staring at her in silence, looking concerned. She hurriedly brushed aside her worried thoughts and feelings and exclaimed:

"What lousy weather! Next time I won't leave the house without an umbrella."

"These microclimates are crazy," added Gus with an inscrutable smile. "There can be a downpour in one place and not a drop a hundred yards further away."

"Gus…" muttered Oksa.

"Don't worry, I understand. Drink your hot toddy."

39

An Unhappy Friend

That evening Marie and Pavel Pollock telephoned and, with an enthusiasm tinged with euphoria, Oksa talked to them for ages about everything she'd learnt in just two days.

"You are being careful, aren't you?" asked her father anxiously.

"Of course, Dad! You should see how well Leomido looks after me—frankly he's worse than you."

"Just listen to the way this insolent girl talks to her poor old father, who's sick with worry! Poor me, no one understands me…"

"Oh Dad, why do you always have to be so OTT?" replied Oksa, laughing.

Oksa could also hear her mother laughing behind Pavel's pathetic wails.

"Dad, can you do all these things?" asked Oksa, becoming serious again.

"Hmm… I wonder whether I shouldn't take it up again in view of your mother's lack of compassion, just to get my own back. She'll soon see who she's dealing with," replied Pavel Pollock, sidestepping his daughter's question.

Oksa heard her mother laughing even louder as she came to the phone.

"How are you, my little witch? Are you having a good time?"

"Amazing! It's totally intense, but I love it. You'll get to see everything I can do, Mum. I've improved my Magnetus no end and now I know how to Vertifly.

"Oh my goodness, it sounds terrifying," she murmured. "Be careful won't you, and don't overdo it."

"Okay."

"We'll call again tomorrow, love you, darling."

After hanging up, Oksa went back to join Gus in the huge living room. Huddled in an armchair facing the window, he was gazing outside and stroking the baby Lunatrix, who was stretched out on his lap, snoring.

"You okay, Gus?" asked Oksa, going over to him.

Gus just shrugged, huddling deeper in his armchair.

"Is something wrong?" insisted Oksa.

"Er… nothing important," grumbled Gus.

"There is then," remarked Oksa, kneeling by her friend.

"Well yes, there is—me," replied Gus, not looking at her.

"What on earth do you mean?"

"I mean… I don't know how to do anything," he said, trying to keep his voice down so he didn't wake the small sleeping creature. "I mean, if I call my parents, what am I going to talk about? About my best friend who's learning to fly and summon storms? Or about incredible creatures from an invisible country? About me, who can't do anything except watch and applaud your amazing feats? About how useless I am? About how pathetic I am?"

Gus was speaking through clenched teeth, his jaw set. His scathing words cut Oksa to the quick. Her eyes filled with tears.

"Pathetic? Are you crazy? You're not pathetic, you're not useless!" she cried with a lump in her throat.

"Oh, right? You think? Even the Incompetents are more useful than I am! You do everything better than I do. And I'm not just talking about Vertiflying or the Magnetus, I'm talking about the rest too: rollerblading, school, karate, friends, EVERYTHING. I'm always lagging behind. I always am and always will be Gus-the-loser."

Oksa was amazed by Gus's words. She'd known for years that he didn't have a very high opinion of himself, but she'd never seen him like this.

What saddened her most wasn't his harsh, uncompromising words. No: the worst thing was that Gus really believed what he was saying. This was really the way he saw himself.

"But Gus, *you're talking rubbish!*" she exclaimed. "You've got loads of great qualities. You're loyal and intelligent, you're super-talented at all kinds of things, computers, video games. You know everything there is to know about manga, and you're a model student."

"You must be joking," moaned Gus bitterly. "You get better marks than me."

"And what about karate?" continued Oksa, without breaking stride. "I'm sorry but you're doing yourself down with that, as with everything else. Anyone who looks closely can see immediately that you've mastered it better than me. You know me, I always big myself up, but there are tons of things I can't do. Unlike a certain Gus who is effective without drawing attention to himself, discreet as anything—which is a *fantastic quality*! And what's also super-cool about you is that you never lose your head. If you weren't there, I think I'd have got myself into really hot water. At least you think before you act, whereas I'm the complete opposite. Do you realize how important that is? I need you to be my friend... and anyway I like it that you're my friend, and that's all there is to it. You're just as important to me as my family. You are family! Honestly, you do *get on my nerves* when you say things like that..."

Oksa looked away in exasperation and gazed outside. She felt a painful mixture of anger and sadness seething inside her. Struggling not to let these feelings overwhelm her, she took a deep breath and tried to calm herself down.

"Okay, okay," conceded Gus, still staring out of the window. "But it doesn't alter the fact that you're a queen, a sorceress and someone totally exceptional. And I'm a complete zero. I'm not jealous, Oksa, I just feel *totally pathetic.*"

"Oh yeah? And being a queen's best friend doesn't count for anything at all, is that it? You really do take the biscuit!" replied Oksa, tugging a strand of Gus's long black hair. "Do you really think that someone of my calibre would waste her time on a *total loser*? Really?"

She pulled a face at him, careful not to let him see how deeply his words had affected her. Gus gave the ghost of a smile.

"I'd give anything to be like you, though."

"No way, Gus, no way. You're fine just as you are, believe me," murmured Oksa, blushing to the roots of her hair.

And the two friends sat there quietly, side by side, as darkness filled the living room. The rain had stopped as suddenly as it had started and the only sound was the gentle snoring of the little Lunatrix still asleep on Gus's lap and Leomido's faint voice as he chatted with the Lunatrixes, who were slaving over the stove. As for Dragomira, leaning against the door of the living room, she was watching the two youngsters, whom she could only see from the back. She'd been deeply moved by the conversation she'd just overheard. She wiped away a tear and tiptoed off to join Leomido in the kitchen.

40

DISAPPEARANCE
ON THE MOOR

WHEN OKSA WOKE, SHE COULD HEAR RAIN BEATING
steadily against the windows. A chilly light was filtering through
the curtains and it felt as though the morning was well advanced. Tangled
up in her sheets, Oksa was drenched with sweat. She extricated herself
somehow and, as she'd done the morning before, rushed into Gus's room.
He was still asleep—or pretending to be—his breathing shallow and half
his face hidden by a strand of hair. As she looked at him, Oksa caught
herself noticing his perfectly regular features. He looked just like one of the
enigmatic heroes in the manga that she read by the dozen. Gus. Her friend
Gus. Suddenly, he threw his thick eiderdown to the other end of the room
and leapt up giving a loud yell. Surprised and embarrassed, Oksa screamed.

"Were you spying on me?"

Oksa pulled a face, before replacing the eiderdown on the bed. With
no more than a glance, naturally.

"Show-off," said Gus, smiling.

They were interrupted by three taps at the door.

Opening it, Oksa found herself face to face with Leomido's Lunatrixa,
wearing a chef's hat and an apple-green apron.

"Young Gracious and her young friend, the clock is about to strike ten
times in our ears, that is the information which all stomachs await! But rest

242

assured! The Lunatrixes are able to foresee this type of inconvenience and have prepared saucepans of food which will lick your chops."

"You mean we should come down and eat, is that it?" asked Oksa, bending over to be on a level with the creature.

"That is a statement of perfect accuracy, Young Gracious!"

"Where are Dragomira and Leomido?"

"Oh, Young Gracious! How may I give you an answer without falling into a risk?"

"A risk? What risk?"

"A risk for me to deliver information which I should shroud in secrecy," replied the Lunatrixa, looked around in panic and twisting her long arms.

"Tell us, Lunatrixa, please. We won't say anything, you can count on us, honestly!"

Gus came over and knelt down next to Oksa in front of the creature.

"Well, now I have the difficulty of presenting the Young Gracious with a refusal…"

The Lunatrixa took a deep breath then continued in a low voice:

"An intruder took nocturnal liberties."

"An intruder?"

"Yes, Young Gracious, an intruder walked round the residence of our Master! His large feet imprinted marks on the soil of the vegetable plot and the cemetery. And his curiosity at the window created disturbances for the Goranovs, which have collapsed in a terrible panic attack. Another problem has been identified in addition: the abominable Abominari has engineered a disappearance."

"What on earth do you mean?" asked Oksa. "It has escaped?"

"Most certainly, it is no longer in our vicinity! Bah! The disappearance is not regretted because the companion was hateful. But the Master's anxiety has registered an increase. He has made some explorations but detection is negative. He has the concern that the Abominari has roamed and the thought full of hope that the hiding place is still on the estate and that the empty stomach of the ungrateful creature will cause its return.

With regard to the tracks around the abode, my ear has heard the words entrusted to the Old Gracious: the opinion of the Master tends towards a prowler and, this night, some Tumble-Bawlers will make the alarm if he pokes the tip of his nose in here."

"Tumble-Bawlers?" asked Oksa.

"Tumble-Bawlers give mighty shouts to warn the Master," explained the Lunatrixa. "Then the Master motivates the intruder into flight."

"I'd be interested in seeing that," said Gus.

"So would I! Anyway, I hope it isn't anything serious," said Oksa. "Lunatrixa, we'll be right with you, if you don't mind giving us a few minutes to make ourselves presentable."

Five minutes later, after promising the Lunatrixa for the umpteenth time that they wouldn't breathe a word about the information she had given them, Gus and Oksa walked down the stately staircase of dark wood. Hearing music, they immediately headed for the living room where Leomido was sitting at a massive grand piano which took up a large part of the room. He was playing a beautiful piece with a slow, haunting melody. In front of him, a couple of inches from the black and white keys, the two Goranovs were swaying their leaves in time to the music with great conviction. Suddenly the pace speeded up and the hyper-sensitive plants fervently straightened their leaves. Then the cadence slowed and they resumed their gentle rocking.

"Come over here, youngsters," invited Leomido softly. "The Goranovs are extremely nervous this morning and, when they're in this state, Chopin is the only thing that can calm them down."

Gus and Oksa glanced at each other, trying not to laugh. Leomido was also looking somewhat amused at their surprise and at the sight of the two plants, which were humming—or rather moaning—their stem and stalks trembling.

"Oh… life, life!" they sighed. "A constant torment."

The two friends leant their elbows on the piano and enjoyed the short recital. Gus was fascinated by Leomido's talent. His eyes riveted on the elderly man's hands, he felt bewitched by the music, like the Goranovs, which gradually sank into a deep and comforting torpor. Their leaves trembled less and less and soon steadied to become perfectly still.

"You must be starving," whispered Leomido, gently closing the piano. "Dragomira is waiting for us in the kitchen. Let's go."

※

"I propose a lighter schedule for today. You will have noticed that the weather is offering you its local speciality," said Leomido, indicating the window, against which the rain was pattering. "So, no outside activities. We'll just go over a few things inside, in the warm. Anyway, my dear, you look a little tired and I know a certain Pavel Pollock, who will curse me to the end of my days if I hand back his daughter with even a hint of dark circles under her eyes."

Hearing this, Dragomira almost choked—to the great alarm of her Lunatrixes, who raced to her aid, wailing:

"Oohh! Our Old Gracious, is your food nauseous? Oohh, your disgust is our regret..."

"No, my Lunatrixes, everything is as delicious as usual," spluttered Dragomira, gently patting their heads. "It's just Leomido making me laugh. You're not implying that my son has a tendency to overreact, are you, dear brother?"

"No more than you or your Lunatrixes, dear sister," retorted Leomido with a chuckle.

"Your family is a bunch of nutters!" chortled Gus, glancing merrily at Oksa.

※

The day was largely spent in the refectory of the former monastery. There, the Young Gracious spent ages polishing her Magnetus, moving

245

increasingly large and heavy objects, like the volumes of an encyclopaedia, pot plants and even a bike. As for Gus, while watching his friend out of the corner of his eye, he struck up a friendship with some of the creatures, particularly the Squoracles, to whom he described a trip he'd made to Australia with his parents, providing details about the climate and opening up new horizons for the tiny creatures, which felt the cold so keenly.

"Those atmospheric conditions would be ideal for us!" they said enthusiastically. "Why is our Master so determined to live in the northern hemisphere when the southern hemisphere is so welcoming? The Australian desert is just as sparsely populated as the Welsh moors, if that's what he's looking for. Oh, young friend of our Young Gracious, tell us more about the desert and those idyllic temperatures."

Oksa allowed herself a short break when her thoughts strayed to the Granok-Shooter which she hadn't yet used. She raced up to her room to fetch it and began examining it with Gus.

"It doesn't work!" she exclaimed, seeing Leomido and Dragomira approaching.

"Of course it doesn't, Dushka. And all your attempts will come to nothing while your Granok-Shooter remains empty," announced Dragomira.

She looked at the two friends, hesitated for a second then said:

"Do you want a small demonstration?"

They nodded eagerly. Dragomira took her own Granok-Shooter from the folds of her capacious dress and said in a low voice:

"Reticulata!"

Then she blew gently into the tube, causing a sort of gelatinous bubble, like a jellyfish, to swell from the end.

"Look," she suggested, beckoning the children over to the window.

Gus and Oksa rushed over and saw with amazement that everything in their field of vision had been made a hundred times larger by the Reticulata, from the delicate blooms of the heather to the tiniest ant threading its way between the blades of grass.

"Wow, amazing!" cried Oksa.

Dragomira swung the large bubble round to bear on the Lunatrix. This time, the two friends could examine the smallest details of the creature's skin as if it were under a magnifying glass—they could see each pore, each downy hair and each small wrinkle in close-up.

"Do you want to try?" asked Dragomira, seeing Oksa's enthusiasm.

"Can I? Really?"

"Yes, you can. I'll give you a few Granoks, my dear. But from the moment they are inserted into your Granok-Shooter, you must remember that you're the only one who can use them," explained Dragomira, darting a look filled with kindness at Gus.

"Don't worry," said Gus in a resigned voice. "I am and will always be the loyal assistant of her Young Gracious, which isn't so bad after all," he added, looking down.

"Oh, I think you're much more than that," replied Dragomira, looking at him shrewdly.

Then, moving her Granok-Shooter near to Oksa's one, she summoned a Reticulata which dropped into the palm of her hand and was immediately sucked up by the girl's instrument.

"Here's your first Granok, Oksa. If you want to activate it, you must say this little rhyme:

> By the power of the Granoks
> Think outside the box
> Reticulata, Reticulata
> Things far away look larger.

Oksa repeated obediently.

"When you want to use it, you just have to say its name, either in a low voice or inside your head. I'd say the second solution is the best, particularly when it's an emergency or you're defending yourself. Saying the name out loud gives your adversary a valuable clue, which will enable him to defend himself. For this attempt, it won't be hard, particularly as the Reticulata is a simple tool which doesn't belong to the category of offensive or defensive Granoks. But imagine you have ten or twenty different Granoks: you must remember the name of each one and particularly their usage. Abakum mentioned a few to you, didn't he?"

"Yes, the Dozident and the Stuffarax—"

"What!" shouted Leomido in a panic, looking at Dragomira with amazement. "She knows about the Stuffarax?"

"Just by name," said Oksa in her own defence.

"Your grand-niece is very inquisitive and has an excellent memory," said Dragomira. "She doesn't miss a thing."

Oksa felt her cheeks turn crimson and looked at Gus for support. He smiled and shrugged with a resigned expression.

"It's true that, ever since you were a little girl, stopping you from finding out our little secrets has really taxed our imagination!" admitted Leomido.

"Little secrets? That's an understatement," remarked Oksa. "State secrets, perhaps!"

"Hey, Oksa-007," broke in Gus, "let's see what you can do. C'mon, show us a good Reticulata!"

The demonstration was beyond their wildest hopes: the jellyfish-bubble spurted from Oksa's Granok-Shooter as soon as she uttered the phrase and blew into the small tube. In a few seconds it had doubled, tripled, quadrupled in volume until it had filled half the room. Gus roared with laughter, holding his sides.

"Everything in moderation as usual, I see!"

"It's wicked! But what do I do if I want some different Granoks, Baba?"

"We'll talk to Abakum about it later."

But, seeing the disappointment on Oksa's face, she continued: "Okay, fine—I'll have faith in you, even if you do sometimes totally abuse my trust. Let's see what I've got in stock. Watch and, above all, listen carefully," said Dragomira, pronouncing the phrases for the Granoks clearly as the Granok-Shooter sucked them up.

"Cool," said Oksa, proudly tapping her Granok-Shooter. "Thanks for all this ammunition."

"Please, just promise me you won't use them recklessly."

"You know me, Baba. I'm the soul of discretion!" said the girl reassuringly, ignoring Gus's amused expression.

*

The highlight of this uneventful day undoubtedly came from an idea that occurred to the Young Gracious. Early in the evening, exhausted by all her diligent revision, she went looking for Gus and saw him at the far end of the large living room, near the hearth, surrounded by a good twenty creatures, which were gathered around him and listening very closely. It was an incredible scene. Gus looked up in her direction and his expression shocked her: her friend seemed so elated and yet so sad. He ran his fingers through his hair and gave her a smile which immediately dispelled this impression of bitterness. Oksa had a wild idea: she went over to Gus and told him to follow her into the middle of the large room.

"Stand behind me and put your hands on my shoulders!"

"What are you doing, Oksa?"

"Hold tight and don't let go, okay?"

"I won't let go," he said, surprised at how embarrassed he felt touching her.

They rose above the floor, first by a few inches, then quickly ascended the twenty-four feet or so to reach the high ceiling. Clutching Oksa's shoulders and pressed against her back, Gus let her carry him, murmuring:

"Amazing! I'm Vertiflying! I'm Vertiflying!"

They flew back and forth like this in the air, which filled Gus with happiness, until Oksa, with aching shoulders but a joyful heart, landed them both back on the floor.

"Wow, thanks so much!" said Gus shyly, his cheeks scarlet and his grateful eyes fixed on the floor. "Thanks…"

41

A STRESSFUL TRIP

"CHILDREN, WE HAVE A SMALL SURPRISE FOR YOU, WHY don't you follow me," said their host, leading the little group out of the house.

Outside the weather was marvellously mild, the sky was clear and the mood was high. This was Gus and Oksa's fourth day with Leomido and they were already excited by the discoveries they were bound to make. Gus began running through the grass, which was still wet from the day before, with Oksa in hot pursuit. Brimming with energy, they both let off steam by scaling the low hills that extended across the estate. They then rolled around on the heather-covered moor, laughing until they were breathless. Leomido and Dragomira were walking arm in arm at a much more sedate pace, following the barely visible path across the rolling hills. Dragomira's long turquoise dress floating behind her was the only splash of colour in the autumn landscape. Soon they branched off towards a deeper valley than the others, sheltered by gorse rippling in the light breeze. Two huge birds more than six feet tall were gliding on a lake lined with reeds at the bottom of the valley.

"Let me introduce you to my Gargantuhens," announced Leomido.

The Gargantuhens, one white and the other russet, turned towards their visitors and cackled noisily, flapping their wings frantically.

"They're enormous!" remarked Oksa.

"Be careful what you say, my dear, they're very concerned about their appearance and they don't take criticism well," warned Leomido. "Do you fancy a short trip on their backs?"

A minute later, the Gargantuhens drew alongside the small wooden landing stage and docilely allowed the four to sit astride them. Leomido clambered onto the russet Gargantuhen with Gus, Oksa climbed onto the white one with her gran, and the unusual craft began to drift peacefully on the lake. Oksa and Gus were having great difficulty suppressing their hilarity. They were actually bent double with laughter and this didn't seem to go down well with the large birds, who showed their annoyance by giving ear-splitting squawks.

With their hands muffling their ears, they were advised by Leomido to pet the annoyed Gargantuhens by stroking the mottled feathers at the base of their necks. With sparkling eyes, Gus and Oksa exchanged looks, biting their lips to stop themselves roaring with laughter. Then, obeying Leomido, they plunged their hands into the plumage which emanated a gentle warmth. The Gargantuhens, surprised by their attentions, stopped swimming. A few minutes later, peace and quiet had been restored on the lake and the boat trip continued.

"How soft they are," remarked Oksa, still stroking the feathers, which were over twenty inches long. "They feel like silk! They're magnificent creatures. Can we fly with them?"

"Well, we're in danger of attracting attention with creatures like this," replied Dragomira. "If someone saw us flying in the Welsh sky, perched on giant hens—dear me, no, I'd rather not think about it... Anyway, the Gargantuhens are expressly forbidden to fly without permission from one of us. We occasionally allow them to on very dark nights, even though they have very poor night vision. Otherwise, they have to stay away from prying eyes on this lake and in the hennery built specially for them over there," she said, pointing to a wooden cabin the size of a house further along the bank. "But let's enjoy our trip."

This was such a delightful excursion that their thoughts soon began to drift and they slipped into a trance-like state. Gus felt so relaxed that he was almost asleep, his body limp on the comfortable back of the giant bird. With one cheek against its silky neck, he gazed dreamily at the rolling hills and the cloudless sky, thinking about the fantastic, thoroughly enjoyable adventure he was having, thanks to the generosity of his friend and the Pollock family. And what an amazing family it was! He was lucky to know them, very lucky. On the other Gargantuhen, Oksa was so happy that she felt as though her muscles, veins and even her bones had turned to jelly. Copying Gus's lazy pose, she leant forward to let her head rest against her mount's warm, downy neck. All they could hear was the soft rustling of the gorse and the reeds along the bank and the faint lapping sound of feet moving in the water. The Gargantuhens were gliding past the opposite bank to the landing stage when the one carrying Dragomira and Oksa suddenly screeched piercingly, as if in terrible pain. It began to thrash about frantically on the water, beating its wings wildly as though it could no longer control its movements.

"Baba! What's going on?" shouted Oksa, trying to keep her seat on the giant bird.

"I don't know! Stay calm, Dushka, we're going to take it back to the bank."

Dragomira leant over the Gargantuhen, putting her arms part-way round the rotund body of the hen, which was squawking and struggling harder and harder. Leomido and Gus tried to draw nearer to it, but the white Gargantuhen was beating its wings so hard on the water that they had to keep their distance to avoid being capsized. Dragomira, still holding on tightly to the feathered body, was finding it harder and harder to keep her balance.

"Oksa!" she shouted. "Hang on! Keep hold of its neck, I'm going to dive in!"

"Baba! The water must be cold as ice!"

Dragomira didn't heed this warning in the slightest: she had already jumped into the water. With her dress spread out around her body like a blue water lily, she swam round until she was behind the Gargantuhen and began kicking her legs furiously, pushing the poor creature with all her might. Unfortunately, the Gargantuhen didn't budge an inch.

"Fine, desperate times demand desperate measures," muttered Dragomira, her hair dripping down her face.

Oksa turned round and what she saw almost knocked her sideways. Dragomira had given up swimming and had adopted a completely different mode of transport: Baba Pollock was now walking on the lake, as if its surface were solid ground. Standing on the water—*standing on the water*—she was leaning against the Gargantuhen and shoving with her entire body, as if pushing a wardrobe or a broken-down car, relying on her feet for purchase. This proved to be much more effective than swimming. Leomido, understanding his sister's tactics, quickly guided the russet Gargantuhen behind its companion to help complete the manoeuvre. With a lot of pushing and shouting, they soon reached the bank. Leomido leapt to the ground and helped Gus and Oksa to dismount.

"Stand back, children!" he told them sharply.

"We'll help you."

"NO!" he snapped. "Get away from the bank."

And he somehow hauled the Gargantuhen onto solid ground, pulling it by the neck while Dragomira pushed from behind.

"Phew, I didn't think we'd ever do it," she sighed, soaked from head to foot.

Leomido rushed over to drape his velvet jacket over her shoulders. Then he turned to Gus:

"Gus, my boy, would you run to the hennery? You'll find a cupboard in there. Open it up and bring back all the blankets inside."

Gus didn't waste a second and ran off at top speed—the sprint of the century! Three minutes later Dragomira resembled a mummy, completely swathed in rugs which stopped her body from shivering and her teeth from chattering.

"But what's wrong with it, Baba?" asked Oksa, looking at the Gargantuhen, which was writhing uncontrollably.

"I don't know. This is the first time a Gargantuhen has reacted like this. Oh, look! It's injured."

And it was. But this was no ordinary injury—far from it: one of its legs seemed to have been turned to glass. The poor creature tried to move its limb in vain and its cries of pain, which had been piercing at first, gradually turned into long, pathetic whimpers.

"Leomido? Are you thinking what I'm thinking?" said Dragomira to her brother, unable to take her eyes off the Gargantuhen.

"I'm afraid so…" he replied with a grave expression.

"What is it?" asked Oksa in turn. "Baba? Leomido?"

There was a heavy silence, which made the Gargantuhen's whining sound even louder.

"Tell us what's going on!" insisted Oksa, tensely.

Dragomira and Leomido seemed at a loss, as they frowned and stared at the vitrified leg. Leomido finally raised his head, looked at Gus, then Oksa, and said in a dull voice, which shook despite his attempts to control it:

"A Colocynthis… a Black Globus."

❋

Leomido had stayed with the injured Gargantuhen while Dragomira, struggling to walk because of the blankets wrapped around her, had escorted the children back to the house, trying her best to hide her agitation. With their hearts pounding, the three of them were now in the large living room.

"Gus, Oksa, wait for me here," said Dragomira, sounding grave. "I shall lock the doors and I don't want you to go out for anything. If there's the

254

slightest problem, send this Veloso to tell me, okay? As its name suggests, it's very fast. It can warn me if need be."

An eight-inch-long creature, similar to a weasel, with two long striped legs, rushed over to stand proudly in front of them, ready for action.

"I'll be back in half an hour at the most. I'm going to change, this is really no time to catch pneumonia," said Dragomira, as if talking to herself.

Then, addressing the two friends:

"I'm going to take an ointment to Leomido to treat that poor Gargantuhen's leg. Lunatrixes, I'll leave these children in your capable hands."

Oksa wondered what this mysterious Colocynthis might be but, from the strained look on her gran's face, she guessed it might be better to leave her questions until later. Anyway Dragomira had just turned on her heels, carefully locking the door behind her. Astounded, Gus and Oksa looked at each other.

"Well! I'd really like to know what's going on," remarked Gus.

"I'll tell you how I see things," continued Oksa in a low voice. "From what I know, Black Globuses are very dangerous Granoks; some of them are even lethal. The Felons perfected them to attack Edefia. I've already seen a man hit by one of those Granoks on the Camereye and it was horrific. This Colocynthis obviously belongs to the same category. And that would mean that the Gargantuhen was attacked by a Felon."

"A Felon! You're out of your mind. How could that be?"

"I don't know, Gus. Lunatrixa?" asked Oksa, suddenly turning to the little creature, which was staring at her. "You did say that someone broke into the estate last night?"

"Yes, Young Gracious, the truth is thus," replied the Lunatrixa.

"What else do you know? Tell me! I'm the Young Gracious!" ordered Oksa more curtly than she would have liked, which made her flush slightly.

This was the first time that she had flaunted her status and she felt slightly ashamed at taking advantage of such a considerate creature as the Lunatrixa. She was about to apologize when the little steward, her eyes filled with panic, began speaking nervously:

"The Master and the Old Gracious had a great vocal anxiety yesterday, their fear could be measured. I have already made the explanation to the Young Gracious of all the details which were in my head and I do not know any supplementary information, that is my promise!"

"Okay, Lunatrixa, calm down," replied Oksa, patting her head. "Thank you for your help."

Then, turning to Gus, she continued excitedly:

"You see! Something is going on. I'm sure that the intruder the other night has something to do with this business of the Black Globus. If that's the case, he's still in the vicinity, I'm sure of it. And don't forget that the Abominari has disappeared—there may be a connection."

"You're probably right, but what I'd like to know is why that poor Gargantuhen was attacked," added her friend.

"The Gargantuhen may not have been the target."

"You mean—"

The front door banged heavily. The children fell silent and Oksa put her index finger over her lips to warn the Lunatrixa to keep silent about what they had just said.

"Yes, my Young Gracious, I have understanding."

Leomido came into the living room, looking drawn. He seemed to be making a great effort not to show how worried he was, but his eyes kept scanning the room from left to right, without coming to rest on anything. His obvious anxiety didn't escape Gus's or Oksa's attention.

"Well, Leomido? Is the Gargantuhen feeling better?" asked Oksa, getting up from her armchair to come over to him.

"Yes, much better," he replied, pouring himself a glass of brandy which he knocked back in one.

"We were able to save its leg, it has almost returned to normal, thanks again to Dragomira and Abakum's talents. I'd never have thought that I'd have to use that ointment…"

"What ointment?" asked Oksa. But Leomido didn't seem to hear the question. Looking distraught, the elderly man stood near the hearth, holding his empty glass.

"Did Baba stay with the Gargantuhen?" continued Oksa, in a fresh bid to rouse Leomido from his daze.

"Yes, to keep an eye on it," he replied finally in a dull voice. "The poor bird has had quite a shock."

Oksa looked at Leomido even more intently. Although the Gargantuhen was feeling better, her great-uncle didn't seem to be doing so well.

"Isn't that a little dangerous? I mean… Baba… all on her own there? What happened exactly, Leomido?"

Leomido sat down in an armchair and leant back, once again totally lost in thought.

"What did you say, Oksa?" he responded. "Sorry, I was miles away."

"Isn't Baba in danger, all on her own there, after what happened?"

"Everything's back to normal, don't worry," he said weakly.

Oksa glanced sceptically at Gus, who shrugged his shoulders in irritation. He gestured back, indicating that it might be better to leave it there, even if it meant trying to get answers to their questions later, possibly by other means. Agreeing with this suggestion, Oksa continued:

"Talking of Baba, she did something completely amazing back there!"

"I couldn't agree more," added Gus enthusiastically. "How did she do that? It was incredible!"

"You mean the Aqua-Flottis?" asked Leomido, who was now giving them his full attention. "I knew that would surprise you."

"Us? Surprised? You're not kidding," exclaimed Oksa. "We were completely blown away!"

"It's one of the Gracious's powers," explained Leomido, with a faint smile. "It's a great privilege for Insiders and much more than that, surely, for Outsiders. So mum's the word, as you can imagine. You can talk to Dragomira about it, she'll be able to explain it better than I can.

257

But I wanted to make a suggestion, because we shouldn't interrupt our schedule. Would you like to go for a short flight?"

"Are we going to Vertifly?" cried Oksa.

"No, not this time," replied Leomido. "We're going to take a ride in a hot-air balloon."

"Whoa! I'd love that!" exclaimed Gus, jumping up from his armchair.

Oksa echoed him, clapping loudly.

"Thanks, Leomido. That's so great!"

"I'm going to change into some more suitable clothes. I won't be a minute, wait here for me."

As soon as the elderly man had disappeared upstairs, the two friends began talking ten to the dozen.

"Well, that's a bit strange, all the same! We've just been involved in something weird and Leomido wants to carry on as planned, as if nothing untoward has happened... and yet he looked really upset. Honestly, don't you think there's something peculiar about that?"

"Yes," agreed Gus. "But I'm sure that from the hot-air balloon we'll be able to see who fired the Black Globus—he must still be on the estate. So, even though it might seem odd to take this trip given the circumstances, it's actually quite a good idea, isn't it?"

42

A STRANGE ENCOUNTER

"THIS IS SUCH FUN!"

Gus and Oksa were full of enthusiasm. They had a breathtaking view from the basket of the yellow and red hot-air balloon, which was floating over Leomido's estate. The sea was sparkling just a few miles away.

"Can we go there, Leomido?" asked Oksa, thrilled by this trip.

"Your wish is my command, Young Gracious. Setting our course for the sea!" said Leomido.

While working the controls, Leomido kept gazing around, studying the hills and valleys with a furrowed brow and narrowed eyes, as if on the lookout for something. This was not lost on Oksa, who murmured knowingly to Gus:

"I'm sure he's looking for the intruder—or our attacker. It's bound to be the same person, I'd stake my life on it. And don't forget that the Abominari is also lurking around here somewhere…"

"It's obvious that this trip is no coincidence," agreed Gus, in a whisper. "There's something very fishy about setting off like this now, of all times."

The balloon glided slowly and silently above the hills they'd been walking across two hours earlier. The gorse and tall grass rippling in the breeze made it a beautiful sight. The sea was drawing closer. Oksa and Gus could already see the overhanging cliffs, and the small cove below was just a hundred yards away. It was then that the uninjured Gargantuhen suddenly emerged from the sheltered cove. The two friends gave a shout of amazement.

"What on earth is it doing there?"

Leomido immediately busied himself with the controls, as if he'd expected this slightly peculiar surprise.

"Hold on tight, children, I'm taking it down!" he shouted.

Oksa and Gus soon realized that he was right to think ahead: the Gargantuhen's powerful wings were beating hard a hundred feet or so from their craft, and it looked as if it might collide with them. Leomido opened the valve and they all gripped the basket tightly as they watched the creature advancing on them. But despite their efforts to manoeuvre away from the Gargantuhen, the bird was drawing closer and closer to the balloon. As if it were following them. OR EVEN PURSUING THEM. Whether Leomido veered to the right or left, whether he gained height or descended, the giant hen immediately mirrored his movements. Suddenly the three of them heard faint shouts and, despite their indistinctness, Oksa thought she could make out her great-uncle's name.

"Leomido, I think someone's calling you from the Gargantuhen!" she exclaimed.

"What? That's impossible!"

But it wasn't. She'd definitely heard Leomido's name. As the Gargantuhen drew closer, their doubts vanished. Leomido took out his Granok-Shooter and summoned a Reticulata in an attempt to see who might be calling him so persistently. With the jellyfish magnifying glass in front of him he paused for a moment, unmoving, his eyes wide with amazement. Then the colour drained from his face as he gripped the rim of the basket.

"No, it's not possible! It can't be him," he muttered, as if he'd just seen a ghost.

They could clearly see a dark figure moving around on the Gargantuhen's back—a figure which looked strangely familiar to Gus and Oksa. But no—it had to be a vague resemblance. A hallucination. Something

260

wrong with their eyes. *Seriously* wrong with their eyes. *Very seriously* wrong with their eyes.

"Gus, I think we have a problem," murmured Oksa, gesturing at her ashen great-uncle.

"Yes... and we also have a problem over there," replied Gus in a dull voice, pointing at the Gargantuhen which, as it came closer, confirmed their initial impression. "LOOK!"

Oksa turned and had the shock of her life. A horrifying sight. A waking nightmare. There was Dr McGraw! Horrible, revolting, unbearable McGraw, dreadfully close! Riding on the Gargantuhen's back in the Welsh sky, a couple of hundred miles away from home!

"McGRAW!" chorused the two friends.

"ORTHON!" said Leomido in a hollow voice.

The giant hen with its terrible rider drew nearer, dispelling any remaining doubts. McGraw bellowed Leomido's name and Oksa looked at her great-uncle in complete confusion, her eyes beseeching him for some kind of explanation, however minimal it might be. Time seemed to stand still for a fraction of a second as his eyes met hers and Oksa read the terror in them, as if Leomido were facing his last moments on Earth. He pulled himself together and shook his head, trying to banish his frightening thoughts.

"Get down, children, stay out of sight!" he snapped, sounding unusually curt and looking distraught.

He hurriedly worked the burner of the balloon, which rose sharply but, as feared, McGraw manoeuvred the Gargantuhen perfectly and followed hard on their heels.

"Leomido!" he yelled. "Give me Oksa. You owe me that much. I've dedicated my whole life to this moment, that child is my key!"

"You're mad, Orthon!" replied Leomido.

"You're a fine one to talk about madness. You're living a life of mediocrity. Join me! I've discovered a world here on the Outside which is worthy of my ambitions, a world in which I've been planning my return at the head of an army. This is the start of a new era, an era of power and light. Don't stand against me, Leomido. My powers are immense and your only choice is to co-operate with me if you want to live!"

"What is he saying? What does he mean? How does he know you?" screamed Oksa in terror, clutching at Leomido, who immediately pulled away to concentrate on the controls.

She huddled at the bottom of the basket and darted a panicked look at Gus, who came to crouch down beside her. "*We're done for!*" she was screaming inside her head.

"See? I was right! McGraw was looking for me, he's not a teacher, he's here to abduct me! I was right, oh Gus—"

"Orthon!" shouted Leomido over the rim of the basket. "Give up! Oksa will never come with you. NEVER. Do you hear me? Go back to where you came from!"

"What about all your promises? I'm here to make sure you keep them. Give me Oksa!" replied Orthon-McGraw.

Oksa was baffled and panic-stricken by what she was hearing. Her whole body was shaking in despair. She cowered back in a corner of the basket, with Gus next to her.

"What's all this about? Why is Leomido calling him Orthon? I don't understand—I'm scared stiff."

"Oksa, did you bring your Granok-Shooter?" asked Gus hurriedly. Oksa nodded.

"I think it's time to show what you're made of. C'mon! It's up to you now," he encouraged her forcefully.

"You're right!" she said, getting a grip on herself.

She took out the slender tube, which she kept in the inside pocket of her jacket, and sat up a little straighter. Raising her head just above the rim of the basket, she saw McGraw a few yards away with something glinting in the sun aimed at the balloon envelope. Was it a weapon? A gun? She tried to concentrate, but everything had been driven from her mind by the terror, making rational thought impossible.

"Oksa!" Gus shook her. "Quick! You've got to do something!"

But Oksa's mind was a complete blank. No matter how hard she thought, she couldn't remember the slightest thing that Dragomira had told her a few hours ago. On the verge of tears, she looked at Gus in panic.

"I can't remember anything, Gus, I've forgotten it all!"

Gus leant over and whispered a few words in her ear. Just in time. With her heart brimful of rage and fear, deeply grateful for Dragomira's incredible intuition and Gus's amazing ability to keep a cool head, she spoke the name—which she'd just recalled thanks to her friend's prompting:

"Tornaphyllon!"

Then, aiming directly at McGraw, she blew into the Granok-Shooter. As soon as the Granok was expelled, the Gargantuhen began spinning madly and was swept away by a whirlwind which had suddenly formed and carried off everything in its path.

"Oksa, you did it! You're amazing!" cried Gus exultantly. "Oh! What's that?"

A worrying black patch was coming closer. Like a thick, shifting cloud of starlings, the patch suddenly surged towards them.

"Watch out, children!" yelled Leomido. "Death's Head Chiropterans! Get down and cover your heads. Don't let them bite you at any cost!"

Gus and Oksa just had time to see a hideous swarm of mutant insects heading for their balloon. They crouched down while Leomido defended them by throwing large fireballs. In the basket, the two friends could hear the sickening crackle of the insects being burnt by the flames—but also the terrifying buzzing of the survivors, which were still managing to attack them against all odds. Copying Leomido, Oksa concentrated and threw a few fireballs which hit their target. Immediately the charred bodies of these repulsive Death's Head Chiropterans, the largest specimens being almost three inches long, plummeted to the ground. One, tougher or more stubborn than its counterparts, managed to get through the barrier of fire created by Leomido and Oksa and raced ferociously towards Gus. Its wings began smoking, there was the stench of burning flesh and the hideous insect gave a bloodcurdling scream of agony.

"How can it still be alive?" hissed Gus. "It's on fire! It's burning right before our eyes!"

At the sight of its gaping mouth, which showed a glimpse of razor-sharp fangs, the boy panicked. Before he had time to react, he felt a sharp pain near his ear: the foul creature had bitten him. He crushed it with a violent slap of the hand, as a greenish, viscous substance trickled down his cheek. He grimaced, wiping his face nervously and picked up the insect with his fingertips to examine it more closely. When he saw its horrible little head, he realized immediately where it had got its name and, feeling sick, threw it overboard. On the other side, the poor Gargantuhen was losing speed and height as it was buffeted by the tornado. It was uttering heart-rending cries and struggling to throw off its rider. Suddenly, it unseated him with a mighty blow from its wing. Stunned, McGraw lost his balance as the Gargantuhen fell towards the sea and they both unceremoniously crashed into the water. Meanwhile, tensely clutching the controls, Leomido guided the red and yellow balloon inland as McGraw's loud threats rang out over the moor.

43

A BLEAK REPORT

"**A**LARM! ALARM! AN ACCIDENT HAS BEFALLEN THE friend of our Young Gracious! He has plunged into unconsciousness and a bad injury has stained his face with blood! Alarm!"

Leomido's Lunatrix was wailing and wringing his hands. Standing opposite him, the Lunatrixa turned so white that she looked almost translucent. Then she started reeling from the shock. Tottering dangerously from one foot to another, she stammered:

"He... he has undertaken a fall from the balloon?"

"No, my Lunatrixa," replied her companion gravely. "The wound has been attributed by a monstrous danger... a Death's Head Chiropteran."

"A Death's Head Chiropteran? But the Chiropterans come from Edefia! The Felons—"

The Lunatrixa didn't have time to finish her sentence: overwhelmed by anxiety, she collapsed on the floor. The Lunatrix rushed over to her and without further ado blew on her chubby face until she came to her senses. At that moment, the heavy front door swung open on its hinges with a hideous squeal. Leomido's tall figure appeared on the doorstep, to the relief of the panic-stricken little creatures. Unfortunately, as the Lunatrix had announced, this was a grim homecoming: Leomido was cradling the unconscious Gus, who had an ugly mark like a snakebite on the side of his face. All around it the swollen skin had turned the disturbing colour of rotten fruit, which extended down the left side of the boy's face. Oksa, feeling nauseated at the strong stench from the wound, couldn't take her eyes off her friend and was struggling to combat feelings of panic.

When Leomido laid the injured boy on one of the sofas in the large living room, Gus's eyes half opened to reveal white, milky eyeballs that looked lifeless and had rolled back in his head. For a minute, Oksa thought the worst had happened—Gus would never get better. She groaned and her nostrils pricked violently as her entire body felt as if it was filling up with bitter tears. But after a few seconds, which seemed to last for hours, Gus's dark-blue eyes began to regain their normal appearance. For a few seconds more there was no expression in his eyes, as if his brain had stopped functioning. Then a gleam appeared in their depths: he was coming round.

"My Lunatrix, run and get Dragomira," ordered Leomido. "Don't worry, Oksa," he added, turning to his great-niece. "Dragomira will know what to do, Gus will be okay."

It was close on midnight when the last Runaways finally filed into the living room. Arriving shortly after Mercedica, the proud Spanish woman who was a member of Baba's Band, Naftali and Brune Knut, Tugdual's eccentric grandparents, removed their heavy overcoats and greeted their friends.

"You're all here," murmured Naftali. "Good evening, Young Gracious," he added, staring at Oksa.

Oksa hadn't met the Knuts before and she was amazed by their imposing appearance. She'd never seen such an astonishing couple. Naftali was unusually tall and bald, and the lower part of his face was covered with a fine, almost translucent down. His black velvet clothes were adorned by a single ornament: a necklace of tiny gleaming green pearls, which set off his enigmatic emerald-green eyes. Staring at Oksa, he put his hand on his wife's arm and she bowed slightly, saying in a guttural voice:

"Delighted to make your acquaintance, Young Gracious."

Brune Knut was just as striking as her husband. She looked around seventy, perhaps even eighty. Wearing trousers under an asymmetrical dress, she cut an eccentric figure. Her snow-white bobbed hair showed an ear pierced along the rim with at least ten small diamonds. The top of her upper lip was also adorned with a little stone which glinted when she bowed to Oksa.

"Good evening," said the girl, awed at being treated with so much respect by such an elegant woman.

She sat on the carpet, her arms clasped round her knees, and tried to hide her embarrassment. Around her, despite the warmth of that splendid room, the mood was serious and expressions grave. Clustered in a semicircle in front of the huge hearth, they exchanged remarks in low voices, glancing at her in concern. She felt the weight of their gaze upon her but her angry thoughts were erecting a barrier between them and her. Instinctively, she looked up at the ceiling with its stucco tracery. Gus's room was just above them. He was feeling better thanks to Dragomira's salves and concoctions, each more mysterious than the last. But he'd had a terrible shock and he needed to rest. Anyway he'd soon fallen into a deep sleep. Oksa had watched over him for a while, worried and upset by her friend's drawn features and his deathly pallor. The image haunted her. She shivered and looked around for her parents, who had arrived only two hours after the terrifying accident, together with Pierre and Jeanne Bellanger. She couldn't understand what Gus's parents were doing here—particularly in these somewhat unusual circumstances. Apart from Gus, no Bellanger had any reason to be at a meeting for Runaways, and yet no one seemed surprised. Oksa had dragged Dragomira to one side in an attempt to question her briefly, but Baba Pollock had merely waved her hand vaguely in what was supposed to be a reassuring manner: she had to be patient, she'd have answers soon enough.

Dragomira sat down stiffly, her voluminous plum-coloured dress flaring out around her, and began nervously fraying the silk fringes of the armrest with her fingers until she'd reduced them to fine threads. Then she cleared her throat to attract the attention of everyone there.

"My friends," she said finally, sounding tense. "For over fifty years we've feared it might be so, but today, alas, we had it confirmed: at least one of the Felons managed to pass through the Portal. The son of Edefia's worst enemy is on the Outside and has succeeded in getting very close to the heart of our hope," she added, looking at Oksa.

A wave of panic swept through the entire room. The Lunatrixes uttered a shrill cry, echoed by Jeanne and Marie.

"What happened exactly? Tell us, Leomido!" said Pavel, his voice shaking.

Beaded with perspiration, Leomido closed his eyes for a brief moment, then reopened them.

"He first attacked in the early afternoon," he said in a hollow voice. "One of my Gargantuhens suffered the consequences. But that was nothing compared to what we had to face two hours later…"

Leomido fell silent and swallowed with difficulty.

"He attacked again?" prompted Naftali.

"Yes," continued the elderly man. "With a strength that staggered me. I really thought we weren't going to be able to outmatch him. Fortunately, Oksa and Gus were very brave," he added. "Otherwise he would have got his hands on Oksa. She reacted quickly by firing a Tornaphyllon Granok at him, but he retaliated by sending a swarm of Death's Head Chiropterans against us."

A shudder of concern ran through the Runaways.

"How terrible! You were lucky to escape!" said Jeanne Bellanger in alarm, appearing to know what they were talking about, much to Oksa's puzzlement.

"Yes," agreed Leomido. "As you know, Gus was injured, but the bite is superficial. Dragomira has done what was necessary and he's out of danger."

"What about after-effects?" asked Naftali hastily, looking concerned. "Chiropterans are extremely—"

"Let's not complicate matters for no reason," said Leomido curtly, cutting her off.

"How were you able to escape the swarm of Death's Heads?" continued Mercedica, staring at Leomido.

"We threw Fireballisticos at them and burned those horrors to a cinder. But it's Oksa who should take all the credit for our escape. Thanks to her, the Gargantuhen was carried off in the direction of the sea."

"And thanks to Gus," murmured Oksa.

"You're right!" agreed Leomido. "They were both remarkably cool-headed. For my part, I couldn't believe my eyes when I saw we were being attacked in the sky. It was stupefying. It had obviously been carefully planned. And what looked at first like a mistaken target during the attack on my Gargantuhen was actually intended to draw me into the sky. He always found me so predictable."

"It was really him then? You're sure?" butted in Naftali.

"Yes, there's no doubt about it, it was Orthon, Ocious's son."

"No, it was McGraw, our maths teacher!" said Oksa loudly, interrupting him.

All eyes were suddenly on her. Pavel gave a shout of rage. White as a sheet, Marie caught hold of his arm, her eyes open wide. Jeanne and Pierre looked at each other in amazement.

"Your maths teacher?" stammered Dragomira, sounding at a loss.

"Well..." replied Oksa hesitantly. "He's not a real teacher."

Everyone stared at her.

"Oops," said Oksa, with the unpleasant sensation of having said too much. "Sorry."

"What do you mean?" insisted her father in a broken voice.

Oksa hesitated for a second. Then, encouraged by her father, she explained almost inaudibly:

"Until today, Gus and I thought that McGraw had been sent by the secret services and that he wanted to abduct me to experiment on my brain."

"WHAT?"

Everyone in the living room had shouted in unison, including the Lunatrixes, who were wringing their hands in the corner. Oksa looked down, embarrassed at being the focus of attention, as well as the subject of conversation and the cause of all these problems.

"Wait!" said Marie, sounding frightened. "You mean that since you started school, you've both thought that your maths teacher was some kind of mercenary, who was planning to kidnap you?"

"What made you think that?" asked Abakum, his resonant voice calm.

Oksa glanced at Dragomira in desperation.

"We investigated him."

"What on earth do you mean?" grumbled Pavel, frowning.

"Everyone hates and fears him," continued Oksa. "We always thought there was something fishy about him, and not just because he's an awful teacher, whatever you may think. It was because, right from the start, it was as if he knew everything about me, as if he'd always known who I was! A few days ago, we managed to get hold of his administrative file."

"I'd rather not know how," muttered Pavel.

"There were notes to the effect that he worked for the CIA and NASA. He specialized in photoelectricity and is fascinated by Einstein's work on light."

"Oh come on," grumbled Abakum.

"Straightaway, we thought it was unlikely that someone would leave NASA to come and teach maths to high-school students," continued Oksa, with a brief glance at her father. "Then we discovered that he'd applied to St Proximus College for personal reasons—and his personal reasons were ME! That's why we thought he was a secret agent who was looking for me; but we never thought he might be a Felon!"

It would have been an understatement to say that the Runaways were rooted to the spot with amazement. They were all paralysed by Oksa's and Leomido's revelations. Breathing hard, their eyes anxious, the Runaways were all trying to take in this incredible information. As for Oksa, her mind was working overtime and everything was falling into place. Her slate-grey eyes widened as all the pieces fitted together perfectly.

"Oh dear," she exclaimed suddenly. "I don't believe it!"

44

WORRYING REACTIONS

I F HER OWN CONCLUSIONS WERE ANYTHING TO GO BY, Oksa had the awful feeling that they were getting mixed up in something much more dangerous than they might have thought.

"Are you going to tell us what you're thinking?" asked Pavel tensely.

Oksa looked at him mechanically, her face expressionless. She shook her head to pull herself together and blinked.

"At St Proximus, there was a maths teacher called Williams," she began hoarsely. "Just before we started school, he was found dead in the Thames—murdered. This appears to have been a horrible murder, and one shrouded in mystery, as our friend Merlin Poicassé told us."

"My goodness!" exclaimed Dragomira. "And... does anyone know how the man died?"

This was clearly the question on everyone's lips—a crucial question with a frightening answer.

"Er, no," muttered Oksa. "But I have a few thoughts on the matter."

With that, she jumped to her feet and rushed into Leomido's office, which was adjoining the large living room. She turned on her great-uncle's computer and, a few seconds later, was on the net. All the Runaways had gathered around her, their eyes fixed on the screen, which they could only partly see. A page from a newspaper, taken from the *Times* archive, flashed up. Oksa moved closer to the screen and scanned the article at top speed. Never had she read so quickly.

When she had finished she gave a low whistle, her hands tense on the computer keyboard.

"Tell us now!" said Mercedica curtly. "We want to know."

"Well, not only is McGraw a Felon, he's also a murderer!" exclaimed Oksa, looking both triumphant and terrified. "He killed Dr Williams to take his place."

"But that's terrible!" cried Dragomira in alarm.

"And that's not all," continued Oksa, fidgeting. "He also killed the journalist Peter Carter because he was becoming too dangerous. And here's the proof."

The Runaways felt their blood run cold. The *Times* article they were reading provided horrific details about the death of Lucas Williams, the highly respected maths teacher from St Proximus College, found in the Thames two weeks before school started. Scotland Yard detectives said that the cause of death was a mystery: the victim's lungs had literally been dissolved by a substance whose origin had not yet been identified by any scientific laboratory. The foremost international specialists had studied this unknown toxin, but had been unable to determine its strange composition. No one had managed to shed any light on the murder of Lucas Williams when another, strangely similar, case had occurred. The body of Peter Carter had been found. And the famous American investigative journalist had died in exactly the same way as Williams.

"Dad?" said Oksa, when everyone had finished reading the article. "Remember when you said it *had* to be one of you who killed Peter Carter? Well, you were right, it was a Runaway—but that Runaway is a Felon: it's McGraw! Or Orthon, if you prefer... he's the one who fired a Pulmonis at Lucas Williams and Peter Carter."

Everyone seemed glued to the spot in amazement as they tried to assimilate this incredible theory.

"Wait..." broke in Leomido unsteadily. "How can you be so sure when you're just basing your theory on supposition; this is a very serious matter."

"I'd swear to it or stake my life on it—anything you like—that McGraw did this," retorted Oksa angrily, her hands on her hips. "He had one big fat motive, whether it was Williams or Carter."

"A motive, however genuine it might be, doesn't make someone a murderer," replied Leomido sternly.

"That may be true," admitted Abakum, looking at him. "But if it wasn't him, then it was one of us. And frankly, my dear Leomido, I would doubt that. Oksa's theory seems to vex you, but it appears more than likely to me. The death of Lucas Williams allowed Orthon to get close to Oksa. As for Peter Carter, he was about to discover our origins. He was becoming a danger to Orthon as well as to us, because we share the same secret, remember. However, even if he removed the threat of Peter Carter, Orthon still poses a very real danger for us. What happened today is clear proof of that and adds more weight to the case for the prosecution: unleashing Chiropterans on someone is not a trivial act. Particularly when used against children and his former best friend."

A few of them exchanged worried glances without saying a single word. In the leaden silence, Oksa became aware of the seriousness of the situation and particularly of the consequences of the day's revelations.

"I have to show you something!" she cried, whirling round so fast that she knocked over the Lunatrix, who was in her way.

Watched inquisitively by the Runaways, Oksa raced out of the room, almost tripping over her undone shoelace. She stuffed it into her trainer and rushed upstairs, taking the steps four at a time. A door slammed and she soon reappeared triumphantly brandishing a small piece of paper folded in eight.

"Gus and I found this in McGraw's wallet," she said.

"*Found?*" repeated her father, rubbing his chin with his hand.

"It's some sort of list," continued Oksa. "It's very odd, I'm at the bottom. There's also your daughter, Leomido… and you, Jeanne," she added, looking at Gus's mother.

The Runaways watched even more attentively as she unfolded the piece of paper and handed it to Dragomira. Then they gathered around Baba Pollock, who softly read out the mysterious list drawn up by McGraw:

G.L. 19/04/54 Kagoshima (Jap.) 10/67+08/68
G.F. 09/06/60 London (Engl.) 09/73+05/74+01/75
J.K. 12/12/64 Plzeň (Czech.) 04/77+02/78
H.K. 01/12/67 Mänttä (Finl.) 11/79+10/80
A.P. 07/05/79 Mýrdalsjökull (Icel.) 01/91+06/92
C.W. 16/03/88 Houston (USA) 12/99+05/01+10/01
Z.E. 29/04/96 Amsterdam (Neth.) 07/08
O.P. 29/09/96 Paris (Fr.) 05/09

From the first lines, there was unanimous consternation.

"Incredible..." said Dragomira with difficulty, laying the piece of paper on her lap. "How did he do it?"

Oksa waited, feverishly biting a nail. Finally Dragomira looked up and everyone stared at her.

"What you have found here is worth its weight in gold," she said, trying to control her excitement.

"But what is it exactly?" asked Oksa.

"The list of girls who had the potential to be a Gracious."

"Wow!" said Oksa, dumbfounded.

"Exactly, Dushka," agreed Dragomira. "The information you've just given us is priceless. Orthon, or McGraw, which is the same thing since he's actually the same person, has obviously dedicated his life to finding out how to return to Edefia. Firstly, through his scientific work on light, which has a direct connection with the Portal—the only way into Edefia, remember—and then by constantly searching the world for the Gracious who might be able to give him access. This list sends shivers up my spine, but it's clear proof. We know most of the people on it and they are all the daughters or granddaughters of Runaways."

"My daughter's there," confirmed Naftali, without taking her eyes off the list.

"Mine too," muttered Leomido.

Oksa began thinking aloud:

"I'm so stupid not to have understood earlier… really stupid. I was so sure that McGraw was a secret agent that I just saw this as a list of people in our circle of friends and family whom he could use to get to us."

"But that's the case, Oksa!" broke in Pavel. "Most of the names on this list are known to the Pollocks. You couldn't have realized that they were Runaways."

"You don't say…" remarked Oksa, gazing into space.

"Whether he's a secret agent or a Felon, Orthon-McGraw is here for you, Oksa, this proves it," explained Abakum. "You're clearly in great danger—he won't let you go. All his scheming and those terrible murders were just a way of getting to you."

"Yes, and he's succeeded perfectly!" added Dragomira.

"So, if I understand you correctly, you mean that this Orthon-McGraw, our children's maths teacher, is a Runaway who is a Felon, as well as a dangerous murderer?" summed up Marie in a flat voice, addressing Leomido and Abakum.

"I wouldn't call him a dangerous murderer," remarked Leomido bitterly.

"You're very lenient!" retorted Naftali.

"The reason I wanted you all to come here today," continued Leomido without reacting to this remark, "was to keep you informed and also to reassure you. Even if many years have passed, I know Orthon well. Don't forget that we were very close in Edefia, we were almost raised together. He's not the person you think he is; you mustn't judge a book by its cover."

An agitated hubbub broke out and grew louder. Everyone was talking at the same time and the tone of the conversations made it clear that not everyone agreed with Leomido. Abakum was the only one who didn't say anything—he just looked at him with deep disapproval. Leomido appeared unsettled, but he managed to continue in a dull voice:

"I know Orthon wouldn't harm Oksa."

"But he did try to kidnap her!" shouted Pavel. "And, in case you're forgetting, let me remind you that he set Death's Head Chiropterans on them!"

"That's true," acknowledged Leomido, almost reluctantly. "But they weren't intended for Oksa, Orthon needs her too much. He'd never do her any harm, that's for sure. She's too valuable to him."

"Well, you wouldn't think so," grumbled Marie.

"I agree with you, Leomido, we can't judge by appearances," interjected Abakum, smoothing his short beard with his fingertips. "Those who knew him know that Orthon wasn't always a cruel man. But face facts, my friend. You may remember the boy he was, but don't ignore the man he's become."

Leomido, his eyes unblinking, looked even more unsettled. He stiffened in his armchair, then slumped down suddenly, distraught. None of the Runaways dared to speak and silence descended on the large room. A log crackled in the hearth, making some of them start and others cry out.

"The boy he was?" whispered Oksa, turning to her gran. "What was he like?"

Dragomira's only reply was to get up heavily from her armchair and take down a picture. She sat down again and stared at the bare wall. Immediately, some images appeared.

"The Camereye!" murmured Oksa, impatient to see this live broadcast of her grandmother's memories.

The first scene which appeared on the wall seemed to date back to when Dragomira was still a child. The Runaways saw a birthday cake decorated with seven candles and Oksa recognized various people sitting around a heavily laden table from previous Camereye screenings: Gracious Malorane—Dragomira's mother—her husband Waldo, as well as three young men.

"There's Abakum," explained Dragomira, "and that's Leomido and Orthon."

277

The latter boy looked about fifteen. Slender, almost puny, in appearance, he had a sweet face framed by brown hair. Oksa shuddered: since Dragomira was the focus of Orthon's attention, the young man appeared to be looking straight at Oksa and everyone else watching the Camereye. There was nothing unsettling about his gaze, though; quite the opposite. Full of kindness and affection, it formed a complete contrast with the expression Oksa had seen that very afternoon.

"Come on, blow out your candles! And don't forget to make a wish!" Orthon cried out to little Dragomira.

The Camereye broke off for a moment to move on to another sequence, this time a more athletic scene in the air: Dragomira was probably flying, with Leomido and Orthon.

"Leomido's going to win again!" called Orthon cheerfully. "Quick, Dragomira, we've got to catch him!"

But Dragomira's memories were racing past and no one ever discovered the outcome of that chase: the Camereye was already showing a third sequence. Orthon was sitting opposite Leomido and looked terribly sad.

"I'm far from being the perfect son for a man like him," he said to his friend. "He can't bear who I am. You're the son he would have liked— someone brave with a strong, determined character..."

A fourth scene appeared on the wall and Oksa recognized the setting as the Glass Column, the residence of the Graciouses. A stormy conversation was shaking the glass walls and they saw the frail young Orthon rush out of a room. It seemed as though Dragomira wasn't supposed to be there, because they couldn't see part of the scene, as if she were behind a pillar.

"How could you hide something like that? Do you realize that *they* are the ones who're paying for it today? You and your damn secret are entirely to blame. If anyone is immoral, it's YOU, not them!" yelled Orthon, slamming the door behind him.

A weeping Malorane came out of the room and walked over to Orthon, who was shaking all over. She tried to get near him but he shoved her away roughly.

"I'll never forgive you!" he yelled. "Do you hear me? NEVER!"

The last image shown by Dragomira's Camereye was still clear in Oksa's memory: a young man in a leather helmet was confronting Malorane's supporters, who were trying to escape. Orthon. The Great Chaos. Of course… There was no kindness left in the face of the man who had become a Felon. Much to Oksa's surprise and confusion, his hard, cruel eyes seemed to hold great suffering, something which she hadn't noticed during the first screening of her gran's memories. The Camereye went totally blank and Dragomira kept her eyes shut for a few seconds, looking totally unreachable. Opposite her, Leomido seemed to be having difficulty breathing.

"That's what Orthon was like," remarked Dragomira, coming back to herself. "A charming young man broken by his father; a fragile, unhappy man who was our best friend and who became our enemy. Will we ever know what happened?"

She gazed intently at her brother with moist eyes. Leomido opened his mouth but nothing came out. He swallowed with great difficulty and his face looked even more drawn.

"All I know," he managed to murmur, "is that after his audience with Malorane, everything deteriorated. Orthon was never the same."

The elderly man stood up and heavily walked out of the room, watched by the Runaways.

⁂

"Leomido is right," said Abakum after a few long minutes, "Orthon can't afford to hurt Oksa, that's for sure. But he can do a great deal of damage to obtain his ends—he has already proved what he is capable of, both in Edefia and on the Outside. You only have to look at what he did to Gus to be convinced of that. I don't think his character has softened over the years. He may even have become harder… he's a bitter, ambitious man who knows what he wants and will do anything to get it. His dearest wish is to return to Edefia. After all, don't forget that his father Ocious is still there."

"That guy is the Devil incarnate," Tugdual said coldly, ensconced in a love seat well away from the rest of the group. "Haven't you realized that yet? What he wants is to conquer the world and make us all grovel at his feet."

"ENOUGH!" thundered his grandfather, Naftali. "You don't know anything."

"Tugdual is right!" cried Oksa suddenly, meeting the boy's steely eyes. "When we were in the hot-air balloon, Orthon said he was preparing to go back to Edefia at the head of an army and that this would be the start of a new era."

Abakum looked dispirited.

"Leomido neglected to tell us that small detail," he said.

Oksa chewed her lip, feeling embarrassed at betraying her great-uncle. But this was terribly important.

"Orthon has the means to dominate us all, and you know I'm right," added Tugdual, his eyes blazing. "The countdown has begun."

45

THE BELLANGERS' SECRET

A FROSTY SILENCE DESCENDED ON THE GATHERING. Everyone was lost in thought. As for Oksa, she was dumbfounded: horrible McGraw and Leomido had been childhood friends! It was strange to think of that sensitive, mixed-up boy as the man who'd caused all her problems since starting school. She was also beginning to have her doubts about Leomido. In particular, she thought it odd that he'd played down the danger posed by Orthon-McGraw, when he'd been in an ideal position to observe the Felon's persistence and his violent attack. The two men might have been close friends once, but the encounter this afternoon had proved that their friendship was now a thing of the past. Orthon-McGraw had changed long before the Great Chaos, everyone had seen that. So how could her great-uncle be really sure that the villain didn't mean to harm her and her family? What if he hurt them? Or Gus? Abakum was right: even if McGraw didn't seem to be the secret agent she'd imagined, the fact that he was a one-time Felon didn't bode well at all. In some ways it was worse. Making the most of everyone's preoccupation, Oksa got up and walked out of the living room. She had to move or she'd go mad! She went to the kitchen and gulped down a glass of water, then retraced her steps, feeling uneasy about being on her own. Walking through the hall, she noticed Leomido's Lunatrixes deep in conversation under the stairwell. She tiptoed over and listened.

"The Felon Orthon carried out a double murder, that is a certainty!" whispered the Lunatrix to the panic-stricken Lunatrixa.

"So the evidence is that Orthon, son of Ocious the hated Felon, experienced departure from Edefia? Like us with our accompaniment of the Old Gracious?" she asked, her complexion more chalky white than ever.

"The truth is disastrous but implacable, my Lunatrixa. The Felon Orthon has settled his life near us and is preparing plans of great ugliness. Courage and strength must be mustered to fight Felony. And, above all, the hope of return to Edefia must be preserved despite cunning ambushes."

"Cunning but powerful," corrected the Lunatrixa. "You have a hollow memory."

"It is the Young Gracious who possesses the supreme power, my Lunatrixa. Keep trust warm in your heart."

The Lunatrix broke off. His chubby face immediately turned an incredible purple, a sign of extreme embarrassment.

"The ears of the Young Gracious have absorbed our words, her presence is in proximity…"

Oksa was now able to understand the convoluted language of these estimable creatures, so she knew full well what this last remark meant.

"Ahem," she said.

"Young Gracious, your domestic staff has carried out zealous surveillance of the boy named Gus, who is confined to bed," announced the Lunatrix, emerging from his refuge. "But the Young Gracious must receive the information that the one who is her friend has encountered resuscitation. He lives again!"

"You mean Gus has come round?" exclaimed Oksa. "Brilliant!"

And before the Lunatrix could say a single word, she ran upstairs.

"Gus! Are you okay?" she said, sweeping into her friend's room like a whirlwind.

His head resting on three pillows, his left ear and cheek covered by a thick dressing, Gus looked at Oksa and his handsome Eurasian face lit up with a big smile.

"I'm okay," he replied. "I thought I was going to die in agonizing pain when that revolting insect bit me. I feel awful and I may be turning into a mutant without realizing it, but otherwise I'm fine. What about you? What's new?"

Oksa couldn't help laughing. She felt both alarmed and relieved, two conflicting emotions that only increased her agitation.

"Oh Gus, if you only knew!"

And she began telling him in minute detail about the revelations of the past few hours. Sitting up in bed, Gus listened closely in amazement without interrupting.

"We've got ourselves mixed up in one hell of a business here," he whistled, as soon as Oksa had finished. "McGraw? A Felon from Edefia? This is bad."

The two friends looked at each other for a moment, their thoughts racing.

"You know, something is going on with Leomido, it's very odd," said Oksa moving closer to Gus. "It's almost as if he's trying to defend McGraw, it's as if he's on his side."

"But you don't think that he's the one who led him to you?" asked Gus breathlessly.

"No! Why would he have defended us like that, otherwise? He would have just handed me over, no questions asked. It doesn't make sense. There's something else going on... but what?"

"And did you notice that McGraw looked a whole lot younger than your great-uncle?" added Gus in concern. "But they should be about the same age, shouldn't they?"

"Yes," replied the girl, intrigued. "That's weird."

"There's something else too..."

Gus closed his eyes, overcome with emotion. When he reopened them, Oksa could see he was upset.

"I was semi-conscious, but I'm sure I saw my parents here," he stammered.

"Your mother—" began Oksa.

"…is a Runaway, is that it?" continued Gus, his voice cracking.

The sound of someone clearing their throat made them both jump. They spun round to see Abakum leaning against the doorjamb. His arms crossed, the stooped, elderly man gazed at them both with penetrating grey eyes.

"Abakum! Oh no, you must have heard everything," wailed Oksa.

"Don't worry," he replied amicably. "You know you can trust me. I've never betrayed anyone."

Oksa pulled a face.

"Can I give you some advice, my dear? Just be careful of passing judgement without knowing all the facts. Things aren't always as they seem."

"Okay, Abakum," said Oksa, hanging her head.

"All the same, your gut feelings and your instinct can sometimes be just as accurate as knowing certain facts," added Abakum mysteriously. "It's all a question of balance."

He looked at the two friends for a long time before continuing:

"I thought I heard you talking about Orthon's appearance. What did you mean exactly?"

"Well, he looks much younger than Leomido, which is really odd," explained Oksa.

"How much younger?" asked Abakum, inquisitively.

Oksa glanced at Gus.

"Thirty years younger, easily," she replied, and Gus nodded in agreement.

"As much as that?" said Abakum in astonishment. "Then I understand your surprise."

The elderly man narrowed his eyes and stroked his short beard absent-mindedly for a few seconds.

"What does that mean, Abakum?"

"I have my own thoughts on this, but it will wait until later. For the time being, I think Gus would like the answer to a more pressing question: you're intrigued by your parents being here, aren't you?"

"Yes!" exclaimed Gus, tossing back a strand of hair that had fallen over his face. "Anyway, my mother is on the list, which means she's a Runaway, doesn't it?" he added, sounding vexed.

"Your mother is one of the descendants of the Runaways and, as a result, there was a chance that she could one day be our Gracious. That's why her name appears on that list you... um... *found*. Only she wasn't the one who was chosen," he added, giving Oksa an affectionate smile. "But don't you think it would be better to talk to your parents about it?"

Abakum helped Gus out of bed and offered his arm to go down to the living room, with Oksa leading the way.

"Jeanne, Pierre, here's a young man who'd like to ask you a few questions."

"Gus!" exclaimed Pierre.

The man whom everyone nicknamed "The Viking" wore a sheepish expression on his face, which was somewhat at odds with his impressive girth.

"Well," he muttered. "Since the time has come for revelations..."

He finally looked straight at Gus, who was in agonies.

"As you've realized, we're here, son, because we're no strangers to Edefia. Like Pavel, your mother and I weren't born there and we've never been there. But our parents were part of the group of Runaways who passed through the Portal on the day the Great Chaos started."

A terrible shooting pain made Gus put his head in his hands and slide down the wall. His father rushed over to hold him up and then carried him to the sofa, next to his mother.

"Take this, dear boy," said Dragomira, holding out a small bluish phial. "I don't think another dose would do you any harm—quite the reverse, in fact."

Gus closed his eyes, downed the contents of the phial in one and pulled a face, shaking his head.

"This stuff will certainly clean out my stomach!"

"The taste is not filled with excellence, but the action is triumphant over poisonings," said the Lunatrix encouragingly.

Gus smiled weakly at the little creature, then turned to his mother.

"Explain everything to me, Mum, please. I want to know."

"My father was called Tempel," began sweet-natured Jeanne Bellanger. "He was the Sylvabuls' representative in the High Enclave, Edefia's government. Pierre's parents were Firmhands, in charge of supply at the Glass Column. All three were very close to Gracious Malorane, which is why they enjoyed her protection as far as the Portal. Like everyone lucky enough to benefit from this, they swore to take care of Dragomira. But unfortunately, when the Runaways were ejected from Edefia through the Portal, they were scattered throughout the world. Only those who were next to each other managed to stay together: that's what happened with Dragomira, Abakum and Leomido. My father and Pierre's parents formed another group; they were ejected into Czechoslovakia, a couple of thousand miles from Siberia. They integrated quickly and always remained very close. My father married a young Czech woman and I was born twelve years later. During the events of August 1968, when the Russians invaded Prague, my parents were killed. Pierre's parents took me under their wing and treated me like their own daughter. Soon after, we went into exile. This was the second time for Pierre's parents. Instinct took them to France and, as luck would have it, they met up again with Dragomira, Abakum and Leomido a few years later."

"How did they do that?" broke in Oksa, captivated by the story.

"When my family were still in Czechoslovakia, the country was closed and it was hard for us to find out what was happening in the West. But a few months after our arrival in France, Pierre's father chanced upon an article about Leomido who, as you know, had become a renowned conductor. He immediately recognized him from the photo, like other Runaways who lived in countries with greater freedom of information. So a few of them were reunited as a result of your great-uncle's reputation,

Oksa: first-generation Insiders, like Mercedica in Spain, Naftali and Brune in Sweden, Cockerell in Japan."

"How many of you are there? Do you know?" asked Gus.

"At present, we know ten Runaways. Without counting Orthon, whom we could happily have done without," replied Pierre "The Viking" bitterly. "The list you've just given us will provide information that will help us to find others. There were thirty-five in the group which accompanied Gracious Malorane, but we don't know how many managed to pass through the Portal. It's even harder when it comes to the second and third generations, because not all of them necessarily told their children about their origins."

"Like you," muttered Gus.

"Oh, Gus!" exclaimed his mother, trying to draw him closer.

"Which means that for a few weeks you've known that I know the whole story and you've acted as though nothing had changed!" shouted Gus rebelliously, pushing her away.

"Don't be angry..." said his father gently.

"I'm not angry," grumbled Gus, "I feel humiliated. You must have been falling about laughing!"

"Really, Gus!" cried his mother indignantly, sitting up straight. "Why would we have been laughing? Do you really think this is a laughing matter?"

"Yes, you're right," conceded Gus belligerently, "it's not funny at all. It's even worse than I thought it was."

"Why is it worse, Gus?"

"Because now I'm even more of an *outsider*!" he exploded.

"Oh no, he's off, screwed-up Gus strikes again... why don't you give it a rest? I've had it up to here!" yelled Oksa. "You're with us because you're my friend, the best friend I could ever hope for. What more do you want? And if that's not enough for you, remind me who made it possible for us to get all that information about McGraw? Who prompted me with the words of the Tornaphyllon spell when my mind was a complete blank?

Who is *always there* to help me see things clearly? YOU ARE, FOR YOUR INFORMATION!"

With a crimson face and tears in her eyes, Oksa glared at Gus, then whirled round and hurried to the far end of the living room, where she threw herself down on a sofa.

"I've had as much of this as I can take," she muttered.

46

A Cry for Help

THE ENSUING SILENCE WAS DREADFULLY EMBARRASSING, particularly for Gus, who felt humiliated and ashamed. His parents gazed sadly at him, feeling hurt and helpless. Their son would need some time to come to terms with being kept in the dark about their past. But he'd come round. Later. He was taking it hard now, though. *"Completely understandable, really—I would have acted the same if I'd been in his shoes,"* thought Pierre, trying to make himself feel better.

"We have to decide what we're going to do about Orthon!" Brune Knut said suddenly in her incredibly deep voice, as she sank back in her leather armchair. "This is very serious."

"What can we do?" said Marie.

"Not a lot, I'm afraid," replied Abakum. "Informing the police is out of the question, they'd think we were mad."

"Certifiable," muttered Tugdual, in his corner.

"Or worse, we'd become laboratory rats in the hands of the scientists," continued Abakum, ignoring the boy's remark. "We all know that. It would certainly be difficult to take the children out of school."

"And, anyway, it wouldn't make any difference now that Orthon knows that Oksa has the Mark," added Dragomira. "Look how he managed to track down some of us," she said, indicating the list that she still held in her hand. "Unless we change identity and flee to the far ends of the earth…"

"We've already done so much running, and for what?" cried Pavel angrily. "We're in even more danger than before!"

"No, we must stick together," continued Dragomira, glaring at her son. "Stick together and remain true to ourselves and to each other. We must be prepared for the worst. We must join forces to fight Orthon and, most importantly, to defend Oksa. The fate of everyone here hangs in the balance."

"But Oksa doesn't belong to you!" roared Pavel, making everyone jump. "It isn't up to you to decide her destiny. Stop yoking it to yours!"

"Pavel, please, this is neither the time nor the place," replied Dragomira curtly.

"I'll say it again: Orthon won't harm Oksa," said Leomido in a cracked voice. "He has a vested interest in keeping her safe. He wants the same as us: to go back to Edefia."

"And that's out of the question!" retorted Pavel.

He got to his feet and began pacing up and down some distance away from the group. From where she was, Oksa could see him perfectly. His face ashen, he kept glancing at Marie in despair. He looked so weary, so anguished. All because of that damned Mark. "*I should have kept quiet instead of showing it to Baba,*" she said to herself, chewing her lip. Finding out the secret of her origins had led to nothing but trouble and danger for her family. Edefia just created problems for them. And she, Oksa, the girl they now called "The Last Hope", was only making a difficult situation worse. Despite the best efforts of the Curbita-Flatulo, fear and anger were forming a painful ball in the pit of her stomach. A ball which was swelling and swelling as it spread bitter bile through all the veins of her body. Then, like a raging storm, her distress overcame her resistance.

"IF THIS GOES ON, I WON'T DO ANOTHER THING!" she yelled, at the end of her tether.

The room rang with her words. She couldn't bear being the focus of attention again so she jumped up from the sofa to make her escape.

But she was stopped by a mighty flash which suddenly illuminated the room, shaking the walls and ceiling. Particles of plaster showered down on her, covering her with white powder, while electric filaments began crackling and zigzagging towards the Runaways, although they never touched them. Marie screamed as a golden filament brushed past her face, bathing her in a ghostly light. Oksa froze, awed but not in the least afraid. She knew what this was. She recognized these sensations because she'd already experienced them. There was no doubt about it: the Ageless Fairies were there, inside her. She was hearing their voices deep within, close to her beating heart. But, unlike the other times, she wasn't the only one to be aware of their presence: all the Runaways were witnessing this. It seemed to fill them with amazement.

"Don't be afraid," murmured Abakum, taking her hand, "they mean you no harm."

"I know, I'm not afraid," replied Oksa.

"What are they saying?" whispered Dragomira.

The filaments were still crackling around Oksa, who was about to answer her gran when she was lifted into the air by a phenomenal force. Marie put her hand over her mouth, her eyes filled with panic and fear.

"Oksa! Stop that immediately!" she hissed through clenched teeth.

"She's not doing it," whispered Abakum. "It's the Ageless Ones, they want to say something."

Oksa didn't fight it. Halfway up to the ceiling in the huge room she hung in the air, motionless and self-assured. Incredibly self-assured. The voice of the Ageless Ones spread through her, coupled with an unfamiliar feeling of strength and certainty. Suddenly the crackling stopped and the electric filaments vanished. All the Runaways stiffened and looked at each other. That's when they heard a warm, enchanting voice which seemed to be coming simultaneously from inside them and from the four corners of the room:

291

The curse is drawing to its end
Because the Last Hope bears the Mark
Which will lead to the land Inside.
Its might and the two Graciouses allied
Are the hope that can save the world and its heart.
The power of darkness cannot vanquish its strength
And we will keep watch to the end.

In the next second, everything stopped and Oksa found herself back on the ground, feeling dazed but strangely calm. A myriad sparks were spinning around her. No one said a word; all eyes were on her face. Dragomira drew her granddaughter closer, put a hand on her shoulder and pressed gently to reassure her.

"Dushka," she began.

But she broke off, too choked with emotion to continue what she was saying.

"Wow, that was something else!" exclaimed Oksa, brushing off the plaster dust. "Did you see that?"

"It would have been hard not to," said Marie, with some difficulty.

She looked down and sighed deeply, as if to quell her mounting panic. Cautiously, Pavel put his hand on her arm. The immense anxiety they shared had brought them even closer.

"It was the Ageless Fairies, Mum," explained Oksa, feeling drained by what had just happened. "I think they…"

For a brief moment, she searched for the right word. She couldn't make up her mind between "are guiding me" and "are summoning me" when Gus, his eyes bright with excitement, broke in.

"…they know," he said simply.

Oksa looked at him gratefully, glad that the friend she respected so much was back to his old self.

"Exactly, Gus," said Abakum in agreement. "The Ageless Ones know who you are, Oksa. And, more than that, they know your power better than anyone, better even than yourself. What just happened is exceptional: it's the first time the Ageless Ones have ever spoken *directly* to more than one person at a time. It has never happened in the Insiders' memory! And it's probably a sign that they're desperate. This is a cry for help, my friends."

"I never thought I'd live to see this," remarked Naftali. "The Ageless Ones… incredible… do you realize what just happened?"

"It is amazing," added Mercedica, "but it's also very worrying."

"What does it mean?" asked Oksa, anxiously.

"Nothing good, I fear," replied Abakum, looking sadly at Dragomira. "'*Its might and the two Graciouses allied are the hope that can save the world and its heart*' is what they said."

"If we have to save the world, then it's in danger! That sounds serious—"

"Particularly as the world in question may not just be Edefia."

47

A Nocturnal Chat

H UNCHED ON THE STAIRS, HER ELBOWS ON HER KNEES, Oksa was trying to control the waves of anxiety sweeping over her. Her blood was thumping at her temples, causing a blinding headache. She closed her eyes for a few seconds, briefly taking some time out from the world and everything around her—and, as a result, didn't see the dark, shadowy figure slip right past her and stand motionless in the dark recess of the stairwell…

"I have to get a grip," she groaned.

She felt the Curbita-Flatulo moving on her wrist and lifted her sleeve. The small bracelet-animal was squirming vigorously in an attempt to calm her down.

"I'm making a lot of work for you at the moment, Curbita," said Oksa, gently stroking it.

She chewed a nail, then stood up and decided to go outside for a breath of fresh air. The night was pitch-black, the air was bracing and there was total silence. Just what she needed. She sat down for a moment in the deserted vegetable plot, unaware that the mysterious figure had followed her and was sitting a few yards away. Letting the stillness of the night wash over her, Oksa stretched out in the fresh, damp grass. She stayed there for ages gazing at the moon, which kept appearing and disappearing among the clouds. She was so lost in thought that it took her a few minutes to hear the sweet melody coming from the old cemetery behind Leomido's house. She sat up and listened: the voice was low, muted and terribly sad. Oksa shivered, more from cold than fear; even though it sounded less than inviting, her curiosity was aroused and took the upper hand. As usual. She turned round and noticed some small lights shining in the cemetery. She hadn't been mistaken! Drawing nearer, she recognized Tugdual, leaning against a crooked, ancient gravestone covered with moss. He was dressed in his customary black, with a variety of strange silver necklaces around his neck. He had headphones over his ears and he was singing. A Polypharus was waving its luminous tentacles in time with the melancholy young man's voice. It was a striking, beautiful and frightening sight. Tugdual looked up, revealing his dark, almost hostile eyes. The tiny diamonds in his ears and nostrils glittered in the darkness. Oksa was glued to the spot, fearing the intimidating youth's reaction. But instead of rebuffing her, he beckoned her over:

"You can join me, if you want,"

"Er... I don't want to disturb you," murmured Oksa.

"You're not disturbing me. Sit down," he said, making room beside him against the gravestone.

Oksa swallowed with difficulty, but complied. *Damn my curiosity... I'm far too inquisitive for my own good,* she thought to herself.

"Do you like cemeteries?" asked Tugdual point-blank.

"Er, I don't know; I don't think so," replied Oksa who, at that precise moment, felt like a prize idiot.

"I love them," he went on. "I find them soothing. All that silence and stillness. People think I'm unhealthy, but they're wrong, they don't understand. All they see is the veneer I choose to show them, when all they have to do is look at what I *really* am! I mean, look below the surface."

"Are you unhappy?" ventured Oksa, glancing at him out of the corner of her eye.

To her immense surprise, she realized that Tugdual was carefully considering her question before answering and he was clearly taking it seriously, so she felt less stupid.

"No, I'm not unhappy. At least, I don't think so… I think it's more that I don't have a gift for happiness, cheerfulness, all that, you know."

"But that's awful!" exclaimed Oksa, genuinely sympathetic.

"No, don't get me wrong. I'm not saying I'm happy or unhappy. I just don't have any great expectations, that's all."

Oksa was upset by the young man's words. Her shoulders sagged, as if bearing a heavy burden of sadness and compassion.

"I spent a long time wanting to have powers which would make me stronger than other people," continued Tugdual. "I pulled out all the stops, I did everything I could."

"My father told me about it," admitted Oksa, grimacing at the memory of the vile potions drunk by Tugdual and his followers.

"When I found out that all these gifts were innate, I thought I'd achieved my goal. But I soon felt suffocated by the power, so I buried it deep inside me so that it would never see the light of day again."

"But why?" exclaimed Oksa.

"Because power, lil' Gracious, represents pure danger. Anyone who isn't afraid of anything is invulnerable, nothing can stop them. It's fear that makes men weak. But it's also fear that makes them men. I mean human."

"What about you? Aren't you ever afraid?"

"Not really… that's the problem," admitted Tugdual, looking down.

Troubled by this strange conversation, neither of them said anything for a moment.

"What are you listening to?" asked Oksa to change the subject. "Satanic music?"

"No, I loathe that," replied Tugdual, with a light laugh which lit up his pale face. "I listen to the most magnificent music ever. Music which is full of the tragedy of mankind and the profound meaning of life. Do you want to listen?"

With that, he gently placed his headphones over Oksa's ears and she immediately understood what he'd meant. A glorious voice poured into her ears and then into her mind, flooding her heart and turning it inside out. Was it because she'd had a really bad day? Or because of the words of the Ageless Ones? Or her argument with Gus? Or this poignant music? She didn't know. All she knew was that she really wanted to cry. She restrained herself, shutting her eyes so tightly that she saw a multitude of little electric dots dancing in front of her. In the end, it was stronger than she was: a huge sob swelled and burst out in a loud throaty wail. Tugdual took off the headphones and put his hand discreetly on hers.

"Go on, lil' Gracious, let it all out."

"I'm finding things a bit hard at the moment," she hiccuped, her face streaming with tears.

"I understand."

The tears continued to flow, bearing her worries away with them and lightening her heart. Finally they dried and Oksa's breathing became calmer.

"Tugdual?"

"Yes, lil' Gracious?"

"Is there anything I could do to help you?"

"No," he replied, looking even more melancholy than ever. "No one can help me. But thanks all the same. You need to concentrate on what's going on at the moment and, above all, you must have confidence in yourself. The Ageless Ones are right: you'll come out on top of all this. You're the only one who can."

This was unexpected, but Oksa attached more importance to the remark than she would have done if anyone else had made it.

"That Orthon-McGraw is evil incarnate, I just know it," continued Tugdual. "And evil too often triumphs over good; it's sad but that's the way it is. Only you're not like the others, I know that too. I realized it immediately, the minute I saw you. And I know how to spot that kind of thing, believe me. You will succeed."

They stayed sitting against the crooked gravestone until Oksa's feelings were completely under control. Then the Polypharus guided them back to the sleeping house, where they took leave of each other in peaceful silence. The mysterious figure, which until then had been crouching, perfectly motionless, by the low wall of ancient stones, watched them go by, then stood up too in a fluid movement. There was a strange gleam of excitement mingled with anxiety in the depths of its eyes. Suddenly, a bird took flight in a loud clatter of wings. The figure turned its back on the house, stepped over the low wall and disappeared into the vast darkness of the night.

48

A Hare Called Abakum
or Abakum the Hare?

"**G**US! GUUUS!"

Oksa was shaking her friend, who groaned, reluctant to wake from his deep sleep.

"Gus! Wake up, you sleepyhead!"

Oksa's eyelids were still puffy from all that crying, which only Tugdual had witnessed in the cemetery. Tugdual... he was so fascinating. If only she could do something for him.

"What do you want?" grumbled Gus. "What time is it?"

"Four o'clock."

"Morning or afternoon?" asked Gus, yawning.

"Morning, of course!"

"Of course," he muttered. "Stupid question."

"Do you feel up to getting out of bed?" asked Oksa, looking at the dressing that still covered the left side of his head. "I heard some funny noises and voices, we have to go and see!"

How could he resist? Gus got up and followed Oksa, seizing the opportunity to repair their close bond after the angry words they had exchanged a few hours ago. Creeping quietly downstairs, they could definitely hear someone speaking in a low voice in the back room, where Leomido's creatures were housed.

299

"Hey, you must have really good hearing if you heard this from your room," remarked Gus in a whisper.

"First of all, I heard a bell around 3 a.m.," explained Oksa. "I wonder if it was that alarm-creature the Lunatrixa told us about the other day?"

"The Tumble-Bawler?"

"I don't know—perhaps. I listened but all I could hear was footsteps and Dragomira's and Leomido's voices. I wonder what's going on. C'mon, let's try and find out more."

"Oksa…" sighed Gus.

He felt much too shattered to try and stop his friend—to do that, he'd have to be in tip-top form, at the very least; and at four o'clock in the morning, after being attacked by a furious Felon and bitten by a Death's Head Chiropteran, he might as well accept that it was mission impossible. They tiptoed towards the room at the end of the long corridor on the ground floor. The light filtered through the half-open door and they could vaguely hear the muffled voices of Dragomira, Leomido and Abakum. Oksa crept even closer, dragging Gus by the arm. The boy raised his eyes skyward and let her pull him along. When Oksa got an idea into her head, good or bad, nothing could stop her. *"She won't let anything stand in her way when she's set her mind on something,"* Gus thought to himself.

Standing behind the door, the two spies huddled against the wall in the corner to peer inside the room. They couldn't see a great deal, but they could make out Dragomira and Leomido in profile, sitting round a table on which crouched a huge, magnificent hare with greyish-brown fur.

"I covered the entire estate to the sea first, but I didn't find anything. Oh, my legs are aching like mad, it's been a long time since I've run like that."

It was Abakum's voice. *"Where is he?"* wondered Oksa. *"He must be sitting on the other side of the table."*

"Do you want some water? You must be exhausted, dear Abakum," said Dragomira, putting a bowl in front of the hare and stroking it.

Dragomira was talking to the hare? Oksa frowned, looking completely baffled. Abakum? Abakum the hare? A hare called Abakum? What on earth did that mean? As for Gus, he was just thinking that he was still asleep and was having a really odd dream in which a hare called Abakum was speaking, talking… in Abakum's voice. "*Rubbish!*" he thought to himself, leaning against the wall. "*I'm delirious.*"

"But I followed my nose to the village and there I saw and heard something very interesting."

Oksa stared wide-eyed: it really was the hare talking! With its long ears pricked up, the animal was conversing seriously with Dragomira and Leomido at that very moment, there was no question about it. The hare and Abakum were one and the same! Indeed, McGraw and Orthon, Abakum and the hare—it was a string of double identities. Oksa squeezed Gus's arm in amazement. He felt as if he'd been transported to another dimension and couldn't believe he was wide awake. But, after drinking a few sips of water, the hare continued its tale, dispelling any doubts Oksa and Gus might still have had:

"I saw Orthon in front of the Dirty Liar Hotel. It was very dark, but I recognized him, mainly by his voice, which was as hard and curt as it was fifty years ago. He was loading the boot of a car. He looked as though he was injured and having difficulty carrying his bags. A young boy was helping him, his son… I heard them arguing. Apparently the boy wanted to stay and '*make one last-ditch attempt*', those were his words. Orthon didn't agree; he replied that things were more complicated than he'd expected and that he had to come up with a more effective plan. Then they got into the car and drove off."

"Well done, Abakum!" Dragomira said to the hare. "That's really interesting. If Orthon has gone we can rest easy for a while, but none of this bodes well and we'll have to get ourselves organized before he attacks again, which he will."

"Oh—and I also saw the Abominari with him," added the hare.

"I suspected that and now I understand why it had become so

aggressive lately," said Dragomira. "It must have sensed its master was in the vicinity. I should have thought of that before. Anyway, it's no longer roaming the countryside, that's one good thing, at least. It was so furious that it could have given itself up to one of the Outsiders, just to make trouble for us."

"We've avoided the worst, that's for sure," confirmed the hare, its muzzle quivering.

"So Orthon has a son," murmured Leomido, his hands steepled in front of his face, lost in thought.

"Why wouldn't he have?" remarked the hare gently. "He's made a life for himself on the Outside. Like you. Like all of us."

Aware that the conversation was drawing to a close and that it would be rather tricky if they were caught blatantly spying, Oksa and Gus chose to make a swift retreat and tiptoed back to Gus's room. There, they threw themselves on the bed breathlessly, their cheeks flushed.

"What do you think about that, Gus? Abakum is a hare!"

"It would be more accurate to say that the hare we've just seen is Abakum," corrected Gus, who was now wide awake.

Oksa gave a jerky laugh.

"Whatever. It's amazing, isn't it?"

"Not really," retorted Gus, pretending to be blasé, "I really can't see why you're making such a big deal of it. Talking hares are ten a penny, after all! Just like girls who shoot into the air like rockets, hens six feet tall and plants that faint when they get stressed. For someone like me, this is all pretty run of the mill. But you let any little thing impress you! Honestly, you should try to get out more."

Her only reply was to hit him over the head with a pillow, to which he retaliated by throwing a bolster at her.

"You're lucky you're injured," growled Oksa with a laugh. "Otherwise I'd make your life hell."

"I'm not afraid of you!" retorted Gus, throwing a sock at her. "Go back to bed and try to get a few more hours' sleep."

"Fine," whispered his friend with a shrug, throwing back the sock lying on the floor with a flick of her eyes as she left the room.

"You're nothing but a big show-off," accused Gus, smiling.

❁

When the two friends went down to the kitchen, all the Runaways were having breakfast around a vast table.

"What's for lunch?" asked Oksa, sniggering. "I wouldn't say no to a tasty hare stew…"

Dragomira suddenly glanced over at Abakum, who looked down with a knowing half-smile.

"With carrots? Wouldn't that be nice? Carrots are so tasty! And crunchy," continued Oksa, delighted with her veiled allusions and her ready wit.

"Stop it, Oksa," whispered Gus, as Dragomira hurriedly changed the conversation. "You're pushing it…"

"It's just my nerves," she replied in the same tone. "I can't control them any more."

"That's because you're mental. You really are a nutter."

"My Young Gracious!" called out the Lunatrix, alerted by Oksa's culinary suggestions. "I have the fear that the tasting of stewed hare is impossible to delight your stomach. But I make the suggestion of taking enjoyment in fillets of fish and garden peas in the proximity of thirteen hours. Oh! The dishwasher has rung the bell, the preparation is complete."

"The dishwasher?" asked Oksa in astonishment.

Everyone turned to watch the chubby little creature open the dishwasher and take out a plastic box. The Lunatrix opened the container and a cloud of steam escaped—as well as a delicious fishy smell.

"Don't tell me you cooked the fish and the garden peas in the dishwasher!" exclaimed Oksa.

"Young Gracious, the dishwasher brings to perfection steamed cookery, the certainty is tasty."

"That Lunatrix is incredible," remarked Gus in surprise. "I love him."

"If the Young Gracious communicates the desire, some carrots can experience this cookery to make accompaniment with the fish. The wish must be told to be added to the next round of the dishwasher."

"Okay," agreed Oksa, "carrots get the thumbs-up from me! You're a genius, Lunatrix."

"The Young Gracious gives incredible honour," replied the Lunatrix, flushing purple with pleasure.

Leaving the Lunatrixes to their domestic chores, the Runaways exited the kitchen, accompanied by Oksa and Gus. After a short, but refreshing, night's sleep, they were less emotional and more thoughtful. Sitting in Leomido's large living room, again doubling as their headquarters, they made the most of them all being there to confer at length, taking decisions and assigning activities: analysing the list, actively searching for Runaways—and Felons—who might still be anywhere in the world, keeping Orthon-McGraw under surveillance—the most important of all these measures being to train Oksa so that she could control her new skills and acquire others.

"And don't forget: while there are people around, you aren't in any danger. But we mustn't let Orthon find any of us on our own when he comes calling," continued Pavel.

"Hey, I know how to defend myself!" exclaimed Oksa. "You must admit that my Tornaphyllon was rather successful."

"Yes, and let me take the opportunity to congratulate you on that right now," replied Dragomira. "With everything that has been going on, we forgot to praise your magnificent first attempt! You controlled your Granok perfectly, well done Oksa."

Everyone clapped fervently and Gus whistled loudly. Oksa's face lit up in a big grin, but her satisfaction was tinged with bitterness, because it was Gus who should really have taken all the credit for her success. He'd remembered the words which had enabled her to shoot the Granok, when she had been in such a panic that she couldn't think straight. She looked at the Runaways standing there in front of her, so full of hope and so confident. McGraw's menacing shouts echoed again in her head and she was more aware than ever of how much rested on her head. What if they were all wrong? And what if she wasn't as strong as they thought?

49

FROM FLOOR TO CEILING

As the Runaways had announced, one of their urgent priorities was to consolidate Oksa's powers. As soon as the Pollocks got back to London, Dragomira took things in hand.

"Come with me, Dushka."

Dragomira walked into the double-bass case and led Oksa up the spiral staircase to her workroom, which smelt sweetly of the bergamot-flavoured tea that had been prepared for the two Graciouses. Everything had finally found its rightful place in the attic room, which looked neat and tidy. The scene was no less animated, though, because the creatures were busily doing chores on petrol-blue floor cushions.

Oksa headed for the darkest corner of the workroom, which was dominated by a giant alembic with countless brightly coloured glass pipes, some reaching as high as the ceiling.

"I've never seen anything like this! What do you use it for? Do you make bootleg alcohol?"

Oksa was feeling in a decidedly impish mood that day—which did not escape the creatures' notice.

"Al Capone!" cried the Getorix. "Watch out! Eliot Ness is getting close! Beware of the Italian Mafia!"

Dragomira burst out laughing, and Oksa immediately followed suit.

"You're very well informed," said the old lady merrily. "I can see that everyone has benefited from the book on Prohibition I lent to the Lunatrixes."

"It's always this crazy then, is it?" remarked Oksa, indicating the Getorix, which was raking the soil around the Goranov with tiny gardening tools.

"Who's Eliot Ness?" asked the Incompetent, standing bolt upright in the pink velvet armchair.

"Eliot Ness? He's a detective who tracks down bootleggers and hideous creatures," replied the Getorix. "And the ones he hates most of all are Incompetents. That's hard luck for you!"

"Is Eliot Ness a hideous creature? Well, well! Poor thing," said the Incompetent compassionately.

"And the Incompetent is just as slow on the uptake, from what I can see," remarked Oksa, bursting out laughing. "No, Incompetent," she continued, addressing the wrinkled creature. "Don't listen to that naughty Getorix, you're very attractive and I'm very fond of you."

"What! What!" exclaimed the Goranov in its turn, coming late into the conversation. "Is the Italian Mafia distilling alcohol in the house? That's extremely dangerous, you know."

Its leaves shivered violently, threatening to collapse at any second. The Getorix rushed over, imitating an ambulance siren.

"Emergency! We must hoe the soil quickly, its roots have to breathe. Stand back, give it some air, give it some air… hang on Goranov, breathe deeply!"

And it began hoeing at top speed, as Oksa roared with laughter, holding her stomach.

"They're mad, completely mad. I just love them!" she exclaimed, wiping her eyes. "Oh, Baba! What are you doing?"

What Dragomira was doing was very simple: she'd prepared a little surprise for Oksa.

"What? What's the matter?" she asked, sounding disconcertingly matter-of-fact.

"But, but, Baba…"

"Not very original, Dushka, if I may say so. Your replies aren't usually quite so vague," remarked Dragomira mischievously. "Has something given you a shock, perhaps?"

That "something" would have shocked anyone—even Oksa, who had seen worse over the past few weeks. Dragomira had adopted a most unusual position: standing with her feet on the wall and her body completely horizontal, she was looking at her granddaughter with a completely straight face. Only her eyes betrayed her amusement. Oksa was flabbergasted. She was even more surprised when Dragomira walked along the wall as easily as if she were walking across the floor. She zigzagged between the pictures whistling, a feather duster in hand, and casually began dusting the giant alembic, as if it was the most natural thing in the world.

"Oho! You could knock the Young Gracious down with her Baba's feather duster," said the Getorix with uncharacteristic wit.

"Phew," sighed the Goranov, which had regained consciousness.

The Croakettes, inspired by Dragomira, began beating their beautiful translucent wings and gracefully fluttered around their mistress.

"Would you be a great help, Dushka, and bring me a rag?" asked Dragomira innocently.

"Could I? *Really*? I've always dreamt of doing this. It's… *MAGIC*!"

"Of course. Anything I can do, you can do! Empty your head of all thoughts that stop you believing it. I'm not saying that's the answer to everything or that it's the secret to doing anything you want… but when it comes to what I'm asking you to do, you'll see it's very good advice. Before you join me, take a white Capacitor from the jar on the table."

"What's a Capacitor? What's it for?"

"There are a great many Capacitors," replied Dragomira, still horizontal, turning to look at Oksa. "You'll get to know some of them during your training. Generally, I'd say that they're used to boost human abilities: balance, thought, speed—it's extremely varied. The one I'm giving you is a Ventosa. You'll find out what it's used for in a second. All I can say is that it's made from a base of puréed climbing insects and ivy."

Feeling rather sick, Oksa hesitated. The mental image of repulsive teeming insects crawling up tree trunks made her grimace. She turned the white capsule over in her fingers and held it to her ear to check for any signs of life inside. She really wanted to cut it in half, just to check, but Dragomira looked at her, smiling with amusement.

"You know how much we respect life, Dushka," she explained to Oksa. "We would never harm a living thing. Never. It's a fundamental principle."

After shaking the Capacitor and inspecting it one last time, Oksa finally swallowed it with her eyes shut. Her mouth and throat were flooded with an incredible taste of blue cheese—those insects must love smelly cheese. But the most important thing was in front of her: the wall.

"I'm going to crash and burn, that's for sure," she muttered, beginning by putting one foot on the vertical surface. She attempted to lift her other foot, trying hard to picture it next to the foot on the wall.

"Not bad, Oksa, not bad!" said Dragomira encouragingly.

But Oksa was racked with doubt. She shut her eyes, tried to concentrate and felt… as if she was walking. One foot in front of the other, nothing to it—nothing to make a song and dance about.

"Well done, Dushka, you did it first time!"

Oksa felt vexed. Her gran must have lost her marbles. When she realized that the wall opposite her was actually the ceiling, though, she gave a cry of joy. She'd done it! A shiver of excitement ran down her spine and almost made her lose her balance—if you could talk of balance when you were horizontal. After her initial hesitation, she began moving with mounting confidence. So much so that it wasn't long before she became more ambitious.

"What about the ceiling, Baba?"

Dragomira chose to reply with a demonstration and, standing with her two feet glued to the ceiling, she drew Oksa closer.

"Wow! Magic! This is great. It's as if my feet are magnetic!"

"That's exactly what the Capacitor does," confirmed Dragomira.

"Fortunately we're wearing trousers," laughed Oksa. "You obviously anticipated this, Baba."

With a wink, the Old Gracious straightened her embroidered kimono trousers.

"Do you want to try with your hands now?"

With growing astonishment, Oksa crouched down in a fluid movement and put her hands on the ceiling. Her two palms immediately adhered to it.

"This is amazing," she exclaimed enthusiastically. "Look, Baba, I'm a giant spider!"

"Very good, Spider-Girl," said Dragomira, congratulating her, her feet still on the ceiling.

"And how do we get down?"

Without waiting for an answer, Oksa pulled away from the ceiling and performed a backflip which allowed her to land on her feet.

"Woohoo!"

Dragomira couldn't hold back a scream.

"Quite risky for a first attempt, you could have hurt yourself badly," she said with a frown. "Risky, but very spectacular, I must say!" she added, her eyes twinkling.

"Shall we surprise Dad and Mum?"

A couple of minutes later, they both went downstairs—without using the staircase, of course, that was far too boring. Oksa knocked at the door and found herself face to face—although upside down—with her father.

"Hi, Dad! You okay?" she said, trying to act naturally.

Pavel decided to play along.

"Come in Oksa. Oh Dragomira, you're there too, what a surprise! Come in, ladies, come in."

The ladies in question came into the room, stepping over the space between the top of the door and the ceiling.

"Your place isn't very convenient, my boy," remarked Dragomira, her plaits hanging down towards the floor and brushing her son's face. "Hi there, Marie!"

Marie looked up and lifted her arm to ruffle Oksa's hair.

"Oksa, could I interest you in a nice cup of spiced hot chocolate?"

"For sure!" exclaimed Oksa, repeating her brilliant backflip to get down from the ceiling and land at her mother's feet. "Did you see that, Mum? Isn't it brilliant?"

"Er, that's pretty basic for any self-respecting witch, isn't it?" remarked Marie, sounding unperturbed. "No, I'm teasing," she continued with a wan smile. "Of course it's brilliant!"

Then, turning to Dragomira, who had come back down a little less athletically:

"So? How do you rate your student? Is she being careful, at least?"

"She's excellent, Marie, don't worry."

"I always worry, you know that. Always."

50

SKELETON AND CURBITA-FLATULO GO MAD

H ALF-TERM WAS OVER. SO MANY THINGS HAD HAPPENED that Oksa felt as if it had lasted months. It seemed very strange to be putting on her school uniform again—sweater and trousers for winter—and pulling on her rollerblades that Monday morning to meet Gus, who was waiting outside her house. He wasn't alone: both sets of parents, the Bellangers and the Pollocks, had agreed to take it in turns so that the two children never had to go to school on their own. "*We can kiss our freedom goodbye,*" Oksa had lamented. That morning, Gus's father was going to be taking them.

"Hi there, Pierre, how are you?" Oksa said in greeting. "That's a cool bike!"

"Hiya, Oksa! Yes, I got it out of the cellar just for you and Gus. I just hope I can keep up with you…"

"We don't need an escort to get to school! We're not kids any more, you know. We know how to defend ourselves."

This was the umpteenth time that Oksa had returned to the subject since they got back from Wales. And Pierre Bellanger gave her more or less the same answer as always:

"That's not the problem, Oksa. It's better to be doubly cautious when dealing with people like Orthon."

"Tell me about it, Dad," added Gus. "I'm worried sick at the thought of seeing him again. With a little luck, he may not be there any more."

※

But they were totally out of luck that day. The students in Year 8 Hydrogen hung their heads and dragged their feet as they did every Monday morning on their way to the classroom, as if they'd been condemned to hard labour. McGraw was writing jerkily on the board and did not turn round when the students came in.

"Sit down in silence!" he thundered by way of a welcome. "*In silence*, I said. Or isn't that a word in your vocabulary? Miss Beck, is there any point in hoping that the half-term will have done you some good and that you're not going to inflict countless falling pencils on us, as is your wont?"

Poor Zelda blushed to the roots of her hair and sat down, holding both her breath and a pencil which had already been rolling towards the edge of the desk. Oksa smiled at her and pretended to wipe her forehead with the back of her hand. Yet she didn't feel in top form. Thanks to her victory over Orthon-McGraw, she was dreading seeing him again. When he turned round, she pursed her lips to hold back a cry of surprise: the much-hated teacher's left arm was in a sling and he had a black eye! Gus elbowed his friend and whispered:

"McGraw doesn't look too clever."

McGraw looked round at the class, carefully avoiding eye contact with Oksa and Gus, then said in a bleak voice:

"Get out some paper for a written class test."

A ripple of disapproval ran through the class. A written test on the first day back at school, that was typical McGraw. But it didn't make it any easier to stomach.

"I won't stand for any argument or any mark below average," he announced coldly. "You've had all half-term to revise, you have no excuses!"

They bent over their papers and concentrated on answering the questions on the board. When she raised her head, Oksa tried not to look at the teacher, who was sitting at his desk. She felt strong, and thought that the effort McGraw seemed to be making to avoid her was a confirmation of her power. Such a new and exciting power! She certainly didn't lose any time in using it again. Her irresistible urge for action was prompted by the skeleton hanging in the corner of the classroom between the window and the board. The skeleton began to move one hand as if waving to the students. Attracted by the movement, some of the students raised their heads and looked around to see who was playing a prank on McGraw. The latter, puzzled by the class's growing restlessness, looked up. But the skeleton remained motionless, like all self-respecting skeletons. As for Oksa, she was diligently bent over her test, her face partly hidden by her hair. But the moment McGraw went back to his marking, she used her power again, even more boldly. This time, the skeleton put its hands on its hips and squatted down, raising one leg after the other, as if performing a traditional Russian dance. Gus elbowed Oksa hard as half the class burst out laughing and the other half waited with bated breath for their terrible teacher's reaction.

"In case you'd forgotten, let me remind you that you're taking a written test!" yelled Dr McGraw immediately. "Why are you clucking like hysterical hens? Miss Guckert, can you give me an explanation?"

The girl struggled to stop laughing long enough to reply:

"The skeleton, sir..."

"Miss Guckert," sighed McGraw contemptuously, "your answer is not even a proper sentence, let alone a straight answer. The skeleton what?"

"The skeleton is dancing, sir."

"SO WHAT?" bawled McGraw, suddenly slamming his book down on his desk so hard that all the students jumped. "Some boy or *girl* is playing with the skeleton and not a single one of you is capable of concentrating on your test! Do you think you're in the school activity centre? Given the standard, I'd say it was more like kindergarten."

His sombre glare scanned the class, skating over Oksa as if she didn't exist. She realized from McGraw's feigned indifference that he knew she was to blame for this joke, which was intended to provoke him and make him fly off the handle—and this gave her immense pleasure.

❊

At eleven o'clock, the science lesson was spent in the same way: doing a written test. The sighs were even heavier and the complaints even more audible, which made McGraw literally roar:

"I am your teacher! I decide how I will run my lesson. If you can't cope with two written tests in a row, I don't set much store by your schooling. Your comments and your opposition are the least of my worries. But the next person I hear complaining will get three hours of detention, mark my words. As for you, Mr Bellanger, I haven't forgotten how much you benefited from sharing a desk with the brilliant Miss Pollock last time… so please go and sit on your own at the back of the class."

Stiff as a post and flushed with anger, Gus stood up and went to the desk at the back, trying not to lose his temper. Oksa looked up and glared at McGraw, but he was still avoiding her gaze, preferring to attack Gus instead. Which didn't bode well at all—she didn't want her friend to suffer instead of her. She turned round and gave him a sign of encouragement before buckling down to her science test. But she was soon distracted by her Curbita-Flatulo, which was squirming on her wrist. *"But I'm perfectly calm! What's wrong with it?"* she wondered in amazement. She lifted her sleeve discreetly and saw that her living bracelet was pulling an odd face: its tiny tongue was lolling to one side and its eyes were terribly dull. She stroked it but that didn't seem to help. Then some rather uncouth, suggestive noises began reverberating furiously around the room. There was no room for any doubt, it sounded like someone breaking wind. Some of the students looked at each other suspiciously, others ventured a snigger. As for McGraw, he raised his head and looked round to see who was

315

producing the loud succession of farts, without managing to discover who was to blame. *"Oh no, I forgot its granule!"* thought Oksa in a panic. *"How stupid can I get? I understand what Abakum meant when he said its displeasure doesn't go unnoticed... I'll have to last it out till lunchtime!"* And she literally buried herself in her paper, pressing herself flat on her arms to try and muffle the Curbita-Flatulo's intestinal noises. There was no doubt about it, the Flatulo was aptly named.

❊

When the bell rang for lunch, the students took only a few seconds to hand in their papers and get their things. Impatient to get away from McGraw as quickly as possible, they all left the room without saying a word to their teacher, except for one or two who never missed an opportunity to ingratiate themselves. Oksa was the fastest out of the classroom. She raced to her locker, where she retrieved the reserve of granules that she'd fortunately kept in case of emergencies. And this was a matter of urgency! The Curbita-Flatulo wolfed down its daily granule and the farting stopped immediately, much to its forgetful mistress's relief.

"I'm sorry, Curbita," murmured Oksa, closing her locker. "I'll be more careful in future, you can count on me."

And she at last made her way into the courtyard, where all her friends were waiting for her. Their commentary was in full flow.

"When the skeleton squatted down and began to dance, I thought I was going to wet myself," exclaimed Zelda.

"I was pinching myself and trying to think about sad things to stop myself laughing. But even thinking about the mark I'm going to get for maths didn't stop me getting the giggles," added another student.

"Was it one of you?" asked Merlin Poicassé.

The students shook their heads. Oksa was a little more evasive and just lowered her eyes innocently.

316

"I'd really like to know who it was," said Merlin, his eyes resting on Oksa. "Just so I could ask them how they did it. It must have been a really ingenious device, I couldn't see any trace of a thread. Perhaps they controlled it remotely with magnets, a radio signal or electromagnetics? Anyway, no one saw a thing, it was just like magic."

Oksa pretended to ignore Merlin's remarks, which were so near the mark. It wasn't the first time he'd dropped hints like that. Every time, her heart raced and she broke out in a cold sweat. What if he'd guessed everything?

"Magic or no magic, whoever did it deserves a medal," added Zelda.

"All the same, McGraw really excelled himself!" exclaimed Gus, changing the subject. "Two written tests on the first day back at school, how crap is that?"

"You can say that again. He's a real head case," added Zelda. "And he's really starting to bug me with all his comments about dropping pencils. I may be a little clumsy, but that's no reason to make such a song and dance about it. He stressed me out so much that my whole pencil case almost landed on the floor. Can you imagine? Sheer purgatory—I'd rather not think about it."

"What about me? It's just as bad for me," moaned Gus. "He's still coming out with his pathetic accusations. I don't copy! I've never copied! I'm fed up with it."

Oksa draped her arms affectionately around Gus's and Zelda's shoulders, McGraw's two favourite targets.

"I don't know what stopped me giving him another black eye," continued Gus.

"I don't know how he broke his arm, but it serves him right!" remarked Merlin. "Pity it didn't make him any nicer. And did you hear? Someone must have overdone the baked beans at breakfast, what a laugh!" continued Merlin, chortling.

"It was hilarious," added Zelda. "McGraw's face!"

"It's just as well he hasn't found out who it was, take my word for it," said Oksa, feeling her wrist. "C'mon, let's go and get something to eat."

The small group headed merrily towards the cafeteria.

"It was your Curbita-Flatulo, wasn't it?" murmured Gus in Oksa's ear, drawing her slightly away from the group.

"Yes, the 'Flatulo', you said it!" she replied, with a peal of laughter.

"It wasn't just McGraw who really excelled himself today—I think you beat him hands down. Your dancing skeleton was amazing! I loved it."

"I'm sorry you had to pay the price," said Oksa, looking down in shame. "If I'd known he would take it out on you, I would never have done it, honestly."

"Don't worry. He's so mean that I'm sure he'd have made me change seats anyway. It had nothing to do with the skeleton... or you," he added, with a reassuring smile.

※

Oksa felt gloomy all afternoon. Unlike Gus, she wasn't convinced that McGraw would have decided to make her friend change seats if she hadn't given into the temptation to provoke him. And when she thought about Gus's kind words, and the generous way he had of raising her spirits and making her feel less guilty, she was dismayed at her own behaviour. Had her actions been those of a true friend? Seeing McGraw's lack of interest in her, she should have suspected that he'd find another target and turn on Gus as soon as the opportunity arose. He hadn't only separated them—he'd publicly insinuated things that were untrue and slanderous, and Oksa knew how hurtful those kinds of hints could be. If only she'd thought before she'd acted; she still had a great deal to learn. And not just about Granokology.

51

AN UNFRIENDLY ENCOUNTER

THAT MONDAY, AT THE END OF THE AFTERNOON, OKSA had a chance to show her friend that he could count on her. As they were putting their sports kits in their lockers, Hilda Richard—alias Cave-Girl—came up behind them and gave Gus a violent punch in the small of the back, bellowing:

"You should be ashamed of yourself, nasty little copycat!"

Gus whirled round immediately. Swallowing his rage, he chose to reply with mockery, eyeing her dumpy figure up and down:

"Oh look! It's the very kind, very thoughtful Hilda Richard. How delightful to see you, dear Hilda, to what do I owe the pleasure?"

"You'd better not copy from me, or I'll smash your face in," she continued, provocatively.

"I'm not likely to copy from you," retorted Gus, scarlet, "unless I want to get below-average marks *all the time…*"

"Shut your mouth!" answered Hilda. "Why don't you run along with your little Russian doll, that show-off who thinks she's so clever?"

"Clear off, Cave-Girl!" broke in Oksa, her eyes blazing.

"Why don't you try and climb a rung or two up the evolutionary ladder, you don't want to spend your entire life in the Precambrian," added Gus.

"Precambrian yourself, you dirty Chink!" she shouted, before turning on her heels.

319

"Right, that does it," murmured Oksa, beside herself with anger, "she's going to get what's coming to her."

And she put her hand in the inside pocket of her school blazer to take out her Granok-Shooter.

"Cover me, Gus!"

"You've got to be kidding! You brought your Granok-Shooter to school? Are you mad? You can't use it here, like that," muttered Gus, trembling. "What if someone sees you?"

But it would have taken much more than that to stop Oksa, who was hell-bent on revenge. She smiled with a vengeful gleam in her eyes and, before bringing the slender tube to her lips, said the accompanying words to herself:

> *Dermenburn, Dermenburn*
> *When this sap is received*
> *You'll scratch till you bleed.*

Then she blew in the direction of the spiteful student who was walking away from them down the corridor. Immediately Cave-Girl began to writhe about and scream:

"Something's making me itch. Help me, I'm itching!"

All the students nearby gathered round her, laughing instead of sympathizing, as they would have done if it had been anyone else.

"I've got an itch. A terrible itch!" yelled Cave-Girl, her face and arms—along with the entire surface of her body in all probability—covered with bright red blotches.

"It's her nastiness rising to the surface," said one voice.

As for Oksa and Gus, they kept their distance, while laughing heartily and making the most of the sight.

"An irritating Granok?" asked Gus quietly.

"Dermenburn," confirmed Oksa, putting her Granok-Shooter away.

She raised her hand and her friend gave her a high-five with a knowing—and grateful—look.

The rest of the week was less eventful. Oksa, who had learnt her lesson after the embarrassing episode of the famished Curbita-Flatulo, had decided not to risk being caught off guard in future and had put all the tools needed by a Young Gracious in a small embroidered bag which she now wore slung across her shoulder. She'd also included the brand-new mobile that her parents had just given her as part of the Runaways' new security measures. On top of that, every morning Pierre Bellanger accompanied the two children to school. In the evening, Pavel or Marie would be waiting at the exit for them to come out.

"Is Orthon-McGraw over there? I'd like to see what that traitor looks like," asked Pavel one evening.

"Oh Dad, he disappears the minute lessons are over. He doesn't seem to get on terribly well with his colleagues, he rarely eats with them at lunchtime, and he's never in the staffroom. Given how friendly he is, I'd say they're well out of it!" she added with a laugh. "But you'll soon have the chance to meet him."

"Will I?"

"Yes. Don't you remember? The parent-teacher meeting is soon. Next Friday, to be exact. Are you going?"

"I wouldn't miss it for the world! I hope Pierre and Jeanne will come too," added Pavel, looking at Gus.

"I think they're just as keen as you."

"Well, we'll go mob-handed and get a closer look at this former CIA or KGB spy masquerading as a teacher," added Pavel, with a merry glance at his daughter.

"Oh, don't fret, Dad. Everybody makes mistakes," replied Oksa, shrugging and suppressing a smile at the memory of what had, in the end, been a rather comical misjudgement on his part.

The parent-teacher meeting a few days later was attended by something which was more like a commando unit than a small group. Once in the school's beautiful cobbled courtyard, the order to spread out was given. And while the Pollocks climbed the impressive stone staircase to the first floor, a shadow which had appeared out of nowhere crept furtively behind, following hard on their heels…

Oksa's parents had no concerns about their daughter's academic progress, nor did any of the teachers. Miss Heartbreak congratulated Oksa on her keen interest in history and geography and her excellent marks. And she wasn't the only one: every single teacher was full of praise for her, which was no surprise to Oksa's parents, but they were still highly delighted by it. They had two teachers left to see: Mr Lemon and that Despicable Man, as Oksa's father now called him.

"You will be careful not to call him 'Dr Despicable' won't you, Dad?" Oksa had warned.

The two teachers were sharing the same room, Mr Lemon near the board and McGraw, dressed up to the nines, right at the back, where he had now relegated Gus for every lesson. The English teacher was just as laudatory as his colleagues and praised Oksa's standard—three cheers for Poluslingua!—as well as her admirable accent, which he thought might reveal a slight Welsh brogue. It was now McGraw's turn.

"The best for last," muttered Pavel through gritted teeth.

Suddenly feeling weak and light-headed, Marie took his arm to steady herself. Looking tense, Pavel nervously clasped his wife's hand and they both resolutely walked to the back of the room, followed by the mysterious shadow which slipped over to a cupboard and stood there motionless. McGraw looked up and curtly invited the couple to sit down.

"You are?" he asked.

"Marie and Pavel Pollock, Oksa's parents. Good evening Mr Orthon," replied Pavel, coldly but firmly.

Dr McGraw crossed his hands in front of him.

"I see—"

"Is Oksa's work satisfactory in the subjects that concern you, Mr Orthon?" said Pavel, cutting him off frostily.

Marie glanced anxiously at her husband and saw the blood vessels throbbing at his temples. Although she felt weak, she could see the rage taking hold of every fibre of Pavel's being. His eyes must have betrayed how he was feeling, because McGraw's face became more strained.

"Her work is exemplary. I simply object to—"

"Yes?" broke in Pavel mockingly. "What do you 'simply' object to?"

Sitting there perfectly still, his hands flat on his knees, Pavel turned his gaze to the bottle of water on the desk. With his eyes, he unscrewed the lid and sent it spinning towards the ceiling. Then the bottle rose and floated behind McGraw. Amazed, Marie looked again at her husband, simultaneously alarmed and delighted at what was bound to happen. Obeying Pavel's silent orders, the bottle tipped its contents down the teacher's back, soaking his dark suit. McGraw glowered, then gave the ghost of an unpleasant smile.

"So childish," he murmured.

Staring at Pavel, he raised his fist in front of him and suddenly opened it, releasing a nasty-looking insect which flew straight for the Pollocks. A Death's Head Chiropteran! A few inches from Pavel's face, the insect stopped and opened its monstrous jaws, revealing two rows of tiny, razor-sharp teeth. Marie put her hand over her mouth to stifle a scream of fear which was bound to draw attention to their strange threesome. A revolting stench of rotting meat escaped from the Chiropteran's maw and Pavel instinctively swatted at it, as he would have done at a wasp flying around him. But the Chiropteran immediately vanished, as if it had been nothing more than a hallucination or a nightmarish mirage. Getting the better of his agitation, Pavel snarled:

"So what do you object to about Oksa?"

"Her handwriting is a mess," replied McGraw defiantly.

The knuckles of his tightly clasped hands whitened under the pressure.

"You're the first person to mention this… *mess*," stressed Marie ironically.

"Mr Orthon," continued Pavel in a low voice, leaning closer to his enemy, "let's be very clear. As you've realized, we know who you are, just as you know who we are. You should also be aware that we hold several trump cards, starting with our numbers…"

"Mr Pollock," snapped Orthon-McGraw, just as quietly, "I can match your trump cards, believe me. You should also be aware that I'm not in the habit of giving up at the first hurdle."

"We are much more than a hurdle, Mr Orthon. And I very much doubt that you'll achieve your end, this time."

"Doubt on, Mr Pollock, doubt on…"

With that, Marie and Pavel Pollock stood up abruptly, favoured Dr Despicable with one last icy look and walked out of the room, followed by the enigmatic shadow.

※

"Well, it seems obvious that we must be even more vigilant than before. Orthon really has some nerve!"

As arranged, the Pollocks and the Bellangers had met up after the meeting to share their impressions while they were still fresh in their minds. Abakum was also there.

"I think we must be careful not to underestimate him; his confidence is not a bluff. We must never lose sight of the fact that he's a very powerful man," stressed Dragomira. "He was already very proficient in Edefia. We witnessed that, didn't we, Abakum?"

"Yes, you're right. And I think he's spent all these years honing his powers, unlike many of us. Also, there's no proof that he's working alone. What was he like with you?" the elderly man asked the Bellangers.

"Unruffled, cynical and very self-assured," replied Gus's father. "We told him to leave the youngsters alone and he just replied: 'Or else what?

Will you set the police on me?' He's aware that we have to be as discreet and circumspect as he is about our origins and powers. We didn't talk for long because we didn't actually have much to say to each other. We were just squaring off like fighting cocks."

"Our minds are made up then. We'll continue to keep constant watch over the youngsters. Also, I think it might be a good idea to take Oksa back with me for the weekend, what do you think?" asked Abakum.

Everyone nodded gravely. Except for Pavel, who still looked very drawn. He put his hand on his wife's arm, glanced at her in anguish and said in a broken voice:

"Don't we have any say in this? We are her parents…"

Dragomira looked at her son and daughter-in-law sadly, then gave a long sigh.

"We're out of options, Pavel. We can't turn the clock back."

"Who's talking about turning the clock back?" snapped Pavel. "We need to stop everything!"

"Say we did stop everything, here and now," replied Pierre Bellanger. "How would we go about persuading Orthon-McGraw? As Tugdual said, the countdown has begun. Our future has been set in motion, Pavel. And we have no choice but to follow our destiny."

"That suits you down to the ground, doesn't it?" replied Pavel bitterly, giving in.

"Oksa? Do you want to come out of your hiding place? And you, Gus," continued Abakum without turning round.

A little sheepishly, the two friends, who'd hidden behind a sofa to eavesdrop on the discussion, stood up. Their hands behind their backs as a sign of obedience, they walked over to the little group.

"It's time to give you some weapons, my dear girl."

52

THE FAIRYMAN

THE LAST TIME OKSA HAD GONE TO ABAKUM'S, SHE wouldn't have suspected that her gran's godfather—her Watcher, as Dragomira called him—was so full of surprises. Quite apart from his mind-blowing transformation into a hare, which she'd witnessed with her own eyes, Oksa had discovered that this discreet, mysterious man was the very embodiment of trustworthiness. Malorane had counted on his loyalty and she'd been right to do so. Keeping his word despite all opposition, he'd dedicated his life to protecting Dragomira—even after she'd become a woman quite able to defend herself. Had he ever been married? In love? Oksa didn't know, but she promised herself to ask him one day. As he drove his motorbike and sidecar along the narrow road leading to his farm, she watched him out of the corner of her eye. Every move he made was unhurried, calm and above all reassuring, just like his everyday behaviour.

As far back as Oksa could remember, he'd been regarded as one of the family. It was Baba Pollock who'd given the impression of being the pillar of strength in the herbalist's shop that she and Abakum had run for thirty years. Her eccentricity and charisma had made her the focus of attention and, as a result, she'd received all the credit for their hard work—particularly over the past few years, when the small company's reputation had spread abroad. Despite his remarkable savoir-faire, Abakum had done everything in his power to restrain Dragomira's enthusiasm for the press, making no secret of his dislike for any kind of marketing. Oksa had in fact overheard some fairly animated discussions on this subject and she'd thought at the time that the old man had been overreacting. She'd wondered why he had to be so cautious. Now she understood better: any article on Dragomira and her talents as a herbalist could fall into the wrong hands. Like those of Orthon-McGraw, for example. She recalled the last article published in an American specialist journal, just a few months before they left for London. The journalist had heaped praise upon Dragomira, describing her as a "genius of alternative medicine" and "a sorceress with plants". The sorceress in question had refused to be photographed, but her name had appeared clearly in print. Now she knew more about Abakum, Oksa understood what a vital role this wise, secretive man performed. He might remain resolutely in the background but he was, above all, a shrewd protector.

The motorbike and sidecar drove through a village, then turned into a lane lined with hawthorn bushes. At the very end, they stopped in front of a tall gate. Abakum got down from the bike, removed his helmet and, from his saddlebag, took out a small box and released some kind of bright green scarab beetle. He introduced this into the keyhole and the gate opened immediately. "*Wow!*" thought Oksa in astonishment. "*A live key! How interesting…*"

Abakum parked the motorbike in the yard, then carefully closed the gate and retrieved the squirming beetle. The land on which the main building stood was surrounded by a very high wall of flat overlapping stones with what looked like two steel security doors in it. Abakum's house was just as remarkable as Leomido's, although very different in style. For many years, this splendid modernized farm had been Abakum's holiday home. But since they had left France he'd been living there full-time, preferring the English countryside to the hustle and bustle of London. Oksa had come with her family last summer to spend a few days here and the farm had lost none of its charm. Shaded from dark red to brown to faded pink, its brick walls were covered by wisteria and roses climbing to the first floor. On one side, a former grain silo that

Abakum had refurbished from top to bottom was connected to the farm by an enclosed gangway. Oksa had never been inside this annex. Perhaps Abakum would let her visit it this time.

"Oh Abakum, your house is even more beautiful than before!"

Sitting in an armchair shaped like a shell, Oksa gazed at the interior of the building while Abakum prepared a welcome snack. It was in stark contrast to the exterior: Abakum had gone for a very different look to the predictable rustic décor.

"You could almost be in the Museum of Modern Art!" exclaimed Oksa, with a whistle of appreciation.

Abakum put a tray down on a small table with striped legs, filled two cups with hot chocolate and sat down opposite Oksa.

"You may not know this, Oksa, but my adoptive parents were what they call interior designers in England. My father and his parents designed furniture and my mother was the best interior designer in Edefia. She was the one who entirely furbished Malorane's suite of rooms in the Glass Column. I've gone for a layout in this house which is very similar to the typical Sylvabul dwelling in Edefia. The house where I lived when I was young looked a lot like this, apart from the fact that it was built in a gigantic tree—a Colosso—a hundred feet or so above the ground. My family always attached a great deal of importance to the aesthetic appearance of things, particularly everyday objects, and I'm very glad this is something you notice."

Oksa listened attentively. She loved one-on-one conversations.

"Edefia must be really beautiful," she said in a low voice, dreamily. "Abakum, I'm sorry, but you mentioned your adoptive parents. Are you like Gus then?"

"Yes. And, like him, I was very lucky because I was taken in by some remarkable people with hearts of gold."

"How old were you?" asked Oksa, emboldened by the elderly man's peaceful smile.

"Only a few hours old."

"You were a tiny baby then!"

A shadow of sadness passed fleetingly over Abakum's face. He closed his eyes for a moment, before continuing:

"Oh, young Oksa… I'm going to tell you a secret that few people know."

"One of your parents was a hare—I'm right, aren't I?" asked Oksa with her customary spontaneity.

At that Abakum gave the loudest snort of laughter she'd ever heard. It was so loud that it made her jump and spill some of her hot chocolate over herself.

"I knew you knew about—how should I put it—my animal side," said Abakum, wiping the tears from his eyes. "But this is the first time anyone has ever suggested that my parents might have been hares!"

"So you know I know," said Oksa miserably, despite being terribly amused at the sight of Abakum shaking with laughter. "I'm a dead loss when it comes to spying."

"I wouldn't say that—but it wasn't hard to put two and two together with your remarks that morning. Anyway, that's what you were driving at, wasn't it, you little minx? I know you. No, Oksa, my parents weren't hares. But what they were was just as incredible."

"Oh, tell me, Abakum," begged Oksa, "please!"

"My father was a Sylvabul beekeeper called Tiburce. I know very little about him, except that he was a good and humble man, a nature-lover who enjoyed his own company. One day, an Ageless Fairy noticed him in the flower-strewn clearing where he had set up his hives, and immediately became enamoured of him. This was extremely rare, and it may even have been the only time this had happened in the history of Edefia. Because of her feelings, this Ageless Fairy, my mother, revealed herself to my father. It was love at first sight for both of them. Despite the exceptionally pure nature of their love, this union led to their ruin: a man and an Ageless Fairy weren't allowed to meet, let alone fall in love."

"What happened?" asked Oksa breathlessly, hanging on Abakum's every word as she watched him with her big grey eyes.

"They were vaporized when I was born," said Abakum gloomily.

"Oh!" exclaimed Oksa, putting her hand over her mouth. "That's horrible! You mean your mother died just after giving birth to you?"

"So to speak," replied Abakum with a sad smile. "Apparently, the Ageless Ones don't have the same constitution as human beings because I was born immediately after my conception. And that brought about the death of my parents."

"That's horrible," repeated Oksa, a lump in her throat.

"I think it's a rather beautiful story," said the old man, his eyes shining. "They both knew they were taking an insane risk. But even the threat of death couldn't stop them loving each other. Their love was absolute."

"What happened then?" asked Oksa, sounding choked.

"The next day, alerted by my hungry cries, two neighbours found me in my father's house. I was alone, naked and dirty. Not knowing what to do, they fed me, then took me to Gracious Malorane, who gave orders for a search. No one knew that a young woman had come into my father's life and had won his heart; everyone was at a complete loss. For a few days, scores of men scoured the forests and clearings, dragged the lakes and explored the caves. But no trace was ever found of my parents; they had disappeared into thin air. This was a great mystery in Edefia for a few weeks. Everyone had their own theory about what might have happened, particularly as there'd been no reports of any missing girls or any births. Some thought my parents had been attacked by the bees; others believed that the girl had given birth secretly to escape her parents' anger; and yet others thought that Tiburce had tried to get onto the Island of the Fairies and that, due to this foolhardy act, he'd become an Attendant for ever."

"An Attendant?"

"They are little men, half-human and half-stag, imprisoned by a magic spell in punishment for their curiosity."

"What do you mean, their curiosity?" exclaimed Oksa. "What did they do?"

"They wanted to see the Fairies."

"But there's nothing wrong with wanting to see the Fairies, is there?" the girl cried indignantly. "It's cruel to punish them for that!"

"Maybe so," agreed Abakum. "But you have to consider that the punishment inflicted on them also brings them great happiness. The lower part of their body may be that of a stag and they may bear antlers on their heads, but they're permitted to live with the Fairies on the Island until the end of their days. And that was their dearest wish. As for my father, you'll realize that this theory was the closest to what really happened. Much later, I was able to consult the archives of *The Enlightened*—Edefia's newspaper—and I can you tell that every single possibility was considered, from the most absurd to the most romantic. But no one ever found out what had really happened or located my parents. Then Malorane gave me to the Sylvabul couple I mentioned before, Mikka and Eva. They loved me as their own son and I owe them a great deal. It wasn't easy to for them."

Oksa looked at Abakum with intense curiosity, impatient to know more.

"By agreeing to take me in, they also accepted the mystery surrounding my birth. When a child is born in Edefia, an identity ring is made by combining his or her DNA with Goranov sap, which is the same process used for the Granok-Shooter. When they tried to make my ring, they found out that my DNA was totally abnormal and didn't match anything that had been seen before in Edefia. Only four people knew about this: Malorane, my adoptive parents and the ring-maker, who was bound by professional confidentiality not to breathe a word about the manufacture of his rings. I must say Malorane and my parents watched me closely throughout my childhood. No one had ever been born from such a union and all three were worried and curious about me, which wasn't always easy to deal with. Also, they soon realized that I had singular abilities."

"So you're a Fairyman?" broke in Oksa, almost jumping out of her armchair. "A FAIRYMAN!"

53

THE REVELATION OF THE SINGING SPRING

A BAKUM STROKED HIS BEARD WITH HIS FINGERTIPS FOR a long time, intrigued by this remark.

"I've never thought about it like that… but why not? My parents said I was a sorcerer. Which is also the view of your gran, your father and Gus's parents, who know about my unusual origins. But I have to admit that I really like the idea of being a 'Fairyman'!"

"But how do you know all this? How can you know that your mother was an Ageless Fairy?"

"I remembered my birth," replied the elderly man simply, the depth of his feelings making his eyes gleam.

"Abakum, I'm sorry but no one can remember their own birth!" replied Oksa abruptly.

"You're right, no one can remember that far back. Even a Fairyman/hare," he said with a wink. "No, I was just lucky enough to win the draw to visit the Singing Spring."

"Win what draw?" asked Oksa in amazement.

"Every year, at the huge party for the Summer Solstice, a draw was held to decide which inhabitant of Edefia would be taken to the mysterious Singing Spring, not far from the Island of the Fairies. Believe it or not, its waters allow the drinker to remember and relive a lost or impossible memory. And I can tell you that this was a highly coveted privilege! I remember it as though it were yesterday… It was my twelfth birthday. When Gracious Malorane dipped her hand into the immense crystal jar which contained all the names of Edefia's inhabitants and called out my name, I thought I was dreaming. She took me to the doors of a vast maze which concealed the entrance to the Singing Spring and slipped a holographic map into my hand, which imprinted itself on my palm. I wandered for hours among hedges of plants and stone walls, exhausted and anxious, before I found the exit. And finding this exit was vital— not only to escape the maze, in which some people had been trapped for ever, but most importantly to reach the Spring! When I finally got out of that diabolical maze, the hologram vanished: I had reached my destination. Two monsters with a woman's head and the body of a lion were guarding the entrance to a cavern—I was face to face with the fearsome Corpusleoxes. Like all Edefian children, I'd heard about these creatures. People told terrible tales about them—tales, or legends, which were mainly intended to scare young children. But at the age of twelve, I still believed them and I remember I was petrified: the two Corpusleoxes stared at me with their yellow eyes, their claws so sharp that a single blow would have ripped me to shreds! I didn't know what to do, I was terrified that my slightest movement might annoy them. I found out later that the pitiless Corpusleoxes are there to chase off any uninvited visitors who might have found the Spring. Fortunately they were expecting me so they let me pass safely—my journey through the maze had given me the right to enter. As I was standing paralysed with fear in front of the mouth of the cavern, those terrible creatures bowed their heads and beckoned me inside with their upper paws. Inside, I found a place of great opulence. The glittering walls of the grotto were made entirely of lapis lazuli. Their surface was covered in reflections from the translucent waters of the Singing Spring, which were a beautiful pink colour, and the air was warm with a sweetish smell. I stretched out on the floor and stayed there for an hour, a night, I have no idea how long…

I'd lost all sense of time and space. I just had the incredible feeling of being in the middle of a giant precious stone. I'd never seen such pure, vibrant colours as those in that cavern. I fell asleep, lulled by the song of the Spring, and when I woke up a large iridescent shell was lying beside me. A clear, sweet voice called me by my name and told me to drink its contents. And that was how I came to taste the incredible waters of the Singing Spring. They tasted like slightly sparkling lemonade, and the limpid bubbles popped deliciously in my mouth, as if stars were exploding inside me! From the very first mouthful, I immediately returned to the day of my conception—which was also that of my birth. And I finally found out who I was."

Oksa was filled with wonder at Abakum's story.

"The mystery was instantly solved," continued the Fairyman. "It was so obvious once the truth was known. Even though I was a very pampered child, I suffered a great deal at being kept in the dark. No one had ever hidden anything about my origins, but a good part of my history and identity was unknown to everyone, including me. There, in that amazing cavern, I travelled twelve years back in time and saw my mother, the Ageless Fairy, and my father, Tiburce the beekeeper. They looked... how should I put it... so radiant! As soon as my eyes focused on them, my father picked me, his baby, up in his arms and my mother leant towards me. Her dark hair framed her dazzling face; she was extraordinary, her beauty radiated from her as if she were suffused with light. Gently she placed her lips on mine and, with infinite tenderness, she breathed her life and her innermost essence into me. Immediately after, my parents exploded in an intense shimmer. It was so beautiful that all my suffering immediately disappeared. I'd found peace at last, because I now knew what had happened. Before leaving this magical place—which it was, make no mistake—the soft voice spoke to me again and guided me towards a waterfall, ordering me to put my hand through the curtain of water and grasp the object behind it. I obeyed without question, as you can imagine, and when I brought my hand out of the water, I was holding a wand. The voice told me that this was the wand that had belonged to my mother, the Ageless-Fairy-Who-Died-For-Love, as she was now called by the Fairies.

Abakum fell silent, overwhelmed by his own story. Oksa was amazed and moved.

"Wow," she murmured, "this is incredible! But it's so sad it makes me want to cry."

There was a distant look in Abakum's kind eyes.

"It's a very long time since I've spoken about all this... but don't be sad, my dear," he added, turning to Oksa. "Just tell yourself that I'm a child born of love. I know it's hard to think of me in that way when you see my beard, white hair and deep wrinkles, but that's what I am, nevertheless."

Oksa looked at him with deep affection and gratitude. A lump in her throat, she was fighting back a flood of tears welling up inside. Abakum seemed to hesitate for a second, seeing how moved she was, then he got up from his armchair and said as steadily as he could, given his own heightened emotions:

"Would you like to take a look at the wand in question?"

"What?" exclaimed Oksa with a start. "You mean the real, authentic, one and only wand of the Ageless Fairy straight from Edefia?" she added, regaining her natural sparkle.

"Exactly," replied Abakum in the same tone, "the very same!"

"And you're asking me if I'd like to see it?" continued Oksa, raising her voice, her hands on her hips. "You bet I want to see it, I'd give anything to see it!"

A few seconds later Oksa cried out in admiration as the elderly sorcerer placed the precious object on the table with striped legs. Just over a foot long, it was made of light wood and carved in a barley-twist design. It became progressively thicker at one end, like a walking cane, and a white gold ring around the thick end was finely engraved with the inscription "The Ageless-Fairy-Who-Died-For-Love".

"I don't believe it. A magic wand. Tell me I'm not dreaming!"

"I thought I was dreaming too, when I held it in my hands," said Abakum. "For weeks, I looked at it and analysed it. I discovered it was made from the wood of a Majestic—a noble species of tree—and that its tip contained a magnetic stone from the highest mountains. But I also turned it this way and that in an attempt to understand how it worked. And I must say it sorely tried my patience! I became so frustrated with it that I almost snapped it in two. I tried out thousands of random incantations, but they all failed dismally. Then, one day, I realized: I merely had to express myself harmoniously—in other words, by singing or using poetical language—to make the wand work."

"So it's a lyrical wand," breathed Oksa, her cheeks flushed.

"Exactly. And that was how I discovered that I could change shape. To do so, I have to look in a mirror so that I can cast the spell on myself."

"Is that how you change yourself into a hare?" asked Oksa, her cheeks flushing redder and redder. "That's incredible. Now I know why Dad said you were the strongest one of us all!"

"Oh, you know, I very rarely use these powers now. But I must admit they have come in very handy in some rather extreme situations!"

"Like when, for example?"

"Particularly when we were escaping from the Soviet Union and had the KGB hot on our heels. Metamorphosing certainly saved my life. I remember one soldier who had problems with his telephone just as he was about to give the alert. The cable had been severed, gnawed through by an animal with long teeth which had somehow found its way beneath the desk... That allowed us to board the plane which was taking Leomido to the West with the members of his orchestra and three stowaways, including your father hidden in a cello case."

"Yes, he told me about that. You escaped by the skin of your teeth!" added Oksa with relish. "But I didn't know all these practical details. You've certainly inherited one hell of a genetic legacy, Abakum; I hope you've never had to have a blood test, because you must be a real scientific enigma."

The elderly man's face lit up and his eyes sparkled.

"You think of everything, don't you? No, fortunately, I've never had anything to do with the medical profession and I hope I'm spared that necessity until the end of my days. I can't even imagine the consequences."

"You're not kidding!" said Oksa. "Er... Abakum, what about that? What's that?"

She pointed to the fat book that Abakum had brought over with the wand, an impressive-looking book bound in worn pale-pink leather and inlaid with metal threads.

"Aah," sighed the elderly enchanter, "that is the Book of Shadows. When I left the cavern of the Singing Spring, one of the two Corpusleoxes handed me a piece of fabric. As soon as I took hold of it, a shadow passed over the place where I was and I remember shivering. I was very surprised; I didn't understand what it might signify. Then I discovered a book on the floor at my feet. The Corpusleox which had given me the piece of fabric, one of my mother's scarves, explained that this was a Book of Shadows. Each Fairy has her own; in it, she writes recipes, incantations, spells and charms. The book I was holding, the book you see before you, belonged to my mother. Now the secret of my birth had been revealed, I was permitted to have it. There, my dear, now you know everything."

Oksa carefully turned the pages of the incredible book. Obscure incantations, mysterious designs and cryptic poetry had been written on the thick yellowed paper in brightly coloured ink. But Oksa was not so much fascinated by the book as by its origins. A book which had belonged to a fairy was hardly something you saw every day! And, leafing through these extraordinary pages, her heart swelled with excitement and delight.

54

An Amazing Alarm

"S HALL WE MOVE ON TO PRACTICALITIES?" ASKED ABAKUM after about ten minutes. "I've prepared a room specially for you: a forest room. Do you want see it?"

"You bet!"

They climbed the metal staircase which led upstairs and Abakum opened a sliding door.

"Wow!" exclaimed Oksa. "This is amazing, I feel as if I'm climbing in the trees."

This was because two of the room's four walls were picture windows overlooking a copse of trees so close that it was like walking into a forest. Virginia creepers climbing up the outside wall and hanging down over the glass added even more to the natural beauty of this extraordinary view.

"You're right, this is definitely a forest room," remarked Oksa.

"Don't forget," recalled Abakum, "in Edefia, the Sylvabuls traditionally lived in the trees in the region of Green-Mantle. Or rather, they had huge houses built in the trees. I wish you'd seen Leafhold, our capital, my dear. I'm sure you'd have loved it. It was suspended in trees whose branches were so wide that they provided a vast surface area to build on, like Colossos and Feetinskies—banyan-like trees with aerial roots. It was a city of more than 500 houses linked by monkey bridges and giant zip-lines. Those who weren't so athletic could travel between the trees on solar-powered cable cars."

"All mod-cons, then!" remarked Oksa.

"Of course," replied Abakum with a smile. "We'd left the dark ages behind us a long time ago!"

"I didn't mean that," said the girl a little defensively. "I know your civilization was really high-tech."

"Exactly right. Although I'd say green technology was more our thing— we've always known how to safeguard the best of our environment and show infinite respect for nature as we've developed. The natural world is our ally. It's a pity that the Outsiders haven't done the same, a great pity."

"What about the houses in Green-Mantle? You said they were similar to yours?"

"Yes, that's right. The houses were made of wood, glass and metal, and each one gave the impression of being moulded to fit the branches of the particular tree it was built in. Over the past few years, I've noticed that the Outsiders have been adopting construction and planning principles similar to those that have been observed by the Sylvabuls in Edefia for over a thousand years. At last people seem to be understanding the advantages of ergonomics and eco-design. Better late than never, don't you think?"

Oksa nodded thoughtfully.

"Well, my dear, I'll leave you to unpack... come and find me when you've finished," suggested Abakum.

❊

A few minutes later, Oksa went back downstairs. Proud of the latest skill she'd learnt, she made an impressive entrance into the large downstairs room, her feet stuck fast to the wall and her body horizontal. Lying in a hammock stretched between two columns, Abakum was surrounded by creatures, some of which Oksa had never seen before.

"Welcome, Young Gracious!" they chorused.

Oksa laughed and, after performing a perfect backflip, thanked the creatures for their welcome.

"I see Dragomira hasn't been wasting any time," noted Abakum with a grin. "Well done, Oksa. Magnificent entrance and what a landing! There's a definite kung-fu influence there, which has a certain style... why don't you come and sit down, so that I can introduce you."

Oksa sank into a soft armchair shaped like a pear and put her elbows on her knees.

"You won't see any Lunatrixes at my house. As you know, they're exclusively for the Gracious's family," explained Abakum. "But I have thirty or so small companions, some of which you may be familiar with: Poliglossiper, Getorix, Incompetent, Tumble-Bawler, Squoracle..."

"Have you any Goranovs?" asked Oksa, casting an eye over the creatures which were staring at her. "They're hilarious!"

"Yes, one, from which I've managed to grow a few young plants. As you might imagine, cultivating them is extremely complicated. They're still nurslings and, even though I hardly ever get the chance to make Granok-Shooters or identity rings, they come in very useful—for example, when a new Young Gracious is revealed."

Oksa smiled and looked at the old man with deep affection. She felt very close to him. Even closer than before.

"Yes. Thanks for my Granok-Shooter."

"Do you use it much?" asked Abakum innocently.

"Er... a little," she muttered.

"Never in public, I hope?" he added, staring at the girl.

His tone was meant to be serious, but his eyes betrayed his amusement at torturing her.

"Never!" exclaimed Oksa, feigning a shocked expression.

"Just as well," replied Abakum, teasingly. "We all know how sensible you are..."

"It's *formidable*! It's *wunderbar*!" said a spindly creature, letting Oksa off the hook.

"Oh! You're so funny!" she exclaimed.

"Do you mean I'm *absurde*? *Grottesca*? *Löjlig*? Boohooboohoo..."

Suddenly the Poliglossiper began weeping copiously. Its lanky body, full of holes like a piece of Swiss cheese, began inflating to huge proportions then subsiding to its original size. Oksa opened her eyes wide in amazement.

"Don't worry, Oksa," said Abakum reassuringly. "As you can see, Poliglossipers tend to use a mixture of languages but their main trait is a keen sense of tragedy. Like several of the creatures who shared our exile, they're much more sensitive than they were in Edefia. This may be because of the climate on the Outside or our long stay in Russia. No one really knows... so you'll often witness tragic scenes on a grand scale."

"...or comic ones," suggested a Getorix. "Because we, at least, haven't lost our sense of humour, unlike some I could mention!"

It started dancing round the blubbering Poliglossiper, which suddenly divided itself into several strips and began chasing the mocking Getorix, lashing its back.

"A whipping—that's what you deserve, *très mauvaise* thing!" shouted the Poliglossiper, spluttering and spitting.

The Getorix took refuge behind Oksa and the Poliglossiper stopped dead.

"Just what I said, no sense of humour!" yelled the Getorix, mockingly.

Oksa couldn't help gathering the little creature in her arms and the grateful Getorix laid its head on her accommodating shoulder.

"You're tickling me," said Oksa, wriggling.

"That's because of its *démoniaque* hair," said the Poliglossiper, which had resumed its initial shape. "*Achtung*, beware, Young Gracious, of the filth from that *capella*!"

"Comic scenes?" broke in the Incompetent, after a time lag of several seconds. "Because you think a Young Gracious with long hair is funny?"

"We don't like filth and we don't like the cold," chorused the Squoracles, taking a more personal approach.

"You know, Abakum," said Oksa laughing, as she put the Getorix back on the floor, "your creatures are as incredible as Dragomira's and Leomido's. But I've never seen a Poliglossiper before, it's astonishing!"

"It's an extremely interesting creature which is in service to Sylvabuls like me. You've had a glimpse of what it can do but, believe it or not, it can change into absolutely any utilitarian object, a ladder, a chair, a piece of rope, anything. Its body is made from a solid yet malleable material, similar to modelling clay or rubber. Handy, isn't it?"

"You're not kidding! What about the Getorix? What are its qualities? Apart from clowning around and annoying the others, I mean."

"You see that generous mane of hair it's so proud of? Well, we use that with other ingredients to make Excelsior Capacitors, which speed up thought processes. As for the Incompetent, its crest is used to make an anti-stress salve."

"Oh yes, I saw that at Leomido's. Dragomira had brought some with her to massage the leaves of his Goranov when it was over-anxious—which seems on average to be about fifty-two times a day, doesn't it?"

"Very observant," said Abakum with a laugh. "But Incompetent crest is also used to make the Memory-Mash Granok, whose effects I'll leave you to imagine, as well as the granules you feed your Curbita-Flatulo every morning. How is it, by the way?"

In answer, Oksa smiled and raised her sleeve to show him her living bracelet, which was in fine shape and purring quietly. Abakum went over to her and gently stroked its sleepy little head, causing it to purr even louder.

"It's doing great," replied Oksa. "It played a nasty trick on me one day at school. But it was entirely my fault: I'd forgotten to give the poor thing its granule—what a noise it made, I can tell you!" she explained, laughing. "It was certainly an explosive experience. Since then, I keep the tools of a perfect future Gracious on me: my Granok-Shooter, my anti-farting box, my Ventosa Capacitors," she added, patting the small canvas bag she wore slung over her shoulder. "I always have it with me now, even when we have games. I'm petrified someone might find it."

"You have every reason to be cautious, particularly with Orthon in the vicinity," remarked Abakum gravely. "But I'm going to give you something that will help put your mind at rest. Come over here, please, Tumble-Bawler."

A creature less than three inches tall fluttered over to him. Its slightly conical mauve body was rounded at the base, which gave it the appearance of a tumbler toy—no doubt where its name came from. Rising out of the astonishing head which surmounted its strange body were two big eyes. These seemed to swivel a full 360 degrees, giving it a perpetually alarmed expression. Two long arms hung at its sides, counterbalancing the large body.

"Master? A mission?"

"Yes, an important mission," replied Abakum. "You will now offer your services to this young person here. Oksa, may I present your own personal Tumble-Bawler."

Intrigued and amused, Oksa looked at the creature which had landed on her lap and was gazing intently at her. The Tumble-Bawler greeted her, rocking back and forth, then steadied itself with what it used for hands. Abakum continued his introduction:

"Tumble-Bawlers are faithful, powerful alarms which can adapt to all kinds of situations and all kinds of needs. You can give them a mission to detect anything and order exactly the type of alarm you want. I advise you to ask the Tumble-Bawler to watch your bag. If someone wants to look inside, through curiosity or malicious intent, the Tumble-Bawler can warn you or activate an alarm, which will make any approach impossible. For example, you can choose a shrill, ear-splitting bell or a sharp scratch on unduly bold hands, it's up to you."

"Come here, little Tumble-Bawler," called Oksa, "come here…"

The little mauve creature fluttered onto Oksa's outstretched palm and began rocking again.

"Young Mistress, I await your instructions!"

Abakum winked at Oksa encouragingly.

"Listen carefully then," she continued, putting the Tumble-Bawler in her bag. "You'll guard my bag and scream very, very loudly if anyone other than me and Abakum tries to open it. We're going to give it a try, okay? I'll pretend to be someone nosy…"

Immediately Abakum put his hands over his ears. Oksa opened the fastening of the small bag and an alarm as loud as the siren of a fire engine blared out. Oksa dropped the bag and put her hands over her ears, like Abakum—the old man had obviously learnt from experience. A few seconds later, the dreadful alarm stopped and the Tumble-Bawler emerged with an enquiring look on its face.

"Young Mistress, was the alarm suitable?"

Oksa, a finger in each ear, her eardrums ringing, tried to laugh off this violent assault on her hearing.

"Perhaps something a little quieter? I don't want to alert the whole school!"

"Oh, Tumble-Bawlers aren't exactly overburdened with subtlety," grunted the Poliglossiper, which had rolled into a ball in a corner of the room. "*Villano!*"

"Okay, okay, message received loud and clear, young Mistress," promised the Tumble-Bawler, crawling back into the bag.

"That's a good job done," said Abakum. "Now, would you care to move on to something a little more serious? Follow me."

344

55

THE SECRET SILO

ABAKUM TOOK OKSA UPSTAIRS, FOLLOWED OBEDIENTLY by all the creatures. At the end of the corridor, a steel security door opened onto the gangway which led to the mysterious silo. As with the outer gate, the door opened as soon as Abakum introduced the green scarab beetle into the lock. They walked along the gangway and came out into the silo, which had been converted into a giant hothouse. A translucent domed ceiling bathed the entire space in a milky light, and some tiny golden birds welcomed the master of the house and his guests by singing loudly.

"Hello, Ptitchkins," said Abakum, greeting them.

"Hey! Baba has some bird-shaped earrings exactly like these," blurted Oksa, blinking as she tried to focus on them.

"I wonder if they're not actually *real* birds," replied Abakum with a mischievous grin.

"Oh, Abakum, stop pulling my leg!"

"Look a little more closely next time your gran wears them," he advised.

"You two are unbelievable," said Oksa. "Arrrgh, what's that?" she yelled, suddenly grabbing Abakum's arm.

An enormous swarm of insects had taken to the air and were abruptly changing direction like starlings as they flew. Oksa went white, her heart pounding with terror. The swarm reminded her of something that she'd rather have forgotten for ever—and certainly had no desire to relive.

The image of the Death's Head Chiropterans was still very traumatic. Abakum immediately realized she was panicking.

"They're not what you think they are," he said, squeezing her shoulder reassuringly. "Watch carefully."

The swarm was magnificent. Except that Oksa hated insects—particularly when they travelled en masse and seemed to be taking a malicious pleasure in heading straight for her, only swerving right or left at the last moment, making her shudder each time they flew past. Realizing the effect their comings and goings were having on his young guest, Abakum whistled noisily between his fingers and the swarm immediately flattened itself against the wall of the silo to form a shifting picture, which spelt out the words:

WELCOME, YOUNG GRACIOUS!

"Oh, Abakum! What does that mean?"

"It means that my Invisibuls are welcoming you, can't you read?" replied the Enchanter, smiling widely.

"Your *what*?"

"My Invisibuls. They aren't insects, despite what you may have thought at first, but tiny creatures similar to flying tadpoles. In fact, they're perfect little winged chameleons which can assume any colour they want. Watch."

There was no longer any trace of the presence of the swarm on the wall. But in the next second, a new picture had formed—this time Oksa's face surrounded by exploding fireworks. She burst out laughing:

"They're incredible! I love them."

"But, you know, their primary function isn't artistic," explained Abakum. "The Graciouses mainly use them as an invisibility cloak—they cover themselves with them and can go anywhere incognito owing to their imitative abilities."

"Can I try?" asked Oksa enthusiastically.

"In due course, yes, you can," replied Abakum.

"It's a real tropical forest in here," continued Oksa, looking around.

The silo contained scores of plants, each more luxuriant than the next. After the first rather suffocating and unpleasant impression, visitors became acclimatized to the mugginess and were enchanted by this remarkable place. A staircase ran around the walls of the silo and made it possible to descend to floor level, where most of the plants were kept. Oksa had always suspected that Abakum was hiding all kinds of mysteries here; but the sight of the plants nattering to each other like old ladies in a tearoom was enough to leave even the most experienced Young Gracious open-mouthed with astonishment. Some of these incredible plants were placed on the floor or on long wooden tables; others were hanging from the staircase banister. Oksa recognized some Goranovs, a few of which occupied a huge console table. They were bound to be the nurslings. When she went over to them, the biggest Goranov—the mother, without a doubt—shuddered in distress.

"Who goes there? It's a strange girl! A strange girl bringing all manner of disease! Bacteria! Viruses! What are the Tumble-Bawlers playing at? A stranger has got in! Watch out! WATCH OUT!"

Abakum came over and stroked its leaves, murmuring a few words that Oksa could barely hear. The silo was in a state of excitement and all that could be heard was the growing noise of rustling leaves and whispering. The murmur grew louder and louder. The plants leant towards each other as if to pass on a message until one of them, the largest plant, which was sitting prominently in an enormous pot in the middle of the silo, yelled hoarsely:

"It's the Young Gracious! IT'S THE LAST HOPE!"

Immediately the rustling stopped then picked up again furiously a few seconds later. The plants were clapping their leaves, banging them together like cymbals.

"They're applauding you," Abakum whispered in Oksa's ear.

Not in the habit of being applauded by plants, Oksa blushed and waved to them in acknowledgement.

"That large plant is astonishing. What is it?"

Before replying, Abakum whistled again through his fingers to ensure silence and the plants immediately went back to chatting more quietly.

"Oh, I see you've spotted my Centaury. It certainly doesn't pass unnoticed. And it isn't even fully grown. In a few months, it will be fifteen feet high."

"It seems to be laying down the law for the others, doesn't it? It's like a plant-sheriff," remarked Oksa, watching the Centaury with curiosity.

"You're not entirely wrong. A Centaury helps to regulate the atmosphere in a glass-roofed environment by absorbing or releasing water vapour or carbon dioxide, depending on requirements. But that isn't its only function. You may have noticed that our creatures are very resilient. Well the same holds true for the plants, except that they're immobile and confined to this space. They possess certain gifts, although unfortunately not the ability to move. As a result, disputes are a little harder to control. The Centaury acts as a mediator if things get out of hand and can calm everyone down. Did you see how it dealt with the situation a minute ago?"

"You can see straight away that it's a tough customer. What about this fragile-looking one?" asked Oksa, going over to a plant with delicate mauve flowers blooming at the end of long, slender stems.

"That's a Nobilis. The pistil of its blossoms produces a sort of golden dust used to make a Granok causing blindness."

The Nobilis bowed one of its long stems to stroke Oksa's hand gently with the tip of its petals. Surprised, Oksa jumped and took a step back. Then, seeing Abakum's unruffled smile, she allowed the plant to continue. The Nobilis wiggled, chuckling with pleasure. Further away, another bushy, garrulous plant tried to attract her attention by waving its leaves in all directions. Inquisitively, Oksa walked over and the plant, crying shrilly with enthusiasm, immediately clutched her wrist to stop her moving off.

"This is the Pulsatilla, Oksa," said Abakum by way of introduction. "As you can see, it's pretty vivacious! I discovered its use following the

Chaos in Edefia, after examining those terrifying Granoks used by the Felons as weapons."

"The Black Globuses?" asked Oksa.

"Yes, particularly the Colocynthis, which turns limbs to glass, as you saw with Leomido's poor Gargantuhen. I can make an antidote neutralizing the effects of the Colocynthis with the Pulsatilla. That's what Dragomira gave the Gargantuhen to heal its leg."

The Pulsatilla was still holding Oksa by the wrist and didn't seem inclined to let her go.

"It's also a very affectionate plant. But you probably don't need me to tell you that... Pulsatilla, would you please give me back Oksa? I'd like to show her something."

"Come on, lettuce, let go of the Young Gracious!" broke in the Getorix, pulling on the stem clutching Oksa's wrist with all its might.

"I'm not a lettuce, Hairball!" cried the Pulsatilla indignantly. "I'm a very useful, very noble plant, that's what the Master said. And I need affection to blossom! Does anyone know what that means? What is affection?"

Abakum leant over to hear what Oksa was whispering to him.

"Of course you can!" he said approvingly.

Oksa bent towards the Pulsatilla and placed a light kiss on its largest leaf. The plant immediately let go of her wrist with a sigh of satisfaction, which sent its neighbours into raptures. Abakum made the most of this display of emotion to take Oksa to the small mezzanine halfway up the silo. This platform held a workshop equipped with a worktop laden with instruments and huge cupboards with drawers, like the one Dragomira had in her living room. Abakum ushered Oksa to a chaise longue and took a seat beside her in a sort of rocking chair.

"That's incredible!" exclaimed Oksa, her large grey eyes open wide. "A plant which feels and expresses emotions—that's mental! Is everything like that in Edefia?"

"Yes," replied Abakum. "We are so attentive to the natural world, so respectful of life in all its forms, that we've become mutually receptive. Gradually, over the centuries, the differences disappeared and we've reached a state of perfect understanding. In Edefia, the plants communicate with human beings quite simply because human beings listen to them. Few Outsiders can open their minds and senses enough to commune with the natural world. Vladimir, Dragomira's husband, belonged to the category of people who could, along with his grandfather, Metchkov, the Siberian shaman who took us in when we arrived. You know, Oksa, respect and the ability to listen are—or used to be—fundamental to the way Edefia operates. Society was also based on need, not on people's desires or greed, as is too often the case on the Outside. For example, in Edefia the sole purpose of work was to meet our requirements, without any concern for accumulation, profit or superiority. There was no social hierarchy: a baker was the same as an architect, a sewer worker was no different from a dignitary in the High Enclave. Every person did what he knew how to do for the common good. This is how we lived, with a well-balanced system that was beneficial to us all, until Malorane showed us that society could be structured differently. Malorane committed a serious error of judgement when she showed us the Outside. Everything was going so well before… It's such a pity and such a waste. Who knows what state Edefia is in today."

"What did you do before you had to leave?" asked Oksa, fascinated by Abakum's story. "You were a herbalist, weren't you?"

"Yes, I was the Granokological Master of Edefia and the official herbalist-apothecary to the Gracious's family. When I was very young I already had very obvious gifts; I had always been passionately interested in plants. I could spend hours on my stomach observing them in the forest grass, in hothouses or in the fields. When I was around seven, I began creating original mixtures and producing simple remedies. It was at that age that I even invented my first Granok—out of unrequited love, believe it or not!"

"Tell me, Abakum," begged Oksa.

"At that time I was in love with a young girl who only had eyes for another boy, whom I hated, of course. Then, to get my revenge, I created the Laughing-Rill. Nothing like that to get rid of rivals, I thought!"

"You were the one who invented the Laughing-Rill? At the age of seven? But how did you do it?"

"Observation, Oksa, observation. That is often the most effective way of understanding and learning things. I'd noticed that the sheep were particularly cheerful after grazing on a certain plant in the fields. They gambolled about in all directions as if they were having a fit of the giggles and then, how should I put it, they seemed to lose control of their bladders. That gave me the idea for an experiment, and there you have it! Simple."

"Simple? Easier said than done," remarked Oksa, sitting up straight on her chaise longue. "In any case, I really like the sound of that invention. What about the girl? Did she fall in love with you after that?"

Abakum gave a small laugh.

"Not at all. She flew to the assistance of my damp rival and completely ignored me. Oh, don't worry, I recovered. In any case, my disappointment at least made it possible to confirm one thing: Granokology was in my blood."

"What did your parents think about that?" asked Oksa.

"They were a little surprised at first; they thought I was going to follow in their footsteps and take up design. But my passion for plants was so strong that they let me do what I wanted. When I was eight, I began my apprenticeship with Mirandole, the best master of Granokology in Edefia at the time, an old man who was over 150 years old. He was a follower of Hildegard von Bingen, whose name was given to the Healery of Edefia—that's the equivalent of a hospital, as you will have guessed. Hildegard was a remarkable Outsider. Gracious Annamira discovered her existence in the twelfth century during her Dreamflights. Hildegard von Bingen was a mystic poetess, but she was also known for her extraordinary talents as a physician because she knew the secrets of plants. Annamira carried out a great number of Dreamflights in Europe at that time and her observations inspired a large number of Granokologists, including good old Mirandole, who taught me so much. And eight years later I entered the service of Gracious Malorane."

"You were very precocious, weren't you!" exclaimed Oksa.

"You don't do so badly yourself," said Abakum pointedly.

He stood up and went over to one of the cupboards containing a large number of tiny drawers. He opened about ten of them and took out what looked like pills, then arranged them inside a tube which had been cut in half lengthways. There were all different shapes and colours—round, flat, elongated.

"Come over here, we're going to move on to some practical exercises. Would you take out your Granok-Shooter, please?"

56

Crash Course
in Granokology

For almost two hours, Oksa diligently recited the magic words, functions and names of the Granoks. They were both concentrating so hard that they didn't even see the Centaury standing up on its roots to watch them and then give a detailed account to all the other plants in the silo.

"Well!" exclaimed Abakum. "You're a really good pupil and a fast learner; I give you twenty out of twenty."

"This was so much fun!" replied Oksa, stretching her arms above her. "I think Granokology has become my favourite subject. Thanks Abakum."

She threw her arms around the old man's neck and he hugged her warmly, touched by his young student's spontaneity and affection.

"Er, Abakum... I was wondering..."

"Yes, I'm listening."

"You were talking earlier about the mutual respect between plants and the Insiders, and I was wondering how you went about using their leaves, roots or sap. Doesn't that hurt them? Isn't that against your beliefs?"

Abakum fixed his grey eyes on Oksa's and replied:

"Very well observed, my dear—it's a good question. For my part, I've always taken care to ensure that the plants and creatures living under my roof are treated with as much esteem and kindness as they were in Edefia. And I know that Dragomira and Leomido take just as much care as I do. As for using their leaves, I simply cut them off and I think that if it's done gently, the plants don't suffer any more than when you go to the hairdresser to have your hair cut. As for the roots, I proceed in the same way and then it's as if I were cutting their nails. It's the same thing for the Incompetent's crest. Although it does grow rather slowly…"

"Like its brain!" remarked Oksa with a peal of laughter.

"Yes, like its brain," laughed Abakum in turn. "Its crest is like our nails: it must be trimmed regularly. It's more complicated when it comes to the sap of the plants, particularly that of the Goranovs, which is extremely precious. For decades, Insiders have made tiny incisions on their stem to gather the sap and you can imagine how painful that could be for the Goranovs. This may be why they're genetically so stressed. One day, a shrewd botanist found another way, and since then we have milked them."

"What?" blurted Oksa, flabbergasted. "You milk the Goranovs? That is what you said, isn't it?"

"Yes, that's right. The technique is fairly complicated, because with the Goranovs nothing is ever simple. But that is effectively the principle."

"Goranov-milking—that's super-cool!"

After this discussion, Abakum stood up and closed all the small drawers from which he'd taken the Granoks. He opened another cupboard and took out a round tin.

"Didn't you say earlier that you had some Capacitors with you?" he asked. Oksa nodded and, with the agreement of the Tumble-Bawler, which was ready to sound the alarm, she took out an old metal cigarillo tin she'd used to store Dragomira's Capacitors.

"Here, take this Caskinette," said Abakum, holding out a small round box. "I made it specially for you with the same materials as your Granok-Shooter—and after milking the Goranovs long and hard," he said with a wink. "You can use it to store your Capacitors, starting with the Ventosas that Dragomira gave you."

The Caskinette was a very attractive object made of meerschaum and measuring about three inches in diameter. Oksa took it from Abakum with a grateful look and ran her fingertips over its smooth, matt surface. Then she pressed a tiny rose-gold fastener in the shape of an interwoven O and P and the box opened, revealing about ten mini-compartments. Abakum again searched through the drawers of another cupboard and brought over enough capsules in different sizes and colours to fill the little box. The following hour was devoted to an in-depth lesson on Capacitors during which Oksa carefully assimilated all this new information.

"What's in that cupboard over there?" she asked, pointing to a much smaller cupboard than the others, hung on the wall almost six feet off the floor.

"You don't miss much," remarked Abakum, his eyes twinkling. "That little cupboard contains ingredients for some very special preparations."

"Really? What kind of special preparations?"

Abakum suddenly looked cagey—which, of course, didn't escape Oksa's notice and heightened her curiosity.

"Tell me, Abakum, please!" she pleaded, putting her hands together. "Please tell me!"

"With you, it's all or nothing," he sighed, stroking his beard. "I should know that by now," he added, smiling. "That said, I understand your curiosity. In that little cupboard—which is reinforced, I'd like to stress—are plants and grasses which mustn't fall into the wrong hands."

"You mean they're dangerous? Poisonous?"

"No, not exactly. In their natural state, almost all of them are harmless. But depending on the blends or doses, they can be lethal. This applies to many things found in nature: remedies and deadly poisons are often made from the same plant. My little cupboard holds henbane and monkshood, whose properties range from causing a curative drowsiness to paralysis, for what I'd call my more aggressive preparations. Of course, I also have belladonna and mandrake, which I use for different Capacitors, sleepy nightshade (whose use isn't hard to guess), stramonium and purple foxglove, two plants which can be highly toxic, and a few others, which I hope you'll allow me not to name, my dear."

"Wow," said Oksa, looking impressed and thoughtful. "Tell me, Abakum: have you ever made poisons?"

"Oh, Oksa, Oksa," replied Abakum, tapping the edge of the worktop. "Will you allow me to plead professional confidentiality and not reply to your question?"

"That's a pity," sighed Oksa. "But I'm sure you have. In any case, I know you can make Black Globuses."

Abakum's only answer was to give an almost imperceptible nod with a faint smile, which Oksa interpreted quite rightly as the end of the "toxic plants and poisons" chapter.

"Hey Abakum," she cried, totally changing the subject, "look! I haven't shown you yet. I can do something really cool. And without a Capacitor, what's more."

Oksa climbed onto the railing of the mezzanine and sat down on the outer edge, more than twelve feet above the floor. The mother Goranov gave a cry:

"Watch out! The Young Gracious is going to squash me. I'm going to die!"

Oksa stood up on the narrow edge, blinked and stuck her right foot out over the empty space, her arms by her sides. Then she put her left foot forward and began slowly descending, regulating her speed so as not to frighten the Goranov, which had already curled its leaves against its stem. Leaning his elbows on the railing, Abakum clapped wildly, accompanied by the Getorix and the Poliglossiper, which had changed itself into castanets. Carried away by this applause, Oksa took off towards the top of the silo, only this time much faster. She was travelling so fast that she reached the glass dome in a flash—which was not something that Oksa had factored into her calculations. Her head smacked against the transparent ceiling. Totally stunned, with blurred sight and ringing ears, she felt as though she were plunging into a huge black hole.

57

PIERCED THROUGH THE HEART

WHEN OKSA CAME ROUND, SHE WAS LYING ON THE BED in the forest room. Abakum was sitting in a canvas chair opposite one of the two picture windows, an Incompetent on his lap. As soon as he realized Oksa was awake he set down the creature, which began placidly watching the trees, and came over to sit beside her.

"How do you feel, my dear?"

"Ashamed," replied Oksa, staring at the ceiling.

"Don't be. We all learn from our mistakes. You were just carried away by enthusiasm, which is hardly unusual when you're thirteen; you simply need to get into the habit of thinking about the potential risks of your impulsive behaviour. That's not something you can do overnight, I'll tell you that right now. The lesson you should learn from today's mishap is that it's better to check whether there's a ceiling before you Vertifly."

"You're not kidding," grumbled Oksa, blushing. "Was it you who came to... get me?"

"No, Oksa, it was the Croakettes. They flew to your aid and brought you back down to the ground. I can't Vertifly."

"What? Can't you? But you can do so many things!"

Oksa propped herself up on one elbow, astonished by this news.

"No. I'm a Sylvabul and Sylvabuls don't Vertifly, they keep their feet firmly on the ground, literally and figuratively. But don't worry, they can do other things. Like this, for example…"

Abakum held his arm out over Oksa. With a degree of scepticism, she thought to herself that there wasn't anything particularly amazing about that. But she soon changed her mind when his arm lengthened impressively, first by a couple of inches, then kept growing until it had reached the door handle on the other side of the room. Wide-eyed, Oksa whistled in admiration.

"Well? What do you think about that?" asked Abakum, retracting his arm to a more normal length.

"What do I think? I saw you do that before, when Baba showed me your escape from the Glass Column on the Camereye. You stepped over the balcony and your arms lengthened until you reached the ground. That was cool, but it's even better in real life. I'm blown away, that's what I think."

And she fell back heavily on the pillow, impressed and exhausted.

☀

Oksa was lying on her bed, looking out at the trees swaying gently in the breeze. She rubbed her eyes, took a deep breath and let her arms fall back to her sides in a state of complete relaxation. While thinking back over everything that had happened during this extraordinary day, she thought she heard someone tapping at the door of her room.

"Yes?" she murmured, sitting up.

The door slid open and, to her surprise, she saw Tugdual Knut.

"Hiya, can I come in?"

"Of course!" replied Oksa in some amazement.

Tugdual turned round the chair in which Abakum had been sitting and sat down opposite her. He seemed much more relaxed than when Oksa had seen him last. He'd cut his hair and was wearing no eye make-up, which made his face look brighter and rendered him virtually unrecognizable. He was still dressed in black, apart from his jeans, but he no longer wore his many necklaces and crosses. His make-over had left him with just two piercings—one on the arch of his eyebrow and one on his left nostril. Oksa stared at him, captivated by his chilly good looks and intrigued by the air of deep sadness which he made no effort to hide. A few weeks earlier, he'd told her that he wished people would see beyond his appearance. And, at that precise moment, she understood exactly what he'd been getting at. But, to her own surprise, the idea that she was seeing him as he really was, stripped bare of all pretence or façade, was deeply unsettling. Was she more perceptive than before? Less blinded by her own concerns? Or was Tugdual just showing his true colours?

"I didn't know you were here," she said, blushing.

"Convalescence," he replied tersely.

"Well, you look well."

To her surprise, she was glad to be chatting to this strange, disconcerting boy again. Very, very glad.

"Do you feel… better?" she ventured, trying to hide her excitement.

"Better? Yes, you could say that," replied Tugdual, stretching his arms out in front of him. "What about you? How are you?"

"Me? I just knocked myself out like an idiot against the ceiling of Abakum's silo. I took off at top speed, then bang! Otherwise, my life has been totally crazy over the past few weeks. I feel like I'm in a film or something."

"You're not kidding," agreed the boy. "You have to be made of pretty strong stuff not to go stir crazy. I wasn't strong enough. But I've got nothing on you."

"Why?"

"Because you're the *Last Hope*! You're the strongest one of us all, you're the one who's going to save us."

"I don't think so…" stammered Oksa.

"Course you will, it's obvious!" retorted Tugdual, gazing at her intently. "Think about it. The Runaways have been like cats on a hot tin roof since they've known you have the Mark. They can't do enough for you."

"I don't understand what you're saying—I'm not going to save anyone!"

"Yes, you are, Young Gracious, I had good grounds for saying what I said to you last time, believe me. I've thought it over: although you don't seem to realize it, you're the one who'll save us because you're the last key. The one that was missing. And the last key holds supreme power. Orthon-McGraw has realized that. He's all set to plunge Edefia into complete chaos and I'm sure there are quite a few people in this world who'd rally to his cause. To say nothing of the army he mentioned... I know what I'm talking about, believe me. Look after yourself, lil' Gracious. I wouldn't want any harm to come to you."

Oksa shivered. Tugdual was talking so calmly and there was no trace of the underlying exultation she'd sensed during their previous conversations. She could even see concern in his eyes.

"Do you... do you feel all right, Tugdual?"

"Are you referring to my acute paranoid psychosis and my chronic morbidity?" he replied mockingly. "Well, believe it or not, I'm feeling a lot better. I made life rather difficult for Abakum, but he's the only one who really understood me. He's a star, you know."

✻

When Abakum summoned Oksa and Tugdual downstairs for dinner, the huge ground-floor room was in an unusual state of uproar: the Getorix was playing table football with the Poliglossiper. A small band of supporters comprising the Incompetent, the six Croakettes, the two Squoracles and the Tumble-Bawler had gathered around them in excitement. Abakum, meanwhile, was quietly busying himself in the kitchen, clearly accustomed to the noisy outbursts of his creatures. Various utensils, such as an egg whisk, wooden spoons and butter knives, floated around him, shooting straight into his hand when he needed them. But unfortunately not everyone was as laid-back as he was: sitting on the worktop near the master of the house, the mother Goranov was listening with growing alarm.

"No one will ever convince me they don't want me dead! What is the reason for all this noise? A riot? A revolution? A bloodbath?"

"Not at all, Goranov, not at all," replied Abakum calmly, as the stone of the avocado he was preparing flew over his head and landed in the rubbish bin.

Oksa and Tugdual exchanged amused looks: a Fairyman in the kitchen was definitely a sight worth seeing.

"Take that, you peanut-faced Poliglossiper!" yelled the Getorix suddenly.

As dishevelled as always, the hairy little monster was excitedly twisting the handles of the football game. Oksa and Tugdual went over to them, intrigued. The game was in full swing.

"Do you want to hear what this peanut has got to say to you, *sale* hooligan?" replied the outraged Poliglossiper, hopping around frantically.

"Peanuts are grown in a hot country, aren't they?" commented the Squoracles, wrapped in tiny multi-coloured mohair scarves.

"Oh, what pretty scarves you're wearing!" remarked Oksa.

"They're not scarves, they're beak muffs. The Master knitted them for us as part of the 'winter cold' project," explained one of the Squoracles. "To tide us over until we migrate to a hot country for ever."

This short chat about the weather was interrupted by the hysterical shouts of the Getorix, who had just scored. The Croakettes beat their wings in exultation and the Tumble-Bawler, like all football supporters, screamed loudly.

"Well?" asked the Getorix. "Who's the best, Poliglossiper, let's guess, you pest!"

"Oh! *Ta gueule*, you crap poet!"

"The Getorix has taken it into its head to start rhyming," explained Abakum, from the kitchen. "But be lenient, it's only a beginner."

"Oh, I understand now," said Oksa laughing.

Inspired by this answer, the Incompetent came over to her, looking even more confused than usual.

"Oh, you understand something about all this, do you? I don't."

"Hey, Incompetent," cackled the Getorix. "The day you understand something, it will snow in August!"

"Oh no! Oh, please no!" said the Squoracles, their teeth chattering at the mere mention of snow.

But the Incompetent, in fine form, ignored the remarks of the other creatures and continued to think things through very slowly.

"I don't understand anything about this game. What do you call it? The peanut game?"

"No, it's table football," explained Oksa, politely suppressing her laughter. "It's very simple: there are two teams, blue and red. The aim is to kick the ball into your opponent's goal. The winner is the person who scores the most points."

The Incompetent paused for a moment, during which it seemed to be deep in thought.

"That seems very complicated... and why do you need to wear a beak muff knitted by the Master when you play? Can I have one?"

"Haha, you'd need something more like a feather muff for a featherbrain!" sniggered the Getorix. "Haha, a featherbrain muff for the Incompetent!"

Oksa turned to look at Tugdual for some kind of help in stifling her mounting giggles. But he merely winked at her with a smile. Further away, the Goranov was complaining about these violent exchanges and the strain this commotion was putting on its fragile nerves. As for the Getorix and the Poliglossiper, they were both frantically cheating to win the game.

"I'll scalp you, if you do that *encore une fois*," screamed the Poliglossiper. "*C'est illégal* to pick up the ball and put it *directement* in the goal!"

"Here's what I'll do with your wet threats, you pest. I'll clean up my mess!" replied the Getorix, screaming with laughter. "Haha, I'll clean up my mess with your threats, you pain in the neck!"

"Hey, I've never noticed how much hair that creature has, it's astonishing," remarked the Incompetent, so guilelessly that Oksa couldn't help exploding with laughter. "This game is very funny, isn't it?" it added, seeing the tears rolling down Oksa's cheeks.

"This is hilarious!" remarked Tugdual, holding his stomach. "They're all totally bonkers."

"Come on, creatures," broke in Abakum trying to sound serious. "We're about to eat. No more table football tonight."

The creatures obediently went upstairs, squabbling all the way, except for the Incompetent, which gazed at Oksa with large, bulging eyes full of uncertainty.

"I've seen you before somewhere," it muttered.

"Me too, Incompetent, me too," replied Oksa between peals of laughter.

Without taking its eyes off Oksa, it sat down near the hearth to explore the complexities of its hazy thoughts. Nearby, the Young Gracious relaxed and enjoyed the evening. But her good mood wasn't just down to the excellent meal, she realized. Something had happened to her. Something totally unexpected. She tried to catch Tugdual's eye to confirm what she, at least, no longer doubted. The young man seemed to be concentrating on his plate, his lips curved in a half-smile. He stayed like this for seconds on end, torturing Oksa. Suddenly he raised his head and looked deep into her eyes. Oksa trembled, blushed and felt her stomach lurch, but she managed to maintain eye contact, even though his look was more intense than any she'd ever experienced before. She felt as though her heart had been pierced right through.

58

EMERGENCY!

WHEN THEY ARRIVED IN BIGTOE SQUARE ON SUNDAY evening, Abakum and Oksa immediately saw an ambulance's flashing light intermittently illuminating the façade of the Pollocks' house. In a panic, Oksa leapt out of the sidecar and rushed into the living room. Not a soul. The kitchen was empty too. Then she spotted some ambulance men on the upstairs landing, carrying her mother on a stretcher.

"MUM!"

Marie's long hair hung down untidily, revealing her drawn, white face. She was lying there motionless with her arms at her sides. Only her eyes wandered vaguely. The ambulance men stopped for a moment and Oksa dashed over to her mother.

"What's happening? Dad? Where are you?" she yelled in alarm.

Pavel Pollock appeared suddenly at the door of the bedroom, an anguished expression on his face and a travel bag still open in his hand.

"Oksa, sweetheart! There's something seriously wrong with your Mum. She has to go straight to the hospital."

"You don't look in a fit state to drive, Pavel, I'll take you," suggested Abakum, looking at Oksa's father in concern. "You can explain what happened on the way. Where's Dragomira?"

"I'm coming!"

Baba Pollock came out of the bedroom too and rushed over to hug Oksa. She looked worried and her hands were shaking so uncontrollably

364

that she was finding it hard to do anything efficiently, which was highly unusual for her. She walked over to Abakum and whispered something in his ear which made the blood drain from the old man's face in an alarming manner.

All four of them climbed into the Pollocks' car. Abakum quickly moved off and followed the ambulance through the traffic, which immediately gave way on hearing the siren. Sitting stiffly in the front seat, Pavel finally explained in a dull voice what had happened.

"She didn't say anything to you but she's not been feeling herself for a few days now. It started with painful joints as if she were suffering from rheumatism. I even teased her about her age, as usual," he admitted with a choked sob. "And then on Friday, she began feeling terribly giddy. We thought it was due to the parent-teacher meeting and particularly because of the interview with Orthon-McGraw. She was a bit tense, I could sense how apprehensive she was all day… I was fairly anxious myself and I didn't look for any other explanation. On Saturday, her dizziness worsened and her eyes began to hurt. She couldn't tolerate the light any more and she could barely see anything, even in the half-light. We thought it was a really bad migraine. Dragomira prepared a powerful decoction to try and relieve the pain, but it was no good. Marie was too dizzy to stand up. She dozed off and slept until mid afternoon. Dragomira and I took turns to watch over her; we were both very worried. When she woke up, she was paralysed—she couldn't move the left side of her body! All she could say was that she was hurting all over. I called an ambulance and you got here just after."

Pavel put his face in his hands, looking worn-out with worry. Oksa, sitting just behind him, threw her arms around his neck to comfort him. But tears were rolling down her face, and she felt totally helpless in the face of this tragedy.

"Here's the hospital," said Abakum, breaking the silence. "They'll look after her here and this will all just be a bad memory in no time, you'll see."

There was a hint of pessimism in his voice, though, which he couldn't voice openly. Gripping the steering wheel with his hands, he met Dragomira's anxious eyes in the rear-view mirror, which only served to confirm his worst fears.

※

The next morning Oksa had to go back to school with a heavy heart and her mind light years away from her everyday student concerns. This wasn't a normal Monday. She was relieved to learn that McGraw had called in sick. She was in no mood to put up with him, or his sarcasm. Merlin and Zelda, whom Gus had told about Marie Pollock's illness, rallied around their friend as warmly as they could, but Oksa seemed miles away, cut off from everyone. Words rolled off her like water off a duck's back. Nothing and no one could give her any comfort. During Dr Bento's lesson she couldn't help thinking dark thoughts, which plunged her into suffocating despair. She'd thought about death before, of course. She'd known people who had died in her family but, when she thought carefully, it had never been anyone she was close to. She'd never lost anyone she loved. Never. Death had always been an abstract idea, a pain which she imagined was deep and lasting. A feeling of terrible emptiness. But today, things were very different. And very *real*. It was not so much pain she felt, as a silent, uncontrollable terror which was invading every inch of her heart. At break she ran to take refuge in the Statues' Den, where she cried heavy, racking sobs. When she emerged, her eyes red and swimming with tears, her friends were waiting for her, looking concerned and helpless. Just before lunch Mr Bontempi came to the prep room to find her and took her to his office.

"Oksa, I'm aware that your mother has been taken into hospital. I know how hard this is for you, because I had to cope with the same thing when I was your age. I think it would be better for her, and for you, if you spent a few days with her. You won't find it hard to catch up on the lessons you'll miss. You have friends you can count on, which is one of the benefits of being so popular, isn't it?" he added with a smile that was meant to be comforting. "Your gran is coming to get you. Oh, there she is now!"

Seeing Dragomira come in, Oksa jumped up, toppling her chair over, and rushed over to her.

"Baba! Have you seen Mum? How is she?"

"She's had a lot of tests," replied Dragomira, after greeting Mr Bontempi. "We know a little more today. She is suffering from some sort of hemiplegia, which has paralysed the left side of her body. But there's another neurological problem which the doctors are looking into. It's a bit too soon yet for them to know exactly what's going on. But your Mum is feeling better, Oksa, she's in much less pain and she'd like to see you."

"Then don't keep her waiting, Mrs Pollock," said Mr Bontempi encouragingly. "Go quickly. And be strong, Oksa—your mother needs you."

❀

The next few days were nerve-racking for the Pollocks. Taking Mr Bontempi's sound advice, Oksa tried very hard to build a shell around herself and to deal with the constant aching sadness that ate away at her. Every day she spent hours at the hospital with her mother, along with her father. Hiding her anguish as best she could, she'd lay out all the gifts she and her father had bought in town that morning on the bed: nightgowns, each prettier than the last, eau de toilette, flowers and gizmos to brighten up the room, crystallized fruit—Marie's guilty pleasure—CDs of relaxing music, etc. She'd read aloud from celebrity magazines to take her mum's mind off things and tell her whatever came into her head, from the morning news to the latest funny stories she'd heard. In the evening she'd come back from the hospital, wrung out by the effort of not crying. She'd throw herself on her bed, often in tears, her heart in pieces. Her father would come and do his best to comfort her, although he was also bitterly upset. As for Dragomira, she'd sit up with her in a chair next to her bed. But a gran, however caring she is, isn't a mother. Overwhelmed by sadness, Oksa would eventually sink into a fitful sleep, plagued by her worries about a dismal future.

When she'd been admitted to the hospital, Marie Pollock had been in a critical condition. Her family was shocked at the contrast between Marie's appearance before the illness and the gaunt, ashen face of the woman lying in her hospital bed. As Dragomira had said, she wasn't in so much pain now; but it was so hard to see her looking so weak and sapped by this disease, not to mention the bouts of nausea caused by the strong drugs they were giving her. At the same time, the medical diagnoses had confirmed that she was seriously ill and that it was proving hard to find a suitable cure. Everyone was distressed by the mood of unspoken pessimism which hung over Oksa's mother. Yet, a few days later, to the doctors' great surprise, her condition altered drastically.

59

A CONSPICUOUS
RETURN

THE FOLLOWING WEEK OKSA WENT BACK TO SCHOOL. Gus, who was waiting to see her, made no attempt to hide his impatience or his joy.

"Hi there! I'm so glad you're back!" he exclaimed.

And he rushed over and kissed her on the cheeks. Two sincere, clumsy and totally spontaneous kisses. What a first! Oksa couldn't remember Gus ever kissing her, not since they'd known each other—in other words, not since they were toddlers. Taken aback, she looked down and flushed. She didn't go as red as Gus, though, who had turned so scarlet that he seemed about to go up in flames.

"Hiya, Gus," she said. "My mother's home, I'm so happy! The doctors weren't keen, they thought it was too early, but Dad insisted on having her discharged so that he could bring her home. I really thought they were going to come to blows."

"Yes, I know," said Gus, his cheeks and forehead still bright red. "My parents called your father yesterday evening, they've just told me. How is she? She looked as if she was in so much pain when we came to see her the other day."

Oksa's face darkened.

"She can move her left arm a bit now. She can't walk, but she can stand up; she's gradually regaining her balance, she's got her sight back, and she doesn't get dizzy any more. I hope it continues... I was so afraid Gus, you have no idea!"

"What about the doctors? What are they saying?"

"They think it's multiple sclerosis. I did some research: it's a serious disease which attacks the nervous system by forming lesions which alter the neurological functions. It mainly affects women. Abakum is staying with us for a few days and he and Baba make a pretty formidable team, I can tell you. I was aware they were clued up on alternative medicine, but I had no idea how much they knew. Believe it or not, Baba injected my mother with some Vermicula!"

"Er... what are Vermicula?" asked Gus.

"It's top-secret information," murmured Oksa, looking around cagily. "Vermicula are a widely used remedy in Edefia, particularly in micro-surgery. I don't have to tell you that the doctors here aren't in the know. Abakum explained to me that, instead of operating on people, they inject them with a substance which contains worms the size of human cells. They make their way to where the illness has taken hold and treat it—No kidding! It does sound a little disgusting, I agree, but I think it's worked well on my mother. In her case, it seems that lesions have formed on her nerve centre and, according to the doctors, we don't know what the long-term effects are. From what I've read, the damage is usually irreversible, since it's a degenerative disease: the affected cells don't regenerate, you never get back what you've lost. That's why the doctors have described the results of the last tests they did on my mother as a miracle. They can't get over how much she's improved in just a few days; this is the first time they've seen a case like this. We can't say anything to them, but I'm telling you in the utmost secrecy that Abakum and Baba's Vermicula went straight to the root of the problem: they're the reason my mother is feeling better. Admittedly she's not cured, far from it; but, given the extent of the damage, she should be far worse, according to the doctors. I just hope she continues to get better..."

"That's so typical of the Pollocks—microscopic worms the size of cells! If you didn't exist, someone would have had to invent you. What about you? How are you?" asked Gus, moving closer and stealing a glance at Oksa.

"Oh Gus, you've got a blackhead on your nose!" said Oksa, trying to change the subject. "Only joking… things are better now my mother's back, even though she's far from well. You know Dad, he won't leave her side by so much as an inch. Otherwise, you would get a look at the Lunatrixes! Dragomira has given them permission to come downstairs in view of the special circumstances, and they're as busy as… as…"

"As Lunatrixes?" said Gus helpfully.

Oksa laughed heartily for the first time in days.

"Exactly. They're more bonkers than ever, their vocabulary is all over the place. But it's lucky they're there because my mother loves them and so do I. They give us a good laugh and they make themselves very useful."

She paused for a second, then asked:

"What about… McGraw?"

"McGraw? Well… he asked where you were, believe it or not, you'd almost think he missed you! Apart from that, nothing special, he's just the same as usual. Despicable, like your father said. Other than that, someone else has really missed you—"

He was interrupted by the arrival of Merlin Poicassé, who gave a loud shout of joy when he saw that Oksa had come back. He also came over to kiss her clumsily, but boldly, on the cheeks. Blushing furiously again at more hugging and kissing, Oksa wondered: *What on earth is going on with those two? Did they make a bet or something?* But if she'd seen Gus's crestfallen expression, she'd have realized immediately that a bet was well wide of the mark—that the "someone else" who'd missed her was perhaps not who she thought it was.

As Mr Bontempi had anticipated, her week away from school didn't have any effect on Oksa's work. Gus had emailed her the homework she had to do along with the lessons she had to learn every day and she soon caught up. All the teachers were very kind and asked after her mother. Unfortunately McGraw hadn't changed and was just as mocking and contemptuous as ever.

"Oh, Miss Pollock is back, just when we'd given up *our last hope*," he said, with heavy emphasis on these words. "A week away from school for a hospitalized parent! How long would you have been off if it had been *you* taken sick? A year-long sabbatical, at least…"

A shocked murmur ran through the classroom. Oksa was literally speechless. Sitting on her own at her desk, since Gus had been relegated to the back of the class, she felt the Curbita-Flatulo firmly squeeze her wrist. She was *SO* angry. She put her hand on her small shoulder bag and felt for her Granok-Shooter. She wanted to use it so badly. A good Muddler or Dermenburn would teach that arrogant McGraw to be sarcastic! The pressure from the Curbita-Flatulo increased and the rage which was burning Oksa up inside was quickly extinguished, as though quenched by a cool breeze—helped by the fact that she had a small act of revenge up her sleeve, just in case… a doubly satisfying act of revenge, since there was nothing magical about it at all. And McGraw had just unwittingly given her a great opportunity. As he was writing on the board, she raised her hand and called out:

"Please, sir?"

McGraw turned round in astonishment, looking tense.

"Yes?"

"Sir, there's something odd in the last exercise you gave us," she explained innocently. "You seem to have reversed the abscissa and the ordinate. The way it is now, the problem can't be solved."

An ominous silence followed this remark which was, after all, totally justified. At the back, Gus decided there was absolutely no point trying to make his friend see reason. In expectation of the catastrophe that was bound to befall the class in the next few minutes, some of the students were gnawing their bottom lips, while others wisely lowered their eyes. Oksa kept hers firmly fixed on McGraw. It was hard, but she was determined not to be the first to look away. All kinds of thoughts helped her to keep her resolve. Specific images, like Gracious Malorane endangering herself for Dragomira, the man with the decomposing arm writhing in pain, flames emerging from the Glass Column in Edefia, her mother lying on the stretcher. Even if this last mental image had nothing to do with him, it gave her more courage than all the rest combined. McGraw had belittled her mother's illness and she wasn't going to put up with that! The teacher rummaged through his papers and took out the exercise in question. He reread it quickly, but Oksa was confident she was right, so she didn't take her eyes off him. Finally he looked up and fixed his dark gaze on her:

"Fortunately the brilliant Miss Pollock is here to point out her teachers' mistakes! Perhaps I should let you take my place?" he said stiffly, his thin lips pursed in rage.

"But Dr McGraw, I'm not a teacher, I'm only thirteen!" she retorted, a hint of irony in her voice. "I just wanted to make sure it was a mistake because, otherwise, we might have found it confusing."

"Your classmates have probably already corrected it. I'm sure everyone picked up on such a glaring mistake well before you mentioned it," said McGraw icily, putting an end to the conversation.

Oksa smiled mockingly at him, noticing that a few of the students in the class had grabbed their pencil cases and notebooks to correct the faulty logic of the exercise and were hurriedly trying to come up with a coherent answer. Their hasty diligence and Oksa's provocative smile didn't escape McGraw and he spent the whole hour looking daggers at her.

※

Needless to say, she was given an ovation at break. The students in Year 8 Hydrogen were gloating: once more, Oksa had managed to stand up to the hateful McGraw. She slipped away just in time to avoid being carried shoulder-high in triumph, because her victory, far from going to her head, didn't dispel her worries.

"I must phone home to find out how my mother is, I didn't see her before I left. I'm going to get my mobile, I left it in my locker."

"Do you want me to come with you?" Gus asked hurriedly.

"No, don't bother. I won't be a minute."

The corridor was deserted, since everyone was outside in the court-yard enjoying the winter sun. Oksa fetched her phone and called home. Dragomira picked up immediately and reassured her granddaughter: Marie was fine this morning, she'd even managed to take a few steps leaning on Pavel's arm. The Vermicula seemed to be working miracles. Her mind put at ease, Oksa hung up. But when she turned round, her relieved smile quickly vanished: she found herself face to face with the Year 9 Neanderthal, no more than a couple of feet away.

"Well, well. If it isn't my favourite loser! You don't seem so full of yourself without your pathetic little band of brats following you around," he said provocatively.

"Not so full of myself as who?" retorted Oksa belligerently, massaging her wrist to relieve the pressure of the Curbita-Flatulo, which found itself in demand for the second time that morning.

"You think you're so clever, don't you, Miss I-can-do-everything-better-than-anyone-else! Do you really believe I don't know who you are? You're living in cloud cuckoo land. You're nowhere near as strong as you think you are, my father is head and shoulders above you. He could flatten you and your whole family to a pulp if he wanted!"

"Oh yeah?" said Oksa, determined not to be overawed. "Is your father a bulldozer then?"

"You pathetic moron, you still haven't realized, have you? MY FATHER IS MCGRAW!" yelled the Neanderthal.

60

Three for
the Price of One

WHEN SHE HEARD THIS, OKSA COULDN'T RESTRAIN
herself: her Knock-Bong somehow thumped into the boy she
now knew as McGraw's son with incredible force, sending him flying.
He landed heavily on the flagstone floor sixty feet away with a stifled cry.

"*Wow*," thought Oksa, rubbing her wrist, "*that was worth a little pain
from the Curbita-Flatulo!*"

But the thick-set lout was already struggling to his feet, looking a little
dazed but hell-bent on revenge—Oksa could see that clearly from his
furious face, which didn't bode well at all. Bent double, rubbing the small
of his back, he lumbered closer with a threatening expression. Suddenly,
like a flash, he lunged at Oksa before she could react, crossing the sixty
feet between them at a phenomenal, totally unreal, speed. Less than a
second later he pounced on her, slamming her against the ground, his
speed increasing the impact. Crushed under her attacker's body, Oksa
gave a deep groan of pain mingled with rage.

"You didn't think," spluttered Mortimer McGraw, "you were the only
one who could—"

He didn't have time to finish his sentence: Oksa had just delivered a
relentless blow which weakened his resolve. Using the fingers of her right
hand like the talons of an eagle swooping on its prey, she'd hit him hard

on the temple. Then she rolled to one side, athletically freeing herself as her father had taught her to do in karate, capitalizing on the boy's surprise at her counter-attack. She was about to defend herself from a fresh attack from him when someone suddenly jumped on her back, pinning her to the ground. She had just enough time to put her hands out in front of her to break her fall.

"Don't you dare lay a finger on Mortimer, understand!" hissed a voice.

With her face against the floor, Oksa couldn't see who was speaking. All she could see were McGraw's son's shoes just in front of her. There was a savage kick to her right side. Making a superhuman effort, she tried to turn over. The grip on her relaxed and Oksa was able to sit up, her ribs hurting, to see who had spoken.

"ZOE? I thought it sounded like you! Help me!"

"Leave Mortimer alone! Don't touch my family!" snarled Zoe in return.

"You mean… that Neanderthal is your brother?"

One by one, the pieces of information slotted into place, to her total incredulity.

"That means McGraw is your father too! But I thought you were an orphan. YOU LIED!"

"No, you don't know anything," muttered Zoe.

She released Oksa and ran off. At the same time, Gus suddenly appeared in the corridor, worried that his friend hadn't yet come back. Oksa raised her head just enough to see her friend charging at the Neanderthal like a wild animal. The two boys were glaring at each other, eye to eye, and Mortimer McGraw had adopted the stance of a boxer about to throw a lethal punch. But Gus intercepted his move, blocking his sworn enemy's throat with his right arm, then hooked his leg. Despite his massive build, the Neanderthal staggered and almost lost his balance. He stopped himself falling just in time by catching hold of Gus's uniform tie.

"I'd advise you to let me go," said Gus through gritted teeth.

But instead of following this sound advice, Mortimer McGraw tightened his grip and was clearly about to throw Gus against the wall. This wasn't something the boy fancied at all, his rage giving him the strength of ten men. Catching hold of the Neanderthal by the arms, he vigorously propelled him over his hip, and threw him to the ground like a sack of potatoes.

"Are you hurt, Oksa?" panted Gus, rushing over to her as the Neanderthal ran off.

"No, I'm fine... well, actually, no, I'm not fine all," she said, sitting on the ground with her head in her hands. "Ow!" she cried, holding her ribs, as she tried to stand.

"What's going on?" asked Merlin, who'd just turned up with a few other students alerted by the din. "Are you hurt, Oksa? Can I help?"

"Leave it, Merlin," replied Gus breathlessly. "I'll look after her. Come on, Oksa, I'm taking you to the infirmary."

❄

Matron refused to believe Oksa when she claimed she'd broken a rib falling over and badgered her for the truth. Confronted by the student's stubborn refusal to change her story, she called Mr Bontempi, who got there a couple of minutes later.

"Oksa, you have to tell me who did this to you," he said, sitting down by her bed.

"I fell over, sir, honestly," she added, seeing his unconvinced expression. Mr Bontempi sighed.

"Oksa, it's very hard to break a rib just by falling down in a corridor. Personally, I think that some student or other was bullying you and you don't want to give me their name for fear of reprisals."

Oksa shook her head: her answer was final. Mr Bontempi turned hopefully to Gus.

"Gustave, did you see anyone?"

"No, sir, when I arrived, Oksa was on the floor and there was no one around."

"I see…"

Mr Bontempi stood up and said one last thing to the pair before leaving the infirmary:

"You know where my office is if you want to speak to me. Let me say again that what just happened is very serious. I could punish the person who did this to you very harshly if you would only co-operate. All I need is a name! The ball is in your court, kids."

He turned on his heels and they heard his heavy footsteps going downstairs. Matron came over:

"You can go back to the classroom, Gustave; thanks for your help. Oksa, I called your home and your father is coming right away to collect you and take you to the hospital. I think you've broken a rib, but you'll need an X-ray. Stay lying down while you wait, okay?"

And she went back into the small glazed office from which she kept an eye on her visitors.

"Thanks Gus," whispered Oksa in her friend's ear. "Thanks for not saying anything!"

"Oksa, I wasn't dreaming, was I? It was Zoe who stopped you defending yourself, wasn't it?"

"It's even more serious than that, Gus."

His ear practically glued to Oksa's lips, Gus was completely taken aback when his friend told him the unthinkable news. In the space of a few seconds, they both realized that the number of McGraws had just tripled.

61

THE POISONED GIFT

FOR FEAR OF BEING QUESTIONED ABOUT THE STRANGE mark around Oksa's belly button, Pavel took the injured girl straight home and didn't go anywhere near the hospital. With her ribs tightly bandaged, Oksa was welcomed by Dragomira and the Lunatrixes, who had now taken up residence on the first floor.

"Oooohhhh! The Young Gracious has encountered an accident! There are great health deficiencies in this family, it's a phonebook of disasters and we are held in the pincers of a total melodrama!"

The Lunatrixa began sobbing noisily while her companion hastened over to help Pavel support Oksa.

"Rest Your Graciousness's hand upon my head, I will become a cane for you, that is my ambition."

"Thanks, Lunatrix. Where is Mum?"

"She is seated at the table in the kitchen and awaits your accompaniment," replied the Lunatrixa with a loud sniffle.

"In here!" rang out Marie's voice.

Oksa and her father found her sitting in the kitchen with a fragrant cup of tea.

"You're here at last!" exclaimed Marie. "How do you feel, darling?"

Before replying, Oksa kissed her mother, pulling a face at the pain, and asked for her news first.

"I'm okay, honestly. But we'll talk about me later, tell us what happened to you."

"I fell over and broke a rib," replied Oksa softly.

Even breathing gently caused her a great deal of pain. She grimaced, and tried to breathe as shallowly as possible.

"A broken rib!" exclaimed Dragomira. "Don't move, I've got just the thing for you."

She leapt out of her chair and they heard her steps echoing up the stairs to the second floor.

"Don't say anything, don't do anything, don't move. Wait for me!" she shouted in a ringing voice.

They heard a faint commotion and, a few minutes later, Dragomira reappeared holding a small jar.

"Take that bandage off now," she said, beckoning to Oksa to come and lie down on one of the sofas in the living room.

"Are you going to give her a Bonigonum?" asked Pavel, seeing the bottle his mother was holding. "It's a very long time since I've seen that, it's a great idea. That will have you back on your feet in no time, Oksa."

"Anyway, if it's as effective as the Vermicula are, I advise you to have it, darling," said Marie.

Dragomira opened the small pot and took out a large bright-blue slug, about three inches long and thick and shiny. *Very* thick and *very* shiny. Oksa cried out in horror, then immediately cried out again at the pain caused by the first cry.

"I'm going… you're going…" she muttered.

"You can conjugate the verb 'to go' very well, Dushka," remarked Dragomira smiling, the slug wriggling feebly between her two fingers.

"Have I got to *eat* that revolting thing?" continued Oksa, swallowing with difficulty.

This question caused general hilarity. Dragomira and Pavel exploded with laughter and the Lunatrixes, purple to the top of their heads with their mouths wide open, slapped their thighs frantically.

"Eat a Bonigonum? Distance that thought from your stomach, Young Gracious! The Bonigonum is not to be eaten and does not eat anyone, it will be the repairing of your bone."

"Is that true, Baba?"

"Completely true."

"Then you're going to inject me with it like the Vermicula, aren't you? I don't want that, no, no, no," panicked Oksa, imagining the size of the syringe that would be needed for such an injection.

"Don't be afraid, my dear. It's much simpler than that, just relax."

Dragomira put her hand on Oksa's forehead and, with her other hand, placed the revolting slug directly onto her bare skin, exactly where the pain was at its worst, the place where the broken rib was bulging under the swollen flesh. At first Oksa looked away, feeling totally nauseated. Then curiosity got the better of her and she ventured a glance. The slug's eyes were bulging and were striped with little black veins. It had also started to produce an impressive amount of saliva: an abundant froth was spreading from beneath its glistening body and seeping into Oksa's skin.

"You see, the Bonigonum acts like a powerful poultice," explained Dragomira, gently pressing on the wiggling slug. "Its saliva has the power to make bones knit faster and, as you can see, your skin absorbs it immediately like a sponge. In a few hours, your rib will be as good as new."

"The doctors would give their right arm for this!" remarked Oksa.

"Very true, darling," agreed her father, "so we'll stay away from the medical profession for a few days in order to avoid any embarrassing questions."

"Can you imagine replying to concerned enquiries?" enthused Oksa. "My broken rib? Oh yes, I did have a broken rib this morning, but it's ancient history now, you know!"

Oksa began to laugh and immediately grimaced: the pain wasn't ancient history yet, she'd have to wait a few hours with that revolting, slobbering blue slug stuck to her side.

"Yes, let's avoid attracting the doctors' attention, they're already asking far too many questions about me."

And Marie explained to Oksa that her condition had improved at a pace that defied medical opinion: the lesions paralysing her nerve centre were visibly receding, which was unheard of according to the doctors. Also, in view of the severity of those lesions, whose cause was still unknown, she shouldn't even be able to move a toe, let alone take a few steps, even with the continuous support offered by Pavel and Dragomira.

"Hurrah for the Vermicula then!" said Oksa cheerfully from her convalescent sofa. "And hurrah for the Bonigonum! You should patent it, Baba, you could be the queen of the pharmaceutical industry. You'd become a multimillionaire."

"Probably," agreed Baba Pollock, smiling. "Given everything we can do, Abakum and I could have founded an empire. But that's never been our ambition. We've stayed true to our principles, which were shared by many Edefians: live and work according to our needs—no more, no less—and never abuse our powers. That is our rule."

"Not everyone can say as much," said Oksa, her face suddenly darkening.

"You mean Orthon? Or… McGraw?" asked her mother.

"Yes."

"You mean your injury has something to do with him?" exclaimed Pavel, abruptly jumping up from his seat.

"Yes… well, no… It's always the same snide comments with him, we're starting to get used to it. It was his children who caused the problems today," admitted Oksa, hanging her head.

"*WHAT?*"

Everyone immediately looked astounded. With her hand on her heart, Dragomira shut her eyes and tried to take in this shocking piece of news. Marie gave a cry and Pavel, standing behind her, clenched his fists in a gesture of rage. His face twisted in a grimace, betraying his anxiety. They all looked at each other, then stared at Oksa.

"His children? You mean that Orthon's children are here? At school?" asked Dragomira, breathlessly.

"You remember the Neanderthal? I already told you about him," said Oksa, realizing the effect that these revelations were having on her family.

"That rough older boy who keeps picking on you, the one you drenched with balls of water one day?" continued Dragomira. "You mean he's Orthon-McGraw's son?"

Oksa nodded and decided to tell the truth. Lying was too much of an effort and she felt so tired.

"His name is Mortimer. And I didn't fall over. He broke my rib," she blurted out, trying to stop her voice trembling. "He cornered me in the corridor, just after my phone call. He told me who he was and threatened to flatten all of us to a pulp. I hit him with an amazing Knock-Bong, I couldn't help myself!" she added, chewing her lip.

"You attacked McGraw's son with a Knock-Bong? In one of the school corridors?" exclaimed her mother in dismay.

"Oh Mum, you should have seen how powerful it was!" said Oksa excitedly, perking up at the memory. "He was thrown a good sixty feet. It was great! The problem is that he seems to have terrific powers too. He came for me at tremendous speed, I've never seen anyone move so fast. We fought, then his sister came up behind me and jumped on my back. I found myself flat on the ground and while I was down, Mortimer recovered. He kicked me in the ribs. That was when Gus arrived, and used one of those amazing judo holds on him. Which was just as well, because I don't know what I'd have done to those two—I could have killed them," she said angrily, blithely ignoring the gap between desire and reality.

"Or they could have killed *you*," stressed her father, looking even more anxious than ever. "But you mentioned that boy's sister. Is she also at St Proximus? Do you know her?"

"Yes. And so do you—it's Zoe."

"ZOE? The Zoe who came to your birthday party?" asked Dragomira in alarm.

"Yes," replied Oksa angrily. "Now I'm convinced she became friends with Zelda just to get at me. I never liked that girl, I told you that, Baba. When I think that she gave us the impression that she was an orphan! I'm disgusted."

"But that means Orthon-McGraw's daughter has been in this house, doesn't it?" her father said slowly.

Silently all four looked at each other gravely, thinking about the implications of this new and surprising information. Suddenly Dragomira cried shrilly:

"The SOAP!"

"The soap?" echoed Pavel and Marie in their turn, as Oksa nibbled at her last remaining nail.

"Where's the soap that Zoe gave Oksa for her birthday?" demanded Dragomira hastily.

"Oksa gave it to me, because of her allergy to glycerine," replied Marie dully. "I've been using it for the past few days."

⁂

Abakum and Dragomira were adamant: their analyses of the remaining piece of soap proved that Zoe's gift had been poisoned. Originally intended for Oksa, with the aim of weakening her and making it easier for Orthon-McGraw to get near her, even kidnap her as he'd apparently planned, the soap had found another victim: Marie Pollock. It was easy to understand now why she'd suddenly been taken so seriously ill.

"This is very clever," explained Abakum. "Orthon added essence of robiga-nervosa to it. This is a highly toxic, very rare plant whose cells immediately attacked your nervous system, Marie. They act like rust. It's lethal. I'll take what's left of that soap to examine it and I'll try to find an antidote. Luckily we had the Vermicula, my dear Marie, because otherwise I think you'd still be paralysed in your hospital bed without any hope of remission. The Vermicula seem to be working, they've stabilized

384

and improved your overall condition. But there may be something more effective that will allow you to regain full use of all the functions you've lost. The doctors didn't beat around the bush about their pessimistic prognosis, did they?"

Marie shook her head and Oksa felt tears pricking her eyes. Would her mother have to stay like this for the rest of her life? That would be awful, particularly as she was the one who'd given her the poisoned soap, all because of her damned allergy.

"It makes me so livid to think that this was aimed at you," murmured Marie, moving closer to Oksa.

"But you're the one who's ill!" retorted Oksa, swallowing back her tears.

62

CAUGHT OUT
BY THE ALPHABET!

"IT'S NOT THAT I DIDN'T UNDERSTAND, I JUST DIDN'T LISTEN!"
The Incompetent was standing in the middle of Dragomira's strictly
private workroom, arms dangling at its sides. In front of it stood the
Getorix and a Squoracle, wrapped in a big woollen scarf.

"Then you're not just soft in the head, Incompetent, you're hard of
hearing too," said the Getorix, looking even more dishevelled than ever.

"Who opens a window in the middle of winter?" continued the
infuriated Squoracle. "Did you ever hear anything like it? What were
you thinking, Incompetent? I said: whatever you do, please don't open
the windows. It's not exactly complicated. It's snowing outside, I saw
that and, more than that, *I felt it*… If you want me dead, then say so!" it
bawled through chattering teeth. "And did you even consider bird flu?
Haven't you ever heard of medical confinement?"

"What's going on here? Why are you arguing?"

Oksa had just walked into the room after slipping inside the double-
bass case, which had been left open. Dragomira was hard at work in
front of her giant alembic, ignoring the creatures' squabbling which
had stopped bothering her a long time ago. Bluish wisps of smoke
rose from the pipes and filled the workroom with their sickly sweet
perfume.

"Hello, Dushka, how are you? I'll be with you in a second, do sit down."

"Young Gracious, do you have the wish to acknowledge receipt of my homage?"

The Lunatrixa was bowing so low as she approached Oksa that she overbalanced and crashed to the floor at the girl's feet—which didn't escape the Getorix's notice.

"Haha, what a ridiculous bow! Do you think you're at the Austrian Court?"

From the back of the workroom Dragomira, who'd been listening with at least one ear, provided Oksa with some useful clarification:

"I should explain, Dushka, that yesterday evening, the Lunatrixes watched a film on the life of Sisi, Empress of Austria. Since then, they've been totally obsessed with—how shall I put it—matters of etiquette."

"Young Gracious, Old Gracious, would you be consenting to make me a crinoline? The dream is intense in my heart."

Oksa burst out laughing, as the Squoracle came over shivering:

"And if you could make me a fur bodysuit, maybe I could survive the winter."

Oksa picked up the poor frozen creature and rubbed its back to warm it up, while the Lunatrixa backed away, lifting the folds of an imaginary crinoline.

"What are you making, Baba?" she asked, going over to the giant still.

"Granoks, Dushka, Granoks... I have a small stock of them, but we're all going to need ammunition in the coming months. I'll have to work flat out."

"Because of the McGraws?"

"Yes, because of the McGraws. We have to be ready to defend ourselves," replied Dragomira gravely.

"Do you think Mortimer and Zoe have Granok-Shooters too?"

"No—or, at least, it's very unlikely. As you know, Goranov sap is a key component in the composition of Granok-Shooters. When the

Great Chaos descended on Edefia, my mother, Malorane, was able to plan our escape, which is why Abakum took the Boximinus containing plant cuttings and creatures—"

"Like Noah's Ark!" Oksa butted in.

"Exactly. But there's no way the Felons could have foreseen that some of their number might be ejected from Edefia, no way at all. They passed through to the Outside with what they had with them: their clothes, their Granok-Shooter—and their dark ambitions. No, Abakum is the only person capable of making Granok-Shooters. Anyway, as I said, you'd need a Goranov to do that."

"But there are quite a few Goranovs."

"Yes, we shared the plants between us, just to be on the safe side. A single plant in a single place would have been short-sighted. What's happening at the moment proves it," sighed Baba Pollock.

"I saw some at Leomido's house too. Don't you think that's a bit dicey?" added Oksa, gazing intently at her gran in the hope of finding out more about her great-uncle's relationship with the sworn enemy of the Runaways.

"Why?" asked Dragomira, narrowing her eyes. "Because he lives alone in that massive house in the countryside? Don't you worry about that. Leomido's place is very secure, just like Abakum's house, you can depend on that."

Her gran clearly didn't understand what she was driving at. Oksa had complete confidence in Abakum, no worries there. But she didn't feel the same about Leomido. An image of the old man handing McGraw a phial of Goranov sap flashed through her mind…

"What are you thinking about, Dushka?" asked Dragomira.

"Oh, nothing, Baba, I was just frightening myself."

"Ah, I think the Arborescens has finished distilling."

The two Graciouses bent over the mouth of the smallest pipe of the still, where a thick, yellowish liquid was oozing into a small dish. When the last drop had dripped out, Dragomira poured the substance into the lower part of a small apparatus which looked like an Italian coffee-maker, then put this on a portable stove. The blue flames licked up the side of the utensil and after a few minutes they could hear rattling noises. Reading her granddaughter's thoughts, Dragomira explained with a smile:

"No, I'm not making popcorn for you!"

She took the weird coffee-maker off the stove and opened the top part: a large number of tiny Granoks were vibrating in the heat. Oksa looked at Dragomira in astonishment.

"Here's a small stock of Arborescens already! Give me your Granok-Shooter, Dushka."

"Oh, I know this Granok; Abakum told me about it. Arborescens, wasn't it? You can tie your adversary up with it, if I remember rightly."

Dragomira nodded, smiling.

"What ingredients do you use?"

"In Edefia, we used mainly roots taken from the Feetinsky tree. But, as you can imagine, we had to find an alternative plant on the Outside. After testing ivy, marrows and brambles, we managed to make Arborescens using the sap of voluble plants like bindweed and clematis. It's not quite as effective as when we use Feetinskies, but it is satisfactory. It's a fairly complicated manufacturing process: the base is made by steeping sap in perfectly pure spring water, in which chrysoprase—a stone which draws its strength from the night—lakeside algae and Croakette sweat have been submerged."

"Do Croakettes sweat then?" asked the Young Gracious in amazement.

"Of course!" replied Dragomira, laughing. "In tiny quantities, certainly... but that's what makes their sweat so valuable."

Oksa pulled a face, while her Granok-Shooter sucked up a good twenty yellow granules. Baba Pollock poured what was left into a small jar, which she locked in a recess concealed behind one of the many paintings hanging on the wall.

"Is that where you hide the Granoks? Behind Dad's portrait?"

"Yes, but I don't need to tell you that this is top secret. Anyway, it's not enough to know the location of this hiding place, because I'm the only one who can open it."

"Oh! It's like the gate at Abakum's house and the back of the double-bass case: the lock only obeys its master."

"Exactly."

After filling her Shooter with Granoks and going over the accompanying words again with Dragomira, Oksa went back downstairs to her room and stretched out on her bed. With her hands behind her head, she stared at the starry sky created on her ceiling. She didn't think she was afraid. With everything she'd learnt these past few weeks, such as the Granoks and the powers—particularly the Knock-Bong, her favourite—she felt stronger and ready to face new ordeals. When Mortimer had attacked her, she'd defended herself rather effectively and if that traitress, Zoe, hadn't butted in she'd have managed quite well on her own. And when McGraw had chased them through the sky, she'd managed to fight back, forcing the elderly Felon to beat a hasty retreat. Then again, thinking it over, her victories weren't all that convincing. If Gus hadn't reached the school corridor in time, Oksa would have been at the mercy of the two junior McGraws. Which might have cost her more than a broken rib. Not to mention using her powers *in school* and stupidly running the risk of being seen—this was not the first time she'd broken the basic rule that had kept the Runaways safe for over fifty years: never attract attention. Thinking about it again, Oksa felt deeply ashamed. Then she thought back to the hot-air balloon episode a few weeks earlier. What would have happened if Leomido hadn't managed to protect her and Gus from the Death's Head Chiropterans that McGraw had unleashed? And, more recently, what if the Croakettes hadn't flown to her aid in Abakum's silo? Her dad sometimes said "if ifs and buts were sugar and nuts, the world would never starve", and that there was no point dwelling on things you couldn't change. But it didn't make her feel any better. She was stronger, much stronger. But Dragomira was right: she had to be careful not to become big-headed about her powers and think too highly of herself, or underestimate the other person, which came down to the same thing—because McGraw had managed to strike right at the heart of her family, despite everyone's vigilance. And what if he weren't the only Felon who had left Edefia? Would the Runaways be strong enough to fight? Did they present enough of a united front? Could they count on Leomido? And her dad? He seemed so opposed to this journey to Edefia... Oksa understood how he felt, really. He'd never seen this land, which was by all accounts fabulous but which wasn't really his. Also, this affair wasn't without its dangers and Oksa was on the front line, which seemed to be the main cause of his anxiety. But she'd never been to Edefia either! And yet she was prepared to brave a thousand dangers to return to the land of her ancestors. Was it because of the Ageless Fairies, who'd made such a strange and compelling plea? Or because of her growing strength and powers? Or because of the Mark—that incredible eight-pointed star—around her belly button, which became more noticeable with every passing day? She was fascinated and frightened by all these questions, in particular the one whose answer remained shrouded in mystery: what was going to happen?

❋

"Class test! Take out some paper, please. Miss Pollock, as Mr Oyster is away, you will help me put the equipment away after the lesson."

Dr McGraw's deceptively casual remark had just taken Oksa by surprise.

"But sir, I have a lesson... a violin lesson afterwards," lied Oksa, with good cause. "I can't stay."

"You play the violin, do you? Well, well, I'd never have thought it of you. I thought you were more interested in kung fu or some other exotic activity. Well, violin or no violin, it's of no interest to me. We all have things to do after the lesson but you'll stay behind and help in line with what was agreed at the start of the school year: every Thursday evening a student will help me put everything away."

"I can stay, sir!" Gus immediately offered.

"Mr Bellanger," sighed McGraw with an exaggeratedly weary look, "we all know how gentlemanly you are. But it's a rather old-fashioned quality these days and you'll have to devise some other tactic to get yourself noticed by girls. Anyway, Miss Pollock comes right after Mr Oyster in the alphabet, which never changes its order and is constant, unlike gallant teenagers. So it will be Miss Pollock."

There were sniggers from a few students, led by Hilda Richard. Embarrassed and furious, Gus hunched at the back of the class. His anger soon gave way to concern: there was no way Oksa could be left alone with McGraw. He gazed at his friend's back and could sense how worried she was. Huddled over her desk, Oksa was thinking fast. She had to call home to warn her father or Dragomira! With the utmost care, she opened her little shoulder bag. The Tumble-Bawler stroked her fingers as a sign of recognition when she took out her brand-new mobile. Keeping an eye on McGraw, who was walking among the desks, she put the phone in her lap and began texting:

5.30pm = on my own…

Suddenly the screen went dead. Edgily, Oksa glanced in McGraw's direction: he was barely six feet away from her, smiling maliciously. He made a small gesture with his fingertips and the phone immediately came on again. It made Oksa's blood boil and she quickly resumed texting. Too bad if McGraw saw her! Which he did, of course; with clear enjoyment he made the same gesture again and Oksa saw a slender thread of light leaving the phone and heading straight for the despicable teacher's fingertips. The power had just been sucked out of the battery! With a smug expression, McGraw continued his rounds, leaving Oksa with her unusable phone. She turned round and tried to catch Gus's eye, which wasn't easy because there were quite a few students sitting between them. It soon became totally impossible, because McGraw kept standing between the two friends, preventing any eye contact. Oksa's stomach churned with panic and her forehead was beaded with perspiration. Her panic was making her feel nauseated. Her head was a jumble of thoughts and she couldn't think straight. The Curbita-Flatulo squeezed her wrist and undulated with increasing force beneath her sleeve. Oksa shut her eyes and tried to breathe in time with the movements of the living bracelet. A few minutes later, she felt a little less scared and more confident. Unfortunately, though, she still couldn't see a way out of this mess. In frustration, she rummaged about in her bag and took a gold-coloured Capacitor from her Caskinette—the Excelsior, which was supposed to boost mental abilities. She hadn't tried it yet, so maybe it would help her make the right decisions? Next to the Excelsiors gleamed the Ventosas, which were a pretty pearly colour. With her fingertips she picked out one of those too. She might need it, you never knew… She'd just swallowed the two tiny capsules when Merlin turned round to wink at her in encouragement. Thirty seconds later, Oksa slipped him a hastily scribbled note:

Merlin, tell Gus, phone dead. Let my father know. Very URGENT. Thanks.

Merlin turned round again and nodded to Oksa: he'd understood, she could count on him.

※

This was hands down the worst test Oksa had ever done in all her school years, given that her mind definitely wasn't on science. The Young Gracious was sensibly preparing for the worst: McGraw was bound to change up a gear, and if he thought she was going to let herself be trapped easily without putting up a fight, he didn't know her at all.

The students scattered immediately when the bell rang. No one ever hung around after McGraw's lessons, particularly not on a Thursday evening when Year 8 Hydrogen was the last form to have a lesson in the deserted school. Only Gus and Merlin didn't rush to put their things away.

Oksa tried to catch Gus's eye but McGraw took a sly delight in standing between them. Oksa twisted round and, against all odds, managed to show her friend her mobile, gesturing that it wasn't working. And when the two boys walked out of the classroom, glancing anxiously at her one last time to show their support, she saw Gus brandishing the scrap of paper she'd passed to Merlin. Then he gave her a thumbs-up and immediately took out his phone, so she realized her message had been delivered. Phew! Gus would go and get Pavel, who was waiting for them as usual at the exit, and they'd both come racing to her aid. She just had to hang in there for a few minutes. Still she watched Gus and Merlin walking away through the windows lining the corridor with a heavy heart. A heavy heart which sank even further when McGraw shut the door, turned the key in the lock and turned round with his Granok-Shooter in his hand and an ominously sardonic smile on his face.

64

THE FELON ATTACKS

"**A**HA, MY DEAR, VERY DEAR OKSA!" BOOMED MCGRAW in his grating voice. "You've led me a merry dance."

"I'm not your dear Oksa. Let me go, you filthy traitor!"

It hadn't taken McGraw long to fire a Granok at Oksa. He'd attacked as soon as the door was closed, and the girl had immediately found herself suspended six feet above the floor by two Croakettes holding her firmly by the elbows. She'd been expecting an attack but McGraw had still taken her by surprise—which is why she was beside herself with rage. How could she have let herself be caught like that? Now she was hanging there helplessly in the air, struggling frantically. She swung her legs back and forth like a pendulum to try and break free, but the winged frogs were phenomenally strong. She reckoned they'd be able to lift the Statue of Liberty!

"Let you go?" retorted McGraw with an evil laugh. "You must be joking! Now that I've got you, I'm certainly not going to let you go just because you tell me to. You may be the Gracious, but you're powerless against me."

"You won't get anything from me. Ever!" shouted Oksa, trying to struggle free.

"Are you mad, you little fool? Do you really think you can stop me? I've been waiting for fifty-seven years. Every single person who's stood in my way has regretted it."

"Yes, and we all know what that means!" yelled Oksa, glaring at him. "Lucas Williams and Peter Carter paid very dearly for it, you monster."

McGraw looked at her in amazement, with one eyebrow raised.

"Lucas Williams and Peter Carter? I'd almost forgotten those two... you're certainly quick on the uptake. But no thirteen-year-old kid is going to come between me and the realization of my dreams. I tried weakening you, but I hit another target entirely. Your poor, dear mother, the delightful Marie Pollock, what a shame," mocked McGraw. "But I've got you at last. There's nothing you can do about it, it's the law of the strongest, my dear. *And I am the strongest!* I'm going to put you into a deep sleep and keep you near me until you and your beloved grandmother open the Portal for me."

Suddenly someone tapped on one of the windows separating the classroom from the corridor. Mortimer McGraw was gesturing to his father from the other side. He flashed a spiteful, ironic look at Oksa, still suspended in mid-air by the Croakettes. McGraw went over to the window.

"All done, Dad! I did what you told me to do," shouted Mortimer.

"Good boy. You'd better be off, now."

"But Dad..."

He clearly wanted to tell him something. McGraw turned round and glanced at Oksa, who was still being held captive by the Croakettes, and went out into the corridor. Immediately his young prisoner, her mind in turmoil, stimulated by her anger and by the Excelsior Capacitor, took advantage of the fact that the elderly Felon had relaxed his vigilance to call to her Tumble-Bawler and her Curbita-Flatulo. She knew Gus and her father wouldn't be long but, in the meantime, the only help she could count on was from those two faithful creatures, which hadn't left her side for weeks.

"Help me!" she murmured to them. "I don't know how, but I'm begging you, help me..."

Immediately the Tumble-Bawler opened the bag's fastener from the inside, climbed out and sprang up Oksa's right side in the direction of her shoulder. When it reached her elbow it savagely scratched the Croakette, which immediately let go with a growl. Oksa suddenly lost altitude on one side and, with her free hand, snatched the Granok-Shooter from her open bag. On the other side, the Curbita-Flatulo uncoiled and crawled hastily up to her other suspended elbow. With a snap of the jaws it dislodged the second Croakette, which hastily flew off, complaining bitterly about the Curbita's appalling manners. The "Free Oksa" operation had barely taken five seconds. The Young Gracious, her feet back on solid ground at last, felt readier than she'd ever been to cross swords with McGraw. Taking no chances this time, she took cover under one of the desks.

"OKSA!" thundered McGraw, bursting into the classroom. "OKSA! You won't escape me, there's no point hiding."

By way of an answer, Oksa took a deep breath to focus her thoughts. She swept the room with her gaze, smashing all the test tubes and bottles on the worktops. Tiny fragments of glass scattered at McGraw's feet and he gave a roar of anger. As they mixed together, the chemicals began giving off acrid fumes and spattered the teacher's spotless shoes. He hurriedly grabbed the first rag he could get his hands on and angrily tried to clean his reeking footwear. During this time, sensibly crouching down, Oksa changed hiding places and scurried under another desk.

"I can hear you, you little pest, I can hear the slightest movement you make, the quietest breath you take. Didn't dear old Leomido—my blood brother—tell you I possess the Volumiplus power?"

At these words, Oksa directed a Magnetus at the taps on the worktops in the middle of the classroom. Jets of water suddenly spurted out with such force that they were almost horizontal. Soaked from head to foot, McGraw performed a reverse Magnetus, turning them off one by one, as Oksa strove to turn them back on immediately.

"You can show off all you want, it won't get you anywhere!"

McGraw went to the back of the classroom and pressed down on a red lever, immediately cutting off the water supply. But now Oksa, whose brain was working overtime, let fly with a Fireballistico, scoring a direct hit on the coat stand where McGraw's hat and overcoat were hanging.

"You've set fire to your favourite teacher's clothes. Are you satisfied now? Not bad, I must admit, I can see that Dragomira has pulled out all the stops… but it's no big deal compared to what I have in store for you," said McGraw with a horrible snigger. "And when you're finally mine, it will be the turn of that decrepit old shrew."

Oksa stood up, taking the risk of leaving herself exposed:

"I forbid you to speak like that about my gran!"

And she aimed her Granok-Shooter at her adversary and blew into it.

"Oho! Little fool! You still have room for improvement."

McGraw had just avoided the Tornaphyllon Granok, but this didn't cancel out its effect. Out of nowhere, a small but very fierce tornado appeared in the lab. It careered around the classroom, overturning all the utensils which were still intact. The sheets of paper left on the desks were blown into the four corners, while the fluorescent tubes and the windows giving onto the corridor exploded. Awed by the destruction she'd just unleashed, Oksa dived under another desk, ripping the trousers of her school uniform on the shards of test tube strewn over the floor. She curled up as small as she could, bending over and protecting her head with her arms. Too late, unfortunately—she had been hit in the face by some splinters of glass. She wiped her hand over her forehead and cheeks and cried out more from fear than pain when she saw it was covered in blood—a fear which increased tenfold when she saw McGraw's shadow looming over her.

"I told you I was THE STRONGEST!"

He immediately blew into his Granok-Shooter and fired a Granok, which narrowly missed Oksa, who took off like a rocket. This time she stopped before knocking herself out against the ceiling, but she was immediately joined by McGraw. Floating six feet from each other, they faced off like wild animals about to attack. Oksa, her heart pounding, stood fast and made a supreme effort not to take her eyes off the vile teacher—an effort which bore fruit, because she suddenly saw a thin ray of light, like a lightning bolt, shoot from her enemy's fiery eyes. She rolled to one side to avoid the electric current, which hit the wall behind her with a hideous crackle. Standing in mid-air, the Felon attacked again and Oksa only escaped by frantically running around the walls to evade the bolts of electricity. After circling the entire room several times, she decided to change tactics and used the momentum from her last leap to reach the centre of the classroom.

That was when she had a sudden flash of memory: in her mind's eye she saw the image of Malorane trapped in the Glass Column by Ocious and his henchmen, just as she'd seen it on Dragomira's Camereye. Obviously, the "Excelsior" effect... doing the splits more than three feet above the floor, the Young Gracious immediately began spinning at a dizzying speed, turning herself into a weapon. She soon felt her foot connect with something, so she stopped spinning and hung there in the air to see the result: McGraw had been kicked to the back of the classroom by Oksa-san, the fearsome human spinning top. With his head lolling to one side and his eyes closed, he looked unconscious.

But this was only a brief respite. The invincible teacher suddenly opened his eyes and immediately brought his Granok-Shooter to his lips. In a fraction of a second the tiny granule had been shot at her as fast as an arrow. Oksa couldn't avoid the Granok and when she saw the state of her knee, she opened her eyes wide in horror as she realized what had just hit her: a PUTREFACTIO. She was going to rot away to nothing! Struck down by the intense pain, she dropped to the floor and crawled behind an overturned set of shelves for shelter, as McGraw gave a sardonic laugh. The lab was now lit only by the dying flames of the burning coat stand, the light from the corridor and one surviving fluorescent tube, which was feebly flickering on and off. The chemicals spreading across the room were giving off acidic, suffocating fumes and strange, dark thoughts filled Oksa's head. Would she ever see her mother again? What would Gus do? What about her father? Why hadn't they got here yet? Had Mortimer somehow stopped them? Was she going to die? Yes, she was bound to die here in this ruined lab, far from everyone she loved… in a few minutes it would all be over and she'd be nothing but a disgusting heap of decayed flesh. At that thought, despite the awful pain, she mustered all her courage, struggled to her feet and aimed at McGraw:

"ARBORESCENS!" she yelled.

And what she saw gave her every reason to hope she might come out of this hellish experience alive: thick, viscous, yellow creepers began vigorously twining about McGraw with a nauseating sucking noise, depriving him of the use of his hands and legs.

"I'll get the better of you! You wai—" he just had time to bellow before the creepers reached his mouth and silenced him.

Wait? No way! Oksa clambered onto a desk which had ended up against the wall in the violence of the struggle. She struggled through one of the smashed windows and let herself slip down into the corridor.

❊

"OKSA!"

Gus was just coming round the corner of the corridor in which the lab was located when he saw his friend, covered in blood, her clothes blackened and torn. Through the tear in her trousers he saw her injured knee, which looked a funny greenish colour. Behind her there was glass all over the floor and smoke was escaping from the classroom. Gus rushed over to help her up. They had barely got to the end of the second corridor when they heard a commotion and a yell which made their blood run cold:

"OKSA! OKSA!"

"He's broken free, quick, we've got to get out of here!" screamed Oksa, terror-stricken.

They began running as fast as they could, but Oksa's pitiful condition slowed them down and they were soon caught by McGraw, brandishing his Granok-Shooter.

"What's going on here?"

"MISS HEARTBREAK!"

The history and geography teacher had just appeared round the corner of the corridor, her eyes popping out of her head.

"Dr McGraw? What are you doing?" asked the young woman in disbelief.

"Mind your own business and shut up!" he spat, foaming with anger.

Making a superhuman effort, Oksa instinctively attempted to stop McGraw one last time, attacking him with a Knock-Bong which sent him flying to the other end of the corridor.

"Run, Miss Heartbreak!" shouted Gus, with a beseeching look.

Miss Heartbreak gave a cry of fear and bewilderment.

Despite the danger, the poor woman was glued to the spot with astonishment. But Gus had another priority: he grabbed Oksa under the arms and dragged her towards the exit.

64

A Series of Set-Ups

P IERRE BELLANGER'S CAR SKIDDED TO A HALT IN FRONT of the school gates just as the two friends emerged from the building, but the heavy front gate was locked and there was no way out.

"Oksa, you're going to have to make one last effort—we'll have to climb over the wall, we're trapped!" stuttered Gus.

The main thing Oksa had to do was try and ignore the dreadful pain and unbelievable terror caused by her injury so that she could concentrate on Vertiflying—she had to succeed at all costs.

"Gus, stand in front of me and hold me tightly."

Gus obeyed and clung to Oksa, putting his arms around her waist. They immediately took off, rising first by a couple of inches, then climbing unsteadily to the top of the wall, which was almost ten feet high. On the other side, Pierre had magically turned off the street lights—a very timely power cut—which meant that the two youngsters could escape under cover of darkness. It would be awkward to say the least if anyone were to see them, and this really wasn't the time to be disturbed by busybodies.

"Well done you," Gus said to Oksa, who was precariously balanced against him on top of the wall. "Just one last push, hang in there!"

Clinging to each other, the two friends came down as unsteadily as they'd gone up. When they landed on the ground, Oksa felt completely drained of strength and would have collapsed on the pavement if Gus hadn't been holding her up. Pierre rushed over, took the injured girl in his arms and laid her on the car's back seat.

"Lie still, Oksa, there's nothing to be afraid of, you're safe now."

Gus sat down in the front, next to his father, who immediately started the car.

"Look, over there! It's Mr Bontempi!"

"We can't warn him, Gus, we have to get away from here. Oksa needs treatment fast."

In the back of the car, the injured girl gritted her teeth to stop herself screaming. She was in terrible pain. An unbearable, terrifying pain that was spreading relentlessly through her body and mind like poison. She ventured a glance at her knee and groaned: the skin was puffy and had turned an awful brown colour. It also smelt disgusting—the stench of decaying flesh, combined with the reek of blood and clothes impregnated with chemical fumes. The Curbita-Flatulo redoubled its efforts, undulating constantly to calm down its panic-stricken mistress.

"Hang on, Oksa, we're there!"

Cradling her in his arms, Pierre dashed up the front steps to the Pollocks' house. Gus, white as a sheet, hammered on the door.

"Children!" cried Dragomira, seeing the dreadful state of her granddaughter. "Good Lord! What happened?"

"Dragomira, go and get some Dermi-Cleaners quickly, I think Oksa has been hit by a Putrefactio," interrupted Pierre.

While Dragomira rushed upstairs, he laid Oksa on one of the living-room sofas with Pavel's help.

"This is all my fault," muttered the latter, his face contorted in anguish. "I'll never forgive myself…"

"Stop it, Pavel!" said Pierre.

"Please, Pavel," broke in Dragomira, coming back into the sitting room, holding a small phial. "This is neither the time nor the place!"

Then, turning to Oksa:

"Oksa, I'm going to put this on your knee…"

Baba Pollock's forehead was creased with worry and she was trembling as she uncorked the bottle. She poured a large blob of an orange substance onto her fingertips and carefully massaged it into Oksa's knee.

"It's burning, Baba!" groaned the injured girl, writhing with pain.

Her mother took her hand and squeezed it tightly.

"Gus, would you stay with Oksa?" asked Dragomira, covering the bad knee with the viscous substance, which looked a little as if it was crawling. "I'll be back soon."

The three Pollocks and Pierre Bellanger went out into the hall. But although they were talking in hushed voices, Oksa could hear every single detail. The Volumiplus power was incredible...

"Marie, I must tell you that this is the first time since the Great Chaos that we've come across a Putrefactio," murmured Dragomira. "We've never had to treat it. The Dermi-Cleaners are excellent at healing wounds and infections, even gangrene. This therapy is starting to be used on the Outside with maggots—you may already have heard of it—but when it comes to Putrefactios, there are no precedents. I can't promise that the Dermi-Cleaners will be able to cure Oksa."

"I understand," replied Marie, trembling. "And I know that you'll do everything in your power."

※

Gathered around Oksa again, they all anxiously watched the progress of the injury to her knee.

"You put worms on me, Baba," said Oksa in a weak voice with an undertone of reproach.

"Yes, Dushka. The Dermi-Cleaners can work miracles with this kind of wound," said Dragomira comfortingly, even though she wasn't sure how effective they would be for such a serious injury. "The worms eat away diseased flesh and regenerate it. Your knee will soon be good as new."

Oksa couldn't help grimacing with pain and disgust at the sight of the hundred or so worms, which could be seen very clearly now and which were lethargically wriggling about on the suppurating skin.

"Do you feel strong enough to tell us what happened?"

Pavel, his eyes wild with worry, had just tensely asked the question on everyone's lips. Oksa took a deep breath and gave them a detailed account of everything that had happened since McGraw had ordered her to help him tidy up the lab. As soon as she'd finished, it was Gus's turn.

"When Merlin gave me the note and I saw that Oksa's phone was out of battery, I ran to the exit to find you, Pavel," he said, looking at Oksa's father. "But you weren't there. Then I tried to phone but there was no answer, either at the house or on your mobile."

"We received a call from the hospital in the early afternoon—Marie's doctor wanted to see us urgently," explained Pavel, looking crushed. "When we got there, we had to turn off our mobiles. We waited two hours before being told that none of the doctors had called us! We thought it was a mistake. But now, it's obvious the call was a set-up, intended as a diversion. There was still enough time for me to come and meet you from school. But when we went back to the car, it wouldn't start. We caught a taxi to go home. The taxi rank was nearby, but the traffic was terrible and it took ages to get back. I didn't think to turn on my mobile until quite late and I tried to call you, Oksa, to tell you to wait for me. But the call went straight through to voicemail. I called Gus, who told me everything, and then I called Pierre, who came to get you as fast as he could. I'm so angry with myself; I was careless."

"Don't blame yourself," said Pierre. "This was just an unfortunate set of coincidences."

"More like a series of set-ups!" retorted Dragomira. "What happened after that, Gus?"

"I wanted to stay as close as I could to Oksa, but there was no way of getting back into the school; the porter had gone, locking the porch gate behind him. I called you at home again, but no one was there and now

I understand why. I got your call, Pavel, and I phoned the restaurant to tell you to get here as fast as possible, Dad. You already knew, because Pavel had just called you. I stayed outside the front of the school—I was worried to death. Suddenly I saw Miss Heartbreak arriving, so I slipped inside behind her when she opened the porch gate and I dashed upstairs. You'd just got out of the lab, Oksa, and then suddenly McGraw appeared, shouting. That's what brought Miss Heartbreak running. I'm so sorry, Oksa, I should never have left you alone and I knew it! I'm such a waste of space…"

"Gus, what happened isn't your fault!" exclaimed Marie. "You did exactly the right thing by warning us. And if you'd stayed, McGraw wouldn't have taken much notice of you. You have to know that all you are to him is a potential bargaining counter."

"I know," replied Gus, hanging his head.

"All the same, without you I'd never have been able to get away, I could barely stand. It's because of you that I escaped McGraw's clutches. You saved my life!" exclaimed Oksa.

Gus blushed with embarrassment.

"What worries me is Miss Heartbreak," he added. "She saw everything and we left her alone with McGraw. He can't allow her to spill the beans. Either he disappears off the scene or she does, don't you think?"

"I'm very much afraid so," agreed Pierre gravely.

"You saw Mr Bontempi arriving just as you were leaving, didn't you? Do you think he saw you?" asked Dragomira.

"No, it was too dark. Fortunately for us all…"

65

WRONG PLACE, WRONG TIME

IT HAD ACTUALLY BEEN TOO DARK FOR MR BONTEMPI TO
see anything when he arrived at the school car park that Thursday
evening. A power cut had apparently knocked out the street lighting and
he parked next to Miss Heartbreak's car in the light from his headlamps,
all the while noticing a third vehicle. *"Well, well! Dr McGraw is still here,"*
he thought, noticing the teacher's car. He slammed his car door, annoyed
he'd been made so late by that stupid phone call telling him that there'd
been a burglary at his home. He'd had to drive all the way to the other
side of the city to find out that someone had been playing a hoax. His
apartment hadn't been burgled at all. That was certainly good news,
but what a waste of time! And just when he'd thought he was going to
spend a long, romantic evening with Benedicta Heartbreak... From the
courtyard, he noticed there were still lights on in the first-floor corridor.
So, before heading for his office to wait for the history and geography
teacher, he decided to go upstairs and switch off the lights.

"Good heavens! What on earth has been going on here?"

The lab was in the same state of destruction as when Oksa had left it.
Mr Bontempi walked carefully over the thick layer of broken glass on
the floor with his hand over his nose and mouth to filter out the acrid
stench which grew stronger as he approached the gaping door of the
lab. The furniture and equipment had been overturned and were dripping with water. It looked like a raging tornado had left behind a trail of

devastation. Mr Bontempi turned off the light and, perplexed, made for his office. On the landing of the main staircase, he almost tripped over a handbag that looked familiar. The Headmaster rummaged around inside and recognized the small purse and a tube of lipstick—it was definitely Miss Heartbreak's bag.

"Benedicta? Are you there?"

The office was empty, and so were the staffroom and school corridors. After exhausting all possibilities, Mr Bontempi flopped down in his armchair and phoned the young woman's home. The phone rang, but no one picked up. He tried her mobile, but heard the ringtone coming from the handbag on the table. *"What would her car be doing in the car park if she weren't here? And why was her handbag in the corridor? I hope nothing has happened to her,"* he thought, picturing the ransacked lab in his mind's eye.

He went to stand in the middle of the courtyard and, cupping his hands round his mouth, he yelled:

"BE-NE-DIC-TA! Where are you?"

But a deafening silence reigned in the building, interrupted only by the echo of his anxious shouts.

"Hello? Police please. This is the Headmaster of St Proximus College. I want to report an act of vandalism—and a missing person."

❉

Benedicta Heartbreak couldn't hear him, although she wasn't far away—just a few yards. When she'd arrived in the courtyard a little before 6 p.m., her attention had been drawn by the first-floor lights and the sound of shouting. She'd hastily gone upstairs and what she'd seen in the corridor wouldn't have been out of place in one of the nail-biting thrillers she loved: two of her best Year 8 students, Oksa Pollock and Gustave Bellanger, were being pursued by Dr McGraw, who was soaked from head to foot and covered in pieces of thick yellow string! Her strange colleague was yelling threats and young Oksa was in a terrible state, covered in blood with her uniform ripped and a nasty wound on her leg. Gus, looking as terrified as she was, was holding her up and helping her escape.

"Run, Miss Heartbreak!" he'd shouted.

At that moment, Oksa had stretched out her hand and McGraw had been thrown some sixty feet backwards, as if he'd just been punched hard by some monstrous force. The teacher had hit the wall with a dull thud and had fallen heavily to the ground, unconscious. Without thinking, Benedicta Heartbreak had gone over to him to help. She'd wanted to question the two children, but they'd already disappeared. She was alone. When she'd got close to McGraw, he'd suddenly opened his eyes and had grabbed her wrists. She'd given a piercing scream and, seeing McGraw's nasty smile, her mounting panic had turned to real terror.

"Dr McGraw, what did you do to Oksa Pollock?"

"Oh, Benedicta, Benedicta," sighed McGraw wearily, tightening his hold on her. "Charming Benedicta Heartbreak, everybody's darling, you've just ruined everything... Oksa is my key, my way in! The one I've waited fifty-seven years for."

"Fifty-seven years? What nonsense is this? You're insane! Have you been drinking?"

McGraw had sighed again, looking at the young woman witheringly.

"How could you possibly understand?"

"All I understand is that you've attacked a student from this school and that's inexcusable, whatever your reasons. That's not the way to sort things out."

McGraw had sniggered as Benedicta Heartbreak struggled to break free. When he'd let go of one her hands, she had a brief hope of freeing herself—a hope which had quickly turned to crushing defeat when McGraw had aimed his Granok-Shooter straight at her and had blown into it... Kind Benedicta Heartbreak had crumpled slowly onto the stone floor. Putting his hands under her arms, her assailant had dragged her somewhere dusty and entirely disused. There, he'd propped the poor woman against a stone pedestal and had carefully closed the creaking door behind him, not forgetting to put back the plank barring the entrance. Then, as if it were the most natural thing in the world, he'd left the school via the narrow service corridor and had got as far as the car park.

"Blast! There's that fool Bontempi. What's he doing here?" he'd grimaced, seeing the Headmaster shut his car door. "Hmm… he must have come looking for his beloved Benedicta." Diving behind a low wall, he'd watched him: Mr Bontempi was peering over at his car parked some distance away in the car park. McGraw had waited a few more minutes, then he'd discreetly crept back to his own car in the dark and, reaching underneath, had ripped out a cable. Finally, casually, he'd stood up and walked resolutely and smugly towards the centre of the city.

❋

After walking around all the school classrooms and offices, the two policemen were standing in the middle of the wrecked lab, taking notes.

"Who were the last people to leave the school?" one of the men asked Mr Bontempi.

"Dr McGraw. He's the teacher who has a lesson with Year 8 Hydrogen until 5.30 on Thursday evenings. Every week, a student helps him to put everything away in the lab. That doesn't usually take more than ten minutes."

"Who helped him this evening?"

"I don't know. As I told you, I wasn't there. I'd received a call about a burglary. I had to rush home—which proved to be a totally pointless exercise since there hadn't been a break-in at all. A bad joke, at a guess. So I came back to school and got here a few minutes after six. I was supposed to meet Benedicta; her car was in the car park and I saw Dr McGraw's car was there too, which intrigued me because no one stays as late as that. The rest, you know."

"Does everyone have access to the school?"

"No. During the daytime you can only get in by ringing the doorbell. Then the porter checks your identity, ascertains the reason for your visit and lets you in. Other than that, a close watch is kept on the students coming in and out."

"Even this evening?"

"A porter is always there until 5.30. After that time, no student has any business being inside the school. Except those who have to help a teacher, like Dr McGraw on Thursday evenings. In that case, he'll accompany the student in question to the exit. All the teachers have a swipe card allowing them to lock or unlock the porch gate."

"So you need that swipe card to get in or out after 5.30 p.m., is that correct?"

"Exactly," nodded Mr Bontempi. "Having said that, I didn't notice anything unusual and no one has reported losing their swipe card. But you can never rule out a break-in. I'm very worried about Benedicta, gentlemen, very worried."

"Do you have any idea what could have taken place in this room? Someone's gone completely crazy in here, everything was destroyed!"

"No idea at all," replied the Headmaster despondently.

The three men looked around the vandalized lab. The reek of chemicals, which was still very strong, pricked their eyes and nostrils. The two policemen conscientiously inspected every nook and cranny, carefully threading their way between the overturned pieces of furniture. Fragments of glass from the broken windows and shattered bottles cracked beneath their feet. Not even the ceramic worktops had survived.

"One last question, Mr Bontempi: do you have an address for Dr McGraw?" asked one of the two policemen.

※

"Dr McGraw? Police. We're carrying out a routine inquiry and we'd like to ask you a few questions."

"Come in, please," said McGraw pleasantly. "What's this about? Nothing serious, I hope."

The two policemen ignored the question and sat down on the chairs he'd offered them.

"What time did you leave school this evening?"

"At about 5.40 I tidied up the lab with the help of Oksa Pollock, a student in Year 8 Hydrogen. Then I accompanied her out and unlocked the porch gate for her. I wanted to take my car, but it wouldn't start, so I left it in the car park. I didn't feel like phoning the breakdown company—it had been a tiring day so I decided I'd rather take a taxi home."

"You did say 'Oksa Pollock', didn't you?" noted one of the two policemen, scribbling in his notebook.

"That's right," replied McGraw, frowning suddenly in concern.

"Did you see anyone before leaving the school?"

"No, no one."

"Did you notice anything unusual?"

"No, nothing. The corridors were deserted like they are on every Thursday evening. I didn't notice anything strange," replied McGraw casually.

"When did you last see Miss Heartbreak, your colleague who teaches history and geography?"

"Miss Heartbreak? Let me think… it must have been after lunch in the staffroom. I may have bumped into her in the corridor, just after lessons started again, at two—I really don't remember. But why do you ask? Has something happened to her?"

"How did you do that?" asked one of the policemen, pointing to the scratches on McGraw's face and hands.

"My cat," replied the man, without batting an eyelid. "Lately the damn thing has been a real handful!"

At that very moment Mortimer McGraw burst into the living room, holding a cat which was struggling furiously.

412

"Calm down, Leo. Dad, this cat is bonkers! Oh, sorry," he said, suddenly breaking off. "I didn't know you had company."

He turned round and headed back out into the hall. Then he unceremoniously pinched the cat, which wailed and struggled to get free.

"Ouch! Horrible creature, you scratched me!" he yelled, loud enough to be heard clearly from the living room.

And if they hadn't had their backs turned, the policemen would have seen the satisfied grin on his face...

66

SUPERIOR SEAMSTRESSES

T HE DERMI-CLEANERS DID AN EXCELLENT JOB ON Oksa's injury. They spent all night meticulously cleaning the suppurating wound, eating away every particle of decaying flesh, while Dragomira and Pavel took turns sitting by the brave patient's bedside. When Oksa woke up Dragomira was nearby, preparing a mixture in a marble pestle.

"Baba?"

"Dushka! How do you feel?"

Pavel, who was lying on a camp bed next to Oksa's bed, opened one eye and sat up. He had large, dark circles under his eyes, and his anxious gaze immediately strayed to his daughter's knee, which looked much less revolting than the evening before: the skin, which was no longer a hideous boggy colour, appeared to have regenerated. And it didn't smell anywhere near so bad. The Dermi-Cleaners went on wriggling slowly, which made Oksa screw up her face. The Insiders' pharmacopoeia—worms and slugs, etc.—took some getting used to.

"Wonderful!" exclaimed Dragomira. "It's worked a treat. No one would think you'd done anything worse than fall over rollerblading. Would you bend your leg for me?"

Oksa obeyed cautiously. The skin stretched, giving a clear view of the writhing mass of mending worms.

"It doesn't hurt so much now. That's fantastic, Baba!"

She threw her arms around her gran's neck, pulling her father over too so she could hug them both very tightly. What a relief! She'd been so scared.

"Now that your knee is out of danger, I'll take care of your face, Dushka."

"My face?" asked Oksa in alarm, feeling her cheeks and forehead with her fingertips. "What's wrong with it?"

Then she remembered the state of her hand when she'd wiped her face with it after the lab windows exploded: it had been covered in blood.

"Am I disfigured?" she asked in a strangled voice.

"No, Oksa, you're not disfigured," said Dragomira gently, making her lie down. "You just have a few scratches from broken glass. I'll deal with those in less than no time. First the cuts, then a cream to make them disappear without a trace. You'll see, it's incredible."

"You're going to stitch me up? No way, Baba, I don't want you to. No needles!"

Oksa squirmed on her bed and her reluctance intensified when she saw *what* was going to be stitching her up: spiders. Minute spiders with ultra-thin legs, admittedly—but still spiders!

"No, no way, I can't, Baba! I'll throw a fit."

To everyone's surprise, this made Pavel roar with laughter until tears came to his eyes. His mirth was so infectious that Dragomira followed suit and the delicate spiders seemed to share their mistress's amusement, jigging up and down on her hand.

"Oh look at them, Oksa-san! They are Spinollias, they're completely harmless," cried Pavel. "And, what's more, they're wonderful seamstresses."

"The son of the Old Gracious possesses truth in his mouth, Young Gracious," broke in the Lunatrix, who had just entered the room bearing a tray laden with bread and butter and steaming bowls. "One day a finger belonging to myself was guillotined by a large kitchen knife during a severing manoeuvre performed on carrots; the Spinollias sewed it back on with the delicacy of lace. Look, my finger belongs to my hand again! Feeling was absent, totally absent, you must have confident belief, accuracy is in my words."

Oksa grimaced, then closed her eyes with a resigned sigh:

"Fine, go ahead, do what you want to me. No one told me that I'd be giving my body to science... and during my lifetime, too."

Pavel and Dragomira exchanged a knowing smile. Then Dragomira gently picked up one of the three spiders stretched out on her hand and placed it on Oksa's face. She shuddered and screwed her eyes shut so tight that her forehead was furrowed with worry lines.

"Relax, sweetheart," said Pavel, taking her hand. "If you tense your forehead too much, the Spinollias will sew the wrinkles together... and thirteen's a bit young for a facelift, don't you think?"

"Great," muttered Oksa between gritted teeth, gazing up at the ceiling.

The three Spinollias were now on her face. She could feel their thin legs busily moving around on her skin. It was a weird feeling. Very, very weird, though not unpleasant, if you managed to forget there were spiders on you. Until then Oksa hadn't realized her face was cut, since all her attention had been focused on her injured knee. The Spinollias' activity refreshed her memory, though, bringing back a handful of images: the whole lab exploding, the disgusting reek of the chemicals, furious McGraw doing his utmost to catch her... and Miss Heartbreak.

"All done, Dushka! Your cuts are a distant memory. Now I'll apply this cream. It'll remove the scars and make your skin as soft and smooth as a baby's bottom again."

"I know someone who'll be very glad to see you looking so... bright-eyed and bushy-tailed," murmured Pavel in her ear.

He unfolded his tall body and left the room.

"Marie!" they heard his voice ringing out in the corridor. "Do you want to see your brave daughter?"

He returned a few seconds later, pushing his wife's wheelchair. Seeing Oksa, Marie's face broke into a broad smile, although her eyes didn't lose their profoundly anxious expression. Pavel pushed the wheelchair over to Oksa's bed.

"Did you see that, Mum?" said the girl, indicating with her eyes the Spinollias which Dragomira was carefully returning to a glass container. "How gross is that! Er, Baba… while we're on the subject of disgusting things, what *exactly* is in this cream?"

"Ever suspicious, aren't you?"

"Well, that is… YES!"

Dragomira and Pavel smiled, while Marie thought privately that she shared her daughter's disgust.

"Don't worry," explained Baba Pollock, "it's just a few dried and crushed yarrow leaves mixed with a drop of Goranov sap and some rose juice."

"Promise?" asked Oksa severely.

"Promise!"

"Fine, then under those conditions, I'll continue to lend—and I do mean 'lend'—my body to science."

And she stretched out on the bed, her arms outspread, in a pose of total resignation.

"I am going to school today, aren't I?" she said hesitantly.

"Yes," replied her father. "We've thought it over and even if you find it very hard after what you went through yesterday evening, we think it would be safer and more sensible for you to go. The police will almost definitely have been called, if only because of the damage to the lab. And from what you and Gus have told us, McGraw is bound to have done whatever he had to do to silence Miss Heartbreak. She saw too much. If anyone asks you, and they're bound to, you must act as though nothing happened, as if McGraw had accompanied you to the exit as he usually does with the others. Do you understand?"

Oksa nodded.

"We know this is hard for you, very hard. But it's essential for all of us that no one knows exactly what happened," continued Dragomira. "Keep your eyes and ears open and you'll see that McGraw will behave in the same way. He can't afford for anyone to guess anything, about him or us. Even if we haven't done anything wrong, you must bear in mind that we'd be in big trouble if anyone discovered who we are and, most importantly, what we can do. You realize now how different we are and what that might mean to those who don't share our abilities... you weren't far off the mark when you thought that people in the secret service or various government agencies would give their eye teeth to examine individuals like us. And when I say 'examine', that would just be the start of it. By saying nothing, by not raising the alarm, we're protecting ourselves and that's your responsibility today. I'm sorry to have to ask this of you—I know it'll be hard. But for over fifty years, we've managed to preserve our anonymity and our secrecy."

"Yes, I know," replied Oksa, sounding overwhelmed. "But what about Miss Heartbreak?"

Pavel replied in a strangled voice:

"We can't do anything for her at the moment, darling."

※

When Pierre Bellanger dropped Gus and Oksa off in front of St Proximus he sensed, as they did, that the whole school was seething with agitation. He gave them one last encouraging look and made sure they were safely inside the courtyard before leaving.

"Everyone seems very uptight," Gus whispered to Oksa, glancing anxiously at her out of the corner of his eye.

Oksa didn't reply. She felt tense and tired and, despite her best efforts, it showed on her pale, unmarked face. The two students threaded their way among the noisily chatting groups of students. The words "police" and "lab" seemed to come up in every conversation, which did nothing to calm Oksa's escalating stress levels. Merlin Poicassé, who was waiting for his friends in front of the lockers, was the first to give them some information:

"Hiya, Oksa! Hiya, Gus! Guess what? The science lab was wrecked yesterday evening, it's a real mess. Absolutely everything was destroyed. Even the ceramic worktops, can you believe it? The police were called; no one seems to have the slightest idea who might have done it. It's crazy, isn't it?"

Although Oksa and Gus thought they did a really good job of pretending to be dumbfounded at the news, it obviously wasn't good enough, because Merlin, gazing shrewdly at Oksa, soon edged nearer and whispered confidingly:

"I know what happened, Oksa... I saw everything!"

Those two short sentences hit the two friends like a bombshell. Gus felt the blood drain from his face as he moved closer to Merlin.

"What are you on about?" he asked with feigned astonishment.

"I followed you when you slipped inside behind Miss Heartbreak after she unlocked the porch gate," replied Merlin, watching his reaction. "I had a feeling that something weird was going on—I saw Oksa send McGraw flying to the other end of the corridor *without laying a finger on him* and I saw you both rise into the air and go over the wall."

"You're talking rubbish!" Gus snapped angrily.

"You looked in a really bad way, Oksa," continued Merlin, completely unflustered. "But I'm glad to see you're much better—the night seems to have done you good. One might almost think it was a magical recovery."

"You're out of your mind, Merlin," muttered Gus, going pale.

"Leave it, Gus," said Oksa in a resigned voice. "You can see he's realized..."

"So you are a sorceress?" continued Merlin.

"You've suspected that for some time, haven't you?" retorted Oksa, looking him straight in the eye. "But please don't say anything. The lives of several people depend on it."

"Really?" stammered Merlin, taken aback by the impassioned appeal in the girl's eyes.

"I promise I'll explain everything if you swear not to breathe a word to anyone about this."

"Oksa!" exclaimed Gus, shocked.

"We don't have any choice, Gus," said the Young Gracious quietly, turning to her friend. "If we deny it, he'll go on nosing around and that'll be even worse... and I'm sure we can trust him," she added in a louder voice, turning to look intently at Merlin again. "Can't we, Merlin? I repeat: if you breathe a word, you endanger the lives of quite a few people, starting with me."

The boy flinched, flustered not only by the solemnity of her request but also by being stared at so intensely by a girl he liked so much.

"I understand," he agreed. "You can count on me. What about McGraw? Is he like you?"

"McGraw? It's worse than that," replied Oksa, seeing the dreaded teacher walk into the courtyard.

"Well, you certainly gave him a going-over," remarked Merlin enthusiastically. "Wow, look at the state of his face! He looks like he fell into a rose bush."

McGraw's gloomy face was covered in scratches. All the students who passed him shot him quizzical glances. Some were even amused and dared to burst out laughing. Gus and Oksa, on the other hand, had no inclination to share their amusement, particularly when McGraw started heading in their direction. Without taking his eyes off them, he slowed down as he drew level with them, and Oksa noticed a hint of surprise in his expression as he glared at her, probably because he couldn't understand how she could appear completely unscathed by their terrible battle of the evening before. He walked past, his head high but his back bowed, and disappeared around the corner of the corridor.

※

Ten minutes after the start of the French lesson, a haggard Mr Bontempi burst into the room.

"For your information, Miss Heartbreak will be absent for the day, so please go to the prep room at ten until noon. Also, Oksa would you come with me for a minute. You can have her back soon, Dr Lemaire," he said to the French teacher with a strained smile.

Oksa stood up to follow the Headmaster, taking care not to limp. Her knee was no longer decaying, but it was still painful. She had to be strong—now more than ever.

"Some police detectives are investigating the damage to the lab," Mr Bontempi told her monotonously. "They'd just like to ask you a few questions, but there's nothing to worry about."

Mr Bontempi didn't say another word before they reached his office and Oksa felt a surge of sympathy for him. He must be very worried about Miss Heartbreak and she knew his fears were justified. Nervously she adjusted her small shoulder bag. "*Oh dear, I hope they don't search me!*" she thought in alarm. "*What if they find my Granok-Shooter and my Tumble-Bawler? No, Oksa, it doesn't bear thinking about, don't even consider it.*" She dug her hands deep into the pockets of her blazer and felt a strange object. She looked at what she'd just found and recognized the talisman Dragomira had given her on her first day at school. She remembered what her gran had said at the time: "If you feel tense in body and mind, hold this and gently stroke it. It will make you feel more at peace with the world, the sky will seem clearer and your path more sure."

"Oh Baba, thank you!" murmured Oksa emotionally, picturing her gran helpfully slipping the little pouch in her pocket just before she left for school.

Her strength and bravery came flooding back with that mental image. Her family was always with her. And she had Gus. She was never alone.

Two policemen were waiting for her in the office, but she had prepared herself and didn't feel as overawed as she thought she would. Perhaps she'd get away with lying to them after all.

"Hello," she said, walking through the door.

"Hello! You're Oksa Pollock, is that correct?"

"Yes."

"Sit down and don't be afraid, we just have a few questions to ask you. You stayed behind with Dr McGraw yesterday evening to put things away in the lab?"

"That's right."

So far, so good.

"What time did you finish? Do you remember?"

Now she had to play her cards close to her chest.

"I didn't look, but it can't have been long. Ten minutes, quarter of an hour, maybe. There wasn't much equipment to put away because McGraw—I mean Dr McGraw—gave us a written class test."

"And then? What happened then?"

"Then? Well we went downstairs, he unlocked the porch for me and we went our separate ways."

"Did you notice anything unusual?"

Oksa squeezed her talisman hard. She had the feeling she was bright red from head to toe. Thank goodness there were no scratches on her face any more! She would never badmouth spiders again...

"No. Except that Dr McGraw called me by my first name and that's totally out of character for him," she said to lighten the mood.

The policemen smiled.

"Did you see Miss Heartbreak before you left school, Oksa?"

"Miss Heartbreak? No," she replied, with a heavy heart. "I didn't see anyone."

The policemen stood up. They had obviously finished questioning her. Phew!

"Good, thank you, Oksa. Just one last question, before you rejoin your classmates…"

At that moment Oksa felt the blood drain from her face. Her thoughts were in a whirl. She squeezed her talisman even harder and fought with all her might against the panic which was in danger of undoing all her good work.

"One last question?" she repeated more firmly than she would have thought.

Through the window just behind the policemen she saw the clouds darken to black in the space of a few seconds. *"Oh no,"* she thought to herself. *"Not a storm! This is really not the time."*

"We'd like to know if you're related to Leomido Fortensky, the conductor?" asked one of the policemen, looking at her intently.

67

A BALL OF WORRIES

"THE YOUNG GRACIOUS HAS A COUNTENANCE COVERED in fatigue," remarked the Lunatrix, staring at Oksa with his big round eyes. "The beverage I offer in suggestion will distil the strength in your veins, you can have unwarranted faith in it!"

"Thanks, Lunatrix. I am really tired," admitted Oksa, taking the cup the creature was holding out to her.

"Juice of rubber repair patch, just the thing when you're tyred!" yelled one of the Getorixes, rolling about on the floor with its customary lack of restraint.

Oksa was actually exhausted. She felt drained by the events of the last few days and could do nothing to combat the overwhelming lethargy that had descended on her since Friday evening. Her eyes vacant and her mind a blank, she spent all Saturday in pyjamas wandering aimlessly around the house or flopped in an armchair, unable to apply herself to anything—although it didn't stop her understanding what was going on around her. She didn't think she was in pain, yet all kinds of vague conflicting feelings were dragging her down to unknown depths. She didn't feel afraid or anxious, or relieved. She just felt desperately empty, and powerless to stop herself from spiralling into a dark vortex of apathy. Her parents watched this unfamiliar behaviour helplessly and comforted her as best they could, but their sincerity and warmth didn't seem able to reach her. She heard what they said, but their words didn't register in

424

her heart, which was beating alone in a vacuum. Sunday began exactly the same: an uncharacteristically silent Oksa stayed in her pyjamas and wouldn't contemplate washing, eating or communicating.

"She's in a state of shock," diagnosed Dragomira. "I think it's time I got the Nascentia out again."

Marie looked at her quizzically, as Pavel exclaimed:

"You still have it? I could have sworn we left it behind in Siberia!"

"Yes, I still have it," replied Dragomira with a wink. "And I'm sure it'll do young Oksa the world of good."

"Could one of you two please tell me what you're talking about?" broke in Marie tensely.

Dragomira's only answer was to stand up and leave the room. She came back a few seconds later with what looked like a tightly folded transparent space blanket, which she laid on the table. Intrigued, Marie touched it with her fingertips, marvelling at its incredibly soft, velvety surface.

"It feels like... *baby's skin!*" she remarked, suppressing a shiver and giving Pavel a horrified and nauseated look.

"Don't worry, darling, it isn't. Although it's not a million miles away from—"

"Not a million miles away?" exclaimed Marie, pulling a face.

"The Nascentia is actually a placenta," continued Pavel. "But no ordinary one."

"I should have known," said Marie, exhaling in relief. "Ordinary and Pollock aren't often spoken in the same breath!"

Pavel gave a wan half-smile.

"You know that Lunatrixes can only give birth once in their lifetime— they live for around 300 years and gestation lasts over two years. But, like humans, they can sometimes give birth to twins. Twins' placenta is extremely precious and has amazing psychotherapeutic powers. I speak from experience, because I used it when I lost my father... It can only do Oksa good, I think it's an excellent idea of Dragomira's. Are you happy for us to try it?"

"Of course I am," exclaimed Marie tensely. "We have to try something, we can't just leave her like this."

"There's no harm in trying."

This was said by Oksa, who had been standing in the doorway of the living room for a short time. She went over to her mother, knelt down in front of her and laid her head on her lap.

"I feel like a total zombie, Mum. It's like I'm completely empty inside."

Dragomira picked up the Nascentia. The delicate, slightly opaque membrane unfolded into a circle around three feet in diameter, then began swelling on contact with the air until it had become a beautiful iridescent globe. The air seemed to condense inside it, filling it with dense vapour.

"Be careful," warned Dragomira, gently patting the globe, "it's very hot—about ninety degrees."

"You're not going to make Oksa go into that furnace?" asked Marie in alarm, her daughter's head still on her knees.

"Don't worry, Marie," said Dragomira reassuringly. "The temperature will drop and stabilize at thirty-seven degrees, which is ideal. A few more minutes and it will be fine."

The Nascentia had now risen and was floating above the floor. Inside, the vapour was disappearing. Droplets of condensation could be seen sliding down the transparent sides. After a few minutes, Dragomira placed her hands flat on the surface of the globe and stroked the membrane.

"She's trying to find the way in," explained Pavel. "Ah there it is, she's found it."

With her hands, Dragomira was carefully widening a slit about twenty inches high to form a passageway.

"Will you come over here, Oksa? The Nascentia is ready."

Oksa stood up and went over to the strange bubble, while Dragomira held it open. She slipped one foot inside, followed by her whole body. Contrary to expectation, the Nascentia didn't sink under her weight but continued to float above the floor. Dragomira relaxed the pressure of her hands and the opening closed. Once inside, Oksa had to crouch down.

She instinctively curled in a ball against the comfortable membrane and let the humid warmth envelop her. As soon as she'd settled down, the Nascentia became covered with fine bluish veins which began to palpitate as if carrying some kind of life form. A few seconds later, it began pulsing with gentle contractions which sent ripples across its silky soft surface.

"It's like a beating heart," murmured Marie, squeezing her husband's arm.

Inside, Oksa soon fell asleep, lulled by the regular beating. Unable to resist the torpor overwhelming her, she had the strangest feeling that the thoughts clouding her mind and dragging her heart down into unfathomable depths were slipping away and dissolving in the damp heat of the Nascentia.

✷

When she reopened her eyes, she was still in the same position, her legs hunched under her chin and her arms around her knees. She had no idea what time it was. Had she been there for an hour? A day? A week? Anything was possible… One thing was sure, though: she felt happier than she had done for a long time, as if a huge, painful weight had been lifted while she'd been in that comfortable globe. Through the membrane, which was now opaque and grey, she could make out the silhouette of her mother, lying on one of the sofas. At her side sat her father, one arm on the armrest and, further off, a large aubergine blotch, no doubt her gran. From the Nascentia Oksa could hear them, and Abakum, speaking. Their voices sounded louder and distorted, as if she were underwater and surrounded by some kind of sea fog. Suddenly, a gap opened in the side and her father's face appeared.

"How do you feel, darling?"

"Fine, Dad. I feel great actually, although it's a little cramped. Have I been in here long?"

"Just over four hours."

Her father grinned at her and, as Dragomira had done when she made an opening for Oksa, he widened the gap to form a passageway. Oksa twisted, put her arms around her father's neck and let herself slide out of the Nascentia. Back on her feet, she stretched and gave a long, noisy yawn as her mother looked at her questioningly.

"How do you feel?" she asked, a little anxiously.

"Oh Mum," exclaimed Oksa, rushing over to her. "I feel amazing. Like I'm… *a new person!*"

"Well, I hope you're still the Oksa I know and love," continued her mother.

"Oh, I don't think you have anything to worry about on that score," said Dragomira with a reassuring smile.

At that moment the Lunatrixa burst into the living room, holding the accessory she and her companion were rarely seen without: a tray heavily laden with a steaming teapot and some mouth-watering pastries.

"Has your sojourn in the Nascentia made the contribution of a beneficial effect, Young Gracious? The impression of relaxation can be read upon your face and brings comfort to my heart."

"You're right, Lunatrixa, I feel much more relaxed. That Nascentia works miracles! Who needs a therapist with something like this."

"You're right," said Marie, with a relieved smile at Dragomira, "that's our very own Oksa."

"You should both take a look over there," said Baba Pollock, pointing.

Abakum was standing in front of the Nascentia, which was still floating in the middle of the room. He had just taken a mahogany case from his jacket and he now opened it and took out an object that was very familiar to Oksa.

"That's his magic wand!" she explained proudly to Marie. "The wand inherited from his mother, the Ageless Fairy-Who-Died-For-Love."

"Oh right," smiled Marie, hiding her surprise. "I was only just thinking… a fairy without a wand isn't the real thing at all."

The man whom Oksa had decided to name the Fairyman put his arm inside the Nascentia and rotated his wand, gently brushing it against the walls. Gradually, the bubble became lighter in colour until it was restored to its milky whiteness. After a few minutes, Abakum removed his wand. The Nascentia immediately deflated and once again assumed the appearance of a piece of delicate fabric, which Dragomira carefully refolded. Abakum went over to Oksa and her mother and showed them the wand; on its tip was a large, dark, almost black ball of down, which looked a little like the clumps of dust that gather under furniture.

"Is that dirt?" asked Oksa, making a face.

Abakum smiled and nodded.

"Yes, in a way. More precisely, though, it's your black thoughts."

"WHAT?" exclaimed Oksa and her mother in unison.

"The Nascentia unburdens the mind of its worries and, more importantly, leads it away from the depths it's drawn towards. Some worries are necessary to move forward but others pollute the mind. What you see at the end of this wand is none other than the darkness taking you away from us and making you forget that there's always light and hope."

Oksa leant over the tangled ball of split filaments and studied it closely.

"You mean all that came out of my head?"

"Out of your head, your body, and your heart, yes," replied Abakum, gazing at her intently.

"Is it… alive?"

"Of course! As much as you are. Thoughts aren't inanimate, they're just as alive as the mechanism which operates our bodies."

"What are you going to do with them?"

"Allow me to show you, my very Young Gracious," replied the Fairyman with a mysterious smile.

With that, he waved the wand carefully over a lacquered box and dropped the ball of black thoughts into it. He then made a hole in a large granule taken from his Caskinette and dropped it inside. Then, after closing the lid securely, Abakum put the box inside his jacket, with his wand case, leaving Oksa in a state of deep astonishment.

68

CAPTIVE IN THE CRYPT

OKSA HAD TO WAIT UNTIL THE END OF THE MORNING TO tell Gus about her remarkable experience in the Nascentia. Immediately after lunch, they decided to give their friends the slip and have a private chat in the Statues' Den, which had recently become Gus Bellanger and Oksa Pollock's Personal and Exclusive Hideout. Unfortunately, the room had been double-locked by Mr Bontempi, who had become aware of these intrusions. Undeterred, the two friends went looking for a new place of refuge. It didn't take them long to find somewhere which had not yet been explored due to its bad state of dilapidation: the tiny school chapel.

"Oksa, we can't go in there," said Gus, standing by the door, which was barred by a single plank nailed across it.

"Yes we can, come on! No one will disturb us here."

"Maybe we could find somewhere else," muttered Gus, who didn't like the idea of going into that gloomy chapel at all. "If a chapel appeals to you so much, we could just go to the new one."

"Are you kidding?" said Oksa briskly. "The school choir will be rehearsing in there now. Listen—you can hear their voices all the way up here!"

Oksa gently tugged at the worm-eaten plank: the rusty nails gave way immediately and it came off in her hands.

"See?" she smiled. "It's a sign."

"Hmm…" Gus coughed softly, unconvinced by his friend's incredible optimism. "A sign, you say? A sure sign of trouble, I reckon!"

430

The Young Gracious pushed open the door with her fingertips and poked her head inside.

"Nothing to report. Don't be such a chicken! It looks perfect."

"It looks a bit scary, if you ask me," retorted Gus.

They walked in and closed the door behind them, checking one last time that no one had seen them. The chapel was stuffy and dark. The air was thick with the dust that also blanketed the pews and a few broken and neglected objects of worship. Outside, the sun must have broken through the clouds, because slender rays of brightly coloured light suddenly filtered through the filthy stained-glass windows above the tiny altar. The two adventurers started in surprise at this startling illumination—it was as if the chapel had just come back to life after years of neglect. Oksa's immediate reaction was to narrow her eyes and assume a kung-fu attack position, with her hands pressed together in front of her and her right leg outstretched. Gus couldn't help smiling.

"Okay? Nothing in sight? You never cease to amaze me."

"Gus! Did you hear something?"

Oksa put her hand on her friend's arm. On his guard again, Gus held his breath and listened, but couldn't hear a thing.

"Perhaps the place is still haunted by an old ghost," he remarked ironically.

Oksa was about to elbow him, but she suddenly froze, all her senses on the alert.

"It's either the Volumiplus or I'm hearing things," she whispered.

"The Volumiplus? That's the power which allows you to hear tiny sounds, isn't it?"

"Exactly," confirmed Oksa, concentrating. "And it appears to be working overtime. Follow me! There's something—"

Gus could think of a good many things he'd rather do than explore this chapel, but he let himself be dragged by his intrepid friend towards the crypt at the back.

"We're not going down there, are we?" he muttered, trying to do an about-turn.

"Oh, Gus," chided Oksa. "It's just a crypt!"

"IT'S JUST A CRYPT? That really takes the biscuit! You know what you get in crypts? Graves. Martyrs' relics. Dead people. Did you hear me? Dead people! Corpses! Skeletons! Stiffs!"

"Okay, okay," she said with a frown. "You don't need to list all the synonyms you know for 'corpse.'"

"You don't really think I'm going down there?"

"You're afraid, aren't you?" exclaimed Oksa, starting to have cold feet herself. "Okay, fine, come on, let's go... AAARGHHH! What was that?"

The sound of singing rose clearly from the crypt. Oksa clutched Gus's arm, while he stood frozen to the spot with terror, his legs turned to stone.

"C'mon, we've got to get out of here, we should never have come in, this is crazy," he stuttered. "We're *totally* not supposed to be here!"

"Don't worry, I'm armed," retorted Oksa briskly, showing him her Granok-Shooter and heading resolutely towards the crypt.

※

It wasn't far off three o'clock that Tuesday afternoon when the students heard the loud, anarchic banging of a drum. In the classrooms the teachers initially tried to maintain order, although it was difficult because they were just as intrigued by the racket as their students. But when the din was accompanied by someone singing an opera aria loudly in the corridors—"Oh! I laugh to see myself so beautiful in this mirror!"—curiosity reached fever pitch. In no time, countless faces were pressed up against the windows overlooking the courtyard or the corridors in an attempt to locate the whereabouts of this strange performance. Some of the teachers thought Mr Bontempi had planned some kind of an event for the carnival, due to take place in a few days' time. Others opened

432

their classroom doors to try and pinpoint the source of the racket and one of them caught a glimpse of a flowing silhouette dressed in blue just turning a corridor. Oksa and Gus were peering out of the window of the English classroom when Merlin cried out:

"Hey, look over there! That looks like Miss Heartbreak near the fountain!"

His eyes met Oksa's. She winked at him; he gave a knowing smile and winked back. A murmur of amazement spread through their class and all the classrooms overlooking the school courtyard. Not one student seemed to be concentrating on their work. Oksa and Gus craned their necks to try and see the courtyard from their window. The angle made it difficult, but they could clearly hear the rasping voice, which was now singing a children's song: 'At the Clear Fountain'. Gus grabbed Oksa's arm and pulled her into the corridor.

Leaning their elbows on the first-floor balustrade, they now had an unobstructed view of the courtyard.

"She did it, Gus!" murmured Oksa. "Thank goodness!"

Miss Heartbreak—there was no doubt it was her—was singing her head off to celebrate her new-found freedom. When Gus and Oksa had glimpsed a shadowy figure in the gloom of the crypt, they'd almost passed out. Gus had nearly dropped dead from fear.

"Miss Heartbreak, is that you?" Oksa had spluttered hoarsely, her Granok-Shooter aimed in front of her.

"Heartbreak? What a pretty name! Pretty, pretty name… no, I don't know any Heartbreak, but I know a heart that's fancy-free," came a sweet, melodious voice, rising from the depths of the crypt, before the two adventurous students had fled.

That was how, a few hours later, Miss Heartbreak came to be sitting on the edge of the central fountain. She had a saucepan fastened across her chest with a dirty rag and she was beating madly on this makeshift instrument, singing nursery rhymes badly at the top of her hoarse voice. With her tangled hair and her face black with grime, she afforded a surprising, and shocking, sight. Her blue suit was torn and her bare legs were covered in bruises and bloody scabs.

"My little sheep, it's time to return to the fold!" she yelled from the fountain, looking up at the packed windows and balustrades. "The big bad wolf will catch you, come, come, my pretty sheep, come hither with your gentle shepherdess."

And she started to whistle through her fingers, to the delight of most of the students, who responded with shouts of joy. Egged on by this reaction, Miss Heartbreak climbed onto the edge of the fountain, then jumped feet first into the icy water. She merrily splashed about in the water, which came up to her knees, singing "There was a shepherdess and ron, ron, ron, little patapon" in a demented voice.

Mr Bontempi, followed by a few of the teachers, ran over and grabbed hold of the poor woman, lifting her out of the water in his arms.

"Benedicta! Calm down, everything's going to be okay!"

But Benedicta Heartbreak didn't seem to agree. She took hold of her saucepan-drum and tried to batter her rescuer who, without Dr Bento's intervention, would soon have been seeing stars. The small group disappeared from the courtyard to the rebellious cries of the drenched shepherdess and the cheers of the laughing students. A few minutes later, the siren of an ambulance echoed off the stone walls, casting a chill over the classrooms and silencing the laughter.

69

FROM BAD TO WORSE

"Yₒᵤ'ʀᴇ ꜱᴀʏɪɴɢ ᴛʜᴀᴛ Mɪss Hᴇᴀʀᴛʙʀᴇᴀᴋ ʜᴀs reappeared? Are you sure?"

"Positive."

Oksa and Gus had dashed home as fast they could, escorted by Pierre Bellanger, who hadn't been able to believe his ears when the youngsters had told him about the highlight of the day. At the Pollocks' house the news was greeted with just as much astonishment.

"This is certainly a big surprise," said Baba Pollock thoughtfully, with a distant look in her eyes.

"It gave us the fright of our lives," explained her granddaughter. "You should have seen how fast we ran out of the chapel!"

"That woman is indebted to you," remarked Dragomira. "Who knows what would have happened to her if you hadn't found her? But I'm amazed, I was sure Orthon had killed her."

"Luckily, he didn't," continued Oksa, deeply relieved. "But she's gone mad."

"You mean she's a complete fruitcake now," said Gus, "stark raving bonkers! But it's hardly surprising, given the terrible state she was in. McGraw must have really gone to town on her. What do you think he used?" he added, turning to Dragomira.

"It might be something like a Muddler Granok, but much more harmful."

Seeing Gus's dubious expression, Oksa explained pedantically:

"The Muddler Granok confuses the brain for a very short period of time, no more than a few hours. The man or woman hit by it becomes muddle-headed and talks nonsense."

"And it's relatively harmless," added Dragomira. "Given what you told us, I think this was something more… aggressive."

"You don't think McGraw could have used a Memory-Mash Granok, do you?"

"There's every possibility that he's combined the two, and I don't think he stinted on the doses. He can't afford for Miss Heartbreak to talk, she saw too much. I'm afraid her condition will be irreversible. Poor woman… where is she? Do you know?"

"An ambulance came for her and I heard the teachers talking about her this afternoon," replied Oksa. "She's at the hospital; the police want to question her, but apparently she's very agitated and the prognosis isn't good."

"No doubt," commented Pavel, squeezing his wife's hand. "We don't exactly bring good luck to anyone we get to know."

Everyone fell silent. Oksa and Gus thought back to how kind and considerate Miss Heartbreak had been and then remembered the last shocking images of her. Nearby, settled comfortably in the wheelchair she'd resigned herself to using, Marie gazed at them sadly, all the while thinking about the damage McGraw had done in such a short space of time. She was a long way from recovering all her faculties, but she was feeling much better. She could now use her hands and arms, and the terrible dizzy spells that had been such a trial had almost disappeared. Only walking continued to cause her concern as well as a great deal of pain. When she put one foot in front of the other, it felt to Marie as if molten metal was flowing through her legs—and the excruciating pain stopped her from attempting the smallest steps. Even when supported in her attempts by one of her family or friends, the pain was unbear-able—as was her bitter disappointment. The rest of the time, it was as if her legs weren't hooked up to her brain. She couldn't stretch them out and they remained unresponsive, even when the doctors pushed needles under her skin to gauge her sensitivity. Marie didn't let it show, but she despaired of ever being able to walk again. And, more than anything, she was afraid that she wouldn't be able to look after Oksa in the years to come. She felt physically sick at such an awful thought. She couldn't help thinking that it was only her deep love for her husband and family that prevented her from abandoning ship. But the Runaways were right: nothing could halt their destiny now. And even if she wasn't technically a Runaway, her fate was now linked to theirs. She was one of them and her daughter was their Last Hope.

Pavel was also having a really bad time of it: his pain was very different but its causes were no less distressing. He was, naturally, desperately worried about his wife—whom he loved passionately and whom he dreaded seeing confined to a wheelchair for the rest of her life—and about his daughter, who bore an enormous burden of responsibility on her shoulders. His young Oksa-san... she was only thirteen! He knew her intelligence and vivacity made her undeniably resilient. She was coping heroically with the many devastating blows she'd been dealt recently—on the surface. Their after-effects had just been removed by the Nascentia, but there was no denying that they had all recently suffered a serious setback. And the future didn't look danger-free either; far from it. They were dealing with a raving madman. Orthon-McGraw wouldn't give up just like that. He'd already gone too far and Oksa was in the firing line. Who would have thought, five months ago, that their lives would be turned upside down by the insane hope of returning to Edefia? And what if this ended in disaster for them all?

Pavel was worried sick. Over the past few days, he'd been overcome by an insidious feeling of uselessness, prompted by his inability to solve anything. His judgement wasn't clouded by his tortured nature and he knew he could do nothing to stop the implacable hand of fate from making his daughter fulfil her destiny. He was well aware that there was no point fighting it. There was no way of turning back the clock or stopping everything. It was impossible. The only thing he could do was protect Oksa. That was what fathers were supposed to do. But what a disappointment he must be—Abakum and Dragomira were much more effective than he was. They always came up with a solution, no matter what. Without them, Oksa would certainly be in McGraw's clutches by now. He, Pavel Pollock, had been absolutely no help. At any time. He'd never been particularly interested in Edefia. For him, it was in the past—ancient family history. Okay, so he did possess a few gifts. He could Vertifly, make a Fireballistico or perform the odd Knock-Bong from time to time. But since he couldn't use them openly, what good were they if they only endangered his family?

That was what he'd thought until today, but the time for such embittered thoughts was past. He had to take urgent action and defend Marie and Oksa—the two people he loved best and who needed him the most. That evening, alone in the kitchen of his restaurant, he was lost in thought and plagued by worries. And these worried thoughts made him explode with anger at the man he didn't want to be: a weak man who shirked his responsibilities and who fled from his origins and his destiny. He was the son of Runaways, he had the blood of the Graciouses running through his veins, his family came from Edefia, and Oksa bore the Mark which would allow them to go back—not to mention the Ageless Ones' prediction about saving the world. He had to stop acting as if none of this were real. That was over. Now he had to face facts! An icy shiver ran through the Insider slumbering within him. With his eyes half-closed, he assumed a fighting position, one leg bent at right angles in front of him. Then he leapt onto a table fixed to the floor and, seizing two long knives, crossed them in front of him. The blades scraped against each other with a sinister screech. Stretching his legs wide, Pavel performed a flying kick, landed on the floor and then leapt again, his body carried forward by the momentum of his legs. He was literally flying over the tables, sinks and worktops with the agility and rapidity of the martial-arts master that he was. Standing opposite the metal door of the cold room, he gazed at his reflection, then gave a long, hoarse yell of frustration and anger. Taking a run-up, he flung himself at the wall and, gaining a foothold on its tiled surface, began running around the kitchen, fuelled by the resentment he'd been bottling up for weeks. Finally, out of breath, he held out his arms and focused all his rage on the enormous copper stewpot which, a few seconds later, found itself thrown through the air and flattened like a pancake against the opposite wall. He had begun his battle against his greatest enemy—an invisible, yet extremely powerful enemy: himself.

70

THE MEMORY-SWIPE

THE NEXT DAY, THE ANXIOUS POLLOCKS AND BELLANGERS were sitting silently in the kitchen of the house in Bigtoe Square, eating a sombre lunch, when there was an unexpected ring at the door-bell. Pavel stood up and came back accompanied by the two policemen who'd questioned Oksa a few days earlier. She swallowed noisily and felt sweat trickling down her back. What were they doing here? Here in her house? She recalled the last question they'd asked her. "We'd like to know—are you related to Leomido Fortensky, the conductor?" She'd answered in the affirmative, of course, intrigued by the question, but more relieved than anything else to be done with this potentially dangerous interrogation. Thinking about it a bit later, she'd told herself that the policemen just might be well-informed music lovers—all the while knowing deep down that their question had to be linked to the murders of Lucas Williams and Peter Carter, what with police logic and all. But she'd been so exhausted in the next few days that she hadn't given another thought to this theory—which was the worst-case scenario. And now look! The police were here. And their presence meant that they were sure her family was mixed up in those terrible events. It was obvious that the noose was tightening.

"We're sorry to disturb you in the middle of lunch," began the police-men, sitting down on a sofa, after being shown into the living room by Pavel. "But we have a few questions we'd like to ask you."

"Allow me to introduce my mother, Dragomira Pollock, my wife, Marie, and my daughter, Oksa," said Pavel, trying to sound laid-back, although his voice was a little shriller than usual.

"Hello, Oksa," said one of the two men, very politely. "We met before at St Proximus College, a few days ago," he explained to everyone there. "May I ask who those people are?" he added, glancing towards the open kitchen door.

"Our friends, Jeanne and Pierre Bellanger, and their son Gus," replied Pavel.

"Bellanger? Did you say Bellanger?" asked the policeman, looking at his colleague. "Our visit also concerns them. Would you ask them to join our little chat."

His mind in a turmoil, Pavel went to fetch the Bellangers from the kitchen. Gus glanced tensely at Oksa before sitting down opposite her.

"What would you like to know, gentlemen?" asked Dragomira cordially.

"Do you know, either well or remotely, a man called Lucas Williams?"

They looked at each other as casually as possible and shook their heads.

"Lucas Williams? No, that name doesn't ring any bells," replied Dragomira, looking convincingly candid.

"Wasn't he a maths teacher at St Proximus?" said Oksa, causing a ripple of surprise among her nearest and dearest who, fortunately, didn't let it show. "A student in our class told us he'd been murdered."

The policemen looked at her attentively.

"That's right, Oksa. You're very well informed. Does the name Peter Carter mean anything to you?"

"He was murdered too!" replied Oksa impetuously, to the policemen's great surprise and her family's utter confusion.

Gus glanced again at his friend and gave a deep sigh. "*What's got into her? She is incorrigible!*" he thought. "*There's no reasoning with her.*" And he lost no time picturing himself handcuffed and thrown in prison for the rest of his days, while the Runaways—specifically his parents and Oksa—would be kept in isolation in high-tech laboratories where they would be dissected by unscrupulous service personnel. *"Well done, Oksa... we're screwed!"*

As for Oksa, she looked perfectly relaxed. Contrary to what everyone thought, she knew exactly what she was doing, as Dragomira soon realized.

"The cause of death was identical in both cases," continued the girl. "Their lungs had been dissolved, it was in all the newspapers."

"That's quite correct," remarked one of the policemen. "And we're here today because we have serious reason to believe that Peter Carter—who was an investigative journalist, as you may know—had been investigating your family for a few months."

"What do you mean?" broke in Pavel, frowning.

"We found a large number of press articles about your uncle, Leomido Fortensky, at his home," replied the policeman, "as well as some documents which left no room for doubt as to the subject of his investigation. That file was unfortunately stolen only a few days after we found Carter's body. We did however have time to examine it. Among other things, it contained an organization chart, photos and highly detailed notes about your friends and family members. About you, Mrs Pollock, and your friend, Abakum Olixone. You ran a renowned herbalist store, didn't you?"

"Yes, we did," replied Dragomira candidly with a forced smile.

"These documents also contained some very odd information about a man called Petrus Prokopius, an art thief by trade, who was killed on a job two years ago in the United States. Does that name ring any bells with you?"

"No, I don't think so," said Dragomira, who seemed to be searching in the folds of her capacious dress rather than her memory. "But what is his connection with that maths teacher? What was his name? Williams?"

"Lucas Williams, that's right. Well, we have serious reason to believe that your family—or at least some of its members—had something to do with the murder of those two men, as well as with the disappearance of

Miss Heartbreak, a teacher at St Proximus," stated the policeman coldly, scrutinizing each of them in turn.

"But Miss Heartbreak has reappeared!" exclaimed Oksa indignantly.

"That's right," retorted the policeman. "But we're regarding her reappearance as suspicious. Quite apart from the fact, as you must be aware, that the poor woman is suffering from serious mental injuries. To sum up, your family seems to be the common denominator in all these cases and we're here to look into this more thoroughly. Lucas Williams was killed just three days after you settled in England and Peter Carter followed you to London, where he suffered the same fate as Williams a month later. What are you doing, Mrs Pollock?" he shouted suddenly, jumping up from his seat. "Please put that—"

The policeman didn't have time to finish. He and his colleague slumped slowly back on the sofa, eyes open wide in the direction of Dragomira, who'd just blown into her Granok-Shooter.

"Well done, Baba!" exclaimed Oksa anxiously. "That was a close shave. They had worked everything out."

"Yes," admitted Baba Pollock. "We're in a tight corner... we have to hurry, there isn't a moment to lose!"

"What have you done?" asked Marie in alarm, her hand over her mouth.

"Don't worry, Marie," said Pierre reassuringly. "I think Dragomira used a Memory-Swipe Granok.

"That's right," confirmed the old lady hurriedly. "And now we must persuade these two men that we have absolutely nothing to do with these events. They must leave here convinced of that."

"Yes, of course," replied Marie uncertainly.

"How are we going to do that, Baba?" asked Oksa quickly, with great interest.

"Like this."

Dragomira put her hands on either side of one policeman's head and, looking him straight in the eye, began frantically muttering some phrases that no one could understand.

"I don't believe it!" muttered Oksa, taken aback by what she was seeing.

A slender trail of bluish smoke was snaking from Dragomira's mouth into the ears of the motionless man. Entering one ear, it emerged from the other a few seconds later and then evaporated gently on contact with the air.

"What was that?" stammered Gus.

"Dragomira has the gift of Thought-Adder," replied her father in a low voice.

"Let me guess," ventured Oksa. "It's a form of hypnosis, isn't it? Baba is persuading those men that we have nothing to do with what happened to Lucas Williams and Peter Carter."

"You're forgetting Miss Heartbreak," pointed out Gus. "The body count is rising."

While they were talking, Dragomira had given the second policeman the same treatment. As soon as the wisp of blue smoke had emerged from his ears, it vanished in the air.

"Quick!" warned Dragomira. "They're about to come round. Go back to your seats!"

They all sat back down immediately. On the sofa, the policemen were nodding gently and groaning. Dragomira brought her Granok-Shooter to her mouth and said in a low voice:

> By the power of the Granoks
> Think outside the box
> Particles of wiped memory
> Remember the words I told to thee.

Then, aiming the weapon at the policemen, she blew into it twice. The two men immediately continued talking from where they had broken off—or rather, from where Dragomira had wanted them to break off.

"Okay," said one of them, standing up. "Thank you for taking the time to answer our questions. We've intruded upon you long enough."

"Not at all, gentleman," replied Dragomira, smiling broadly. "We only wish we could have been of more help."

"On the contrary, madam. The information you've given us will take this investigation in a completely new direction and one we'd never have considered before. We're deeply grateful."

Oksa and Gus gazed at each other wide-eyed.

"Your gran is so cool," remarked Gus as Dragomira showed the policemen to the door.

"I know, I know," said Oksa in amusement. "It's a family trait."

"In the meantime, I really thought you'd lost it when you started giving them chapter and verse."

"You had us all in a real panic!" added Marie. "I thought our last hour had come."

"You should trust me a little more," said Oksa provocatively, and not a little cockily. "Give me some credit!"

"It's a good thing your gran is a fast thinker, all the same," commented Pavel seriously.

"We were exactly on the same wavelength," announced Dragomira, after seeing the two policemen off the premises. "I think the Fairies were on our side."

"You think they had something to do with it?" asked Oksa inquisitively.

"No, it's just an Edefian saying, Dushka," replied the old lady with a laugh.

"Now, mother dear, I'd love you to tell us what wild goose chase you sent those poor policemen on," said Pavel.

"Oh, it's very simple. Remember that Gus and Oksa were convinced that Orthon-McGraw was a secret agent? Well, I used that theory and permanently implanted the following explanation in those policemen's minds. Listen carefully: Peter Carter wasn't a journalist—that was just a cover. In fact, the man was a secret agent working for the FSB, the Russian Federal Security Service, in other words the former KGB. His job was to locate all Russian dissidents in the West. As you know, my dear husband Vladimir was a great shaman. As soon as they found out about his powers, the Soviet authorities regarded him as a potential danger. He was imprisoned in a gulag for his so-called subversive ideas. A few days later, he was killed while trying to escape. Unfortunately, there was nothing imaginary about that bit…"

Dragomira closed her eyes briefly and shook her head to try and banish this painful memory.

"Anyway, following his murder, Abakum, Pavel and I fled the Soviet Union with Leomido's help. Since that day, our family has always been regarded as hostile to the regime. I made the policemen believe that Lucas Williams was in fact Luka Wilenkov, a leading Russian biologist who had also fled for political reasons. Once in England, that man assumed the name Lucas Williams and found a job as a maths teacher at St Proximus—another cover. A few months ago, he contacted us to persuade us to join a group of dissidents who were planning a coup to topple the Russian president. His main asset was a substance he'd invented, a lethal bacteriological weapon developed in the utmost secrecy."

"The Pulmonis!" Oksa butted in.

"Yes," confirmed Dragomira. "You can easily imagine the rest… Peter Carter tracked down Lucas Williams, along with us. He killed Williams with his own weapon, before being killed himself by another dissident from Williams's group—a group to which, of course, none of the Pollocks has even been remotely affiliated. Because the Pollocks, since they were forced to leave the Soviet Union, haven't wanted to get involved in politics, not on your life, thank you very much! Basically, the police now think this is merely a brutal settling of scores by Russian secret agents and naturally we're counting on the British authorities to use the utmost discretion and ensure we're left in peace—after all, we've suffered enough, haven't we?"

Dragomira ended with this question, beaming radiantly at them all.

"So? What do you think?"

"Baba, you are fan-tas-tic!" exclaimed Oksa, flushed with excitement. "Lucas Williams and Peter Carter, Russian secret agents—what an incredible imagination you have! You should write novels."

"Well done, Dragomira! You haven't lost your touch," congratulated Pierre. "You almost managed to convince me."

"Wow," muttered Gus in admiration. "That's top-drawer! It makes me think of all those stories about poisoned Russian spies which caused problems for the British secret service not so long ago."

"Oh, well, Gus, reality is sometimes stranger than fiction," added Dragomira mysteriously.

Only Marie and Pavel remained tense and silent. They weren't finding it that easy to shrug off the feelings of anxiety and panic caused by the policemen's visit.

"What about Miss Heartbreak?" asked Pavel suddenly, gazing intently at his mother. "Is she a dissident too?"

"Who knows," replied Dragomira with a smile.

71

MYSTERY AND LONGEVITY

ISS HEARTBREAK, OF COURSE, HAD NO AFFILIATION
with any group of Russian dissidents or secret agents. And, what's
more, she wasn't dead. Although Dragomira had at first been bothered by
this surprising news, there was a certain logic to it, which Oksa realized
when all the Runaways met once more in the house on Bigtoe Square.

"Of course! If McGraw had killed Miss Heartbreak, he would have
run the risk of drawing more attention to us and, indirectly, to him. The
theories Baba gave the police about Peter Carter and Lucas Williams
hold water. But adding Miss Heartbreak to the mix would've made it
all sound bit far-fetched."

"You have a point, Oksa," agreed Abakum. "Orthon-McGraw has to
protect the Outsiders to protect himself. And vice versa. Our fates are
bound together."

"It's such a hassle," sighed Oksa.

"Has anyone heard anything more about poor Miss Heartbreak?"
asked Naftali, the tall Swede.

Oksa and Gus had found time to learn a few things about their teacher's
condition. By keeping their ears and eyes open and digging around for
information, they managed to gather some interesting titbits, which they
confided to the Runaways.

"Apparently the investigation is tending towards an act of vandalism
gone wrong: the theory is that Miss Heartbreak was in the wrong place at

the wrong time and was attacked. That's what the teachers and the police believe anyway," explained Oksa. "Other than that, I learnt she's been committed to an asylum—Mr Bontempi told Dr Bento yesterday. He visits her every day and he said it's awful because she's totally unhinged. When he arrives, she thinks he's a Chinese mandarin, and a few minutes later she's convinced he's an Egyptian priest."

"You can see she's a history teacher," said Pavel, with a touch of irony. "Sorry, that was out of order," he added immediately, trying to stifle a smile.

"Dad!" said Oksa, her reproachful tone tinged with amusement. "You're in-corr-ig-ible!"

"I was going to get some stuff for Dr Lemaire and I overheard a conversation between McGraw and Bontempi," continued Gus. "It was sickening... that hypocrite McGraw was saying how deeply sorry he was about Benedicta—he called her by her first name, the bastard!—and how deeply shocked he'd been to see her splashing about in the icy water of the fountain and that the image would stay with him for the rest of his life, and blah-blah-blah... It was revolting."

"And in class? How has he behaved with you this week?" asked Abakum.

Oksa and Gus looked at each other, then chorused:

"Good!"

"Good?" asked Marie in amazement.

"Yes, in other words, he's ignored us," replied Oksa. "Which is sheer heaven. It's beyond our wildest dreams. No rage, no persecution; we couldn't be happier. I think we could have danced on our desks and he wouldn't have said a word."

"You really think so?" asked Gus with a smile. "I'm not so sure. Maybe you haven't noticed him glaring daggers at you out of the corner of his eye! You really did a number on him, from the look of his badly scratched face."

"He really did a number on me too," retorted Oksa, serious all of a sudden. "He did a number on pretty much everyone, when it comes down to it."

"What about Mortimer? And Zoe? Have you seen them?" continued Dragomira.

"Zoe came running after me," replied Gus. "But I turned my back on her, saying I didn't want her to talk to me again, or come anywhere near me."

"She tried to speak to me as well, saying she wanted to explain," sighed Oksa. "She had tears in her eyes and looked so sad that I almost felt sorry for her. But in the end I gave her the coldest glare I could manage and walked off without answering. Other than that, I heard Mortimer boasting about an island he's going to on holiday."

"An island?" asked Dragomira, in astonishment.

"Yes, an island which his father has just bought off the coast of Scotland. You should have heard him bragging—'my father's island' this and 'my father's island' that, it was ridiculous. Afterwards he saw me and tried to wind me up, as usual. This time he was making fun of the expression on my face when his father suspended me in mid-air with the help of his Croakettes. He said I was struggling like a worm on the end of a hook and that I looked like a fat leech. I said whatever, and that it was his father who looked ridiculous now, slinking around with his face all scratched up. Then he told me you were nothing but a senile old woman and that you weren't going to be working miracles for much longer, Baba," explained Oksa, sounding choked.

"I see," replied Dragomira, with a knowing look. "Don't worry, I may not be in the first flush of youth, but I still have more than one trick left up my sleeve!"

"Talking about that," Oksa continued immediately, her elbows propped on her knees and her face between her hands, "Gus and I have been wondering about something for quite a while; perhaps now would be a good time to give us an answer."

Dragomira and Abakum looked at each other in resignation, and nodded wearily.

"We know all of you lied to some extent about your identity and your status once you were on the Outside," continued Oksa, heartened by the silence. "You had no choice. And we also know that officially McGraw was born in 1960 although, in fact, he's older than you, Baba."

Gus settled himself comfortably in his armchair, his expression interested and attentive. This matter had been bothering him for quite a while. To everyone's surprise, it was Leomido who spoke:

"Orthon-McGraw is two years older than me and seven years older than Dragomira. So, if I'm calculating correctly, that makes him seventy-seven."

"No way," exclaimed Marie. "Seventy-seven, that's impossible!"

"I knew you were going to say that," conceded Leomido.

"But how can he look so young?" continued Marie, intrigued.

"I'm sorry," added Oksa. "I'm not saying you look old—you're great for your age, but McGraw looks a damn sight younger than you! Seventy-seven, that's incredible! And if he really is as old as that, he would have retired a long time ago."

"Perhaps he's had cosmetic surgery," suggested Gus. "Or a youth cure."

These words seemed to trigger something in Dragomira's and Leomido's minds. They looked at each other in amazement as they registered what now seemed like a blindingly obvious fact. Abakum, on the other hand, had the unruffled composure of a man who'd already spent a long time thinking about this question. He looked at his friends and then broke the silence:

"Do you think that—"

Dragomira put her head in her hands and said quietly:

"No, I can't believe it."

"Don't tell me that you think—" added Leomido, deepening the mystery.

"Think *what*?" ventured Oksa, trying hard not to raise her voice.

Gus's and Oksa's parents watched this mysterious exchange without a word. But the three Runaways were so lost in thought that they were oblivious to the agitation of their friends and family. A concerned Naftali bent down and murmured something in Marie's ear. She replied in a low voice:

"I'd say around forty-five, not seventy-seven, no way!"

Naftali repeated Marie's remark to Brune and Mercedica and the three of them began whispering mysteriously.

"Do they always act like this when someone says 'youth cure'?" Gus whispered to Oksa.

Oksa narrowed her eyes at him and shrugged doubtfully.

"Whatever the case, it looks like it set them on the right track... Well?" she repeated impetuously. "What do you think?"

Dragomira looked up in surprise and stared at them wide-eyed, as if she'd only just noticed her family and friends—and their impatience.

"We may have an explanation... an explanation which isn't a million miles away from your suggestion, Gus, because there was a lot of sense in what you said. I never thought I'd say this, but we're thinking about a rumour which did the rounds in Edefia three or four years before the Great Chaos. There were claims that the Nontemporenta had been discovered."

"The what?" asked Oksa.

"The Nontemporenta," repeated Dragomira, "the pearl of longevity, if you prefer."

"Er, I don't know if I prefer it!" retorted Oksa frowning. "What is it?"

"Until then, the pearl had been a legend. People said that one of the Fairies possessed a shell filled with pearls which delayed the ageing process. But I think Abakum knows more than we do about this," explained Dragomira, turning to her Watcher.

"I've been turning over this matter of appearance in my mind for a while. But I think today all the pieces of the puzzle have finally fallen into place and I can clear up this issue, which has remained a mystery for over fifty years," admitted Abakum, stroking his short white beard. "It's true that I am in possession of several facts which give me an advantage and allow me to come to a very plausible conclusion—"

His eyes gleaming with unnerving intensity, Abakum suddenly broke off, daunted by the magnitude of what he was about to reveal.

"Abakum," said Oksa, beseeching him with her eyes, "Tell us! Do you want us to die of curiosity?"

"In the Book of Shadows inherited from my mother the Fairy, it is written that the fresh waters from the Singing Spring are responsible for the Ageless Fairies' youthful freshness. These waters actually slow down the ageing process, so the Fairies can live for more than 500 years."

"Wow," exclaimed Oksa, "even longer than the Lunatrixes!"

"Oksa, don't interrupt," chided Gus, nudging his friend.

"Yes, even longer than the Lunatrixes," echoed Abakum. "One day, a young boy whom I knew well, Bjorn, confided in me. He'd witnessed something awful a few months previously and he wanted to tell me about it because, he said, it was keeping him awake at nights. He was seven or eight and his mother hadn't wanted to believe him when he'd told her what he'd seen. She'd said he had an over-active imagination, and that had been the end of it. Then Bjorn came to see me. He'd caught sight of an old man in the forest, on the banks of a narrow river. He knew him well: it was Gonzal, a gentle man, well-liked by everyone. He was sitting on the riverbank and weeping because his fifth grandchild had just been born. They were tears of joy and sadness because his fifth grandchild was his first granddaughter, and he would have liked to live longer to watch her grow. I should say that, at that time, he was over 150 years old, and nearing the end of his life... little Bjorn then told me that a shining lady as bright as a glow-worm—almost certainly a Fairy—had appeared and had spoken briefly with old Gonzal. Then she'd given him a shell which shone with a bright pink light. When he told me that detail, it immediately made me think about what I'd read in the Book of Shadows: the Nontemporentas, the pearls of longevity, exactly matched that description.

The little boy continued his story. Unfortunately for Gonzal, someone else had witnessed the scene: a man hidden behind some ferns, who pounced on him as soon as the Fairy had disappeared. Plunging a knife in his heart, he put stones in his clothes and threw him into the river.

After grabbing the shell, of course. It wasn't long before Gonzal's family reported the old man's disappearance. They searched high and low but no trace of him was found. Young Bjorn was terrified and didn't dare breathe a word. As Gonzal was very old, everyone came to the conclusion that he'd withdrawn from the world to die in peaceful solitude, as people sometimes did. I had remembered the story clearly and, even then, I'd had my suspicions about this conclusion. But what my young informer told me later only confirmed my hunch. In fact, a few days later, arriving in Thousandeye City with his parents to sell a harvest of redcurrants, quite by chance he'd seen and recognized the man who'd murdered old Gonzal on a street corner. This had struck fear into his heart and made him decide to speak about it. The man in question was handing a box to someone he knew, a person of importance: Ocious, First Servant of the High Enclave and Orthon's father, as you know. This information started me thinking. When I asked young Bjorn to describe the man talking to Ocious, I immediately recognized Marpel—there was no doubt in my mind. Bjorn had mentioned the green tattoo of an ivy branch snaking up his neck and over his ears, and Marpel was the only person who answered that description. This violent, unsociable man had been imprisoned for several months for robbing the jewellery factory. I secretly tried to track him down, but he'd disappeared. Anyway, his few friends had told the First Servant of the High Enclave, Ocious, that I was looking for him. The investigation didn't come up with anything, so the search was abandoned—rather too soon, if you ask me. Because I'm now convinced that it was Ocious who received the Nontemporentas from Marpel, who had himself stolen them from old Gonzal."

"What an incredible story!" whistled Oksa, shaking her head. "But what do you know about these pearls of longevity?".

"All I know is what I read in the Book of Shadows. The Nontemporentas are found in the depths of the Singing Spring. They're bright pink in colour and they enable the man or woman who swallows them to retain the freshness of youth. It's one of the secrets of the Ageless Fairies' longevity."

"Men would happily kill for that," remarked Pavel.

"Yes, even in Edefia, where we live longer than on the Outside… Anyway, that's probably what happened. Gonzal and Marpel paid with their lives for those fabulous pearls. And the trail leads right back to Ocious."

"And Ocious means Orthon-McGraw!" exclaimed Oksa.

"When I saw him from my hot-air balloon I was shocked," continued Leomido, shaking his head. "I recognized him perfectly, but he looked so young that I couldn't believe my eyes. And, at the same time, it couldn't be his son. It had to be him—too many details confirmed it. I'm totally flabbergasted."

"All this is very worrying. Not to mention that it makes the situation terribly complicated," added Abakum.

"As if it weren't complicated enough," muttered Pavel.

"Complicated perhaps, but you have to admit that it's incredible all the same!" cried Gus with an enthusiasm that surprised everyone. "Pearls of longevity, that's amazing. Do you think McGraw has some with him or that he's hiding them somewhere?"

"Don't get carried away, young man," replied Dragomira, putting her hand on the boy's arm. "This is only guesswork."

"But there isn't any other possible explanation, it's obvious!" said Gus passionately, brushing away a strand of hair.

He was so thrilled by the idea that he was shaking.

"It is a very plausible explanation, I agree, Gus," remarked Abakum. "I think there's a very strong probability that Orthon possesses some Nontemporentas. Or maybe he no longer possesses them—which would explain why he is so desperate to return to Edefia."

Taken aback, Oksa gazed steadily at Abakum:

"That could be a really good reason."

"Yes," admitted Abakum. "Although I do have another theory…" he added.

72

THE OTHER SIDE
OF THE PICTURE

"ANOTHER THEORY?" ASKED OKSA.

"Remember what your gran showed you on the Camereye," continued Abakum. "Ocious wanted to leave Edefia. We don't know the exact details because Gracious Malorane was always very evasive about this subject, even with Mercedica and me, who were her confidants. But we do know, broadly speaking, that Ocious was intending to use his abilities on the Outside to gain power and supremacy. Something we could all have done in the fifty-seven years we've been here. Except that none of us has ever abused our powers, except for the person who paid for it with his life—"

"The art thief!" suggested Oksa.

"Exactly," agreed Abakum. "But if I'm to shed any light on our present concerns, I must go back in time to when Gracious Malorane took the initiative in screening her Dreamflights to the Outside for members of the High Enclave and then all the other Insiders. Those public Camereye shows were a first in the history of Edefia—no Gracious had ever done that before. Most of them had been tight-lipped about the subject and had been careful not to let anything slip. Or they'd give a verbal account of what they'd seen on their virtual travels. But, as a precaution, they carefully selected what they revealed, presenting a version which often strayed far from the truth."

"Abakum!" exclaimed Dragomira, outraged. "How can you say such a thing?"

"My dear Dragomira, I'm sorry but everything I'm saying is the simple truth: the Graciouses weren't always very honest with the people of Edefia when it came to their Dreamflights. Far be it from me to criticize, because they largely hid what they saw out of an instinct for protection. By shrouding the Outside in mystery, they managed to convince our people over the centuries that nothing but danger lay beyond Edefia."

"But Abakum," broke in Oksa, "there's something bothering me. I get the impression that, in some ways, you were... *prisoners* of Edefia!"

"Oksa!" exclaimed Dragomira again, visibly shocked.

A silence heavy with tension descended over the room. Dragomira's breathing sounded agitated and her nostrils were quivering with anger. Abakum looked back and forth between the woman to whom he'd devoted his life—his dear Dragomira—and the girl who was now their Last Hope.

"Oksa is right," he said with boundless tact, gazing intently at the old lady. "Our people have always known about the Outside, but some of them were sure that things were being hidden from them: they believed it was possible to leave. No one spoke openly about it, but this belief only grew over the centuries and a growing number of Edefians felt like prisoners."

"I can't let you say that!" retorted Dragomira with tears in her eyes. "Edefia had reached a state of perfection. I have never seen a more balanced, more respectful and more admirable way of life."

"In the eyes of the little girl you were then, agreed," continued Abakum, with a pained expression. "Obviously Edefia never had anything in common with the dictatorships or totalitarian states that can be found on the Outside. It was a harmonious land where life was idyllic for most of us. But, from generation to generation, we gradually bought into the belief that everything elsewhere was bad. Fear, fuelled by ignorance and rumours, spread through the Insiders' minds over the centuries, allowing the Graciouses to fulfil their wish to protect the people—convinced, I repeat, that it was for their own good. This was all very honourable, I'd be the first to admit it; but Edefia could actually be regarded as a prison by some of its inhabitants. In all honesty, someone has to say this. As far as I'm concerned, Malorane's singular methods proved it. All the problems began when she started showing her unedited Dreamflights—this was the first time a Gracious had shown what she'd *really* seen on the Outside. Some people, led by Ocious, felt deceived by all the Graciouses before Malorane: the view we all had of the world around us was totally false. But should we judge Ocious's supporters? That would be desperately unfair, because not only did the Graciouses lie—admittedly to protect us, but they lied all the same—but also the Outside was nothing like the frightening world they'd described to us before then. Despite the wars, the violence and the injustice, the Outside wasn't at all what we'd been given to believe. In the space of just a few months, it became a land filled with temptation, and the belief we could visit it only grew stronger in some people's minds."

Dragomira seemed totally demoralized by her Watcher's words. Clenching her fists, she jumped up and ran into the kitchen with a stifled sob. Oksa leapt up immediately to follow her, shaking off her father's hand as he tried to stop her.

"Dad!" she said reproachfully. "Can you imagine what she must be feeling?"

And she resolutely followed her gran, watched by the concerned Runaways.

☀

Dragomira was standing by the sink, letting her tears fall freely. Oksa squeezed her shoulder gently.

"Dushka…"

"Don't worry, Baba. It's only natural to be sad."

Dragomira dried her eyes and replied in a strained voice:

"Deep down, I know Abakum is right. I've always known it, but I didn't want to admit it and that's what annoys me most of all."

She turned round and gave Oksa a long look before rejoining the others, who were waiting in silence. She sat down slowly, gazed up at her brother Leomido and asked him dully:

"Is that how you felt too? Were you like them? Did you want to visit other places?"

Leomido looked very uncomfortable. Then, suddenly, he met his sister's gaze and blurted out nervously:

"Yes I did—if you really want to know. I was dying to visit the Outside, explore the deserts and oceans, feel snow on my face, listen to different languages, hear the laughter of people other than those I loved so dearly… yes, I'd have done anything to leave!"

"Would you have betrayed your family and friends?" asked Abakum harshly.

"My family and friends betrayed me."

Oksa darted a glance from Leomido to Abakum. The two men were staring each other down, their eyes filled with resentment and sadness, although there was no hostility—deep sorrow seemed to emanate from this silent confrontation.

"What do you mean?" breathed Abakum.

Instead of replying, Leomido stood up and marched out of the room, leaving the Runaways completely at a loss.

※

"What happened next?" asked Oksa, feeling unsettled, but still impatient to find out more about these remarkable revelations. "What happened next with Malorane's Dreamflights?"

Abakum shook his head and rubbed his eyes as if to banish an unwelcome thought, then continued his story:

"Some men and women, led by Ocious, banded together to study the Outsiders' behaviour and social set-up. You won't be surprised to learn that they were particularly interested in matters of power... I remember an impassioned conversation I overheard between Ocious and one of his friends around the bend of a corridor in the Glass Column: Ocious was fired up about the omnipotence of the oil magnates. He went on to describe the financial mechanisms in minute detail and the influence they had on international political power. I remember clearly how that conversation both fascinated me and chilled me with fear. It was all so different from everything we knew in Edefia! And yet, in a strange way, nothing was really all that different because, deep down, I sensed that we could easily be persuaded to run things the way Ocious admired so much. Apart from our special powers, we weren't so different from the Outsiders: we were all human, driven by the same aspirations, whether good or bad. It was quite a shock. Ocious and his group soon identified the strengths and, most importantly, the weaknesses of those living on the other side of the mantle, our frontier of light. From then on, Ocious pestered Malorane into making other Dreamflights to provide answers to all his questions. He wanted to know everything, absolutely everything, about the Outside. And Malorane—who will ever know why?—gave in to most of his demands."

Abakum broke off again and looked at Dragomira kindly. Baba Pollock cast down her eyes sadly, her lips pursed.

"As you know, the Firmhands possess the power to transform rocks from the Peak Ridge mountains into diamonds. It didn't take long for Ocious and his friends to realize the huge potential of that extraordinary power. Driven by ambition, they tried to find a way out of Edefia, reasoning that if it could be done mentally, by means of Dreamflying, then it could be done physically too. Of course it was physically possible! As you know, that was the legendary Secret-Never-To-Be-Told, the secret of the Graciouses. From then on, things went from bad to worse. Some of the Edefians began expressing their desire to travel to the Outside with increasing vehemence. But these wouldn't have been courtesy visits: they had no desire to be tourists or enter into diplomatic relations. No! They were motivated by notions of power and supremacy, concepts we'd always tried to guard against. Until then, we didn't have a highly developed sense of profit and domination. For centuries, our entire system had been based on principles which were the direct opposite of these and had shaped the way we thought and acted. But, following Malorane's public Dreamflights, people's ambitions and thirst for power escalated, to our great misfortune. As soon as the Secret-Never-To-Be-Told was revealed, we realized with terror why the previous Graciouses had kept us in a happy state of ignorance: leaving Edefia entailed opening the Portal. And opening the Portal was extremely dangerous for Edefia; it made the land vulnerable to the worst possible danger—invasion by the Outsiders! If they'd known about the existence of our land, they would have coveted it and this would have led to exploitation, war and perhaps even our destruction. Because, contrary to the beliefs of many people at the time, the Secret hadn't been introduced to hold the Insiders and the Graciouses *captive*: it guaranteed our safety, and Malorane was the first Gracious to get that wrong. The Gracious's life and Edefia's fate depended on it. Remember the confidential oath that all Graciouses swore during the Cloak Ceremony:

> *Only you the Gracious*
> *Will keep this secret*
> *No one else but you shall know it*
> *Because there is in mankind*
> *On the Inside as on the Outside*
> *Both good and evil*
> *If the Secret be revealed*
> *You will lay down your life.*

"So they were actually being criticized for keeping that oath," deduced Oksa.

"Yes!" replied Abakum. "And there's no doubt that they were in a cruel dilemma: they had to protect the Secret—and consequently Edefia and the people—by hiding things and telling lies. The less they said about the Outside, the more successfully they safeguarded the Secret-Never-To-Be-Told, and the safer Edefia remained."

"No pressure!" remarked Oksa ironically.

"You're well aware, youngsters, that we have gifts that many an Outsider would give their eye teeth to possess. Gifts which would confer undeniable power on anyone who used them unwisely. They are an incredible source of strength, but also a huge weakness. The Runaways know that only too well, since we live under the constant danger of being discovered and captured. But it isn't just these gifts, it's also the diamonds. On the Outside, diamonds are highly coveted gems with which people can achieve the wealth and power they lust after. We think that is bound to be what motivated Ocious. Blinded by ambition, he never weighed up the danger of opening the Portal. He was only interested in leaving with a large stash of diamonds and subjugating the Outside—or at least wielding some kind of power as a result of the vast riches those precious stones would have brought him. As soon as he discovered it was possible to leave Edefia, the Secret-Never-To-Be-Told was doomed, and our country's descent into chaos was a foregone conclusion. But he wasn't the one to leave—his son, Orthon, was. And if Orthon wants to go back to Edefia now, it's because *he knows he can*, that's the first point. When there's no chance of something, you stop thinking about it, or even hoping for it. Secondly, Orthon was sent into exile, just like we were. Quite apart from pearls or diamonds, it's natural he should want to go back, just like we do. But Orthon doesn't belong to our group. He never has and never will. Not just because Ocious is his father—he can't do anything about that, and I think some of us would be prepared to welcome him into our ranks despite his family connections. On the Outside, we're all in the same boat, so to speak... No, the reason he can't be counted as one of us is because he's definitely an enemy of Edefia, as well as an enemy of the Runaways. I shall never forget that he killed my adoptive father in front of my eyes during the Great Chaos and he knows what a bitter grudge I've harboured against him for all these years because of it."

The blood drained from Abakum's face when he said that. His eyes clouded with bitterness and for a few seconds he gazed into space.

"I don't know why he did it," he continued sombrely. "But what we do know for sure is that he wants the Portal open and, for that, he needs to find a way past us to get at Oksa. We're dealing with someone who is extremely ambitious and cruel."

"And totally power-mad!" exclaimed Gus angrily.

"Exactly," agreed Abakum.

"But for goodness' sake, we can't blame him for wanting to return to Edefia!" remarked Mercedica, with a hint of bitterness. "Why is it okay for us to want to go back and not him? I think you're being very harsh, dear friends."

The Runaways stirred in their chairs and murmured in disapproval.

"Permit me to say that I'm surprised at your leniency, my dear Mercedica," retorted Abakum, struggling to suppress his irritation. "We're not questioning his desire to return to Edefia, just the reasons behind it and the appalling methods he uses! Yes, we all want the same thing, but it's Orthon—and no one else—who poses a serious problem for us today."

Dragomira buried her face in her hands with a groan and her Lunatrix, who'd been curled in an armchair since the beginning of the discussion, rushed over and patted her shoulder. Oksa stared wide-eyed at her parents and then Gus, her heart thumping. This was certainly a sensational story.

"I have a question."

"Yes, Oksa?"

"Edefia is invisible from the Outside... so how do you plan to find it again?"

73

THE GUARDIAN OF THE DEFINITIVE LANDMARK

"THAT'S AN EXCELLENT QUESTION, OKSA," REPLIED Abakum after pausing for a few seconds. "And one which has been our biggest concern over the years. A concern which is even more pressing now we hold some of the keys allowing us to return to Edefia."

Dragomira nodded with a sad smile and took over from Abakum, looking mainly at Oksa and Gus:

"Abakum is right. My mother had many qualities and some of them proved fatal for her, as you know. But even though her all-too-trusting nature was disastrous for Edefia and for all of us, she'd fortunately confided a number of things to me before our escape. Otherwise it would be totally impossible to find our land ever again. It was a few days before I was to enter the Cloak Chamber, which should have made me the new Gracious. I didn't know that the Chaos had already begun. The Elzevir had been stolen and the Secret-Never-To-Be-Told revealed to its usurper."

"What's the Elzevir?" Oksa asked immediately. "You've never mentioned that before."

"The Elzevir is a kind of logbook. It's made by the Ageless Fairies, then given to the brand-new Gracious on the day she enters the Cloak Chamber. It's a crystal sheet on which the Gracious notes all the major stages of her reign using a diamond pencil. The Elzevirs function as the

464

Gracious's Archives and are kept in the Memory on the top floor of the Glass Column. As I said, Malorane's Elzevir disappeared mysteriously from the Memorary. The person who benefited most from the theft was none other than Ocious, as you might imagine... From what I know, he was given a great deal of help by an accomplice in Malorane's immediate circle, a vile traitor who plunged us into the Great Chaos, damn him to all eternity. I didn't know this when I was bombarding my mother with questions a few days before our flight. Abakum told me all these details a few years later and that's when I understood why she'd given in so easily. For many years, I was angry with myself for pestering her as much as I did. But now I don't regret it. Perhaps it was instinct that prompted me... or that prompted my mother to tell me her secrets. Because, despite the oath she'd taken in the Cloak Chamber, she told me the biggest secret of all: that the Graciouses could open the Portal of Edefia and pass through to the Outside. I don't know if you can imagine how shocked I was—I'd never imagined anything like it. Like everyone, I knew that the Graciouses could send their consciousness to the Outside. But actually leaving Edefia! Unimaginable. When I realized that Ocious also knew this, I knew how serious it could be and what it could mean to certain people. It was only when I was on the Outside, though, that I really understood the importance of that secret and my mother's mistake. To answer your question, Oksa, the Portal of Edefia will only open if the Gracious orders her Phoenix to activate it. 'How?' you may ask. Every Gracious has a Phoenix which is born—or reborn—from the ashes of the former phoenix when the Mark appears. This legendary bird is one of the two key elements for opening the Portal: its song activates the Portal as the Gracious utters the incantation inscribed on a Medallion that is handed down from Gracious to Gracious. It's as simple as that. My mother then explained that inside the Chamber is a recreation of the universe. It contains a small-scale moving model of the planets, stars and comets in space. The most interesting of these is, of course, the Definitive Landmark: Edefia's position in relation to the universe and the Earth. How I'd have loved to see that," added Baba Pollock with a deep sigh.

She fell silent and closed her eyes. Hanging on her every word, they'd all been listening with intense concentration, but no one dared to show how impatient they were to know the rest of this fascinating story. Oksa was the first to try and attract her gran's attention by gently squeezing her hand. Dragomira reopened her eyes, struggling to shake off her memories.

"Yes, yes, I'm sorry. I was miles away… did you want to say something, Dushka?"

"Yes, Baba: if no one has any information about Edefia's location, it would be like looking for a needle in a haystack! Mission impossible."

Dragomira listened gravely, then her mouth curved into a faint smile and her eyes sparkled.

"The Medallion isn't a problem," she said, bringing out the pendant she wore on a gold chain, safely hidden beneath her dress.

"Wow! Really? Is that Malorane's Medallion?" exclaimed Oksa.

"Yes, Dushka. I've never taken it off since the moment my mother put it around my neck. Anyway, you must have noticed it, when I showed you the day of the Chaos on the Camereye."

"Yes, of course!" exclaimed Oksa, smacking her forehead with the flat of her hand. "Baba, that's brilliant. Will you show me the inscription?"

Dragomira's face clouded over and she gazed at the Medallion desolately before handing it to Oksa.

"But… Baba? There's nothing on it," remarked the Young Gracious, turning the piece of jewellery over and over in her hand.

"That's right, Dushka," said Dragomira sadly. "However, all hope isn't lost, because it's highly likely that the inscription is only revealed when the Phoenix appears. Anyway, that's our continuing belief."

"But how do we find the Phoenix?" continued Oksa, handing the Medallion back to her gran.

"There's no point looking, sweetheart. The Phoenix will come to you. It's as easy as that."

"Is it already born? Or 'reborn', if that's more correct?" continued Oksa.

"Yes. Your Phoenix was born from the ashes of mine the day the Mark appeared on your belly button," replied her gran.

"So that means someone in Edefia may know that there's a new Gracious?"

"That's entirely possible," agreed Dragomira. "The Ageless Fairies, in any case, were well aware that it had happened."

All kinds of feelings assailed Oksa, making her mind whirl. She shivered at the image of a Phoenix flying to her. Red as a beetroot, her cheeks glowing, the Young Gracious was breathing loudly, her chest tight with excitement. A crazy idea formed which she couldn't help voicing.

"Why don't we go there now?" she cried loudly.

Dragomira looked at her with a sad smile.

"No, Dushka, we're no more able to go there now than the last time you asked. You said it yourself, remember: we have no idea where Edefia is."

That reminder immediately dampened Oksa's enthusiasm and dashed the hopes of the more optimistic Runaways. Dragomira's Lunatrixa went over to her mistress and tapped her politely on the shoulder to show her sympathy.

"Our Old Gracious?" called the small creature in her high voice.

"Yes, Lunatrixa, what is it?"

"I have already given my conviction to the Young Gracious and I am going to make the repetition to this gathering," she said, staring at the Runaways with her huge blue eyes. "Gracious Malorane had naïve trust in the nature of mankind and the words you have given are fitting: her mistake brought chaotic consequences down on all of us."

The Lunatrixa sniffed deeply before continuing.

"But the thoughtlessness of her mind didn't form an impediment to anticipation."

"What do you mean?" asked Dragomira, frowning.

"Gracious Malorane entrusted the secret of the Definitive Landmark to some person."

467

The Runaways looked at each other in amazement.

"You mean that… *someone knows where Edefia is?*" murmured Dragomira, a hand over her mouth.

"My confidence in this conviction was filled with hope but it was also very reserved. It was my Lunatrix who gave me the gift of confirmation."

All eyes instantly turned to the Lunatrix, who was making cheese and ham toasties on his ironing board. Sensing he was the focus of attention, he stopped and his pudgy face flushed a strange deep purple.

"My Lunatrix, would you come over here, please?" invited Dragomira.

"Yes, Old Gracious?"

"I'm going to ask you a very important question. Do you know where Edefia is?"

Baba Pollock's voice was hoarse and trembling. An unsettling silence, broken only by the rapid breathing of the members of the group, descended on the room.

"Edefia is along the world and the knowledge of the Landmark is retained with precision in my brain, yes, Old Gracious," replied the Lunatrix simply.

"Good Lord! And you never said anything?" exclaimed Dragomira.

"The promise was vouchsafed to Gracious Malorane that only necessity would release information about the Landmark."

"And what is this necessity?" asked Oksa breathlessly, her cheeks scarlet.

The Lunatrix turned to her and bowed respectfully.

"Necessity means the time when destiny will favour the taking of this decision," replied the Lunatrix calmly. "Giving the Landmark if the time is not right will lead the Runaways into mistakes and failure. And you must absorb the acceptance of this information: knowing the Landmark today is useless."

"How will we know the right time?" asked Oksa.

"The Ageless Fairies will give the signs that will enlighten our Young Gracious. They have already initiated contact with you, this is the truth."

"Yes, that's true," acknowledged Oksa. "What about the Medallion? Do you know anything about it?"

"The conviction of the Old Gracious is shrouded in correctness. The Lunatrix possesses the mystery of the opening with the Medallion: the inscription will reveal its words when the time meets the appropriate occasion."

"Very sensible... but how do you know all this, Lunatrix?" asked Oksa, her voice sounding hoarse with emotion.

"The Lunatrix has the knowledge of all the secrets imprisoned in the depths of the hearts of the Graciouses," explained the Lunatrix. "All the secrets."

74

THE FIFTH TRIBE

THE RUNAWAYS WERE FLOORED BY THIS ASTOUNDING revelation. Everyone was talking agitatedly at once. What an incredible piece of news! And what a relief that someone knew how to find Edefia. Dragomira's Lunatrix! Who would have thought that the Definitive Landmark, the only way to relocate their lost land, was safe inside the head of that whimsical little creature? The prospect of returning to Edefia was more real now than it had ever been. Particularly for Oksa, who was overflowing with enthusiasm.

"I'm ready!" she said enthusiastically to her gran and Abakum. "I know so much more now."

"Yes, there's no doubt about that," replied her gran calmly. "I think we can all understand your impatience. But *look at us*. Some of us are old folk."

"Old folk who could flatten the world boxing champion," remarked Gus.

"Old folk who can fly," continued Oksa in the same tone, "hurl people yards away, manufacture amazing substances… old folk who could have the world at their feet if they wanted!"

"Yes," admitted Dragomira, "but, above all, old folk who are far from being warriors and who aren't ready, physically and mentally, to confront anyone. And, more importantly, old folk who don't know whom they'll have to confront—I'll say it again: this kind of venture cannot be undertaken lightly."

470

"Forgive me," said Naftali suddenly, who had kept silent until then. Everyone turned to look at the Swedish giant whose emerald-green eyes held an expression of great intensity. He clasped his hands together in front of him and darted Brune a look of mingled regret and anxiety. She placed her hand on his forearm encouragingly and gave him a resigned smile.

"Forgive me," he repeated, "but since this appears to be the time for revelations, I have something to tell you—something very important that you should know about Orthon-McGraw."

Leomido stifled an annoyed sigh, which wasn't lost on Oksa. Her great-uncle certainly did react oddly at times. Feeling her gaze on him, he shot her an anguished look and immediately lowered his eyes.

"What do you want to tell us, Naftali?" asked Abakum in amazement.

"I want to tell you about the Secret Society of the Werewalls," he replied staring at the Fairyman.

"The Werewalls?" breathed the latter, disconcerted. "What do you know about the Werewalls?"

Around the table, Brune and Dragomira darted troubled glances at each other, while Leomido's face darkened. Oksa looked questioningly at her father and mother, but they didn't seem to know any more than she did. The Bellangers appeared equally puzzled. As for Tugdual, the phrase "Secret Society" seemed to have caught his attention.

"First of all, I need to go back nine centuries," announced Naftali, taking a deep breath, "and tell you about the Diaphans, who are inextricably linked to the Werewalls, as you'll soon realize. Up until the twelfth century, there were five tribes in Edefia, not four: those you already know, plus the Diaphans. The Diaphans had always lived apart from the others, not far from the Distant Reaches, the most inaccessible territory in Edefia. There weren't many of them, only about fifty in total. These taciturn and unsociable beings, who lived by their own rules in an autocratic society, appeared to be peaceable, if somewhat unfriendly, neighbours. I say 'appeared' because the nature of the Diaphans was actually rather gruesome. In 1145, the Ageless Fairies cast the Confinement Spell, which condemned the Diaphans to an isolated existence in the hostile territory of Retinburn, a place where the stones glittered so brightly that no one could be exposed to their glare without being blinded on the spot. However, the perilous nature of the area actually formed the basis of this Confinement Spell—from that time onwards, the Diaphans couldn't survive outside this incandescent place. The glare from the rocks became essential for their survival. If they strayed too far, the Diaphans ran the risk of being literally extinguished. Over the years, their metabolism adapted to these new living conditions. The entire surface of their bodies became covered with a thick layer of grease which protected their epidermis from the intense light. Their skin, which was already very pale, turned translucent, showing their black veins and hearts. Their faces were reduced to their simplest form: a membrane formed over their eyes, giving them a strangely opaque gaze; their noses virtually dissolved, leaving two small slits as nostrils; their mouths shrank and the outer part of their ears disappeared so that only the auditory canals remained."

"They sound like extra-terrestrials," remarked Oksa, pulling a face.

"Yes, not far off," confirmed Naftali.

"But why did the Fairies cast a Confinement Spell on them?" continued Oksa. "Was it a punishment?"

"Yes, it was," admitted Naftali. "The male Diaphans had a horrible vice. Since they felt no love for their own kind, they'd become expert hunters, specializing in a very particular kind of hunt: the love hunt."

"What does that mean?" asked Oksa.

"Stop interrupting him the whole time and let him speak," grunted Gus.

"The love hunt," continued Naftali, "was simply the means by which these males, who were incapable of experiencing love themselves, stole other people's passionate feelings. For this, they'd travel in the utmost secrecy to Green-Mantle, Peak Ridge or Thousandeye City, where they'd seek out men and women of all ages who were in love. They would then hypnotize them and take possession of their feelings by inhaling them, which earned them the name of Snufflers. For many years, no one was able to explain this strange phenomenon. It was called Beloved Detachment because suddenly, overnight, people stopped loving the man or woman they'd been madly in love with the night before. And no wonder: their capacity for passion and love had been stolen from them for all eternity! In the years before the Ageless Ones stepped in, Edefia was held in the grip of an obsessive fear. No one knew exactly what was going on, so people spoke of a Love Plague and the leading Granokologists tried to invent substances to combat this terrible affliction. However, they met with no success. One day Coxo, the most ravenous of the Snufflers, was caught red-handed: he'd just seized the love of the Young Gracious who was due to be married a few days later. The game was up for them and the Diaphans were for ever banished to Retinburn."

"That's sickening," grimaced Oksa.

"Diabolical," added Tugdual.

"Coming back to the Werewalls: everything began with Temistocles," explained Naftali.

"Temistocles was a Firmhand who was born in 1516 and died a violent death in 1648, as you'll find out. He was a dedicated scientist, who focused his research on the properties of rocks and minerals. His work led to great advances in medicine using stones, but his research didn't stop there. He soon moved on from chemistry to alchemy, particularly transmutatory alchemy."

"What's that?" asked Marie in a small voice.

"Simply put, transmutatory alchemy is the transformation of one material into another. The Outsiders were of course passionately interested in the transformation of base metal into gold. However, in Edefia, the Firmhands could already perform that kind of miraculous feat, because they possessed the ability to transform certain rocks into diamonds. Temistocles wasn't particularly interested in immortality, which was also one of the great utopian dreams for alchemists. What fascinated him was our frontier, that mantle of light which no one had ever managed to cross. This was his ultimate dream, his life's work: to pass through that frontier. His constant search for new materials led him to take an interest in the shining rock of Retinburn. A Diaphan, seeing that he was struggling to get near the rock because it was so bright, made contact with him. It was over 400 years since the Diaphans had seen a living soul! This Diaphan provided his providential visitor with fragments of the blindingly bright rock. Temistocles called it the Luminescent Stone and researched it endlessly, convinced that he had an exceptional material in his hands. And he was right. Shortly afterwards, the Diaphan, aware that Temistocles represented an unexpected opportunity, offered him a deal he couldn't turn down: he would tell him a secret about the transmutation of matter in exchange for a young person's feelings of love. When he heard this, Temistocles rushed to Peak Ridge, drugged a young man who was about to be betrothed and brought him back to Retinburn. The Snuffler went about his awful business, forever depriving the boy of passion, and, in exchange, revealed the secret of the Diaphans: Coxo, the ancestral Snuffler, had developed a fabulous formula which made it possible to transform matter into particles! You can imagine Temistocles' delight—after years of research, his work had just taken a gigantic leap forward."

"You mean he wasn't bluffing?" asked Oksa in amazement. "The formula really existed?"

"Yes, Oksa," replied Naftali simply.

"You… you wouldn't happen to know the ingredients, would you?" asked the Young Gracious.

"Actually, yes I do."

Dragomira couldn't help crying out in surprise. Around her, the Runaways shifted uneasily on their seats, taken aback by these revelations and yet impatient to know more.

"The formula given to Temistocles that day by the Diaphan was incomplete; the centuries had taken their toll on memory. The Diaphan was in no doubt about the first two ingredients: a cube of Luminescent Stone measuring one and a quarter inches across plus 4.2 fluid ounces, or 125 millilitres, of the blood of the person concerned. The third ingredient was much less exact: it was a plant whose roots, stems and leaves had to be crushed and which acted as a catalyst for the previous two ingredients. Then the Diaphan decided to present Temistocles with the fourth ingredient: a small phial of inestimable value."

"What was that?" asked Oksa, holding her breath.

"After snuffling up the loving feelings of their poor innocent victims, the Diaphans experienced a period of euphoria. Strangely this state caused a black, viscous substance to flow from what remained of their noses. And the little phial which was given to Temistocles contained the vile tarry substance collected from the nostrils of Coxo in person, 400 years earlier."

"That's disgusting!" cried Oksa.

"Fascinating," added Tugdual.

"Gross!" added Gus. "It makes me think of 'the love hormone'."

"What's that?" asked Oksa, narrowing her eyes.

"Scientists are studying the phenomenon closely: apparently, when you fall in love, the body secretes a stimulating hormone, which is similar to certain hard drugs. People can even sometimes get totally hooked on it and that sounds like what happened with the Diaphans, doesn't it? And the most amazing thing is that the body is capable of locating this hormone by smell."

"That's incredible," remarked Oksa.

"You've hit the nail right on the head, Gus," added Naftali. "The problem was that the Diaphans had become hooked on the human love hormone."

"But why do you say that Coxo's 'substance' was of inestimable value?" went on Oksa. "What made it more valuable than any produced by the other Diaphans?"

"Coxo was an inventor of genius," replied Naftali.

"A crazy sorcerer, you mean—a psychopath!" broke in Dragomira. "I read a few articles about him in the Memorary. He was totally unscrupulous and capable of boundless cruelty."

"That's true," continued Naftali, defensively. "When I say genius, it's just because he succeeded where everyone else had failed. I'm not denying that he was a contemptible man, but he was the first person to master transmutation. When Temistocles continued his quest, 400 years later, it took him a few years of relentless hard work to reach his goal."

"He discovered the missing ingredient in the end?" suggested Oksa. "It was a Goranov, wasn't it?"

"How did you know that?" asked Gus.

"A plant which acts as a catalyst, Gus, remember..."

"Oh yes, of course!"

"You're right, Oksa," nodded Naftali, "it was a Goranov."

"But that's sacrifice!" cried Oksa indignantly. "That's revolting... the poor Goranovs! Did Temistocles kill many?"

"You can be sure of it," confirmed Naftali. "Until he finally mastered the composition of his elixir, called the Werewall, which reduced the body to particles so that it was permeable to solid materials like stone, wood, metal, etc."

"You mean this Werewall allowed people to walk through walls?" asked Oksa, stunned.

"Exactly," replied Naftali, as all his friends exclaimed in amazement.

"A way of walking through walls," murmured Gus. "Can you imagine what an awesome ability that would be?"

"Yes, Gus, it's an incredible gift," agreed Naftali. "But Temistocles didn't stop at that. After his great success in passing through stone walls, windows, sheets of metal and solid rock, he tried to cross Edefia's mantle—which is what he'd wanted all along. But he struck a wall, make no mistake. A wall of light against which his elixir, despite being ultrapowerful, was no more effective than a glass of water. The alchemist was bitterly disappointed at this, and the defeat almost destroyed him. But he hadn't lost all hope, so he made the last-ditch attempt which ended up killing him: entering the Cloak Chamber to discover the solution to his problem. Of course, he didn't know about the Secret-Never-To-Be-Told, but he instinctively knew he might find some interesting clues in there. One night he slipped inside the Glass Column, avoiding the guards by using his Werewall elixir, and entered the legendary Chamber. What did he find? No one knows, because what came out was a horribly deformed, mindless shell of a man: Temistocles was dead. A few months later his only son, who had helped his father in his research in the last years of his life, secretly founded the Secret Society of the Werewalls and the tradition was carried on. In the gloom of an underground passage in Retinburn, the Society brought together some of the leading chemists in Edefia. Dressed in long robes and masked by cowls, which showed only their eyes, these chemists became alchemists to advance their common cause, driven by a fierce desire to pass through the mantle of light. But, Oksa, to answer your question about the phial given to Temistocles, you should be aware that Coxo experimented on himself extensively, which ended up drastically altering his DNA. And if I tell you that he was the father of human shape-shifting, you'll understand more easily why the small phial given by the Diaphan to Temistocles possessed such singular value."

Naftali broke off for a moment and a heavy silence descended over the group.

"That's incredible," spluttered Oksa, always the first to react. "So, if I understand correctly, the Werewalls used the Snufflers' black mucus to walk through walls... but only Temistocles succeeded in shape-shifting, because of Coxo's mucus, is that right?"

"Exactly, Oksa!" replied Naftali, looking stricken by the tense mood his story had created. "Temistocles and his descendants."

"Naftali, some of us have a broad idea of the Werewalls' history," commented Abakum, looking serious. "But I don't think this part of your

477

story can be found in Edefia's archives, or anywhere else for that matter. So, please don't be offended, but how do you know all this?"

"I know there have been many rumours about the Werewalls and your reactions when I uttered that name a while ago confirmed that some of you knew more about them than you wanted to say. But it's true that no one among you can know the details I've just given you, because I got them from my mother, who was a reformed Werewall."

"You mean?…" said Dragomira disbelievingly, not daring to ask the fateful question.

Naftali fixed his green eyes on her and, in a dejected voice, replied:

"Yes, Dragomira. I hate to say it, but my mother was once a Werewall."

Dragomira gave a cry and everyone looked at Naftali with a mixture of amazement and horror. The Swedish giant's face darkened with deep sadness.

"My mother was a chemist," he continued bravely. "One day, she was contacted by the Werewalls and she joined their Secret Society, seduced by the idea of leaving Edefia. She drank the elixir and, in company with the other members, continued the research carried out since Temistocles. But the Master of the Werewalls wanted to produce greater quantities of the elixir in anticipation of what he believed was their imminent success. This unfortunately meant that the Diaphans had to revive their ancestral vice to provide the legendary black mucus. The early part of the twentieth century was a fairly turbulent period: a growing number of Edefians suddenly stopped loving the objects of their affection and the whole nation was concerned. The terrible history of the Diaphan Snufflers had been forgotten a long time ago—remember, it had happened eight centuries before. But everyone was looking for explanations. Increasingly pessimistic theories gradually created an atmosphere of doubt and fear throughout Edefia. Some people thought our world was on the decline, others that it had been cursed by the Ageless Ones. My mother couldn't tolerate the cruelty of the Werewalls and their alliance with the Diaphans. She left the Secret Society under threat of seeing her whole family massacred if she breathed a single word about them. Unfortunately, all this took place after my birth."

"Why unfortunately?" asked Tugdual sharply.

"It's because of the DNA, isn't it?" broke in Oksa.

"Yes, because of the DNA," confirmed Naftali sombrely. "Once the elixir is ingested, it's passed down from generation to generation."

"Wait a minute," said Tugdual, interrupting him. "You're telling us that you're a Werewall?"

Everyone instantly looked dismayed. Abakum shut his eyes, as if wanting to be left alone with his own thoughts, and Dragomira immediately hid her face in her hands.

"The Werewall gene is in my blood," continued Naftali. "And you can imagine how much I regret that."

"So I'm a Werewall too then!" said Tugdual, sitting up straight in his armchair, his eyes shining. "That's brilliant…"

"Yes," admitted Naftali, looking demoralized. "Like the descendants of every member of the Secret Society, we possess the Werewall gene."

"Good Lord!" exclaimed Dragomira. "But don't worry, my friend, none of us can hold you responsible for mistakes made by your forebears. You're first and foremost one of the Runaways, no one can dispute it. You've adequately proved your loyalty over the years."

"Thanks, Dragomira," murmured Naftali, touched by Baba Pollock's words.

"But you were telling us earlier that you had a revelation to make about Orthon-McGraw," she continued apprehensively. "What's his connection with this story?"

"The connection is, Dragomira, that the last Master Werewall was none other than Ocious. So Orthon is a Werewall—and, what's more, he's descended from the founder, Temistocles, the man who invented human shape-shifting."

75

Hearts and Clubs

O KSA AND GUS SLIPPED OUT A LITTLE LATER, LEAVING
the adults to chat in the living room. Their heads were buzzing
with all they'd seen and heard and they couldn't stop talking about the
day's revelations.

"I don't know what's more amazing," said Gus, lying stretched out
on Oksa's bed. "What with Memory-Swipe, Thought-Adder, Pearls of
Longevity, Diaphan Snufflers and Werewalls—we're spoilt for choice!"

Oksa, on the other hand, was performing a few kung-fu moves, pivot-
ing her body and slowly moving her outstretched hands.

"You're not kidding," she murmured, narrowing her eyes.

"May I come in?"

Tugdual had just poked his head around the half-open door and was
watching Oksa with an intrigued expression.

"What are you doing, venerable lil' Gracious?" he asked, smiling.

Her only reply was to throw her leg out abruptly in his direction as
if to kick him in the ribs. Tugdual sidestepped her attack and, to her
surprise, winked at her. He then joined Gus on the bed.

"So what do you reckon about today?" he said. "Mind-blowing or
what?"

Oksa flopped into her big beanbag and looked at the two boys, twisting the bottom of her T-shirt around her index finger. Gus, her lifelong
friend with so many qualities and hang-ups, her faithful companion...

and, beside him, Tugdual, a strange, gloomy and charismatic boy who made her heart leap every time she saw him.

"That's just what we were saying before you showed up," replied Gus in a dull voice, with just an undertone of aggression.

Oksa felt a surge of agitation at Gus's reaction, as if a small acid bomb had exploded inside her and was eating its way through her heart. Tugdual propped himself up on one elbow and gazed at her with his steely blue eyes.

"I was totally blown away by the Lunatrix," he said, without taking his eyes off Oksa. "To think he's always known how to find Edefia! When it comes to discretion, he really takes the biscuit..."

"Your grandfather doesn't do too badly in that respect either," said Gus disdainfully, staring at the ceiling. "Waiting more than fifty years before you talk about your origins is a little more than discretion, isn't it?"

"Well, everyone protects what they have to protect," replied Tugdual enigmatically.

"What are you getting at?" Gus asked immediately, with an edge to his voice.

"Do you think your parents would've told you about their past, if Oksa hadn't borne the Mark?" replied the sombre young man coldly.

"*Ouch! That will have hurt,*" thought Oksa. Although it was hard to defend Gus when he'd definitely been asking for it. What had got into him? He was usually so friendly... Gus, who was still stretched out on the bed, lost no time in replying.

"Anyway, it's no worse than having blood tainted by sacrificed Goranovs and hormones taken from loads of people who've had their lives ruined," he muttered belligerently. "When it comes to family secrets, I think we're just about quits, aren't we?"

"I guess so," sighed Tugdual. "I don't think there's anybody on this planet who can control their origins... what about you, lil' Gracious? What do you think about all this?"

"Me?"

Oksa felt a hot wave of embarrassment flood her whole body, including her cheeks, which turned scarlet. She felt as stupid as she'd done the day she'd chatted to Tugdual in the cemetery. It was so pathetic! She had to get a grip.

"I think the Lunatrix knows much more than he's letting on," she said, sounding confident despite her agitation. "I trust him, though, because I think he'll know better than anybody else when it's the right time to divulge his secrets. And that's borne out by the fact that he won't tell us anything about Edefia's location until we're ready."

"You're not entirely wrong," agreed Tugdual. "But what would happen if he died?"

Oksa couldn't help giving a small nervous laugh.

"You're unreal! Why would you want him to die?"

"I don't want him to die!" retorted Tugdual, sounding amused. "I'm just teasing, that's all."

"Odd sense of humour," grumbled Gus.

"Anyway, the one big advantage of all these revelations is that the Runaways are now taking Orthon-McGraw seriously. I get the impression that everybody had totally underestimated him before."

"I was the worst offender," admitted Oksa. "Do you really think he can shape-shift?" she asked the boys.

"That would be horrendous," was Gus's reaction.

"I agree," declared Tugdual. "He'd have a sizeable advantage over us all. I've just had a chat about it with my grandfather."

"And what's his take on this?" asked Oksa, fiddling nervously with the seam on her beanbag.

"He thinks the shape-shifting process may not work as well as it did in Temistocles's day. But who knows? With Orthon-McGraw, I told you, we must be prepared for anything. Particularly the worst."

"Good of you to put our minds at rest," Gus couldn't help saying.

"Don't mention it," retorted Tugdual with a scathing smile.

The ceasefire between Gus and Tugdual hadn't lasted long. Now they were getting at each other again, Oksa grumbled to herself. Instinctively she decided to create a diversion by bringing her fizzy drink over from her desk. The glass floated across the room, watched inscrutably by Gus. He seemed too annoyed to appreciate the manoeuvre. Tugdual did nothing to lessen the boy's resentment when he lit the small candle on the windowsill—with his fingertips and without moving from the bed. Two sets of eyes stared at the Young Gracious: Tugdual's gaze knowing and mesmerizing, while Gus looked helpless and, more than that, intensely sad.

"So, Tugdual!" she exclaimed to shake off her confusion. "What does it feel like to be a Werewall?"

"I don't know yet!" he admitted. "My grandfather caught me trying to walk through the kitchen wall just before, and I must admit I didn't lose any time making a fool of myself."

"Why?" asked Oksa.

"Because the only thing I managed to do was graze the tip of my nose."

"Then you're not a Werewall!" remarked Gus challengingly.

"Yes, I am," retorted Tugdual. "I just have to practise. Oksa knows that better than I do: having a gift is one thing, but if you don't do any preparation, it's like having the ingredients without the recipe. So I'm going to slog away at it and we'll revisit the subject later."

"I can't wait," said Oksa.

"Nor can I, lil' Gracious, nor can I."

Saying that, he gave a long stretch and stood up to leave.

"I'm off. See you later."

"See you, Tugdual," said Oksa.

Gus maintained a stubborn silence until Tugdual's footsteps disappeared downstairs.

"*Lil' Gracious*," he spluttered, clenching his fists. "I hate it when he says that."

"I really like it," murmured Oksa, gazing into space.

76

AN INVITATION
FRAUGHT WITH DANGER

"WHAT'S GOING ON, LUNATRIXES? YOU'RE A VERY ODD colour."

Oksa had just got in after being escorted home from school by her father, who'd immediately gone out again to the restaurant. Her mother had been dozing in the living room, her wheelchair beside her and a phone within easy reach. Her face had looked drawn and Oksa hadn't had the heart to wake her. She'd tiptoed across the hall and gone upstairs to her gran's apartment. There she'd found the Lunatrixes in a state of violent alarm, their skin totally drained of colour—a sign of intense panic. And what she saw did little to reassure her: not only had the Lunatrixes become almost translucent, but their reddened eyes were spinning like tops in their big eye sockets. The Lunatrixa went to speak but, instead, she tottered, muttering incomprehensible words, and fainted, collapsing heavily on the rug. The Getorix, usually so quick to make fun of everyone, rushed over to help her without saying a word, which was worryingly out of character. Oksa knelt down by the poor Lunatrixa and gently lifted her head onto her lap. Scanning Dragomira's apartment, she noticed that all the creatures had huddled in the corners of the room. As for the Goranov, its foliage was shaking as if blown by a high wind. The ultrasensitive plant battled with its mounting fear for a few seconds, then all its leaves sagged limply, their weight pulling the stem down towards the floor.

"Has something happened? You must tell me!" Oksa told the pale Lunatrix and the Getorix nearby. "First of all, where's Baba?"

"The Old Gracious? Oh, oh, oh," wailed the Lunatrixa, who was barely conscious.

"Has something happened to her? Tell me!" shouted Oksa, her hands on her hips.

With a great deal of groaning and sighing, the Lunatrix finally launched into an explanation:

"Young Gracious, we should keep the secret buried inside our heads and our tongues dumb with loyalty, but seriousness transcends the discretion which is our habituation. Great danger keeps watch on the Old Gracious and she is meeting with it! The strength of the Graciouses is great, but the Felon has cunning. Cunning is an implement of immense danger! The Old Gracious has this knowledge, but we have the terrifying fear of inadequacy, the terrifying fear…"

Oksa frowned:

"You mean Baba is in danger? And what's all this about a Felon?"

"The Felon Orthon-McGraw has given an invitation to the Old Gracious! He made telephonic communication an hour before the arrival of the Young Gracious, and your household staff, we creatures, had our ears pricked up. They received the comprehension of what the Felon said," explained the Lunatrix, frantically twisting his crumpled ears.

"McGraw phoned Baba? Why?" broke in Oksa, perplexed.

"This is the truth! The Felon Orthon-McGraw wants to give the Old Gracious a secret about her brother."

"But what has Leomido got to do with it?"

"The Felon Orthon-McGraw neglected the details… he put the weight on the brother of the Old Gracious and on an event full of critique."

"Full of critique? What does that mean?" asked Oksa, perturbed.

"Critical, not full of critique, you blockhead!" sighed the Getorix in irritation.

"Mockery is filled with uselessness," retorted the vexed Lunatrix, swinging his small angry fist into the Getorix's face, knocking out the little creature, which crumpled to the floor.

"Hey!" intervened Oksa, picking up the stunned Getorix in her arms. "This really isn't the time for fighting. Let me get this straight, Lunatrix: Baba received a phone call from McGraw, who asked her to come and see him because he has something to tell her about Leomido. Is that correct?"

"That is total correctness, Young Gracious," confirmed the little creature. "The Old Gracious has been forgetful that her Lunatrix knows all the Gracious's secrets. If the request had been made, her Lunatrix would have exposed the fraternal secret! But the Old Gracious has been preferring to hear it in the mouth of the Felon... our anxiety is voluminous, you have our assurance. We have the knowledge of Orthon when he was on the Inside and the very bad memory."

"I understand... but we have to do something. You stay here and look after each other and there will be no fighting!" ordered Oksa, looking at her watch. "And above all—this is very important—if Baba and I aren't back before 8 p.m., you will go and alert my mother, Lunatrix, and you'll tell her everything you've just told me. Do you understand?"

The Lunatrix nodded frantically and took a small, tightly folded piece of paper from the pocket of his dungarees, which he then held out to Oksa.

"What's this?"

"The localization of the Felon Orthon, my Young Gracious. He gave the positioning of his dwelling when he had the telephonic communication. Our Old Gracious is there!"

"Thanks, Lunatrix."

Oksa patted him briefly on the head, turned on her heels and raced downstairs at top speed, mobile in hand.

"Gus! Get over here now. We've got a big problem."

"If our parents discover that we sneaked out, they'll be furious," murmured Gus tensely. "We're going to get it in the neck."

"Tough!" said Oksa. "We don't have a choice, anyway. We can't leave Baba alone with McGraw."

"Your gran's insane going to his house without telling anyone, what was she thinking?"

"C'mon, let's go! We're wasting time."

"What are we going to tell your mother?" asked Gus.

Oksa's only reply was to drag her friend towards the living room, where Marie was now awake.

"Mum! Gus and I have an essay to write, and it'll take us quite a while."

"Okay, darling. I won't disturb you, I understand."

Then, instead of going up to her room, she grabbed Gus's arm and opened the front door, screwing up her eyes and holding her breath. The two friends made their escape, heading for the nearest Tube station at a run.

"I hate this," muttered Gus, shooting a disapproving look at Oksa. "It's rotten having to lie like that to your mum…"

"It's for a good cause, Gus," replied the girl. "Don't forget that Baba is in danger."

※

Twenty minutes later, the two schoolmates, breathless and bathed in sweat, were hiding behind a car on the other side of the street and watching one of the posh houses in this peaceful neighbourhood a few miles from the city centre.

"You're sure this is it?"

"Yes, look, number 12!"

The house opposite them was an old, three-storey building, identical in style to the others on the terraced street. A strip of sandstone rose from the ground to the windows of the raised ground floor, which were adorned with heavy purple curtains. A wrought-iron gate opened onto a narrow lawn with a thick bush planted in the centre. Near it was the front door, sheltered by a small colonnaded porch.

"Have you got a plan?" whispered Gus to Oksa.

"Yes—we'll start with this," she replied, plunging her hand in her shoulder bag.

"Young Mistress," said the Tumble-Bawler, nodding gently on the palm of Oksa's hand. "A request? A mission? I'm at your service!"

"Listen to me, Tumble-Bawler, go over to the front door of the house opposite and see if it's locked. Then come back to tell us, okay?"

"Okay, message received."

And, like a large bumblebee, the Tumble-Bawler flew off. A few seconds later, he landed back on Oksa's palm.

"The Tumble-Bawler of the Young Gracious reporting," he exclaimed, swaying from right to left. "The door of that house is double-locked from the inside, Yale lock, tempered-steel bolt and security latch."

Gus whistled softly, impressed by these technical details.

"You say it's locked from the inside? How do you know?" asked Oksa.

"The key is in the lock, Young Mistress. Do you have another mission for me?"

"No, thank you, Tumble-Bawler."

"So someone's in the house. But that doesn't tell us if we're in the right place," remarked Gus, uneasily.

"Wait a second!" retorted Oksa, showing him her Granok-Shooter. She blew into the small tube and a Reticulata immediately emerged.

"Look!" said Oksa, pointing the jellyfish-magnifying glass at the letterbox, dashing Gus's last hope. "You can make out the name *McGraw*… let's have a look to see where we can get in."

After examining the façade of the house through the jellyfish-magnifying glass, the two friends came to the dangerous conclusion that Oksa had to go in through the first-floor window, which didn't look properly closed, come downstairs and unlock the front door from the inside to let Gus in. The boy was clearly as keen to enter McGraw's house as he'd been to enter the school crypt...

"Don't look at me like that! We don't have any choice—don't be afraid, my Granok-Shooter is full to bursting," said Oksa, winking at him. "And you've forgotten about this."

Without taking her eyes off him, she rose about four inches above the ground.

"Vertiflying in the middle of the street? You don't do things by halves, do you?"

"Hey, desperate times demand desperate measures. Or perhaps I should say desperate McGraws demand desperate means," she added, with a nervous snort of laughter.

"Be careful all the same... I'll keep watch while you get up there."

It was now dusk and Oksa, making the most of the fading light, resolutely crossed the street. The wrought-iron gate gave a soft squeal as she pushed it open, which slightly dented her resolve, but she bravely kept going, even if she felt nowhere near as confident as she looked. "*Go on, Oksa, don't stop now. You're a ninja, don't forget!*" she thought to motivate herself.

Something her father often said during their karate sessions popped into her head: "If you think you can do it, Oksa-san, then you can do it. Otherwise, forget it." So before rising the height of the stone façade, she looked at the wall opposite her and allowed herself to assume a kung-fu pose, hands pressed together in front and her left leg stretched out behind. "*She is incorrigible... Absolutely incorrigible,*" thought Gus, raising his eyes to the sky with an expression that was as much amused as it was despairing. Two seconds later, Oksa was kneeling on the first-floor windowsill. She pushed on the frame and the window, which they'd thought wasn't properly shut, swung open easily. She dived inside the house, as though swallowed up by the darkness.

"What on earth is she doing? Has she fallen asleep in McGraw's bedroom or what?"

Gus was hopping up and down with impatience and anxiety. Once Oksa had vanished through the window, he'd quickly crossed the street and had knelt down on the pavement by the low wall. His attention riveted on the front door, he felt as if he'd been waiting for ages when his friend, eyes sparkling, finally opened the door from the inside.

"You took your time," he muttered, hurrying inside.

"I took the opportunity to look over the house!" replied Oksa impishly. "C'mon, let's go."

"It feels strange to be here."

"You're telling me," murmured Oksa. "I didn't think it would look like this."

"You thought there'd be coffins for beds, did you? Black candles dripping in candelabras and vases shaped like skulls, stuff like that?" whispered Gus, nudging his friend.

If that had been what Oksa expected, she would have been disappointed, because the hall and what could be glimpsed of the living room were decorated in predominantly light shades. The white-painted furniture and walls created an understated, but not austere, effect. Oksa and Gus walked into the living room: two thinly striped beige sofas flanked a round table covered with a spotless tablecloth. Console tables of pale wood lining the walls held lamps with crystal drops or plaster busts. A frame hanging on the wall caught Gus's attention:

"Oksa!" he called in a low voice. "Look, do you think that's the island Mortimer kept going on about?"

Oksa went over and they both gazed at the framed photo, which looked as though it could be of an island. A jagged shoreline with numerous coves was lashed by angry, foam-capped waves. In the distance, a red and yellow lighthouse and a grey stone building could be glimpsed behind treeless hills. But their inspection of the room was suddenly interrupted by the sound of muffled voices, which seemed to be coming from the cellar. Oksa seized her Granok-Shooter in one hand and spontaneously put her other on Gus's forearm. They headed over to the small door under the stairs.

"Are you sure it's coming from there?" whispered Gus, his heart pounding and his face pale—the thought of going down to the basement didn't fill him with any great enthusiasm.

"I looked everywhere, the house is empty, Gus. There's only the cellar left. And the doors leading to cellars are usually found under the stairs," replied Oksa, her tone making it clear she thought she was stating the obvious.

She was right again. As soon as they opened the door, they could hear the voices much more clearly. Voices they knew well: those of McGraw and Dragomira.

77

THE HIDDEN SIDE
OF DRAGOMIRA

O KSA AND GUS WENT DOWN THE FIRST FEW STEPS AS
carefully and quietly as possible, holding their breath and keeping
their backs pressed against the wall. A feeble light was coming from the
back of the cellar but, despite obstructing their view, the staircase was
dark enough to afford them a certain amount of cover. Suddenly there
was a terrible commotion, immediately followed by a stifled scream.
Oksa increased her pressure on Gus's arm, which she was still holding,
and looked at him anxiously. They waited—for what seemed like an
eternity—until they heard a voice.

"So what do you say to that? Don't you think my style has improved
after all these years?"

Oh no! That was McGraw's voice. Oksa inched down a step, then
another, her breathing shallow and her heart thumping against her
ribs. Behind her, Gus was quaking at the knees and he felt his courage
desert him. Their gradual descent into McGraw's cellar was turning into
a descent into hell.

"This whole business has made you into a monster!" retorted
Dragomira. "What a pity—I was so fond of the man you were on the
Inside. You could have been a good person, but you've turned out just
like your father."

"Don't bring my father into this!" grated McGraw in reply. "Our *virtuous* Malorane was no better than him. Anyway, look, I've got something for you, dear little Dragomira. A surprise to celebrate our reunion. I'd despaired of ever being able to use it, but you've provided me with an excellent opportunity."

A loud crash shook the walls and everything began shaking as if there was an earthquake. The whole house seemed to rumble from floor to ceiling. There was a dreadful scream—a scream of sheer terror followed by the worrying din of breaking objects. Oksa shot Gus a panicked look. What if Dragomira was injured? Or worse? Gus pulled on his friend's arm in the hope that he might be able to lead her back upstairs—what was going on down there didn't seem to be a friendly encounter! He was very fond of Dragomira, but it didn't seem very sensible to stay on that staircase. And even less sensible to get involved. It would be far better to leave this nightmarish house and raise the alarm. Oksa didn't seem to share his opinion though. Her Granok-Shooter at the ready, she dragged her friend down the rest of the stairs towards the cellar, where a terrible fate probably awaited them. Once again, his heart beating fit to burst, Gus gave in and let himself be led.

※

They had only gone down a few more steps when the two friends heard the sound of footsteps coming closer to the stairwell. An angry growl immediately told them that the game was up. They froze, unable to go downstairs or run away. A shadow appeared on the floor and came closer until it loomed over the bottom steps. Suddenly the shadow became a person of flesh and blood. Oksa gave a shrill scream of terror and Gus's head swam as the horrible feeling he was about to die washed over him. There was a fifty-fifty chance of it being Dragomira at the foot of the stairs.

"WHAT ARE YOU DOING HERE?"

Luck was on their side. It was Baba Pollock standing there in front of them with a frown on her face and her hands on her hips. Gus preferred not to think what would have happened if it had been McGraw.

"Baba! I nearly fired a Granok at you! I think we've just had the fright of our lives," exclaimed Oksa, throwing her arms around her gran's neck.

"What are you doing here?" repeated Dragomira irritably, disentangling herself from Oksa's embrace.

"I hope you won't be angry with him... your Lunatrix told me that McGraw had called you and that you'd gone to his house. You should have seen him, he was in a right state! So was I. Then Gus and I decided to come and help you, but it looks like we got here too late. You don't need anyone, you're too strong, Baba!"

"Who knows you're here?"

"Er... no one," muttered Oksa, looking at her feet.

"No one?" said Dragomira in amazement.

She paused for a second then continued, gazing sternly at the two friends:

"What you did was very reckless. You could have been injured! Ah well, this is all very unexpected, but I have to admit it couldn't be better."

With this, the old lady's expression changed completely and an unexpected look of satisfaction came over her face. She went up to Oksa and rested an authoritative hand on her shoulder. Then, turning to Gus:

"Thanks for coming with my granddaughter," she said curtly, in a voice that didn't sound like her at all. "You can go home now, your parents will be worried. I've got some things to sort out with Oksa."

Dragomira pushed Gus with the flat of her hand, firmly motioning him to leave the cellar and the house. With growing astonishment, Gus's eyes briefly met Oksa's. Dragomira had never sent him packing like this! She must be feeling a little out of sorts after what must have been a rather violent encounter, if the state of the cellar was anything to go by. She again insisted on Gus leaving the house and the boy didn't have any choice. He climbed the stairs backwards, his eyes fixed on Oksa and a strange leaden feeling in his heart.

"Fine… See you later, Oksa! I'll call you."

But when he reached the hall, he headed towards the front door, opened it and slammed it shut immediately from the inside as loudly as possible. Then, quiet as a mouse, he retraced his steps to the cellar door, which was still wide open, and crept back down the staircase.

"Where's McGraw, Baba?" asked Oksa, once she'd heard the front door slam. "I hope you smashed his face in!"

"You'd like that, wouldn't you?" replied Dragomira, sniggering. "Look! He's over there, cowering on the ground *like a dog*!"

She pointed at a small, very dark room adjoining the main cellar. At the very back of this cluttered storeroom, in almost complete darkness, Oksa could make out a figure lying on the floor, writhing with pain. A guttural groan reached her ears, making her shiver.

"I haven't yet got around to smashing his face in, as you put it," explained Dragomira. "But since you seem to want me to, my dear Oksa, I'll be happy to grant your wish."

"It was just a figure of speech…" remarked Oksa, aghast at being taken at her word and terrified by the thought of watching something like that done, even to vile McGraw.

"Afterwards, since you've come to me," continued Dragomira, ignoring Oksa's remark, "we can finally get out of here. Everything will be much simpler now."

Oksa stared at Dragomira in astonishment. Her gran must have been hit by a Muddler Granok because she seemed to have lost the plot. It was certainly time they got out of here so Dragomira could take one of those excellent tisanes which only she knew the secret of making, and which would unscramble her brain cells. Oksa screwed up her eyes and tried to peer through the darkness, drawn by the sound of McGraw's groans. She was fascinated and troubled by the violent contortions of her sworn enemy's body. The deathly silence was broken by strange, incomprehensible sounds, which seemed to seethe with fury. Dragomira came over and pushed her back towards the stairs.

"Wait for me there! I won't be long."

The old lady stood in the doorway of the small room and said contemptuously to McGraw:

"Look! As you can see, Oksa's here with me. That's fate for you, we've come full circle, haven't we? She'll be able to take me back to Edefia and no one can put a spanner in the works for me now. I've waited for this moment for more than fifty years... What? What did you say? You too? That's as may be, but your plans are nowhere near as big as mine. But before I leave here for good with my granddaughter, I'm going to give you a small sample of hell!"

Dragomira held out her arms and opened her hand, spreading out her fingers. From where she was standing, Oksa saw thin strands of light sizzle from her fingertips and fleetingly made out McGraw's body, which was then hurled against the ceiling. She grimaced at the terrible thud made by the body as it crashed back down onto the ground, followed immediately by a hoarse moan. With a fixed smile on her lips, Dragomira turned round to look at her, and then renewed her vicious attack. The scream McGraw gave was even more agonizing than the last. Icy sweat trickled down Oksa's spine, and she thought she heard a weak murmur, a barely audible voice breathing "Dushka". As if things weren't complicated enough, now her mind was playing tricks! She shook her head and backed away towards the staircase, as Dragomira triumphantly exclaimed to McGraw:

"Ha! Not so proud now, are you?"

Oksa looked at her in complete astonishment: how could her gran, who wouldn't hurt a fly and who advocated respect for all forms of life, take such pleasure in hurting someone? This was a side of her she didn't know—and didn't particularly like. This unpleasant feeling was soon heightened by the Curbita-Flatulo writhing frantically on her wrist, which didn't help matters at all. A wave of panic washed over the girl, as if the process had been reversed: the Curbita-Flatulo was doing its utmost to unnerve her completely! And there hadn't been any cause for concern yet... naturally, she hadn't forgotten she was inside McGraw's house. But Dragomira had the upper hand. And convincingly at that. So long as she was with her, she was in no danger, even if this was a side of Baba Pollock she had never seen. So why was the Curbita-Flatulo so agitated? And now the Tumble-Bawler was getting in on the act too! Emerging from Oksa's small bag, it fluttered up to its young mistress's ear and whispered a few words.

"What did you say?" she murmured, looking at it incredulously. "I don't understand."

"The grandmothers aren't all they seem to be," repeated the little creature.

"This is no time to be making psychological observations, Tumble," retorted Oksa in a low voice. "Things are already complicated enough as it is."

"Oksa! Pssst... Oksa..."

Oksa whirled round: Gus was here! He was standing at the bottom of the staircase, gazing at her. He was pale and breathless and he looked terrified, although determined to stay near his friend.

"Gus! Am I happy to see you!" said Oksa, glancing anxiously towards her gran, who was still busy in the doorway of the other room.

"Something doesn't feel right about this," whispered Gus.

"You're not kidding! We have to look into this," said Oksa, facing dangerous facts. "We don't have a choice. Is that okay?" she added, her eyes searching Gus's terrified gaze.

"I'm scared to death, if you must know," replied Gus. "But you're right. We have to go and see who's in that room. Let's get a move on!"

With Gus a few steps behind her, Oksa stealthily walked over to Dragomira. When they were right by the doorway of the dark room, she took hold of her Granok-Shooter and said to herself:

By the power of the Granoks
Think outside the box
Polypharus, hear what I say
And may your tentacles light my way.

A tiny orangey octopus immediately shot out of the Granok-Shooter and rose into the air, filling the cellar with such a bright light that it blinded Dragomira and Gus, who were taken by surprise. Oksa, her hand shading her eyes, stepped forward and glanced quickly into the room, confirming her awful forebodings.

"BABA!" she exclaimed, panic-stricken.

Oksa had every reason to panic. There, at the back of the room, slumped in a corner, was Dragomira—another Dragomira—her body contorted and her face covered in blood.

78

CELLAR RESCUE

THE DRAGOMIRA AT THE BACK OF THE SMALL ROOM WAS in a dreadful state. Seeing Oksa, she slumped even lower against the wall and tears ran down her cheeks, leaving tracks through the caked dust and blood flowing from her head. She looked up at Oksa and gazed into her eyes. Oksa shuddered, shocked at the pain and sadness she read in that beseeching look.

"Well, well, dear Orthon is resorting to trickery! Very clever, Orthon! My congratulations!"

Oksa stiffened with fright: the first Dragomira had just put her arm firmly around her shoulders and pulled her close. Helplessly, the girl looked up at the old lady who was hugging her imperiously against her—perhaps to protect her?—and then at the second old lady, who seemed to be struggling not to pass out.

"What does this mean?" muttered Oksa.

"My dear girl," replied the first Dragomira, "Orthon has simply used his shape-shifting skills to try and pass himself off as *me*!"

"Shape-shifting? So it works then!" exclaimed Oksa.

"Of course it works. It's incredible, isn't it? Although dear Orthon hasn't been able to resist adding a few melodramatic touches of his own to make you feel sorry for him... Honestly, Orthon, is all that blood really necessary?" she added, looking at the second Dragomira in disgust.

Then, meeting Oksa's eyes, she said fiercely:

"Don't upset yourself, my dear. Shape-shifting is designed to fool the entire world. Don't let yourself be taken in by those tearful eyes. That man has got no more than he deserved. Edefia is ours and ours alone… I won't let anyone stand in my way! Just tell yourself that it was him or me. He wouldn't hesitate to finish me off if I were in his shoes. Isn't that right, Orthon?"

"Oksa, Dushka, for pity's sake, don't listen to him," begged the second Dragomira weakly. "Look at me and you'll know it's me!"

"Shut up!" shouted the first Dragomira. "You can't fool us. I'm the one and only Dragomira Pollock, the real Dragomira."

"What proof do you have that you're telling the truth?" came a shaky voice behind her.

The first Dragomira whirled round, dragging Oksa with her. She peered into the shadows until her eyes had located the person who'd just spoken, standing stiff as a poker in the opposite corner, but trembling with fear.

"Oh, Gus!" she said in irritation, going over to the boy. "Not only have you disobeyed me, but what's more you've picked the wrong side—two mistakes that can still be rectified by joining us while there's still time. Come over here with your friend."

"Oksa! WATCH OUT!" yelled Gus, diving under a worm-eaten workbench.

The second Dragomira had just staggered to the doorway of the small room, blood trickling from the wound in her head. This was a problem, a big problem. Dragging Oksa with her, the first old lady advanced further into the cellar firing bolts of electricity which knocked over everything that stood between her and the second Dragomira. The wooden wine racks laden with bottles leapt into the air, spraying wine over the walls and broken glass over the floor. The light bulb hanging on a flex from the ceiling began swinging frantically, casting agitated shadows. Feeling terrified, Oksa tried to free herself from the "real" Dragomira's grip, but the old lady held her even more tightly. She had to find a way of discovering the truth. She had two Dragomiras in front of her and she knew rationally, and from her own experience, that there was only one Dragomira. But which of them was the right one? Her mind was racing, and her confused thoughts were making it impossible to think straight. She desperately needed to a clear mind at the moment. Since she couldn't rely on logic, she felt instinctively that she needed to act. In a fraction of a second, she executed one of her favourite manoeuvres: a fast vertical take-off. Wrenching herself free, she shot towards the ceiling and performed a backflip to land on a table at the back of the cellar.

"Baba! Show yourself, please! Help me!" she shouted imploringly.

"Oksa, it's me, I'm your gran Dragomira! Trust me," said the first Dragomira, walking slowly towards her with a beseeching look.

"Don't believe that imposter, Dushka, I'm your Baba, your Baba who loves you and who'll always love you," retorted the second trembling Dragomira, her back bowed.

The two Dragomiras aimed their Granok-Shooters at each other and Gus was making signs at her that she couldn't understand. What a nightmare… Oksa rummaged in her bag, without taking her eyes off the two women. They were totally identical from head to toe. This shape-shifting thing was unbelievable! Same face, same hair plaited in a crown, same clothes—it was impossible to tell them apart. Except that one was much more badly beaten and bloody than the other. And that was hardly surprising given the number of violent spells which had been used on her. In fact, it was a miracle she was still standing. Oksa opened her Caskinette and grabbed an Excelsior, which she swallowed immediately in the hope it might help her mind get a better grasp on things. Instinct alone would never be enough to tell the truth from the lies. Her heart told her to believe the second Dragomira, but that was more through a process of deduction than because she had irrefutable proof. Since she'd arrived in the cellar, the first Dragomira had seemed odd to her. What she said and did were in stark contrast to what she knew of her beloved gran. But this was no ordinary situation and it could have had an effect on the soundest of natures. The second Dragomira's pitiful appearance, her ravaged face and body spasming with pain, also influenced the way she felt: she might be a fan of kung fu, but she was still a soft-hearted girl. If the first Dragomira was the real one, Oksa abhorred her gran's vicious attack on a man lying on the ground, wracked with pain. Even if McGraw was the sworn enemy of her family, the Runaways and Edefia, there had to be another way of neutralizing him. The fight had been unfair. And unequal! She would never again view her Baba in the same way… but now was certainly not the time to be thinking like this. Her priority was to find out which of the two women was her gran and to get out of this mess. Alive, if possible.

"What's your husband's name, Baba?" said Oksa curtly to the second Dragomira, who was leaning against a pillar.

"Vladimir Pollock, Dushka, but I think Orthon knows that. Don't rely on my answer…"

"Fine, then, you!" continued Oksa, pointing at the first Dragomira. "Where did Jeanne Bellanger's parents die?"

"In Czechoslovakia, Dushka, during the events of August 1968 in Prague. They were killed by Soviet soldiers. And I don't think Orthon knows that."

"Don't listen to him, Oksa," cried the second Dragomira in a rasping voice. "Orthon could easily know that. He's kept watch on us for years—remember the list!"

"Shut up!" retorted the first Dragomira, brandishing her Granok-Shooter. "All your family has ever done is bring chaos and separate me from my parents. But, today, you will pay for everything your family has done."

"STOP IT!" yelled Oksa, her heart filled with doubt.

She shot a tearful look at Gus, who'd been trying to get her to understand something for quite a while. He was showing her the middle finger of his right hand and discreetly, but eloquently, clasping it with his left hand… and suddenly Oksa realized. The ring! Her eyes flitted from one hand to the other: the ring she'd noticed McGraw wearing on the first day of school, the magnificent twisted silver ring with its shimmering slate-grey stone, was on the first Dragomira's finger. Her head swam with panic. How could she know for sure? How could she be certain that McGraw hadn't done a swap and put his ring on the real Dragomira's finger to plant a seed of doubt? The two women were still standing face to face, their eyes riveted on each other. Tense with agitation, Oksa looked at Gus helplessly. The boy was now blowing into his hand, his fingers curled into a tube. What on earth did that mean? Oksa looked more closely and realized: the Granok-Shooter! What had Abakum said about Granok-Shooters? She had to remember… they were all personal and different, no one could use a Granok-Shooter which didn't belong to them, because they only recognized their owner. Different! Yes! That was the solution. Oksa looked at the precious tubes held by the two Dragomiras. The first had a Granok-Shooter made of dark horn striped with fine silvery lines. The one held by the second Dragomira was a lighter, pinkish white colour, inlaid with tiny gold fragments and precious stones. Oksa concentrated with all her might. *"Ninja-Oksa, try to remember Baba's Granok-Shooter… it's not that complicated!"* Had she ever seen Dragomira's Granok-Shooter before? Aargghh. Oksa searched angrily through a jumble of memories. Suddenly one image stood out among the many rattling around in her head and she was back in Leomido's kitchen a few months ago. Dragomira had taken out her Granok-Shooter to demonstrate the Reticulata. An almost white Granok-Shooter, which sparkled with a thousand tiny little flashes! Yes, but she had the same problem as she'd had with the identity ring: maybe McGraw had been so attentive to detail that he'd switched their Granok-Shooters? There was no end to this question. And no answer. Before Oksa could wonder about it any more, a stooped, emaciated creature surged from the depths of the cellar and leapt on the second Dragomira's back.

"Decaying old hag! I'm going to slit your throat like the sow you are!"

503

Recognizing the Abominari, Oksa quickly held her hand out in front of her and hurled it to the other side of the cellar with a powerful Knock-Bong. But the terrible monster's resistance—and motivation—were equal to anything. It got to its feet immediately and rushed at the second Dragomira.

"Vermin! You're going to die in this cellar and rot here for all eternity!"

Oksa had no time to react before the Abominari violently scratched the old lady's chest with its foul claws, then made its escape up the staircase into the house. Its unfortunate victim gave a cry of pain and her torn dress revealed a Medallion which gleamed brightly. Malorane's Medallion! Without a second's hesitation, Oksa lifted her Granok-Shooter to her lips and blew into it, after saying the accompanying words in her head. The first Dragomira was immediately held tight by a viscous creeper.

"What are you doing, you little fool! Have you lost your head?"

Grimacing from the pain of her wounds, the second Dragomira went over to Oksa and hugged her tenderly, murmuring:

"Dushka…"

"Baba," replied Oksa, in huge relief. "You're really badly injured. We must get out of here so we can get you some help."

Gus also came over.

"Thank you, Gus. You were amazing!" exclaimed Oksa.

"It was nothing. But you're right, we have to get out of here, Dragomira's in a terrible state."

Baba Pollock, leaning heavily on the two friends, seemed to be on the verge of collapse. Opposite them, the first Dragomira was reverting to her original appearance, that of the Felon Orthon-McGraw. The shape he'd assumed was gradually vanishing. The hard, cruel face which Gus and Oksa knew so well had virtually returned. The shape-shifting process was over and they were chilled by the rage burning in McGraw's eyes and radiating from his tense features.

"You really are a monster!" said Oksa, regretting that she'd felt sorry for the man a few minutes earlier—someone as despicable as he didn't deserve her pity. In recent months, the Runaways had seen the great principles of life come under repeated attack.

"You wanted to kill my gran! And you made my mother sick! I hate you. I REALLY HATE YOU!" she yelled, every ounce of compassion deserting her.

Dragomira shut her eyes and, leaning on her granddaughter and Gus, raised her Granok-Shooter to her lips. She was about to blow into it when she met McGraw's eyes. Weakened by pangs of conscience, she lowered her arm.

"I can't," she murmured, slumping against the wall. "I can't kill him…"

"Baba!" cried Oksa, kneeling by her exhausted gran. "Gus! What are we going to do?"

"I don't know, Oksa," replied Gus in a broken voice. "But we're going to have to find… QUICK—" he added, his attention drawn to the staircase.

Oksa followed his eyes and saw a surprisingly dense shadow moving down the stairs.

"What is that thing?" yelled Gus, terrified.

"Abakum… dear Abakum, you're here…" said Dragomira weakly.

"And now your gran's delirious!" said Gus in a panic. "We're finished."

The shadow glided downstairs and reached them in no time. With his hand over his mouth, Gus felt every drop of blood draining from his body as he faced the facts: the shadow didn't belong to a body, or an object, or a creature—it wasn't attached to anything.

"Oh hell!" he muttered. "I think Death is coming for us!"

McGraw, immobilized by Oksa's Arborescens Granok, stared at this strange phenomenon. The shadow came to a halt and, with a silky rustle, materialized. McGraw struggled violently against his fetters, recognizing the man who'd just appeared.

"Abakum! Abakum, is that really you?" exclaimed Oksa, open-mouthed in astonishment. "I knew it!"

"Yes, it's me, dear girl," confirmed Dragomira's Watcher.

"But that shadow—" muttered Gus.

"Fairyman, Shadowman, I keep watch over you," came his simple reply. "Your Lunatrix told me everything," he added, looking sadly at Dragomira. "I shall do what you can't."

He went over and squeezed her shoulder with infinite kindness. His eyes filled with tears and pain as he glanced at her one last time. Then he took out his Granok-Shooter and, without saying a word, blew in McGraw's direction. The Felon widened his eyes as the Granok hit him head-on. Above his head, a dark spiral formed and began whirling unbelievably fast. McGraw craned his neck to try and see what Oksa and Gus were gazing at so intently. And when he managed to catch a glimpse of what was happening a couple of inches above his head, he blanched, groaned and struggled even harder to escape the creeper which was holding him captive. It was a waste of time and effort. The spiral stopped rotating and steadied, becoming a kind of black hole which moved slowly but inexorably closer to McGraw's head. The minute it touched the first of his hairs, the Felon *exploded*. Billions of dark particles flew through the Arborescens and were immediately drawn up into the black hole. A few seconds later there was nothing left of McGraw—only a few fragments of yellow creeper lying on the floor and a strangely shimmering black cloud floating just below the ceiling.

"What was that?" whispered Oksa in horror.

"A Crucimaphila, Oksa," murmured Dragomira brokenly. "The ultimate Black Globus."

An icy shiver ran down Oksa's spine. So that's what the terrible Crucimaphila was! Gus, as overawed as Oksa, staggered, but didn't lose his footing. Abakum carefully put away his Granok-Shooter and lifted Dragomira into his arms. Impatient to leave this nightmarish house at last, the four of them turned, went upstairs and regained the peace and quiet of the street.

"Let's go home, kids."

And as the Fairyman was driving them through the icy rain to the city centre, they had no idea that Mortimer McGraw had entered the cellar a short time after they'd left. At the same time as they arrived in Bigtoe Square, the boy, in tears, his heart filled with rage and insane hope, was clutching a phial filled with the particles of the black hole which was now his father, the Felon Orthon-McGraw.

1

An Unexpected
Connection

Zoe frantically rushed around the McGraws' house, looking in every room. Orthon had disappeared and there was no sign of his wife Barbara or his son Mortimer. She was alone.

"Go to your room, Zoe, don't worry," Mortimer had told her, two weeks ago. "I'll pop up and see you in a bit."

That was the last time she'd spoken to him. She'd waited all evening, then she'd fallen asleep, worn out with worry. The house was empty when she'd woken up. Horribly empty. Again Zoe had waited for hours for Orthon or Mortimer to come back, wandering from room to room and leaving worried messages on their mobiles, which had rung unanswered. Hours had turned into days. The cupboards and fridge gradually emptied, dust settled on the furniture, growing thicker by the day, and spiders' webs formed high up on the walls. With all hope gone, she'd finally had to face hard facts: she'd been abandoned. She was all alone in the world with nowhere to go and no one cared if she lived or died. The house felt as if it were closing in on her like a tomb.

This unpleasant sensation shocked her into action. She packed a small bag with her most valuable possessions: the photo album documenting key events in her short life, a few birthday cards, a pendant in the shape of a clover leaf and her gran's strange-looking flute. Then, with her bag slung over her shoulder, she walked to the Pollocks' house without looking back, her heart in pieces.

✳

When Dragomira opened the door she was astounded to recognize a thin, grubby Zoe gazing at her with desperate, tear-filled eyes ringed with dark circles.

"Mrs Pollock, I'm so sorry for coming here—I didn't know where else to go…"

Then, overcome with emotion, she sank down onto the top step in front of the house. Dragomira, still bruised and battered from the blows she'd received during her encounter with Orthon, summoned the Lunatrixes to help. Zoe didn't resist, too exhausted to show any fear of the remarkable creatures. They carried her up to their mistress's apartment and laid her on a sofa, where she immediately fell asleep, wrung out by sadness.

"Misunderstanding is about to experience mending!" exclaimed the Lunatrix, sounding even more enigmatic than ever.

"Oh, please, my Lunatrix," said Dragomira, rebuking the small creature. "This is no time to speak in riddles!"

"Beware of judgement overflowing with errors and grudges, Old Gracious," continued the small creature nonetheless. "Vast importance must be attributed to this girl because she contains Gracious blood…"

The Old Gracious frowned and slumped down onto the sofa opposite the one where the Lunatrixes had deposited Zoe. Despite her weakened condition and the scolding she'd just given her Lunatrix, she knew in her heart of hearts that this pitiable-looking girl was going to turn their lives upside down.

✳

512

Dragomira was watching Zoe when she woke up, which made the girl feel rather awkward, even though she could see no hostility in Baba Pollock's eyes.

"Hello, Zoe," Dragomira said softly. "Are you feeling better?"

When Zoe replied "no" in an almost inaudible whisper, Dragomira leant towards her and, gently taking her hand, murmured kindly:

"I know you're scared. I would be too if I were in your shoes. I just want to say that I don't mean you any harm—quite the opposite, in fact. You can trust me."

Feeling somewhat reassured and, above all, hopeful, Zoe glanced shyly at Dragomira.

"Why don't you tell me everything from the beginning?" suggested the old lady.

After a brief hesitation, Zoe made up her mind. The words poured from her in their hundreds, tumbling over each other to get out. Her battered heart ached and she was racked by sobs as the painful memories tore her apart. But once she'd started, Zoe couldn't stop. She kept talking through her tears while Dragomira stroked her hand, realizing the magnitude of the mistake mentioned by the Lunatrix.

"So your father isn't Orthon McGraw then!" gasped Baba Pollock in amazement.

"No. He's my great-uncle, my gran was his twin sister. He took me in when she died."

She was now speaking in a tiny voice. Startled, Dragomira looked at her with even greater intensity and murmured:

"Reminiscens… Reminiscens was there, close by, and we didn't realize."

"She told me you'd known each other when you were young and that you alone could help me if I was ever in trouble. She really admired you, you know. I've got some photos of her, if you'd like to see them…"

"I'd love to," whispered Dragomira.

Zoe took the photo album from her bag and handed it to Dragomira, who carefully opened it. The old lady turned the pages, her mind reeling.

She kept looking from Zoe to the pictures and back again, her amazement increasing with every page.

"My gran knew a great deal about all kinds of things, particularly rocks and precious stones," continued Zoe. "She was a diamond cutter. She'd always lived with me and my parents because she adored my dad. He was her only son. When he died, she focused all her energy and love on me. We'd both often hold back our tears to avoid upsetting the other. We had to be strong for each other and that was really hard. I'd lost my parents but she'd lost her son."

"That's awful… Is that your dad in these photos?" asked the old lady pointing to a page of the open album.

"Yes."

"He was very handsome."

Dragomira stared at the photos for a long while, her brow furrowed. Suddenly she was struck by an incredible thought and the blood drained from her face.

"I'd like to ask you something, Zoe," she said, trembling. "What was your father's name? And do you know his date of birth?"

"My dad was born on 29 March 1953 and his name was Jan Evanvleck."

Dragomira sank back on the sofa. All these pieces of information came together in her mind, making her head spin and sucking her into a vortex created by over fifty years of repressed grief and untold secrets. The truth erupted like molten lava from a volcano.

"Leomido…" murmured Dragomira.

She looked at Zoe, her eyes full of tears.

"You haven't lost everything, my child. When you knocked on my door, you found a family. Your own family."

"I… I don't understand!" stammered Zoe.

"My dear brother, Leomido, is your grandfather."

2

A Brief Respite

IT WAS THE END OF TERM AT LAST AND THE STUDENTS OF St Proximus were letting off steam, racing around the courtyard shouting and laughing, their uniforms in disarray and their ties unknotted. Oksa Pollock and Gus Bellanger were more than ready for the holidays—they'd begun to think the school year would never end. So much had happened... What with the revelation of Oksa's mysterious origins and the vaporization of Orthon McGraw, the Runaways' sworn enemy, the last few months had held more than their fair share of exciting discoveries and terrifying ordeals. Determined not to let these thoughts dampen her high spirits, Oksa shook her head and began dragging Gus towards the fountain in the middle of the paved courtyard. Her friend struggled to free himself, laughing.

"It doesn't take a genius to guess what you're up to!"

"How could you say no to a refreshing dip in honour of this red-letter day!" exclaimed Oksa, pulling her friend by the arm with all her might.

"You're making a big mistake if you think you can use brute force. Perhaps you've forgotten that nothing and no one can make me do something against my will!"

He brushed back a strand of dark hair with pretend arrogance. Weak with laughter, Oksa let go—and, losing her balance, crashed into the edge of the fountain.

"Ouch," she yelped. "My elbow!"

A ring of blood appeared around the tear in her blouse.

"That really hurt," she grumbled. "Blast! Look at the mess I've made of myself."

Gus held out his hand to help her to her feet. She twisted round to take off the little bag she wore strung over her shoulder and handed it to him.

"Will you look after this for me while I go and clean myself up?" she asked.

"Wow... the Young Gracious's magical accessories? What an honour!"

Oksa smiled at him and headed off in the direction of the grey stone cloister. Gus watched until she vanished into the shadowy staircase that led into the magnificent building.

※

Twenty minutes later, Gus was still there.

"Come on, Gus!" yelled a golden-haired student. "We're going to play basketball."

"No thanks, Merlin, I'm waiting for Oksa."

Sitting there patiently against a low wall with nothing much to do, Gus gently pressed the bag. Inside he could feel a soft, round shape—the Tumble-Bawler. He hoped it wouldn't kick up a fuss. As if it could read his mind, the Tumble-Bawler said:

"Don't worry, young Master, discretion is my middle name! It has to be, given that high volume doesn't make for a low profile."

This quirky motto made Gus smile.

"Come on, Oksa... what on earth are you doing up there?" he grumbled after a few more moments.

"I can inform you that the Young Gracious is currently in the first-floor toilets, fifty-six yards north-north-west of here," the small creature couldn't help volunteering in a muffled voice.

Gus shuddered uneasily at the thought of someone overhearing this unconventional conversation, but all the other students were having too much fun to pay attention to him. Tired of waiting, he finally stood up and headed over to the staircase.

Walking along the deserted corridor, all he could hear were the sound of his own footsteps and the hubbub from the courtyard. A strange feeling came over him as he remembered the awful events that had taken place just four months earlier—Oksa injured, fiendish McGraw showing his true colours, Miss Heartbreak… He couldn't help glancing inside the lab as he walked past and, as he did so, he heard someone singing a sad, slow song that sounded like a lament. Intrigued, he turned the door handle—the lab was unlocked. Gus walked in and looked around. He couldn't see anyone, but he could definitely hear someone as clearly as if they were standing right next to him. He opened Oksa's bag: the Tumble-Bawler hadn't made a sound.

"What's going on? What is that noise?"

He walked round the room, clutching Oksa's bag tightly. He looked under every desk and opened the door to the store room, then the large cupboard. Nothing. And yet he could still hear the soft, mournful weeping. He stopped searching and stood in the middle of the room listening hard, all his senses on the alert. He could now make out what sounded like faint words amongst the sobs.

"What are you saying? Where are you?" he stammered, looking around despite his fear.

He heard a voice which sounded as though it were coming from a long way off and yet was very close, saying:

"I'm here, right in front of you. I need your help. Please come and set me free… *I'm begging you!*"

❅

Oksa was hurrying back to the courtyard, her shirt still damp, when the wail of a foghorn caught her attention.

"Hey, that sounds like Gus's mobile!"

517

The ringtone grew louder as she walked past the first-floor lab, then cut out. Oksa stopped and listened for a few seconds. With a smile, she heard what she'd been expecting to hear: Darth Vader's rasping voice telling Gus that someone had just left a message. It was Gus's phone. She immediately pushed open the lab door and walked in.

"Gus! Are you in here?"

No answer. Oksa glanced around and looked under the desks. Her friend didn't usually play tricks like this, but you never knew what he might get up to. Suddenly she spotted his mobile on the floor.

"What's his phone doing there?" she muttered with a frown.

She picked it up and looked around again with a puzzled expression, then walked out of the room and went to join the others.

"You haven't seen Gus, have you?"

Zoe looked up, an expression of concern on her pretty face. Oksa kicked herself for worrying her friend for no reason and hurriedly continued:

"What an Incompetent he is. Look, he's lost his mobile!"

Grabbing Zoe's hand, she dragged her after her as spontaneously as ever.

"Come on, he must be hiding around here somewhere. Let's go and track him down."

Since Zoe had been living with the Pollocks, Oksa had discovered how nice it was to be friends with another girl. Real friends. The pity she'd felt for Zoe at first—aroused by the girl's unhappy past—had been replaced by a sincere, mutual affection that had taken them both by surprise. Now they were firm friends, united by a huge secret.

"Just wait till he dares to show his face again..." grumbled Oksa.

After half an hour spent searching fruitlessly for him, the two girls were back where they'd started and they were both feeling more concerned than they cared to admit. It was getting late and the students were beginning to file out of the school.

"You'd better phone home," suggested Zoe, her forehead creased in an anxious frown, which only made Oksa feel more unsettled.

By the time Pierre Bellanger and Pavel Pollock had arrived in the courtyard, the girls were beside themselves with worry. They had spent nearly an hour searching the school from top to bottom again with mounting desperation.

"He isn't at Bigtoe Square, or at home," declared Pierre, sliding shut his mobile.

The caretaker locked St Proximus's heavy gates and they had to face facts: Gus was nowhere to be found. Oksa and Zoe gazed at each other, eyes brimming with tears. The peace and quiet of the last few months had obviously just been a brief respite.

* * *

The Runaways were in shock. Brune and Naftali Knut, the imposing Swedish couple, and Dragomira's brother, Leomido, had rushed over to the Pollocks' house in a show of solidarity. Night had fallen long ago, doing nothing to lighten the heavy mood. Pierre, his face furrowed with worry, had his arms around his wife, Jeanne, who couldn't stop crying. Dragomira walked over and gave them a hug, but couldn't think of anything comforting to say. Standing behind Marie's wheelchair, his eyes fixed on Oksa, Pavel felt paralysed by a creeping sense of anxiety.

"Perhaps we should inform the police?" suggested Oksa hoarsely.

"We can't do that, Oksa" replied Abakum, the protector of the Runaways. "Anyway, we all know they'd just say he's run away."

"Gus wouldn't run away from anything. He's been kidnapped!" cried Jeanne, frantic with worry.

"But by whom?" they all wondered, though no one dared to voice their thoughts. Only Oksa plucked up enough courage to say what they were all thinking:

"You don't think it could be a Felon, do you? Orthon McGraw can't have been the only one to have got out of Edefia; who's to say there weren't others?"

They looked at her with some degree of gratitude. This was the best-case scenario for all of them. It would mean that Gus was going to be used as a bargaining counter by the mystery kidnapper and wouldn't be harmed while negotiations were under way. But what if the kidnapper wasn't a Felon? It didn't bear thinking about.

※

They sat there all night constructing theories and possibilities, mobiles in hand and eyes glued to the front door. Around five o'clock in the morning, slumped on a sofa next to Zoe, who was just as despondent as she'd been the night before, Oksa suddenly discovered what was to be their first lead. She'd kept Gus's phone and was listening for the umpteenth time to the last message that had activated the voicemail alert she'd heard. It was from Jeanne. "Gus, I haven't been able to get hold of you. Your dad will pick you up in an hour. See you soon!" Amazed that she hadn't thought of it before, Oksa carefully examined everything her friend might have recorded. There wasn't anything much of interest in his messages, but there was something weird in the phone's photo gallery: just before his mother had called—the clock on the phone confirmed it—Gus had taken an odd picture.

"Look!"

Oksa showed them the thumbnail on the screen of the mobile.

"What on earth is that?"

Pavel immediately switched on his computer to enlarge the photo and everyone crowded round to take a look. As soon as the picture appeared, Zoe cried out:

"That's my gran, Reminiscens!"

"Are you sure?" exclaimed Dragomira.

"Of course I am!"

They all stared at the screen: the picture showed the upper half of a woman who looked around seventy. She was staring straight ahead, her

520

pale blue eyes wide with despair and fear. She was slim, dressed in dark colours and her drawn face aroused compassion.

"That's my gran…" repeated Zoe, her voice hoarse with tiredness and emotion.

Dragomira and Abakum exchanged surprised looks. Suddenly, a spark of understanding caused them to break their silence and, still gazing at each other, they chorused:

"Impicturement!"

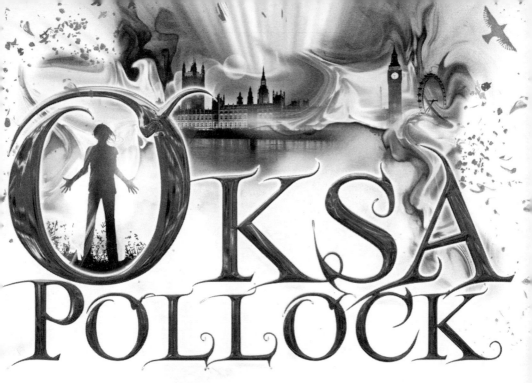

OKSA POLLOCK

Join us.

Become a Pollockmaniac at

www.oksapoLLock.co.uk

The ONLY web destination for Oksa Pollock fans including:

- the latest news

- exclusive character info

- author blog

- competitions & giveaways

PUSHKIN CHILDREN'S BOOKS

Just as we all are, children are fascinated by stories. From the earliest age, we love to hear about monsters and heroes, romance and death, disaster and rescue, from every place and time.

In 2013, we created Pushkin Children's Books to share these tales from different languages and cultures with younger readers, and to open the door to the wide, colourful worlds these stories offer.

From picture books and adventure stories to fairy tales and classics, and from fifty-year-old bestsellers to current huge successes abroad, the books on the Pushkin Children's list reflect the very best stories from around the world, for our most discerning readers of all: children.